THE ANATOMY OF CHEATING

NESLY CLERGE

"The Anatomy of Cheating"

This is a work of fiction. Names, characters, places, and incidents are the product of the author's imagination or are used fictitiously. Any resemblance to actual persons, living or dead, events, or locales is entirely coincidental.

Copyright © 2017 by Nesly Clerge

(Print) ISBN: 978-0-9965017-8-1
(Electronic) ISBN: 978-0-9965017-7-4

Publisher: Clerge Books, LLC

Editor: Joyce L. Shafer (http://editmybookandmore.weebly.com)

Cover and Interior Book Design: Damonza.com

E-Book Formatting: Ebooklaunch.com

To Deborah
I truly appreciate
you as a reader!
Nesly Clerge

ALSO BY NESLY CLERGE

When the Serpent Bites
(Book 1 of The Starks Trilogy)

When the Dragon Roars
(Book 2 of The Starks Trilogy)

End of the World: The Beginning
(Book 1 of a Serial - Amazon #1 Bestseller)

ACKNOWLEDGMENTS

My sincere thanks to my editor, Joyce L. Shafer, for being consistently in my corner and assisting me to reach for the stars.

To my significant other, Tierra Guy--your critiques of my work are always on point. Your encouragement and enthusiasm mean more than I can say.

I give special thanks to my Goodreads reviewers and fans, whose feedback is welcome and invaluable: Diane Lybbert, Lynn McCarthy, Kimberlie Lashley, Julie Green, Tamara Lewis, Brenda Telford, Patricia Brooks, Shannon Fairley, Maxine Groves, Dee Cherry, Irene Appleby, Anthony Richard Parsons, Dianne Bylo, K Morton, Lorraine Sithole, Torrie Angel, Tracy Watson Fisher, Laura Cerone, Russell Dent, Linda Strong, Veronica Joy, Nicki, Lesley Marino, Sue Ward, Kostas Kinas, Sue Leonhardt, Roberson Lapierre, and Hensie Lapierre.

Kay Smillie—your outstanding services and hawk-eyed abilities are always significant. You are the first to read and review all of my published novels, and I truly appreciate you for this. I thank you for being my #1 fan.

My thanks and appreciation to Shayla Eaton for her exceptional marketing skills.

I owe gratitude to the following authors for their esteemed input: Rebecca Mcnutt, C. P. Bialois, J. Kahele, and Rajalakshmi Prithviraj.

CHAPTER 1

INNOCENT OR GUILTY? Dr. Bernadette Moore studied the faces and mannerisms of the people seated and those filing into the room. Seldom did anyone volunteer to admit which category they fit into, at least not in a public forum—not that she ever asked. No *Show of hands, please*, for this type of crowd. However, their questions, comments, and body language informed her of more than they realized or meant to reveal.

A bead of perspiration trickled from her breastbone to the fabric of her bra. It wasn't nerves. She'd gotten used to audiences during her extensive weekends-only book tour that included open forums. Like this one. Inevitable discussions tended to get heated; hence, her request to the manager to adjust the air-conditioner.

This was the last such event before resuming her usual counseling routine at her office. And was why she'd scheduled it in her own town of Waltham, Massachusetts. It would be her bed she climbed into later. Alone. None of the people in attendance needed to know that. Unless someone asked. If asked, she'd answer honestly. It was vital she be an example, not just for the sake of her reputation, but also for the sake of those who sought what she provided.

Dr. Moore shook her shoulder-length blond hair from her face and smoothed the fabric of her jacket and skirt tailored for her tall, slender form. Ready to face advocates and detractors alike, she tapped her pen against the top of the lectern.

Audience members grew quiet as they fixed their attention on her. Dr. Moore's hazel eyes focused on a few faces. "Thank you for joining me tonight. Please respect your fellow attendees and turn off your cell phones now." As nearly every person did so, she added, "That's one of two rules I have. The other is that you never hesitate to ask questions."

A woman in the front row said, "We can ask about anything?"

"Whatever you want. Don't be shy. We're here to discuss and discover intricacies of the compelling and, more often than not, painful topic of infidelity."

Several attendees shifted nervously in their chairs. Others positioned pens over notebooks or tablets opened to a clean page.

Dr. Moore held her book up, showcasing the title, *The Anatomy of Cheating*. "I'm grateful to those of you who purchased my book, and I'm delighted to say it's now a *New York Times* best-seller." She smiled in response to applause that was genuine from some, tepid from others, and made a small bow at the waist.

"I see a number of you brought your copies. Extras are on the table at the back, for those who wish to purchase one either during the break or after the forum." She put the book down. No notes on sheets of paper or index cards were present—she knew the subject and people's natures too well to need them. "Now, let's delve into this topic that affects the lives of so many. Perhaps, even some of you.

"Anatomy is defined as the study of structure, a detailed analysis, rather than solely knowledge of what a body is comprised of. Infidelity—more commonly called cheating—is the action or state of being unfaithful to one's partner when a promise or mutual agreement of exclusivity exists.

"We're here to explore and analyze the internal workings of being unfaithful, as well as the different aspects of such behavioral choices that lead us to the ultimate question: why do we cheat on our spouses or partners?"

The same woman in the front row blurted out, "Men cheat because they're dogs."

Dr. Moore fixed a small smile on her lips and remained quiet.

The woman's face blazed red. "I know how bad that sounds, but I've had some unpleasant experiences with a few no-good, cheating, conniving men."

"It's okay. I welcome the conversation. I'll answer your question, but let me first say that it isn't only men who cheat. Women do, as well; though, there are those who prefer to believe otherwise. And, honestly, women are more adept at it because they're better planners."

Another woman spoke up. "Seems like a blind statement to me." She glanced around to see if anyone agreed with her. No one acknowledged whether they did or didn't.

Dr. Moore took a sip of water. This subject was an uncomfortable one for many, but people in each location she traveled to, showed up and warmed the seats, even if only motivated by vicarious curiosity. "There are any number of reasons why people cheat: Physical gratification, revenge, lack of emotional intimacy in their current relationship, falling out of love with their spouse or partner, lack of appreciation or respect from their spouse or partner, sexual addiction, to list several."

The woman in the front row said, "There's more?"

Dr. Moore nodded. "We'd need to go beyond our scheduled three hours, maybe days, if we were to discuss the myriad reasons people cheat and how they justify it to themselves and others. The bottom line is this: there's a need not being fulfilled, so people look for that fulfillment elsewhere."

Several hands raised. Dr. Moore pointed to a woman in the back. "The lady in red."

"Maybe that's why some women cheat, but we all know men cheat more than women, and why. They want to screw everything that moves. They don't care who they hurt. It's not a big deal for them. Women don't act like that. At least, not the women I know."

A number of women nodded their heads. The men, with the exception of a middle-aged man in the front row, looked at their shoes, the floor, the ceiling—anywhere but at the women—and remained silent.

Dr. Moore said with a knowing smile, "Some women resist owning up to what their gender is capable, as well as guilty, of. It's one reason they get away with it more easily than men. People tend to not expect women to cheat, whereas they do tend to expect it of men. It's one reason why husbands or significant others are so often stunned when it happens to them.

"I've counseled hundreds of couples and individuals over the years, and," she tapped her book, "I've conducted extensive research on the matter. While it's true that most men express themselves through physicality, the consensus is that women cheat for emotional reasons. However," she looked straight at the woman, allowing her pause to hang in the air, "you'd be surprised at how many women cheat solely for sexual satisfaction."

The middle-aged man cleared his throat loudly. He fiddled with his silk tie and said, "Aside from your 'extensive' research—whatever that means, what qualifications do you possess that permit you to call yourself an expert? Personally, I find your position—if you'll pardon the pun—awkward and unsubstantiated."

Dr. Moore grinned. "It's obvious you didn't read my book or, at least, my bio." Light laughter rustled through the room. "I hold a medical degree in psychiatry and a doctorate in human psychology, with emphasis on human sexuality. Additional qualifications are my life experiences."

The man smirked. "I suppose you also consider the fact you were married twice contributory to your expertise. You were married twice, weren't you? Or was it three times?"

Murmurs rippled through the audience.

Dr. Moore did a visual assessment of the man. "May I ask what you do for a living, sir?"

"I'm a psychologist."

"That explains it." Dr. Moore smiled at the people waiting for her response. "Our fellow attendee's demeanor isn't uncommon. People in the field of counseling and psychology sometimes come to my open forums with the intent to discredit me. They say these types of forums are inappropriate; that my public discussions of something so private are unorthodox, even in this day and age. I have nothing to hide, but I can't say that about many of the people who attend."

Some in the room snickered, others sat motionless.

The man leaned forward and aimed a finger at her. "You didn't answer my question, Dr. Moore. In my professional opinion, that's a telling sign. It's avoidance, when called out."

She ignored him. "By show of hands, how many of you are parents?" The majority raised their hands. "How many of you have children involved in sports?" A few hands lowered. "Do you prefer your children to be coached by someone who actually played the particular sport your child is involved in, or would you rather a coach who never played a day in his or her life?" She pointed at a woman in the middle row.

"Someone with experience, naturally."

Dr. Moore turned to the psychologist. "Indeed, because knowing something intellectually and real life experience are two different things. When you combine the two, the result is wisdom."

The man curled his lips in contempt and pretended to evaluate the manicured nails of his left hand.

Dr. Moore stifled a grin. "I don't see a wedding ring on your hand, sir. That could mean nothing," she winked at the audience, "or it could mean a great deal. Don't worry. I have no intention of probing that potential minefield." Most in the audience laughed.

Dr. Moore moved a few feet to her left. "I've been divorced twice, cheated on, and did the cheating. That's why I'm more than qualified to do what I do."

She glanced at the psychologist and said, "I don't hide behind theory," then returned her attention to the others. "I understand exactly what individuals and couples go through when they sit in my office. I understand the pain and humiliation. The devastation. The animosity and bitterness. The mechanism behind it all, and from both sides of the experience. I understand the anatomy of cheating."

CHAPTER 2

THE FORUM CONTINUED in a lively manner, comprised of dredged up emotions, arguments, gender-specific accusations, tears, and occasional bouts of laughter—typical of how they usually went. A half hour past the scheduled end time, Dr. Moore suppressed a yawn and announced the event officially over.

The psychologist stood, adjusted the lapels of his suit jacket, harrumphed and left without saying another word. Several people followed him. About half of the attendees lined up at the back table, book in hand, wallets out. The remainder crowded around the lectern to get their copies autographed. Three men gave Dr. Moore their business cards, accompanied by dinner or drinks invitations.

Dr. Moore smiled at the last two people in front of the lectern as they moved into place. The women were obviously together, and an odd duo. One wore wedding rings, one did not. Only one of them drew lustful stares from some of the men, which was understandable. Men tended not to care if black roots revealed that platinum blond hair wasn't natural. If their eyes even traveled that far up from a stretch of bare legs supported by stiletto heels, and topped off with artificially enhanced cleavage.

The woman with the carat-heavy wedding rings tugged at her too-large, too-long, unseasonable sweater that failed to hide her plump middle and hips. Her cheeks pinked as she held her book out.

Dr. Moore smiled and said, "My mother's hair was almost the same shade of auburn as yours. But her eyes were emerald green rather than blue. Yours is a lovely combination as well."

The woman looked at Dr. Moore then away. In a small voice, she said, "Thank you."

Dr. Moore noted the avoidance, the hesitancy demonstrated by the woman to receive or believe what she'd heard. "If my comment made you uncomfortable, I apologize."

"It's fine. I'm not used to compliments, is all."

Such behavior and its frequent origins were familiar, more common than they should be. Dr. Moore opened the book and poised her pen over the first blank page. "What name should I use?"

"Chelsea. I saw one of your interviews on TV. I got your book just before coming here. After hearing you speak, I'm eager to read it and see what else you have to say."

"Just curious about the topic in general, or do you have a more personal interest?"

The short-skirted woman started to speak then stopped when Chelsea glared at her. "This is my friend Penelope. She's also eager to read what you wrote."

Dr. Moore nodded at Penelope and said, "You're getting approving glances from the men and daggers from the women."

Penelope smirked. "You'd think they'd never seen breasts before. By the looks of this group, the men should get out more and the women should get makeovers."

Chelsea's complexion turned ruddy. "Starting with me."

"Oh, Chels. I'm sorry. I didn't mean—"

"The truth is the truth. Right, Dr. Moore? Who better to tell you than your best friend."

Dr. Moore shifted her gaze from Penelope to Chelsea. "Sometimes, what we call truth is only a perception, or prejudice, in the eye of the beholder."

Chelsea patted her hips. "Or too obvious to miss." She held out her hand for her book. "We don't want to hold you up. The line for your autograph is starting again. I just want to say that I … Never mind. Let's go, Pen."

"I want my book signed."

Dr. Moore scribbled her name in the book then watched the two women leave, Penelope's head high and proud as she swished toward the door, while Chelsea kept her eyes aimed downward. Only one of them was conscious of her deep-seated insecurity. Very few people were willing to admit the truth to others or to themselves.

Especially about themselves.

CHAPTER 3

"NOTHING IS more painful than being disappointed by the one person you thought would never hurt you." Chelsea Hall turned the page of the novel she was reading in bed and said, "He must have been through an agonizing time in his life."

Garrett Hall kept his focus on his iPad. "Sorry. What did you say?"

Chelsea rolled her eyes and adjusted the pillow behind her back. "Someone, at some time, must have crushed him emotionally."

"Who?"

"Luke Thompson."

"Don't know him."

"Of course not. He's the author of this novel." She turned the book to display the front cover.

Garrett gave the book an insubstantial glance. "You know I never read fiction. It's fabrication, Chels. No reason for you to get so caught up in—" Garrett's cell phone buzzed and vibrated on the nightstand. He snatched the phone up and read the name on the screen.

Chelsea wrinkled her brow. "Who's contacting you at this time?"

"I'm on call at the hospital tonight. Remember?"

Chelsea closed the novel and cradled it to her chest. "This is getting ridiculous. You might even say unbelievable. I feel like telling them to hound someone else for a change."

"Here." He shoved his phone at her. "Call the hospital back. Ruin my career or cost some person his or her life."

Chelsea waved him off in a dismissive fashion, but not before she noted the name on the phone registered as Dr. Jacobs.

Garrett hid his satisfaction. He leaned over and kissed her forehead. "Gotta get ready to go in, babe."

Chelsea scooched under the covers and turned on the television. "It's just that you're always working late or being called in. More than you used to be, or ought to be." She chewed on her bottom lip. "Should I be worried?"

Garrett sighed his exasperation, palmed his phone, and left the bed. He knew his wife well: It wasn't his hours at work she referred to. At the doorway of the master bathroom, he turned and said, "Do you have a better suggestion about how I can pay for this extravagant lifestyle you enjoy?"

Her silence was expected, gratifying. He smiled, but not in amusement. "That's what I thought. These late nights and extra hours pay for this small mansion and everything else you couldn't live without. If there are no more complaints, I'll get ready and go do the job I'm paid to do."

He closed the arched double doors of the bathroom then crossed the gleaming marble floor. Matching peach marble continued up the walls and in the shower large enough for four, as well as encased the Jacuzzi. He had to hand it to Chelsea: The exquisite décor in this room and throughout the house was her doing. Sure, he appreciated it, but she'd never have settled for anything less. Nor would he. He never settled for anything less than what he wanted. Why should he?

Garrett sent a text stating he'd be leaving in several minutes. He stripped and admired his toned body in the mirror that spanned one wall then prepped his face and razor. The blade was almost to his skin when the reply to his text message came, asking where he wanted to meet. He put the razor down and typed *Same as last night.*

Quickie or can you stay a while?
I'll call when on my way.

Garrett put the phone down and placed the razor to his cheek. Chelsea screamed his name, and he cursed as the blade nicked his skin. He left the blood to trail into the white foam on his face, ignored the sting of the menthol and opened the double doors.

CHAPTER 4

CHELSEA HUDDLED IN the middle of the bed, her gaze fixed on the TV screen. No fire. No blood spilling but his.

"What the hell, Chels? I cut myself when you shrieked."

She pointed at the TV. "Sorry, but I knew you'd want to see this. It's a special about Frederick Starks. I remember seeing this film clip of when he was being taken to prison after his trial, looking arrogant even then."

"Starks was—is—innocent."

"He was guilty, and you know it. He should never have beaten that poor woman's husband into a coma. Especially not in front of her children."

Garrett grabbed the remote and turned up the volume. A few minutes into the special he pressed the power button and tossed the remote onto the bed. The screen contracted to dark.

"I was watching that." Chelsea scooped up the remote but left the TV off.

"It's bullshit," Garrett said. "They're only interested in sensationalism, not the truth."

Chelsea tightened her grip on the remote. "But we know the whole truth, don't we?"

"You know damn well he went after Ozy Hessinger in self-defense. The man intended to knife him. What those media assholes don't know about Starks is something I do: He's the type of guy who'd give you the shirt off his back, if you needed it. He doesn't deserve what's happened to him."

"He nearly killed a man. And for the most hypocritical reason of all. He deserves what he got."

"You don't know all that I know about what he's been through."

"You're defending him because he was your partner-in-crime. You know the saying, "Birds of a foul feather cheat on their wives together.""

"That's enough, Chelsea."

"I met Kayla Starks socially several times and heard her side of the story. If anyone understands what she went through, I do."

"We agreed not to talk about that time ever again. But, you know damn well, if it wasn't for Starks lining me up with his team of lawyers, I'd have lost my license."

"We could have found someone just as hawkish and less costly. The thousands those high-priced lawyers charged came out of our pockets, not his."

"You mean my pockets."

"I hate when you say that. It's unfair. We agreed it was best I give up practicing law to stay home and take care of Kimberlie. Yes, you pay the bills, but I look after our daughter and manage our home, and I do it mostly alone. If you don't value the contribution I make to ..." Chelsea's chin quivered. She turned away.

Garrett stared up at the ceiling and sighed. "I'm sorry. Of course I value all you do. I'm in a rush, so wasn't thinking straight."

"This isn't the only time you weren't thinking straight."

Garrett threw his hands up. "You won't stop with the needling, will you?"

"Your free time is supposed to be spent here, with us, with me, not screwing around."

"For the thousandth time, I'm *not* screwing around. And, I'm not having this discussion with you yet again. Definitely not now. They're waiting for me at the hospital. I need to take a quick shower before going in. You're holding me up."

Chelsea followed him into the bathroom. "Do men think about their wives when they're screwing other women? Did you think about me? About Kimberlie?"

"I'm way more than damn tired of hearing this broken record. What happened is in the past. Leave it there."

"Last year, Garrett, not years ago. You think I can simply erase from memory that you had sex with that slutty nurse? You'd like me to forget. You want me to act like it never happened. Clean slate and all that. Then you could convince yourself that you're guilt-free. That my pain doesn't exist. That I don't wonder if you compare me to her, and that I lose."

"How is our relationship ever going to heal if you keep bringing up my mistake?"

"Mistake? What a modest word for what you did."

"You're not only not ready to let it go, you haven't gotten your fill yet of punishing me. I understand you're upset that I have to go in, but I don't want this nonsense of yours to escalate into an argument. I don't have the time or the energy for it."

"You never have the time."

"Forget this. I'll shower downstairs. Otherwise, I'll run later than I already am."

Garrett slid his arms into his robe and slipped his phone into a pocket. He grabbed a pair of scrubs, underwear, keys, his wallet, and headed downstairs. He needed distance between him and her accusations.

He got that this wasn't easy for her, but these emotional outbursts were annoying as hell. And getting old fast.

It wasn't his intention to hurt her. But he couldn't seem to help himself: His one great weakness was women. He'd managed to hide his behavior from her until last year, but then she'd found out. Well, there was also the time before that one. He had to be more careful, or he risked losing everything.

Chelsea listened for the downstairs bathroom door to close. A debate went on inside her about whether or not to reach out to Richard. He'd said he was always available for her. She dialed her brother-in-law's number. "Is it okay to call you now? Can you talk?"

CHAPTER 5

GARRETT RESTED BOTH hands on the lavatory countertop and stared disapprovingly at himself in the gilded mirror. "You're a disappointment, son."

He shook off disparaging himself, finished shaving with a fresh razor he kept stashed in a drawer then got into the shower, letting the steaming water sting his skin. It wasn't required that the water be that hot to act as some version of spiritual cleansing. It was that every part of his body had to be all but sanitized. He never knew where *Dr. Jacobs'* tongue would travel.

Of course he realized he asked a lot of Chelsea, particularly because he knew if circumstances were reversed, he wouldn't be able to handle it. Kayla Starks's rampant cheating was well known in their circles, a fact that had crushed Frederick Starks.

That wasn't the worst blow she'd dealt her husband. As Starks's attending physician, he'd found himself unexpectedly thrust right into the middle of that couple's intrigue. What a shitty task it had been to confirm to Starks that his son Blake wasn't his, a thirteen-year deception brought to a gut-wrenching halt. Had Starks not needed a blood transfusion recently, he'd never have had the heart ripped out of him by that revelation. He'd still be blind to the truth.

Thank God Chelsea respected their marriage too much to ever cheat. Kimberlie was his, without a doubt. She'd inherited his ebony eyes and dark curly hair, the latter for which she jokingly chastised him. Had he desired to have another child, he was certain the parentage would have been guaranteed, as well.

His promise to never betray Chelsea again after his last infraction, had been broken almost as soon as he'd uttered the words to her. It was far easier to say the words than to follow through.

His phone buzzed again with a reminder of the anticipated rendezvous.

Did you leave yet?
See you in thirty-five.

CHAPTER 6

I T TOOK TWENTY desire-filled minutes and a heavy foot on the accelerator for Garrett to drive from his home in Waltham to Brookline. The birthplace of one of America's most beloved presidents, whose extramarital activities were well known, seemed an appropriate location for his trysts. And far enough away so that no one who knew him or his family would see him or his car and report his whereabouts to Chelsea.

He sped alongside Olmsted Park, not as famous as Central Park in Manhattan, but still worthy of admiration. When his assignations happened during daylight hours, he took time to give the park its due.

After driving another two miles, Garrett turned his Porsche into the parking lot of the five-star hotel and waited. Minutes later, the car he watched for backed into the space next to his. The woman got out of her car. She flicked her wavy blond hair from her shoulders and smiled at him. Darkness hid the deep blue of her eyes, but the fire in them was evident. She knew how to handle herself. And him.

The woman held up a hand, indicating he was to wait before leaving his car. He complied. She turned in a slow circle, modeling the prize of her body under the second-skin mini. She caressed her breasts then slid her hands to her slim waist and along her hips, turned and bent over just far enough for him to see the only thing between him and euphoria was the flimsy silken sheath she wore.

Her confidence in her sexuality was enticing, his erection demanding. The woman ran her tongue over her rouged top lip then gave her bottom a slap. His expression in response made her laugh. She had him where and how she wanted him. But turnabout was fair play, as the saying went. As soon as he got her into the room, he'd turn her every which way. Or maybe he'd tie her up.

Garrett grabbed the several silk ties and jacket he kept in his backseat for just this reason and got out. He pressed her against her car, bumped his erection against the mound between her thighs for a few seconds then backed away. They beeped their cars locked and made their way to the lobby, his jacket draped strategically in front of him.

CHAPTER 7

THE MAN IN the dark navy suit looked up from behind the reception desk. "Good evening, Dr. Hall. How are we this evening?" As usual, he didn't wait for a reply and kept his eyes respectfully averted from the woman, as he did in regard to any of the women who accompanied his favorite customer.

Garrett handed the night manager his credit card, which was scanned and returned, once again paying for the Presidential Suite reserved by the week, every week, as it had been for at least the six years the night manager had been employed there. The exchange was made of the key to the suite and five hundred-dollar bills for the manager's complicity.

Garrett and the woman moved at a hurried pace to the elevator, silent except for the click of the woman's heels on the faux granite beneath them.

He pressed the button for the top floor. The door eased closed. He pulled her to him. Cupped one of her breasts. Squeezed. Trailed his finger over the nipple responding to his touch. "You're one sexy woman." He pinched the nipple. "Like thimbles. Or gumdrops." He pursed his lips and made sucking noises.

She laughed and pushed him away.

The elevator stopped. At the door to the suite, Garrett slid the key into the slot.

The woman slid her dress over her head.

No way to suppress the hunger he felt at the sight of her nakedness or his admiration for her boldness. He opened the door and let her enter before him.

She tossed her dress onto the nearest chair and sauntered forward in her heels. Stopped and turned, placing her feet shoulder-width apart.

Watching him, she trailed her hand down her abdomen, stroked what he called her *sweet spot*. "Nothing like a fresh wax for your ride, don't you agree?" She laughed as Garrett, wide-eyed, licked his lips. "Maybe next time, I'll let you shave me."

Garrett drew in a breath, threw the bolt on the door and his jacket and ties atop her dress. Forget delaying gratification. He'd save the ties for round two.

It took only seconds to reach her, to grab her bottom with both hands and pull her against him. "Everything about you is luscious. And don't you just know it."

Mouths consumed lips and tongues.

She dragged his scrub shirt over his head.

He yanked his scrub pants and underwear off.

Lifted her so that her legs wrapped around his waist.

Carried her to the bed.

Dived into his need.

CHAPTER 8

THE RED DIGITS on the scale stopped at one ninety-nine. Chelsea shuddered. It was the highest number yet, and way over what her five-foot, six-inch frame was meant to support.

Naked in front of the mirrored bathroom wall, she turned to the right, straightened her posture, and attempted to suck in her belly. Hands placed above her breasts, she pulled the skin upward. Neither effort produced enough of a difference to satisfy her.

Kimberlie was fifteen now. The excuse of reticent baby-weight expired long ago. Garrett had ceased his subtle, and sometimes not-so-subtle, suggestions about how she might lose the weight. With unfounded determination, which she considered a waste of money, he continued to pay membership for her at an exclusive women's health club, despite knowing she had justifications at the ready, if asked, as to why she couldn't make it there. Neither of them had mentioned her lack of attendance for over two years. What was the point?

She'd tried to shed the weight. But it seemed the more effort she made, the more the pounds and inches increased. Bouts of depression hadn't helped. Then she'd caught Garrett cheating on her again, this time with the young, exotic nurse who'd worked at the hospital only a few months. This discovery had sent her to depths she still had no idea how to ascend from.

During the rare times they went places together, his attempts to hide his ogling of other women failed. Garrett's attention landed on women who were young, slim yet curvy. Gorgeous. Sensuality oozed from them. Like nectar to a horny bee whose stinger stayed ready.

How easy it was for those women. They hadn't had a child. Or a husband who cheated on them. They didn't live every moment in a battle with inconsolable pain, anger, and frustration caused by betrayal.

Once, at fourteen, she'd overheard her mother say to someone on the phone, *If you catch them one time, they probably did it a hundred times before they got caught.* How many times Garrett had cheated, and with how many women, was the question that dogged her.

How long had it been since he'd told her she was desirable, that he couldn't wait to have his way with her? Years. Nearly sixteen, in fact.

The only compliment she heard from him these days was about her skills in the kitchen. That is, when he managed to be there for a meal; though, it was more a matter of his occasionally deigning to grace her with his presence.

There was a time when Garrett admired and adored her. Now, she wasn't even sure he still loved her. If he refused to make love to her, as he had for so long, what choice did she have but to find solace in food?

Her appearance was his fault.

The marriage counselor had advised her to put Garrett's infidelities in the past. To trust his promise that he'd never cheat again. How did either man expect her to do that?

This impossible expectation led to her stop the sessions after four months. Hearing week after week after week that she was at fault, rather than Garrett, had been intolerable. And grossly unfair. Having male genitalia shouldn't guarantee entitlement.

Garrett swore he was keeping his promise. She desperately wanted to believe him. To forgive him. But the images that ran on a loop in her mind prevented her from doing that. How could she forgive what she couldn't forget?

She studied the features of her face in the mirror.

I'm still beautiful. A few extra pounds do not classify me as unappealing. I *am* sexy. I *am* desirable. I *am* …

The first tear trailed down her cheek. Staggering to the bed, she burrowed under the silk-covered duvet and wept.

Her cell phone rang. She checked the name on the screen. "Richard." She sniffed. "You're so intuitive."

"What's he done now?"

CHAPTER 9

LUKE THOMPSON POCKETED the generous tip left on the table by a couple of regulars, loaded the dishes onto a tray and took them into the kitchen.

Restaurant manager, James West, leaned against a counter. He took a sip of espresso from a demitasse cup. "How about we hit a bar after work. Pop back a few beers."

"I'll take a rain check for the weekend. I want to get some writing done tonight."

"How's the new book going?"

"Some writing days are better than others."

"That's why you need a break. C'mon, dude. Two brews at the most."

Luke shook his head. "Saturday's better."

"Brandi won't bitch?"

"I'll tell her I'm working late."

James held up his cup in salute. "That's the spirit."

He'd met James at college and formed a solid friendship, for which he was grateful. Only a true friend would accompany a guy to court when he was getting divorced. That day a few years ago had been dismal, appropriately effected by a thunder storm in true novel-like fashion.

After leaving the courthouse, James had dragged him to a nearby bar, not that there had been much dragging to do. He'd been ready to indulge, ready do whatever to numb the hurt that twisted his gut, even for a few hours.

"It's over, dude," James had said. He'd drained the last of his beer from the bottle then gestured for the bartender to bring another round.

"Two frickin' years to finally end this crap. No more back and forth with lawyers."

"Now, it's just a matter of paying them."

"Still. It must feel pretty damn good."

"It should, but it doesn't."

"Aren't you relieved?"

"That'll probably come later. Right now, I'm—I guess devastated—is the word. Conflicted."

"Dude, you know I'm straight. But you're a six-foot good-looking black man with a rock for a body. How can you be devastated or conflicted? That's a waste of energy. Think of all the women who are gonna be eager to play ride the Pogo Stick with you. You're free and clear. A prime candidate for quality sympathy nookie."

Luke shook his head. "You know I'm with Brandi."

"If you like her, keep her. But don't blow this opportunity."

"Infidelity led to my divorce."

James downed a third of his beer. "You had to divorce Tina. Man can't have a tramp for a wife."

Luke glared at his friend then softened his expression. "That may be what she is, but I'd prefer if you didn't call her that."

"I get it. You had that great kid of yours together, so you want to show her some respect. But you gotta call a spade a spade. You gave her seven years, and she expressed her gratitude by cheating on you."

"And in retaliation, I cheated on her, as though payback would solve anything."

"Nothing wrong with a man dipping in some honey here and there."

"Not my nature, James. You know me well enough by now to know that. Infidelity destroyed my family."

"Maybe you're fooling yourself. Maybe you always had the urge, and Tina taking care of hers first was the permission slip you convinced yourself you needed. Got an urge, satisfy it. That's my creed."

"It was a one-time thing, and I'm a one-woman guy. I know that doesn't sit right with you, but it is what it is." Luke turned his beer bottle in half circles. "I don't expect you to understand."

"I understand just fine. Since you have a problem doing the horizontal with more than one woman, pass the beauties my way when they start lining up for some Luke lovin'. I can come out of my state of monotonous monogamy for a little while."

"Since when do you live in that state?"

"Guilty." James chuckled and grabbed a few pretzels from the bowl between them. He tossed one of the twists into his mouth, chewed and said, "You telling me you love Brandi?"

Luke exhaled hard. "I loved Tina, and look how that turned out. From now on, I'm looking for compatibility with someone I can spend the rest of my life with. Love isn't what it used to be. All our married friends but Nara are divorced."

"Doesn't count. Nara's Indian. Arranged marriage, dude."

"Proves my point. He didn't love Danu when he married her, but his parents knew they were compatible. He learned to love her, and she, him."

"Personally, I think Brandi's just filling a void. There are other women with *voids* you could fill, if you'd get over yourself."

"Brandi cares about me. About us."

"Better watch out. Longer you stay with her, the more she's gonna want from you. Smartest move I made was to stay detached after my divorce. Got all the rampant lust out of my system. Took a few years before I was ready to settle down. I'm a married man now, but I ain't dead."

Luke grinned and shook his head. "You'd have sex with an alien if she had breasts, a nice ass, and a place to stick your prong in."

"Damn straight. I'm into the unusual."

"You're what women call a dog, James. Keep your unusual. Brandi's right for me."

"One word: rebound."

"You're wrong."

"I'm telling you the way it is. It's a new relationship. Salve for your wounds and all that jazz."

"It's not that new. It's been a year."

"When that shine wears off, you'll see the real woman. The woman the rest of us see and you don't."

"Again, you're wrong."

"I'm telling it to you straight: there's an expiration date on that relationship."

"Brandi and I know each other. You're not seeing anything about her that I haven't."

"Believe that if you want to. But what happens when she starts pressing you to get married?"

"She won't."

"Bet on it."

"Brandi knows marriage isn't part of the deal. At least, not for a while. If ever."

"You think you're ready for a serious relationship, but you're not. The ink's still drying on your divorce decree. If you were ready, you wouldn't be so morose. You'd have wanted to run home to Brandi and celebrate your freedom between her legs instead of getting drunk with me." James got the bartender's attention and held up two fingers. "Question is, Why didn't you?"

"I can't tell her how I feel right now. It would upset her."

"And, what if she wants a kid, or more than one, then the relationship goes bust? Which it will."

Luke swigged his beer and stayed silent.

"Face facts, dude. She's mid-thirties, never married. She wasn't going to blow her chances by pushing for a ring before your divorce. It's just a matter of time. You watch. Then, again, maybe you really are the kind that needs to be married. Maybe you feel too old to be single, much less horny."

"I'm only forty-two."

"I rest my case."

James had been right. A few months after his divorce, Brandi's hints started gradually. Then she made the subject of marriage a never-ending one. It was something she yearned for, something she convinced him was right for them both. A year after his divorce, he'd obliged her.

CHAPTER 10

L UKE INCHED THE Ford Focus along his street, noting how much the neighborhood resembled the one he'd lived in with Tina, as though repetition was impossible to escape.

Although their relationship had imploded, he missed aspects of it, mostly living with his son, Tim. There were times—more times than he wanted to admit—he wished he could wind the clock back and be in that life again, flawed as it was. Life with Brandi had an unreal feel to it, as though it was an imitation or substitute for something tangible and solid that eluded him. He felt it in his bones.

He pulled into his driveway, turned the engine off and remained in his car. The day of his divorce, he'd told James compatibility was enough. He was no longer certain about that. It wasn't that he missed Tina, so what was it? The answer came to him in a flash, like a sentence for one of his novels: It had been a crushing end of the dream he'd had for his family and his life. It wasn't easy to go through the mourning of that loss or to get over it as fast as a person might prefer or others might think he should.

He'd wanted a stable home for Tim, with loving parents there for him, as he'd had. That desired outcome had ended as soon as he'd learned Tina was raising her skirt and dropping her panties for other men. It was a thread that got pulled. The beginning of the unraveling for all of them.

Worry robbed him of sleep, worry that his sporadic time with Tim might cause his son to go the way of his cousin Jimmy. Jimmy's family had also dissolved. He took up with the wrong crowd at an early age, got suspended from school then expelled. Now he was serving a life sentence.

Most of his own friends from one-parent homes were occupying cells.

James, of course, had taken a different path. His lust for women had saved him. Always too busy screwing to commit a crime.

Luke snickered, released his seatbelt, and got out of his car. He exhaled hard as he unlocked the front door to his small two-story wood frame house and stepped inside.

CHAPTER 11

BRANDI GRABBED A clean platter from the dishwasher and glanced at Luke when he entered the kitchen. "Hi, honey."

He gave her a quick kiss on the cheek. "Hi, sweetheart. What's going on?"

"You got three more letters from literary agents. There, on the counter." She pointed with her chin.

"No doubt, more to add to my rejection collection, along with the electronic ones I've saved for posterity." It took no more than the first couple of sentences of each one-paragraph letter to confirm his expectation. "Sometimes I wonder if I should give up."

"Why won't you consider something more stable? Maybe it's time, or past time, to stop writing and working part-time. Get an actual job."

"I wait tables thirty hours a week. That's almost full-time. It gives me time to write."

"I don't know how you stay focused, much less enthusiastic, after being rejected so often. I also don't get working so hard on something for nothing."

"I don't write to make money."

Brandi cocked her head. "If you're not doing it for money, then you definitely need to give it up. End all the frustration. For both of us."

"Writing is like oxygen for me. I thought you understood that. I love exploring the human psyche. How people think. How they act and react, and why."

"What's to figure out? You know it when you see it. Give me numbers any day, not words about pretend people and situations. The accountant's life is fiction enough for me. Believe me, I learn a lot in my business about people and what they make up."

Luke shook his head. "Words inspire. They evoke feelings and provoke thought. The right words can give people vicarious experiences they'd never want to have in real life. Or make them laugh, or give them strength to make it another day."

"Change 'the right words' for 'the right numbers' and then you'll have something to give you strength." Brandi placed the letters in the drawer half-filled with similar messages. "It would be nice if those words you love paid more of the bills. All those hours in front of your computer. Multiply them by even twenty dollars and we could afford a better home and lifestyle."

"I'm trying to explain why I write, why it matters so much to me, but this conversation seems to be going nowhere fast."

"You're right." Brandi wrapped her arms around his waist. "I don't want to argue. What I want is a date night. We haven't had one in a long time. Get dressed. We're dining out. But first, give me a kiss."

The kiss Luke gave her was adequate, rather than the passionate kind exchanged in the earlier days of their relationship. He wondered if she even noticed.

Brandi stroked his cheek. "Maybe I fuss sometimes. But you know I love you, right?"

Luke searched for the truth in her eyes. "Do you really?"

She punched him playfully on the arm. "Stop kidding around and get dressed."

He started toward the stairs that led up to their bedroom.

"Luke."

He turned and waited.

"You love me too, right?"

Luke smiled, realizing that the gesture occupied the pause that shouldn't have been there. "What do you think?"

Brandi grinned. "Hurry and dress. I'm starving."

Only one of them was satisfied with his answer.

CHAPTER 12

LATE THE NEXT afternoon, Luke switched on his laptop computer. His hand hovered over the keyboard as he pleaded for better results to whomever might be in the mood to grant wishes. Months ago, having grown weary waiting for a literary agent to be interested in one or all three of his novels, he chose the indie route. His patience had faltered as he dreamed of an agent contacting him to state he'd waited his entire career for such a writer. He was far too eager to get his writing out for the world to consume, even if only one e-book or print copy at a time.

He logged onto his Amazon account to check the sales rankings for his books. All three ranked above seven hundred thousand. Equivalent to selling one e-book a month, and so far, resulting in a royalty of a whopping eight dollars and thirty-seven cents.

His Goodreads account revealed one friend request from a Chelsea Hall, which he accepted, and one new review from a different person who'd given his third and latest novel three stars. He browsed some of the best-selling authors' pages, barely suppressing the envy that threatened to surface in reaction to their hundreds of rave reviews and thousands of five-star ratings.

Perhaps Brandi was right. He should quit writing and get a full-time job. His degree in English was nothing more than a framed bit of paper on the wall, unless he could land a teaching job. It wouldn't make him rich, but would give him a decent income and get Brandi off his back about money. The positive would be he'd have summers off to write.

Who was he kidding? It wouldn't be enough time, not the time he needed, and he knew it.

Deep in thought, the knock on the front door startled him. He was nearly to the door when he heard Tim yell, "It's me, Dad," hours earlier than his expected seven o'clock arrival.

Luke shook his head. Tina didn't follow any schedule but her own. She wasn't bothered by defying the court-specified agreement or causing disruption in other peoples' lives. He should be used to it by now, but he could hear James telling him to grow some balls and insist Tina do the right thing. Telling Tina what to do was equal to spitting into the wind.

Luke unlocked and opened the door. He grabbed Tim's bag and said, "Come in, son. Shoes off, please."

Tim removed his runners and aimed straight for the kitchen, brushing by Brandi as though she were invisible.

"Hello, Tim," Brandi said. She waited for acknowledgment that didn't come.

Luke frowned. This again. "When an adult speaks to you, Tim, you answer. Politely. When Brandi speaks to you, you answer promptly."

"I waved. It's not my fault she's blind." Tim opened the refrigerator door, blocking himself from their view as the chilled air escaped confinement.

Luke closed the space between them, taking his position next to Tim. He grabbed his son's arm. "Her name is Brandi, not *she*. Brandi is my wife. You may feel and even be too old for the care a step-mother can give, but that doesn't excuse you from showing proper manners and respect. That goes for anyone who's your elder. If you want to be treated with respect, you have to give respect. That includes in this house. Do you understand?"

"Mom said I don't have to speak to anyone I don't want to," he jerked his head toward Brandi, "including her. You're hurting me."

Luke released Tim's arm. "We teach people how to treat us, son. If you want to be treated like a whiny, petulant child, that can be arranged. If you need a whipping, I can accommodate you with that, as well."

Brandi leaned across the counter. "Everybody calm down. Tim just got here. He's probably hungry." She forced a laugh. "I get cranky when I need to eat. Let's let him get a snack and relax." She faced Tim. "Don't fill up. Dinner will be in about an hour."

Luke turned and pointed a finger at Tim. "Stop acting like a little twit. Especially in my house." He followed Brandi into the adjoining den. "I can't believe he's become so rude."

Brandi placed a hand on his shoulder and lowered her voice. "I've never heard you speak to him that way, or seen you lay a hand on him. What's really going on with you?"

"I'm fine. Just annoyed."

"He's young, and still hurting from the divorce. I know it's been a few years since you and his mother separated, but it's not easy for children. First the split, and then adding another woman into the mix. Kids don't like it if they think someone's trying to replace their mother or father. You need to practice patience with him. Give him time to get to know me better and accept me as a permanent fact in his life. We'll get along. You'll see."

"I understand it's hard on him, but he's fourteen, for God's sake. Hard on him or not, he's old enough to learn respect. If I coddle him, I risk his choosing bad behavior over good. If I have to take my belt to him to make an impression, I will."

"You can't whip a boy his age."

"I don't care if he's fourteen or twenty. What I don't want is for him to go the way of my cousin Jimmy. That's how he started out. Back-talking every adult that spoke to him. I don't want to wait too late to get my son on the right track. I'll teach him respect if I have to beat it into him."

"Something *is* wrong. This isn't like you at all. Tim is likely as shocked by your behavior as I am, though he's doing a better job of hiding it."

Brandi wanted a better explanation for how he was acting. He didn't offer one. Because he didn't know what to tell her.

CHAPTER 13

THE NEXT MORNING, Garrett Hall approached the nurses' station, vacant of the usual crew, with the exception of one nurse scrolling through a file drawer. "Nurse Adams," he said. "New hairstyle, I see."

"Do you like?" She turned in a slow circle.

"Makes me want to mess it up in a bad way." He leaned forward. "A very *bad* way."

She laughed and returned to her task. "I'll take that as a thumbs-up."

"I love this hospital. Everyday, I'm surrounded by angels." Garrett stepped behind the desk, grabbed her by the waist, and moved her away from the filing cabinet. "I need some charts, beautiful; though, I'm more tempted to study you in depth."

She glanced at her watch. "I get off in about forty minutes."

Garrett wiggled his eyebrows. "Good thing I've got stamina."

She laughed. "You're such a flirt."

"I'm a connoisseur of beauty. And just so we're clear, flirtation is usually innocent. We know better, don't we?"

"Careful, doctor. I might swoon."

"I can get you to do that. My office door locks, as you know."

He took several charts, winked at the nurse and left wondering if she'd show up. If she did, the question was, Should he position her on the end of his desk, bend her over it, or do her against the wall. The last time he'd *walled* her, one of his framed certificates had crashed to the floor.

A note telling him to see Dr. Logan was taped to his office door. He dropped the charts onto his desk then quick-stepped his way to the department head's office. He rapped on the door jamb. "You wanted to see me, sir?"

"Take a seat, Garrett."

Garrett lowered into the chair opposite the imposing mahogany desk. "Everything okay?"

Aaron Logan cleared his throat and adjusted his polka-dot bow tie. "We've been reviewing your file. Your performance at this hospital is exemplary."

"Thank you, sir. That means a lot, coming from a doctor of your caliber."

"As you know, I'll be retiring the first of the year. How would you like to be head of the department?"

"I'm honored, but also surprised. I assumed Dr. Williams would move into your position. He's been here longer than I have."

"There are times when that isn't enough. You've accomplished more at forty-five years of age than most doctors have in their lifetime." He tapped the file in front of him. "Your scores on the boards were just short of amazing. You're the only one on staff here with board certifications in radiology, internal medicine, and cardiology. It's practically unheard of, and would be a huge benefit to this department."

"I'm flattered. But I'll have to decline."

"May I ask why?"

"You know my arrangement. I own my radiology practice and work there three days a week, three days here. You need someone who can serve the hospital full-time. Besides, I barely spend time with my family as it is."

Logan waved his hand in a dismissive manner. "It'll be a walk in the park for someone with your skills. Just supervise a few residents and sign a few papers. That's it. You'll have two assistants to help with the administrative duties."

"You make it sound so easy."

"It can be." Logan paused for a moment. "Let me pitch it to you this way. How does an additional two hundred and fifty thousand a year sound? To start, that is."

"Additional?"

"On top of whatever you're currently making here."

"Where do I sign?"

CHAPTER 14

GARRETT RETURNED TO his office. He picked up the first chart but left if unopened. In medical school most students wanted to go into radiology, as it was the only branch of medicine that guaranteed they could also have a life. Few scored high enough on the board to be accepted into a radiology residency, which was a bitch, but came with the territory. He'd made damn sure he wasn't one of them. All his efforts were about to pay off better and sooner than he'd anticipated. An advantage to owning a practice was that he could hire another part-time radiologist. Everything else could be delegated.

Chelsea was going to be thrilled. It was also her birthday tomorrow. And he knew the best way to tell her the news. A celebration was in order. He made a phone call to handle certain arrangements ahead of time, then put his full attention on the charts.

He looked up at the sound of the lock on his office door being clicked into place. Garrett leaned back in his chair. There was more than one way to celebrate a win. "Something I can do for you, Nurse Adams?"

"I need my temperature taken."

"Don't worry. I know just where my thermometer needs to go, to get a proper result."

CHAPTER 15

H IS SPECIAL TASK for Chelsea's birthday had taken about a half hour to complete. A few minutes after six, Garrett opened the front door and called out, "I'm home."

Penelope stepped out from the kitchen. "You're home early. Suspiciously so."

Garrett frowned. Typical of her, her dress was far too short and too low cut, especially in his house, where his daughter could be easily influenced. "Where's Chelsea?"

She pointed straight up.

Kimberlie sped down the staircase. "Dad, you're home early. Mom said you were working late again."

"I decided not to." He hugged her and kissed the top of her head. "Tomorrow's your mother's birthday, you know."

"Yeah, I know."

"Did you get her a gift?"

"Duh."

"What have I told you about using real words?"

From his left a voice that cracked said, "Hello, Dr. Hall."

The young man exited the living room with his hand extended. The anticipated handshake never came. His hand dropped to his side and he shuffled his feet in place.

Garrett studied the boy from head to toe, "Who are you?"

"I'm Mark. Kimberlie's date."

"Her what?"

Kimberlie nudged Garrett. "Be nice, Dad."

Mark cleared his throat. His ears burned red.

Garrett scowled at him. "Even if my daughter were old enough to date, which she isn't, she wouldn't be going anywhere with anyone who wears his pants halfway down his ass."

"Dad, I said to be nice. Everybody's wearing their pants like that. Stop embarrassing me."

Garrett held up a hand to silence his daughter. "Do either of you have any idea how that 'style' got started?" Neither answered. "It's not a damn fashion statement; it's a signal a prison inmate gives to other inmates that he's available for sex." Satisfied at their shocked expressions, he continued. "You're all running around believing you're so cool, ignorant of what it really represents. No boy looking like that is taking my daughter out. End of discussion." He turned to Kimberlie. "Go to your room. We'll talk later."

Kimberlie cried out, "What is *wrong* with you?" She bounded up the stairs, shouting for her mother.

Mark hadn't moved, his confusion about what to do evident on his face. The young man swallowed hard when Garrett faced him, sending his pronounced Adam's apple into a series of bobs.

"Kimberlie is too young to date. I know what boys your age want, and you can forget about getting it from my daughter."

"No, sir. I wouldn't—"

"When she's old enough to date, and if you can dress like you respect her, and yourself, maybe I'll consider letting her go out with you, but not before. The only reason you're still in the running is you were polite when you greeted me. Apparently, you learned some manners along the way."

He escorted the humiliated teen to the front door then stomped upstairs to the master bedroom.

What the hell was Chelsea thinking?

CHAPTER 16

H E FOUND CHELSEA folding and putting away towels in the
master bathroom. "What's going on with your fifteen-year-
old daughter?"

"You ought to know. She's in her room, sobbing because of you."

"Did you meet the thug she brought to our house?" Before Chelsea
could answer, he said, "She's too young to begin dating."

"Kimmie is old enough, and he isn't a thug. He happens to be very
nice. And for your information, it's not her first date. She's been going
on dates since she was fourteen."

"What the hell, Chelsea?"

"Relax. They go with others. I told her no solo dating until sixteen."

"I don't believe this. Why are you keeping me out of the loop?
Forget it. I already know the answer. You both know damn well I
would have said no."

"If you were home more often, you could be involved in your
daughter's life."

"That's no excuse, and you know it. Did you see how he was
dressed?"

"Don't you remember what it's like at that age?"

"That's precisely what I mean."

"Poor Mark. He must feel so awkward waiting for Kimmie to go
back downstairs, especially after what you said to them. I'll go talk to
him."

"He's not waiting. I told him to check back when Kimberlie's old
enough, and if he wears his pants where they belong."

"You are so going to get it from her. Don't you realize you'll only
make it worse if you try to take away her freedom? Not to mention

humiliate her and her friends. You want her to sneak out? It's best to let her be open with us. Give her some space and let her be a teenager."

"Oh sure. But what kind of teenager? I don't want anyone thinking my daughter's a slut."

"Garrett!"

"Speaking of sluts, why is Penelope always here?"

"Don't call her that. And, she isn't always here. She's here now because she's copying some recipes."

His expression was one of genuine surprise. "Penelope cooks?"

"In her own way. That's why she needs a few recipes."

"She's the wrong influence for my daughter. You should know better. I don't want Kimberlie to think it's okay to dress like she's for rent by the hour. She's going to be a doctor one day. Impressions matter."

"You should talk."

"Don't go there, Chelsea. I'm really not in the mood. Definitely not now."

Chelsea propped her fists on her hips. "First of all, you can't micro-manage Kimmie's life. Some of what she does has to be her decision. You especially can't dictate her life as an absentee father."

"Sure. Throw my schedule in my face. Again. But, let me set you straight. As her father, I damn well can tell her what to do. She's too young to know what's best for her. You should know better, too."

"Second of all, Garrett, I really don't appreciate how you treat Penelope. I know she's a bit liberal with her appearance and actions, but she's a good person."

"More like libertine."

"She's been there for me more than you can imagine."

"I want you to stop divulging our personal business to her."

"We've been friends since we were six. Who else am I supposed to talk to? You? You're either working or …" The unfinished accusation hung between them.

"For the thousandth time, I swear there's no woman but you. You're the one I love and the one I come home to every night. But I can stop coming home, especially if it's your intention to punish me forever."

"What a talent you have for always making what you did my fault."

"Look, I'm sorry for anything I've done in the past." He wrapped her in his arms and kissed her forehead. "This wasn't at all the entrance I'd planned. I've got some good news. Change that to great news. Dr. Logan asked me to replace him as department head. It'll mean an extra quarter million a year for us."

Chelsea's body stiffened. "Is that the going rate for more time at work and less time with your family?"

"Just the opposite. I'm going to hire a radiologist to take over my shifts at my practice." He pulled her closer. "There's nothing and no one I care for more than my family. I don't want anything to destroy what we have."

The doorbell jangled. Garrett leaned back, a broad smile on his face. "I believe that's for you, Chels."

"What's going on?"

"Let's go find out."

CHAPTER 17

GARRETT COVERED CHELSEA'S eyes once they reached the bottom of the stairs.

She tried to wriggle free. "What are you doing?"

"Keep walking. I'll make sure you don't bump into anything." When they reached the front door, he said, "The knob's about a foot in front of you."

Chelsea felt for the knob, turned it, and opened the door to a man dressed in an expensive suit. He handed her a key and made a sweeping gesture at the silver Bentley behind him. "Happy Birthday, Mrs. Hall. We hope you enjoy driving your new car."

Garrett said, "Her Mercedes is in the garage. The keys are under the mat by the driver's seat."

The man nodded. "I'll clear the space for you, sir. Ma'am." He tipped a hat that wasn't there and trotted to the open garage.

Garrett put an arm around Chelsea's shoulders. "I know it's a day early, but I couldn't wait. I wanted you to feel special for your birthday tomorrow. I want you to feel special every day, because you are. I love you, babe."

She hesitated then said, "I love you, too."

Garrett let his arm drop to his side. Where was the anticipated screaming and jumping up and down, the hugs, the kisses, shouting for those inside to come see what her remarkable husband had gotten her? "You said this was your dream car. Did I make the wrong choice, choose the wrong color? We can exchange it, if you want."

"No, Garrett. It's the right one."

"What's wrong?"

She recalled his reason for giving her the full-length mink coat, the two-carat diamond earrings, and all the other expensive gifts he thought would make up for his wrongdoings. Chelsea gave him a small smile. "It's nothing. I'm just stunned."

"That's a relief." Garrett yelled for Kimberlie and Penelope. He took Chelsea in his arms. "This confirms I love you, yes?"

"It's a confirmation, all right."

CHAPTER 18

THE FOOTFALLS CLOMPING down the stairs meant it was time. Garrett dreaded having the conversation, but had to engage it—her. It was his obligation to do so. He held up a box of cereal, gave it a shake and asked, "Want some?"

Kimberlie, still in her pajamas, hair mussed and mascara smeared on her cheeks, shuffled to the middle of the kitchen. She plopped onto a stool at the counter and didn't answer.

"I need to talk to you about what I did, Kimmie."

She formed her lips into a pout and shrugged.

Garrett filled a bowl with cereal, added milk all the way to the top, and pushed it toward her. "Just the way you like it." He slid a spoon to her.

Kimberlie picked up the spoon and poked at the contents of the bowl.

"I know you're angry about what happened, but I had to do it. Boys who don't demonstrate proper respect for you, or themselves, have no right to take you out, especially in public."

"It's not right to judge people before you even get to know them. It's not fair."

"Maybe Mark is okay, but there's a fact you have to keep in mind, one I have to keep in mind on your behalf: Boys that age—hell, any age—have one thing on their mind. You know what I mean, right?" Kimberlie shrugged again. "They'll tell you they love you or whatever they think you want to hear, or what they hope will work, just to get what they want. And once they get it, they move on to the next target."

She mumbled something that sounded like, *You should know.* His face grew hot; he wondered how much she knew. Kimberlie's eyes were cast downward as she pushed the sugary circles into the milk and watched them bob back to the surface. He wasn't about to put a foot onto that topic's path, not if he could help it.

Kimberlie scooped cereal into the spoon. "I don't want to talk to you about—you know. Besides, Mom talked to me about it. I've decided to wait till I get married. So, would you just chill, already?"

He sprinted around the counter and hugged her. "That's my girl. Take time to get to know the man you want to spend your life with. You deserve a man who respects you. Adores you. Because you are adorable, you know." He ruffled her hair.

She shifted away. "*Da-ad.*"

"I'm curious about why you thought Mark was someone right to go out with."

"He's real popular. He's also the best basketball player at school. Coach said maybe even good enough for a scholarship to a good college before going pro. Last year he was voted most likely to succeed. All the girls want to be with him, but he chose me."

"Maybe I did misjudge him. But if he has that many girls after him, how long do you think he'll put up with a virgin? You are still a virgin, aren't you?"

"*Eww*, Dad."

"That's not an answer."

"I just said so." She tilted the spoon slightly and watched the milk drizzle into the bowl. "You're so old-school. You probably won't let me date till I'm forty."

"I'd like to protect you as long as I can, but it'll be sooner than that. It's just that I don't want you to do anything, or for some boy to convince you to do something that'll prevent you from getting your degree. A rewarding, lucrative career is what I want for you. You want to be self-reliant and not have to depend on a man."

"Mom depends on you."

"We explained why we agreed your mom would stay home. But your mom, if she had to, can provide for herself."

"It's just that you treat me like a child. Mom doesn't."

He shook his head. "It's not easy for a father to do otherwise. There's nothing easy about watching your little girl turn into a young woman. I'll strive to do better, I promise. But don't expect me to stop trying to do the best for you and to protect you. Can we agree on that?"

One shoulder went up then down. "I guess." Kimberlie dropped her spoon into the cereal. "It's gone soggy." She slid off the stool and did a slide-walk on sock-covered feet until she reached the staircase, taking two steps at a time to the second floor.

Garrett shivered at the sight. When had Kimberlie grown breasts? Terror struck, and he wanted to lock her in the proverbial tower until it was safe to let her out. Until every young man interested in her had been properly vetted, not that any of them would ever be good enough for her.

His daughter was in that precarious between-place with part of her still a kid and another part straining to grow up too fast. A fact of life was that her body wasn't waiting for his permission.

He ate her sodden cereal and wondered if the days were truly over when his daughter hollered for her daddy whenever she got hurt or some possession of hers broke. He'd been too otherwise occupied to notice when it was that she'd outgrown sitting in his lap or cuddling while they watched a movie at home. Nor could he recall the last time they'd done that or anything else together.

The reality of his lack of presence in her life struck him in his chest. If only he could slow time, slow her maturation process. But, Kimberlie would fight such an effort. The last thing he wanted to do was be so strict that he caused her to retaliate, doing everything he said she couldn't and shouldn't.

The thought that followed wrenched him: what if she married a man just like him?

He emptied the rest of the cereal into the garbage disposal, ran the water and flipped the switch. As the grating sound filled the space, he admitted the truth:

You're a damn hypocrite.

CHAPTER 19

THE NEXT MORNING, Chelsea sat on her side of the bed, with her cell phone pressed hard against her left ear. She frowned at the nails on her right hand. One day she'd stop picking at her cuticles, whenever she could get rid of her frustration. That day would probably be the same one as when she wore a size six again. Her manicurist would fuss, but it couldn't be helped.

Janice Johnson answered after the third ring. "Good morning, my darling. I was going to call in a few minutes and wish you a happy birthday. You beat me to it."

"Hi, Mom. Thanks."

"You don't sound as enthusiastic as I would have expected on your big day. Is everything okay?"

"I think Garrett is cheating again."

"Maybe you're just imagining it. It's understandable that you still feel insecure, but—"

"It's more than that. The Bentley I've been saying I wanted? Garrett gave it to me for my birthday."

"How fabulous! It is fabulous, isn't it?"

"Not if he's following his pattern of guilt, like before."

"This is personal—and you can tell me to mind my business—but how are things in the bedroom?"

"Nonexistent. For a long time. I tried to initiate for a while, but Garrett always said he was too tired from working so many hours. I finally stopped trying."

"My mother told me a marriage is as good as what happens in bed. She was right, of course. Although, she did also say if a man isn't having sex with his wife, it's likely he's getting it elsewhere."

"If you're trying to make me feel worse, you're succeeding."

"I didn't mean to say that last part aloud."

"Too late."

"What about going back to counseling? Both of you, that is."

"The only reason Garrett went was because he got caught. Then he said his schedule was too intense and stopped going. The truth is he didn't want to hear how guilty he was week after week. From me, that is. The therapist aimed his arrows at me. If I try to get him to go again, he'll just use the same excuse. He'll argue that he shouldn't have to go if he's innocent, and he'll swear he is."

"Be that as it may, men don't process thoughts and emotions the same way we do. Perhaps he doesn't fully comprehend how you feel."

"He knows. He believes my feelings are my problem, not his." Chelsea brushed at her tears. "My life wasn't supposed to turn out this way. I don't know him anymore. I don't even know myself."

"You should consider counseling again, just for you, but with someone better than that last one."

"And now Garrett is trying to tell me who I can and can't talk to or confide in. I don't know why he detests Penelope, but he does."

"That's because he doesn't understand Penelope, or the fact that women need their friends, especially their closest ones. I know she's somewhat out there, and I also know you need that. You were always so quiet and serious, until you and she became friends. But you also need to understand why a man finds any kind of disclosure about his personal life humiliating."

"Of course you'd take his side."

"I'm not. I'm just more experienced than you are because I've been alive longer. Married longer, too."

"How did you and Dad make it work?"

"I went to my father once, to complain about your father. Dad stopped me and said I shouldn't tell him anything, because I might forgive your father and he might not be able to. Told me to go home and make it right with my husband. You have to find a way to fix it with Garrett, instead of solely talking about it with others."

"I've tried. He's the one who won't make the effort. I refuse to live the rest of my life this way. I'm hurting, Mom. Who knows how many women Garrett has screwed or is screwing now. I'd rather be alone than live like this."

"I wish you wouldn't use coarse language. Never mind. What about Kimberlie? Are you prepared to separate her from her father?"

"She hardly sees him now. For all I know, he'd make it a point to spend more time with her if we split up."

"What about income? You haven't worked since Kimberlie was born."

"He'd damn well pay for our care, at least until Kimberlie finishes her medical training. Believe me, money isn't an issue. Afterwards, I could do what's needed to get back into a practice. I want at least a chance to find true love and happiness. I deserve it."

"We all deserve it, dear, but sometimes you have to pick your battles. You think you're the only woman who's been cheated on? How do you think I managed to stay with your father this long?"

"Daddy never!" When her mother didn't reply, she said, "I can't believe what I'm hearing."

"He gave her up eventually. The reality is you can leave Garrett and find another man. Or you can stay in the luxury your husband provides, keep your home together for your daughter's sake, and find some other avenue for happiness so you don't sit around dwelling on how miserable you feel. The fact is this: The wealthy ones cheat, the poor ones cheat. If you're going to be with a man, you might as well be with a rich one, because they all cheat."

"I refuse to believe that. It's as ridiculous as saying every woman cheats. There has to be a way I can get Garrett to feel about me the way he used to so he doesn't want another woman."

"You read too many romance novels, Chelsea dear. There are no Prince Charmings. Sure, they'll act charming at the start so they can get you into bed. Then they'll either move on to someone else or marry you so they don't have to work so hard for it. Garrett may be flawed, but he does love you and takes care of you. I don't need to remind you how well."

"And yet, you always do."

"Do what you need to, to make your marriage work. It may not be perfect, but it's a matter of better the devil you know. Don't be one of those women who quits whenever the going gets tough. I raised you better than that."

"I'm not like you."

"And if you aren't careful, that may be your downfall." Janice sighed. "I know of a highly recommended therapist here in town. She's considered a bit unconventional, but from what I've heard, she's supposed to be excellent. Dr. Bernadette Moore. She wrote a book called *The Anatomy of Cheating*. It's about the issues and consequences of infidelity and the hardships of marriage. Research the book. Look her up. Maybe she can help you and Garrett."

Chelsea opened the drawer of the nightstand next to her side of the bed and removed the unread autographed book. "I guess I'll try one more time. I'll see you at the party tonight. Give Dad my love."

Everyone was being unfair. They asked everything of her and nothing of Garrett. The therapist had wanted her to forgive and forget. Garrett wanted the same, along with her turning a blind eye to what he was up to, and she was certain he was up to something. Her mother wanted her to find a way to occupy herself so the money train didn't go off the rails.

Chelsea looked at Dr. Moore's smiling image on the book cover and said, "I wonder what you're going to expect of me."

She dialed Richard's number.

"Happy birthday, Chelsea! We're looking forward to celebrating tonight."

"You won't believe what he got me." She told him. Their call lasted a few minutes.

Then she buried her face in the pillow to muffle her sobs.

CHAPTER 20

WHY, CHELSEA wondered, did Monday mornings have to feel more hectic than any other morning of the week. She mentally reviewed her to-do list as she searched for something to wear. Checked the time, swore under her breath, and slipped on the same big-enough pants and shirt she'd worn the day before. If she didn't get a move on, the morning would go to crap in a hurry, starting with the fact that Kimberlie needed to be dropped off early for her school trip.

She snatched up her watch and earrings, putting them on as she rushed to Kimberlie's room. Her daughter had inherited her punctuality from Garrett. Kimberlie, dressed and ready to go, sat cross-legged on her bed, earbuds in, singing along with whatever anthem that had been composed for teens enduring the angst of their age group.

Chelsea charged down the stairs and hurried to the kitchen. She used the single-cup function on the coffeemaker, took a sip, checked the time, cursed aloud. It was a mad dash up the stairs to get her purse, car keys, and daughter. Next to her purse was Luke Thompson's novel, *A Dark Walk*. She made a mental note to check his Goodreads page for updates, and for his approval of her friend request, the next time she thought about it.

She stood at Kimberlie's door. "C'mon, Kimmie. Time to go."

Kimberlie's head bobbed and she sang out loud and out of tune, "You're too illiterate to read my pain."

Chelsea crossed the room and stood in front of her daughter. Kimberlie looked up. Chelsea tapped her watch and said, "Let's go."

They pulled up to the front of the school fifteen minutes early, mostly because she'd sped whenever it was moderately safe to do so.

"Cheek, please." Chelsea kissed her daughter. "Have fun, but be careful."

"You know me, Mom." Kimberlie waved at a friend and slammed the door, now lost in a scenario that didn't include her mother.

There was no point in hoping for a wave from her daughter who was laughing at what someone had said. Chelsea edged her car around the line of school buses and turned right at the street, thankful the superstore stayed open day and night, seven days a week. She drove the few blocks and parked as close as she could to the entrance. She'd likely be walking all day; no point in doing more of it now.

She turned the engine off and stayed in the car, craving a few moments to decompress from rushing around. Her gaze shifted to her purse resting open on the passenger seat. No time like the present. She retrieved her iPhone from the leather *well* filled with wallet, lipstick, and odds and ends, and logged in on her Goodreads account. Keyed in Luke Thompson's name, found his page, his approval, then tapped the mail icon and typed.

Mr. Thompson, I found A Dark Walk *riveting. You're truly talented, and I look forward to reading more of your work. You're definitely a rising star. I'll post a review soon.*

She hit Send. Her phone rang. "Hi, Pen."

"Hey, Chels. Are we still going to breakfast then mad shopping today?"

"Wouldn't miss it. I just dropped Kimmie off and need to get some things at the store. Meet me at my house in an hour."

CHAPTER 21

P ENELOPE RAN A hand along the Bentley parked on the circular drive. She puckered her lips into a pout. "You gave me a ride when Garrett had it delivered, but when are you going to let me drive it? I'd wear this car well, don't you think?" She leaned against the hood and arched her back. "Do I look like a Vargas girl?"

"As usual, you're right on time. Come upstairs while I change clothes. It took a little longer at the store than I thought. I just put away the last item."

Penelope air-kissed Chelsea's cheek then made her way inside and up the stairs.

Chelsea followed her friend, but at a slower pace. "You're in such great shape, Pen. I don't hate you for that, but I envy it."

"Envy-*smemvy*. Think of the shopping we're going to do today. No better payback for a husband who's been naughty."

"Maybe."

"No maybe about it." Penelope stretched across the bed. She lay on her back looking up. "I have an idea about how you could get Garrett's motor running in bed. Put a mirror on the ceiling. He's so arrogant, he'd have sex with you just to admire himself."

"He'd probably prefer to have it alone. I'd spoil the view." Chelsea sighed. "Only a body like yours could pull off wearing a hot-pink bodysuit with a skintight mini. There isn't an ounce of fat on you. Only curves. The right kind."

"Hot yoga, silicone, and liposuction help, as you can see." She stretched cat-like then rolled onto her stomach. "As well as injecting the fat into your derriere for that wasp-waist atop a rounded bottom. It's considered *tres* chic these days, you know."

"I'm not brave enough for those kinds of procedures. The last thing I need is fat added anywhere on my body, and it would be too humiliating to flounder on a mat in a room filled with fabulous bodies."

"You're always so hard on yourself." Penelope sat up. "Chels, what's up? You okay?"

"It's just that yours is the kind of body Garrett appreciates." She grabbed her muffin-top. "Not a blob like me."

"Garrett's your husband and you love him. But he's a prick for what he did to you. Plenty of men would want to be with a beautiful, intelligent woman like you."

"I appreciate your cheerleader effort, but I don't believe it."

"You've let Garrett—the rutting bastard—beat you down. He should get up every morning counting his blessings for having you as his wife."

"That's just it. I don't count. Not anymore. He's even stopped telling me how dissatisfied he is with my appearance."

"Maybe his silence is golden."

Chelsea shrugged. "That's not all he's stopped."

"I thought you were exaggerating about that. No action? At all?"

"Not with me. It's been about three years. Maybe longer. I think he's cheating again."

"I'm sure you're imagining it."

"You sound like my mother."

"Be nice. I think you think he's cheating again because you're feeling so insecure. Which you shouldn't."

Chelsea shook her head. "That Bentley you admire so much? I've told you before: The more expensive the gift, the more egregious the infidelity. At least, that's been Garrett's pattern so far."

Penelope's laugh was hollow. "I'd consider that a fair exchange, as long as the bastard was as good-looking as Garrett and had as much money or more."

"What price can you put on the kind of pain that rips your heart out?"

"Sorry, Chels. Just trying to get you to lighten up."

"I'm either going to follow him or hire a private detective." Chelsea turned on the light in her spacious walk-in closet and began to look for an outfit she might feel less embarrassed about wearing.

"Can't follow him in your new car. You'd have to rent a clunker. He'd find out about a P.I. They're not cheap. Leave it alone, Chels. What you don't know won't hurt you. If it were me in your Ferragamos, I'd fight fire with fire."

Chelsea walked to the door, with a light loose sweater half-slipped on. She pulled the sweater over her bosom. "I'm not following you."

"Get a hot man on the side and make sure Garrett finds out. The old dose-of-his-own-medicine thing. Maybe how that feels will penetrate his thick skull. And you'll have some fun in the bargain."

Chelsea turned and stood in front of the double-wide built-in shoe rack. She stared blankly at the floor-to-ceiling array of expensive footwear. Who'd want her? What kind of man would she want? He'd have to have some of Garrett's more favorable characteristics and be free of the worst ones.

Luke Thompson's handsome face and warm eyes came to mind. If only she could be loved by a man like that, whose keen sensitivity was so beautifully expressed as it was through his writing.

Chelsea felt her cheeks flush. She'd never dated an African American. If she had, what might her family and friends have said? Segments of society had loosened its stranglehold on mixed marriages. Not that it mattered, especially if she cared for the man and he cared for her.

She shook off the useless musing and selected a pair of shoes that matched her slacks and wouldn't hurt her feet if theirs turned into an all-day shopping spree. She eased her feet into the loafers. No way to compete appearance-wise with Penelope. She might as well be comfortable.

Penelope was right about one thing: Garrett had no idea how betrayal felt. She'd made sure of it. She wondered if he'd even care. *Whatever keeps you off my back, babe.* Especially if it meant he wouldn't be expected to put her on her back a couple of times a week, or even just once.

Penelope looked in from the closet doorway. "Are you ready yet?"

Chelsea stared straight ahead. "Maybe I am."

CHAPTER 22

L UKE REREAD CHELSEA Hall's e-mail on Goodreads then clicked on her profile page. Attractive. Not a lot of information about her posted there, but she seemed normal. And sincere.

It was more than a sense of obligation that led him to respond: her comments fed his need to be valued and respected as a writer.

Chelsea, thank you for the kind words. I'm delighted you enjoyed A Dark Walk. *It's refreshing to know someone appreciates my work. Thank you in advance for the forthcoming review. I look forward to reading it.*

Luke startled when the front door was slammed shut with force. He went to the door of the room he used as his office. Brandi glared at him from the den. Her hard gaze met his quizzical one, but she didn't greet him. Face pinched, she made her way into the kitchen and flung her keys and purse onto the counter.

Luke went to her. "What's wrong?"

"Six fucking years."

"What's happened, babe?"

Brandi pulled out a stool from under the counter and plunked onto it. "I got laid off. Without any notice. Got to work and found the pink slip and a check for two month's pay in an envelope on my desk. Then I got politely escorted out."

Luke wrapped his arms around her and held her close. "That's awful. I'm sorry it happened, but it'll be fine. Someone with your skills can easily get another job. An even better one, where you're appreciated."

Brandi shoved him away. "It's hard enough that we're barely making it. I'm the only one bringing in a decent income, and now that's gone."

"I know you're upset, sweetheart, but with what we have put away, the check they gave you, and what I earn at work, we'll be fine until you get another job. I know that won't take long. You're brilliant."

"We've got enough for all of three months. That's it. What you bring in certainly won't make me feel secure in the meantime. Part-time work. Of all things for a grown man with a family to do. Just so you can sit in front of your damn computer hours on end, and for no money. You were offered a teaching job, but did you take it? No."

"I told you it—"

"Takes away from your fucking novels that don't sell. Do you know how much pressure being the breadwinner puts me under? Do you even care? You're so selfish. Irresponsible. You're the one with the balls. Act like it."

"Calm down, Brandi. Before you say anything else you'll regret."

Brandi slid off the stool. "Do *not* tell me to calm down. You want to know what I regret?" Tears filled her eyes. "Never mind. Talking about reality with you is useless. It's like talking to a three-year-old." She sprinted up the stairs and did what he knew she would.

Glasses in the cabinet clinked when the door to their bedroom above the kitchen slammed, shutting him out.

CHAPTER 23

B RANDI HAD PLUNGED the *knife* in deep and twisted it. Another skill she was brilliant at, when she had a mind to use it, which occurred with more frequency these days. James would tell him only a passive schmuck would let his wife talk to him like that.

Luke returned to his office and lowered himself into the chair at his desk. He *should* stand up for himself, but at the moment, he felt defeated. Torn between fulfilling an obligation to Brandi and fulfilling one to himself. He got up and paced.

James had warned him about being pressured to marry Brandi, and doing so for companionship rather than true love, and he'd been right. But he'd stated at the altar that it was for better or worse, and not until death would they part. How many more times would he have to say those words until they stuck?

He wasn't going to go through the turmoil of another divorce. It wasn't worth it. Not this time. Not ever again.

He felt broken. Trounced by Brandi, his harshest critic. She was right, though: He was a failure. His books weren't selling. That was his fault. Because he spent most of his time writing and hardly any on marketing, as though wishing for better results would change anything. Success as a writer was a long shot. He'd known that, but that desired outcome and its companion prosperity retreated further away each day.

His attention returned to the computer screen, still open to Chelsea Hall's message. It seemed the only words of encouragement he'd heard in longer than he could remember had come from a stranger. Now more than ever, he needed some of that kindness. He sat and positioned his fingers on the keyboard, adding to his as yet unsent reply.

Thank you for believing in me. It matters more than you know. I was pleasantly surprised to learn we both live in Waltham. Maybe we can meet for coffee one day (my treat) so I can thank you in person.

He double-checked for typos and hit Send. Then realized such an invitation was probably a mistake. That was the thing about mistakes and missteps, wasn't it? Even a second later was too late to take them back.

What if Chelsea said yes? Brandi's reaction to his meeting a fan was all too easy to imagine. He'd have to lie to her, if he kept the meeting.

It was doubtful that Chelsea would agree. But what if she did?

He'd make some excuse. He had enough problems with Brandi as it was.

CHAPTER 24

A FEW PIECES of leftover chicken were placed onto a plate and into the microwave. Over the hum of the appliance, Luke heard footsteps thump down the stairs. A red-eyed Brandi, without looking at him, opened the refrigerator and stared at its contents. He drummed his fingers on the counter. Watched the numbers on the timer perform a digital countdown. Felt the three minutes last an eternity.

Brandi grabbed a soda and sat at the counter. Luke tucked four chilled beers into the crook of his arm and grabbed his plate with his free hand. No way was he going to eat with his wife's energy nuking him. He'd eat in the basement. In peace or, at least, quiet.

He guzzled the first beer then ate a drumstick, followed by a second beer, a thigh, a third beer, a wing. After he drained the fourth beer can, the effects of the alcohol and Brandi's silent treatment collided. He scrolled to James' number on his cell phone. At "Hello" he began talking non-stop.

After a few minutes, James interrupted him. "Dude, you been drinking. Don't want to be unsympathetic, but let's talk about this shit when you're sober. Maybe in the morning. Get some sleep, man."

Luke turned off the phone and stared at the blank screen, wondering what was wrong with his friend. Probably interrupted him in the middle of doing the horizontal mambo with his wife. Or someone else. It would be a long time before Brandi *danced* with him again.

It was too far to go back to his office for his laptop, and best to avoid Brandi for a while. He'd wait a half hour or so. If she was still in sight, he'd grab the laptop and retreat. Fast.

He turned his phone back on. Went back to his Goodreads page. Maybe it would help to read Chelsea Hall's praise one more time before trying to write amid the tempest threatening to break loose in his house.

She truly was a beautiful woman, with a kind face and enigmatic blue eyes framed by thick shoulder-length auburn hair. He leaned back and closed his eyes. What was it like to caress skin the color of cream? To see the blush of orgasm spread across her skin? These were precarious thoughts. He wouldn't be having them if his life was more fulfilling. And if Brandi didn't consider him a loser.

He opened his eyes. There was another message for him. From her.

Luke—may I call you that?—you obviously have talent. Lots of it. And I'm certain you have many fans who would agree with me. Some people hesitate to post their thoughts about what they've read, for whatever reason. Be patient. The praise will come. You've earned it.

No response from her about meeting for coffee. Relief and disappointment competed inside him. It would mean a great deal to sit face to face with a fan, even for just a quarter of an hour.

Please … call me Luke. Chelsea—means seaport; like a port in a storm. I'm glad you think I have talent and that praise is forthcoming. But my wife thinks otherwise.

He hit Send. He should regret revealing something so personal, especially as a criticism about Brandi. It was disloyal, but he couldn't find it in him to care.

That's because you're drunk, fool, he muttered.

Luke shrugged. Should know better than to drink and write. That only leads to regret. And heavy editing.

CHAPTER 25

U PSTAIRS, A cabinet was slammed hard. Then another. Luke's eyelids felt too leaden to lift. His head drummed. His mouth was like drywall, his breath rank. It was morning, judging by the bit of light fighting its way through the grime on the small basement window.

He sat up, stiff from sleeping uncovered on the ratty sofa. Brandi had left him in the basement. Probably hadn't even come down to check on him. He rubbed his eyes and face. Noticed the shot glass and nearly empty bottle of tequila on the coffee table. When had he gotten the tequila?

His Goodreads page was open on his phone. Why? Then he remembered.

Stupid damn fool. Certain he'd lost his only fan, he typed again.

Chelsea, please forgive me. The message I sent last night was inappropriate. My sincere apology.

He signed out and checked the time: 8:07. Time to pick up the pace. His restaurant shift started at nine this morning.

No way to avoid going upstairs. No way to avoid Brandi. All he knew was that he wasn't in the mood for an argument or to be subjected to more of her vitriol. Not with a raging hangover.

Luke crept up the stairs, each step amplifying the sensation in his head. He heard Brandi in the office, talking on the phone. What he heard halted his steps.

"My life is crap. There's no money. Nor does Luke care about it, not as long as I'm bringing it in. I'm fed up with making his life easy so he can pretend he's a writer. Most of the little he does earn from waiting tables goes to his ex-wife. And that son of his—such a rude little twit. As though my life isn't miserable enough. I'm sorry I ever married him. He's worthless. Refuses to act like an adult."

Her comments should have shamed him. Instead, they enraged him. Luke continued across the room silently then dashed up the stairs and into the shower. No way would he be late for work. In fact, he'd be early. Anything to get away from her.

As his foot hit the bottom step ten minutes later, Brandi came out of his office.

"Where are you off to?" she asked.

"Where do you think? This worthless child-man has to work."

"I didn't realize … Luke, I'm sorry you heard that. I thought you were still—"

"Save it."

This time he was the one who slammed the door.

CHAPTER 26

LUKE AND JAMES sat in silence on a bench in the restaurant courtyard. The ten-minute shift break was welcome. Luke nursed a cup of strong black coffee—his fourth. Even though the sky was overcast, he squinted his eyes against the gray light.

"Okay, dude," James said. "You don't get drunk. Not like that. Start talking."

"Brandi got pink-slipped yesterday. No advance warning or anything."

"That's fucked up."

"Then she dumped on me. Wants me to quit writing and get a full-time job. Wants me to teach kids who think anything more than 140 characters is as much as they can write or read at one time."

"That old horse again. Still, she has a point. The bills have to be paid."

"I overheard her tell one of her girlfriends that I'm worthless; that Tim and I make her life miserable. She's dissatisfied with her life. She's not the only one."

"You hope it was a girlfriend."

"What's that supposed to mean?"

"When's the last time you and Brandi bumped your nether parts together?"

Luke rubbed a vein pulsing at his temple.

"Dude, takes that long to answer, it means you have to *try* to remember. If you haven't asked her for it, you need to ask yourself why. If she hasn't nagged you for it, might mean she's getting tickled elsewhere."

"She's too proper to do that. Too unimaginative, if I'm frank."

"Unimaginative or not, she's the kind of woman who goes after what she wants. And gets it. Who knows that better than you?"

"Still—"

"And to tear you down like she did? To your face and to someone else. When a woman's loyalty and respect slip for her man, she might let someone else slip it to her."

Luke glared at him.

James held up his hands. "Just saying."

Luke propped his elbows on his knees and cradled his head in his hands. "I can't go there."

"I read something interesting in the Bible the other day."

Luke peeked at him from between his fingers. "You read the Bible?"

"I'm a well-rounded guy. As I was saying, I read that men are supposed to love their wives as they love themselves, and that wives are supposed to respect their husbands."

"That's basic common sense."

"And part of the problem. People do love others the way they love themselves. How many people do you know—besides me—who really love themselves? You don't love yourself."

"What's not to love?"

"I'm serious. You wouldn't second-guess yourself like you're doing if you did."

"I'm really not up for this conversation right now."

"Up for it or not, it's gotta happen. We're talking real life, dude. Maybe a woman doesn't love her husband all romantic like after they been married a while, but she's supposed to treat him with respect. Not nag his ass. Man's gotta feel respected first, loved second. Especially in his own home. That's just the way it is. She wanted you to marry her. You did. You're good to her. Brandi ought to treat you like a king."

"She wants me to contribute more financially. She's justified in feeling that way. But she knew the situation when we married. It's not like it was sprung on her after the honeymoon."

"The woman needs to have a little faith in you. And she needs to stop dissing restaurant service. I've been in the biz for years. And I make a damn good living at it."

"The difference is you're a manager, soon to be promoted to area director. I wait tables."

"Customers love you. You're the only one here who gets a twenty-five percent tip most of the time, and has people willing to wait to sit in your section. You know how many diners call to ask us to save them a table for your section when you're working? Some don't even come in unless you're on shift."

"I didn't know anyone did that."

"All the time, dude. They find you charming and love that a one-day famous author takes care of them."

"Nice to know someone thinks I fulfill my obligations."

"What are you going to do about Brandi?"

"The only thing I can. Avoid her as much as possible, until she calms down."

"Brandi don't calm down. Unless she gets her way."

"Then I suppose she'll have to stay upset, and I'll have to see about making the basement more comfortable." Luke groaned. "My luck with women sucks."

"Won't get any argument from me. But I like to be an optimist. Maybe your luck will change."

"Probably around the same time one of my novels becomes a best-seller."

"So, sometime next week."

Luke shook his head. "Maybe you can afford to be an optimist. Despite Brandi's assessment of me, I'm a realist."

"In my experience, we're too easily fooled, by others or ourselves."

"I write fiction. I know the difference."

"Maybe. Maybe not. What's real right now is that this break's over."

CHAPTER 27

J AMES'S WORDS HAD stung. Because there was truth to them. Sure, he understood where Brandi was coming from, but as he'd told James, she knew what was what when she dated him then hounded him to make their relationship official. She'd said what they earned together would cover everything, plus his child support payments. That they'd live modestly until he was a successful author. Then he could buy her a big house with a huge landscaped lawn in a ritzy neighborhood.

Many nights, though it had been a while, they'd snuggled in bed after making love, and he'd talk about his dreams and listen to hers. He told her it might take a while to make it big, possibly longer than they'd like, but when he did …

She'd employed the old trick of blowing proverbial smoke up his ass. Patronizing him for her own purposes, not meaning a word.

Brandi had never written more than a financial statement or a check or a grocery list. No way she could understand the time and energy it took to be a writer who readers wanted to follow. She didn't appreciate what was involved. What was required of him. She didn't appreciate him.

Some writers had a need to feel tortured in order to be creative and productive. Not him. Encouragement inspired him to do better. To aim higher. If only she'd grasp that fact.

During his next break, he slid his phone from his shirt pocket and logged on to Goodreads. There was a new message from Chelsea Hall.

No apology necessary, Luke. Someone with your gift should never let anyone discourage him. Every author who became known started out unknown. Every great writer was a beginner. Thank you for your lovely comment—a port in a storm. With appreciation so lacking these days, especially in our homes, I feel more like I'm on a rowboat in a storm, struggling against the odds to reach a safe haven. Seems you and I are in the same boat (grin—or should that be a frown?).

How long had it been since anyone had engaged in such conversation with him? Brandi couldn't. It wasn't in her.

Chelsea, thank you for the encouragement. But I am dismayed—a woman as beautiful as you, and obviously kind, deserves to be given every reason to smile, and to be appreciated. Please forgive me. It's not my intention to flirt and cause you discomfort. I merely mean to admire you in a respectful manner.

He hit Send. And thought about what he'd written.

You're acting like a fool.

He shut his phone off.

There had to have been an accident somewhere ahead. The traffic was backed up. No one was moving. Luke shifted from Drive to Park, pulled his phone from his shirt pocket and searched for Chelsea on Facebook. Her page was set to Private. He switched to Goodreads. There was a reply from her.

Luke, I took no offense at your compliment. If you meant to make me smile, you succeeded. And I hope you won't take this the wrong way, but I return your compliment. Good face, warm eyes that reflect your sensitivity. The way you write tells me you understand love—what it isn't and what it should be.

Now was the time for caution. Now was the time to put a halt to this type of exchange. There was nothing worth attaining at the end of that road.

Thanks, Chelsea.

She'd see his response as curt, and she'd be right; though, the last thing he wanted to be with her was rude. He added two additional words: *Much appreciated.*

Traffic remained stalled. He dropped his phone into his pocket and stared at the cloudless blue sky. The same cerulean blue as her eyes, if the photo was accurate. Only one way to find out.

Stop it.

His phone was in his hand again. Chelsea's message was on the screen again. He drank in every word then scrolled back and reread each of their exchanges. Until several cars behind him blasted their horns. Traffic had started to move. People behind him wanted to get where they were going; he was holding them up.

He understood their impatience and frustration.

Luke parked his car in front of his home, turned the engine off, and remained inside. Each day it took him longer and longer to leave a vehicle that could facilitate his escape, away from what he knew waited for him inside those walls.

He felt walled in. Caged. Trapped.

The curtain of his office window shifted slightly. Time to face whatever awaited him inside.

Brandi was at the desk computer in the office. He wanted his laptop. There was no way to avoid her.

"What's up?" he said.

"Sending my resume to accounting firms." She motioned with her head toward a small stack of envelopes to her left on the desk. "Those are for you."

Luke picked up his laptop and the envelopes then headed for the basement. He set both next to the opened bottle of tequila. There was just enough of the pale golden liquid left to fill the shot glass. He put the bottle to his lips and drank the contents in one gulp.

He rested back and thought about what James had asked him: What are you going to do about Brandi? A valid question. Now all he needed was a valid answer.

He'd tried to make Brandi happy. Make? Keep? Was he really responsible for her happiness? He didn't feel she was responsible for his. But life was more joyous if shared by two people who were on the same page of life. Who cared about the happiness of their partner. That was the crux of it. They weren't on the same page about that. Nor had they ever been. Not really.

Fulfillment derived from doing something creative, and doing it well, made him happy. Lots of things made him happy. Money, it seemed, was the only thing that would satisfy Brandi. The only way he could accommodate her was to sacrifice himself.

How would he feel about doing that, in order to save his marriage? I'd rather open a vein, he said aloud.

CHAPTER 28

GARRETT LOADED THE film into the view box and pressed the red button on the recorder. "Degenerative changes are noted at the level of L4 and L5. Osteophyte formation is also noted at multiple levels, indicative of—" He hit the Stop button and told whomever had knocked on his closed door to come in.

One of the new residents stuck his head in. "Sorry to bother you, Dr. Hall."

"Not a problem, Kozier. How can I help?"

Kozier pulled out an MRI from the manila folder in his hand. "Heard you're one of the best. Hasn't been a case you couldn't solve, and all that. I hope that's accurate because this one's challenging me."

Garrett took the image and held it up to the light. "What's the history?"

"Seventeen-year-old male. Football player with sacroiliac pain aggravated by activities. No documented injury. X-rays were negative. And this MRI, from what I can see, is also negative."

Garrett exchanged the previous film in the view box with the MRI and studied the image. He pointed. "See this opacity near the sacral region? It's quite faint. Takes a trained eye to see it. It's usually indicative of some type of stress. I'm thinking a possible pars fracture. Often hard to detect. Have radiology run a bone scintigraphy."

"I see it now. Makes sense. Thanks, Dr. Hall." Kozier retrieved the MRI and walked to the door. "Want me to close this?"

Garrett nodded. He was acclimating to his new position as department head. Dr. Logan's anticipated retirement the following year had been moved up to immediately when his wife became ill. The job was more demanding than his predecessor had led him to believe, but he was up to the challenge.

His cell phone rang. "Chels. What's up?"

"Let's do something special tonight."

"Wish I could. Have to work late."

"You said this job would allow you to work less."

"You know how important it is for me to find another doctor for my practice. The process is involved, for good reason. Along with that, I'm still getting my bearings here."

"I know, but—"

"Logan's exit was hasty. For good reason, as you know. Still, there was no training. Just a 'Sorry, my boy. But call me with any questions.' I mean to do whatever it takes to impress the board so I keep this position and the raise that comes with it."

Chelsea stayed silent.

Garrett rolled his eyes. "They chose me over Williams or anyone else from outside who was qualified. C'mon, Chels. You know it's crunch time for me."

"Foolish of me to expect anything else. I'll find something to do. Alone. Again."

Garrett pressed the phone hard against his ear. He hated when she whined. "I promise to make it up to you. Soon as I can. Sorry, babe. Someone's at my door. See you later." He ended the call without waiting for her to say goodbye. Why wait to hear another disgruntled word from her. When had she gotten so needy?

His cell phone rang again. His anger rose. What else was she going to rag on him about?

Caller ID displayed the name *Dr. Kent*. About time she returned his call. His smiled stretched wide. He answered with "If you've got an itch, I've got the motion. And, I make house calls."

"I was wondering when you'd call again, and how convenient that you did. Because I need a specialist's expert touch. Please tell me you called because you're available this evening."

"Available is my first, middle, and last name."

"But no house call. It's the suite or nothing."

"How does seven thirty work for you?"

"Don't make me wait."

"I only make you wait until you can't stand it another moment."

"You're *so* bad, Dr. Hall."

"And you're so glad I am, Dr. Kent. See you then."

Dr. Jacobs was still his favorite. Because theirs was a unique arrangement. Even after all the years they'd been playing together, he wasn't bored with her. He never knew what she was going to come up with.

But every now and then, he needed something different. There was only one thing he'd requested that *Dr. Jacobs* refused to do. So far. He held out on persuading her one day. But not for the full-length mink coat she wanted in exchange. Not when it was so easy to get what he wanted from someone else who was willing.

He sent a text message to *Dr. Kent.*

Bring a friend.

CHAPTER 29

ARRETT CALLED THE hotel to confirm that his usual suite would be held for him. His anticipation of playtime with Suzanne, also known as *Dr. Kent*, and whichever friend she brought with her, amplified as the minutes ticked by.

At six fifty-nine, he got into his car, cranked the engine, and started for the highway that would take him south. At five after seven, his phone rang. His jaw clenched when he checked caller ID. "What is it, Richard?"

"Is that any way to greet your favorite brother?"

"Last time I checked, you're the only one. What do you want?"

"You in a rush or something?"

"I'm at work, and I'm busy. I got promoted earlier than expected."

"Congratulations."

"Thanks. It also means my workload's tripled." An eighteen-wheeler whizzed by in the right lane; the driver blared his horn.

"Sounds like you're in your car."

"Richard. The point?"

"I called at the house and Chelsea said I'd find you at the hospital. But you're not there, are you?"

"I'm running an errand then going back. If you want to play the insinuation game, I'm not in the mood."

"You're very touchy, Garrett."

"Ticktock, ticktock."

"Fine. I called to invite you to our church this Sunday. Anna's getting baptized."

"I thought I made it clear: I'm not religious."

"You don't have to be to attend and show a little family support. But, Garrett, it's time you consider giving your life to the Lord. Get forgiveness for the stuff you've done, especially to Chelsea. It'll keep you from going back to your old ways."

Garrett mumbled, "Self-righteous bastard."

"Say again. I missed it."

"I said I need to go."

"Sure. But first—"

Garrett ended the call. A glance at the digital dashboard clock showed it was seven ten. He swore when the car's Bluetooth picked up another call.

CHAPTER 30

"CHLOE. What is this? Family decided to call and harass me all at once?" Garrett slowed as he approached the highway exit ramp.

"Hello to you, too, G. What are you going on about?"

"Nothing. Talk fast. I'm in a hurry."

"You should always have time for your sister." When Garrett stayed silent, she continued. "I need your help."

"I don't mind helping you, but as I've said a million times, you need to do something constructive with your life."

"If you're going to lecture me, I'll hang up."

Garrett shook his head. "How much do you need?"

"Not much. Two thousand."

"That's not nothing, Chloe."

"I've seen you spend that and more for a jacket."

"Do you really want to go there?"

"Sorry. That was out of line. Because I'm frustrated. I ran into some problems with the rent and a few bills. I swear I'll pay it back."

Garrett rubbed a vein that started to throb in his left temple. How many times had she made the same oath? Twenty? Thirty? "I'll transfer the funds tonight."

"Thanks, G. I appreciate you coming through for me."

"You can't keep going on like this. Come live at the house. We have the room. I'll pay for you to learn a trade. Something useful that's lucrative. We'll get you into a good school."

"I don't know."

"You're my little sister. I love you. There's no reason your life has to be so screwed up when you have two brothers doing well and are willing to help you get on track." After several seconds of silence he said, "Chloe?"

Chloe's voice raised an octave. "This is why I didn't call Richard. He's always preaching and getting into my business. I thought you'd be different. I didn't call you for advice or a damn lecture. Just forget it."

"Wait." He rubbed his face. This wasn't what he needed right now. "We give advice because we care."

"When's the last time you listened to anyone's advice, much less followed it?"

"This is getting us nowhere. I'll get the money into your account as soon as possible, which will be sometime later tonight." He heard her harrumph. "We'll talk more about this later."

Garrett prayed in his own way, for the phone to stay silent. He pressed his foot down on the accelerator and pulled into a parking slot at seven twenty-five. Five minutes to relax and decompress. And get back into the mood.

At seven thirty, a car parked next to his. He got out of his car and leaned over to look at the two women inside the Audi.

This was going to be better than good.

He got his jacket from his backseat and held it in front of him. With a woman on each arm, he took the steps that would lead to his version of nirvana.

CHAPTER 31

CHELSEA SAT ON the edge of her side of the bed. She opened the nightstand drawer, to retrieve Dr. Moore's book, which she placed on her lap. Would anything in the contents make a difference? It was doubtful, but what else was left?

The blurb had been crafted to entice readers, with a promise to solve their problems and fulfill their needs and wants. She flipped through the first few pages, checked segment titles, scanned a few paragraphs. The last thing she felt like doing was reading, even though there was no telling what time Garrett would be home. Just that it would be late. As usual.

The book was exchanged for her laptop computer. An online search revealed that Dr. Moore's office was only fifteen or so minutes away. A click on the Schedule icon brought up a secure appointment calendar. She picked a date and time, entered her name and phone number. A small battle went on inside her then she hit Send. Moments later, a confirmation e-mail appeared in her in-box.

Garrett was working late, or so he'd said, and Kimberlie was doing a study sleepover at her friend Susan's house. Were it not for her daughter's high grades, she'd wonder how much studying was actually getting done.

The house should have felt large with only her in it. Instead, it felt constrictive.

Maybe she should call Penelope for a girl's night out. If, that is, Pen didn't have a date, which she usually did. She picked up her phone then changed her mind. No reason to get Pen to babysit her because she felt like having a pity-party. She did that often enough as it was. Plus, when they went out together, Pen tended to attract people she wasn't in the mood to deal with—men looking for something for nothing more than the price of a few drinks.

Nor did she always want to disturb Richard with her complaints, not that Anna ever said anything. Just hugged her with a sympathetic expression on her face whenever they showed up at the same place.

Chelsea went downstairs to the kitchen, poured a glass of merlot, returned to her bedroom, and turned on the TV.

Garrett had promised the promotion would give him more time to spend with her. He'd said he was getting used to the new position, but she doubted that even once he acclimated, he'd make time for her.

She seriously doubted he was working. She could call at the hospital to check up on him. It was almost a sure bet they'd tell her he wasn't there. They'd wonder why she didn't know. They'd know she was a fool.

He'd promised to love, cherish, and adore her. One thing she could rely on him to do was break his promises.

She muted the TV and pulled her laptop close, logged on to her Goodreads account and read Luke's latest message. She typed, *You're most welcome. What are you doing right now?* And hit Send.

Why had she asked something so personal? It was too late to retract it. She sent a second message that asked, *Writing the next great novel?*

Several minutes later, a reply came in.

Not doing much at the moment. What about you? By the way, thank you for posting your review. And if I'm not sounding inappropriately forward, I'd appreciate input from you. I'd mentioned meeting for coffee. You didn't reply about that—I hope I didn't offend you. I promise it's nothing more than a beginning author's appreciation for a reader who's been kind about his work. That said, do you think it will ever be possible for us to talk rather than messaging back and forth? Humbly yours.

So, he *was* serious about their meeting. She'd thought he was being polite when he'd mentioned it as a possibility. He seemed to genuinely want her input, perhaps might even value it.

Who was she kidding? That's all there was to it.

Was her disappointment because that was the extent of his interest?

Another feeling surfaced: Guilt. What the hell was she thinking?

She turned off her computer and called Penelope. "Sounds like you're at home."

"I am."

"I thought you'd be out. On a date."

"So, because you thought I wouldn't be available, you called me. Okay, Chels, talk."

"Remember the writer I told you about?"

"Luke something."

"He wants to meet for coffee. To get my thoughts about his book. Should I meet with him? Should I give him my number or ask for his so we don't confuse things? You know how text messages leave out the subtleties. Like is he flirting with me or not."

"Stop all this mental chatter. Go ahead and meet with him. By the way, I looked him up."

"Why?"

"You made such a big deal about him."

"He's an exceptional writer."

"He's a hunk. What's the harm in talking with him? What's the harm in feeling flattered by an author who also happens to be a stud? It would do you some good."

"You really think that's all he wants? Because I don't want to mislead him."

"Has he indicated he wants more?"

"No. I think he's too honorable to do that, not that he'd even want more to do with me. Besides, he's married. As am I."

"You don't know whether he's honorable or not. And don't be so sure that his interest in you stops at your praise for his novel."

"It's wrong for me to even wonder about this."

"Chels, are you having any fun?"

"What do you mean?"

"Looks to me like Garrett is the only one enjoying himself. Other than time with me, you're not doing anything for pleasure. Seriously, what's the harm? It doesn't have to go anywhere you don't want it to. Right?"

"Of course. I'm just anxious about talking with him."

"Ha! You decided to meet him. Before you called me. Didn't you?"

"I suppose."

"Then why'd you call me? For approval? You don't need it. Go for it."

"I guess I wanted you to talk me out of it."

"Forget that. It's a little innocent spice added to your life."

"I don't know why I'm making such a fuss."

"Problem solved. And, I do have a date. Gotta run."

It really was innocent. Two people who live in the same town, one an author, one a fan of the author. They could have just as easily met anywhere in town and decided to chat over coffee.

Completely innocent.

Then why did it feel anything but that?

Her mother would say all this pondering was the result of consuming one too many romance novels. That there was no there, there.

She had no intention of mentioning any of this to her mother. She could feel foolish without any assistance.

CHAPTER 32

A S EXPECTED, the lights were off when Garrett arrived home after his liaison with *Dr. Kent* and friend. He'd showered at the hotel. But that had left him smelling like the hotel's bath products. Better that than reeking of the edible body oil the ladies had brought with them.

He'd been concerned that management would disapprove of the quantity of oil left on the sheets—the entire bottle had been used. The women assured him the oil would come out in the wash. Hell, he'd pay for new sheets, if he needed to. Pay to play. It was worth it. Especially with those two voluptuous creatures. They'd soaped the oil off each other in the shower, which had led to his arriving home later than intended.

Chelsea was too suspicious as it was. He went out the back door, stripped, and slid into the swimming pool. After a few laps in the moonlight, he dried off with a towel from the cabana and slipped on one of the several robes kept in there. He grabbed his clothes and went into the library, also used as a home office. The transfer of eight thousand dollars to his sister's account was made. Then he dialed her number.

"I know it's late to call."

"It's almost two in the morning, G."

"I thought you'd sleep better if you knew your account now has money in it. I sent more than you asked for. Figured you'd need it for any overdue bills and such."

"Thanks. Is it polite to ask how much more?"

"I transferred eight thousand." He heard her whoop. "There's a *but* attached. I want you to use the rest to enroll in an educational program. You said you have an interest in massage therapy, right?"

"Right. I just never had the funds to get it going."

"Now you do. Sign up. Tomorrow. Take it from there. I know massage therapists who do really well. Chloe, I want you to be able to rely on yourself. To know you can be independent. My offer still stands about living here, at least while you go to school. Might as well cut down on living expenses as much as you can."

"I appreciate it, but I'd rather keep *some* of my independence." She laughed. "I'll find a school tomorrow. G, I'm going to make you proud."

"I just want you to get some balance in your life and stay there."

"I could say the same."

"Chloe."

"Just saying. I love you, G."

"Me too. Go back to sleep."

He changed into his clothes and dropped the robe into the basket in the laundry room.

There had to be something he could do to get his wife and his family off his back. But what?

CHAPTER 33

TWENTY MINUTES EARLY, Chelsea sat in her car parked outside Dr. Moore's office. Five days had passed since she'd read Luke's message. What must he think of her for not replying to his request. Not even with a refusal. He probably thought she was nothing more than a flighty female. Some kind of flake. Maybe she was turning into one. One whose backbone was missing.

She went inside the office, filled out the necessary forms and waited to be called in.

Several minutes later, Dr. Moore opened the door next to the reception desk. "Mrs. Hall. Please come in."

Chelsea nodded and stood, feeling dowdy in comparison with the stylish doctor.

Dr. Moore extended her hand. "I recognize you from my forum. You asked me to sign your book."

Chelsea shook the hand offered. "I'm surprised that with all the people you come across, you remember me."

"I have a memory for faces. Plus, it hasn't been long enough for me to forget you." She smiled. "And there's the hair. This way, please. We'll talk in my office."

Chelsea followed Dr. Moore to an elegant room, with walls that had a faux finish and furniture that belonged in a magazine that featured exclusive homes. The cherry desk was polished to a reflective sheen, and the few items on it were tidy. And expensive. Across from the desk was a large leather-covered sofa. Adjacent was a large chaise longue, also leather.

Dr. Moore said, "Sit anywhere you'll feel comfortable. I want you to feel relaxed enough to be completely honest with me. And with yourself."

"I understand." Chelsea sat at one end of the sofa, her purse gripped in her hands on her lap.

Dr. Moore sat at the other end, tablet and pen in hand. "Tell me what brought you here."

Chelsea cleared her throat. "I can't shake my depression. I have to try to do something about it."

"How long have you felt this way?"

"Two years." She shook her head. "That's not true. It's been longer."

"Any idea what that's about?"

"My husband cheated on me. Twice that I was able to confirm; though, I'm fairly certain it's more than that. After the second time— that I know about, which was last year, I lost it. I've dealt with the pain by eating, as you can see. I didn't always look like this." Chelsea waved a hand. "Okay, truth is, there's been an issue of baby weight for a number of years, which I struggled to lose and failed. But my husband's disapproval about my appearance, along with his actions, made it worse. And the more I gained the more depressed I got. I can't get myself to stop overeating. It's all stress-related. I'm never not stressed."

Dr. Moore scribbled on her tablet. "We'll discuss that in more depth at another time, but I'd like you to tell me about your husband—when you met, as well as about your children. How many do you have?"

"Just one. Our daughter. I met Garrett when I was a college freshman. He was in pre-med; I was in pre-law. Our daughter, Kimberlie, is fifteen. And the only real joy I have in my life. But she has a life of her own, which means I'm often left alone."

"And your husband?"

"Garrett's always been a hard worker. Graduated top of his class. Went on to medical school the year after we met. He's a radiologist, with certifications in internal medicine and cardiology."

"Sounds like he has a determined personality."

"That's one way to put it."

"How would you put it?"

Chelsea shrugged. "He seems determined to neglect me."

Dr. Moore jotted a note onto the paper. "Have you always felt neglected by him, including as a result of his professional life?"

"Not when we were first married. He was *very* attentive the first few years. His attentions slacked off when I started showing my pregnancy. Anyway, I worked in my own profession until I had Kimberlie. It was a mutual decision that I stay home with her. That's when I began to notice how often he wasn't there. I didn't realize this initially. I was too busy with Kimmie. What was going on became obvious to me after she started school. Then she reached adolescence and didn't need me as much. That's when the reality really hit."

"How did you discover your husband was cheating?"

"The first time it was because he left in a hurry, left his phone at home. I answered when it rang. I didn't recognize the woman's name on caller ID. She hung up when I said hello. I tracked the number on the billing call log and discovered they talked several times a day, and had been for months."

"What did you do?"

"I waited a few hours and called her from Garrett's phone. I lied and told her Garrett had confessed. She admitted to the affair and apologized. Like that made a difference. It didn't stop Garrett, though, despite his profuse apologies and swearing it would never happen again. I chose to believe him. I was desperate to, you see."

"You said that was the first time."

"The second time I found out—the one last year, was with a nurse at the hospital where he works. The woman showed up at my house! Thank God it was while Kimmie was at school. She said she'd fallen in love with Garrett. Said he wanted to leave me to be with her but that I was being difficult. She confronted me at my home, to get me to see logic." Chelsea pulled a tissue from the box next to her and wept into it.

"That must have been a painful time for you."

"Still is."

"Is this the first time you're seeking professional assistance?" Chelsea's sobs grew louder. "It's okay, Mrs. Hall. Take your time."

Chelsea blew her nose. "We went to counseling for a while, but Garrett stopped not long after the sessions started. Said he was too busy. Which was B.S. I continued going for a while then couldn't take it anymore. The counselor didn't understand how I felt."

"How do you feel?"

"Garrett picks women who have perfect bodies. Even if I starved myself to look like them, I don't think he'd be willing to be faithful."

Dr. Moore waited for the crying jag that followed to subside. "Mrs. Hall, the first thing I want you to understand is that you're a beautiful woman. You're intelligent and have a lot to offer. Never allow anyone to take that away from you. The second thing I want you to understand is that those women are not perfect. You're looking at them 'through a glass darkly,' as the saying goes. I promise you they have flaws and shortcomings."

Chelsea sniffed. "Maybe. But I don't think Garrett sees that."

"I'm sure they showed him only what they wanted him to see. Not the whole truth. You can't learn the truth about a person when you engage in nothing more than a tryst. Do you love your husband, Mrs. Hall?"

"God help me, but I still do." She buried her face in her hands.

"Are you willing to forgive him?"

Chelsea's sobs stopped. She glared at Dr. Moore. "You, too? I've had this discussion so many times, with the counselor and with Garrett. Not to mention my mother. How can I forgive what I can't forget?"

"That's not what I asked you."

"Then my answer is that I don't know. I haven't been able to forgive him so far."

"That's something we'll explore in another session, as well. For now, I want you to know that I understand how you feel. You know that's true, from my presentation."

"You said it happened to you. What happened, exactly? I'm sorry. It's not appropriate for me to ask that or expect you to answer."

"It's fine. In my first marriage, we grew apart. I thought I'd find what I was looking for with another man. I cheated. And it didn't take long for me to regret it, especially when I saw and felt the pain it caused everyone involved. I remarried a few years later, not realizing my second husband was a chronic womanizer. I left him."

"I'm sorry."

"Sad, but valuable. I learned it's impossible to run away from pain and the grief we feel for what's lost. Those emotions have to be faced head-on, if we're ever going to get beyond them. Like any form of grief, it takes the time it takes to heal. Denial never healed anything or anyone. You'll never forget what happened, but you can fill your life in meaningful ways so that you don't remember it as often. And at the times you do remember, the pain will be less than before."

"Shades of my mother, again. I suppose I have to take your word about that."

Dr. Moore smiled. "Sometimes, a mother's honesty is difficult to take.

"Our time's up. I think it's best we continue to meet weekly. Please schedule your next appointment before you leave."

Dr. Moore stood. Chelsea did the same, depositing her used tissues in the waste receptacle near the sofa.

"Thank you, Dr. Moore. It makes a difference talking to someone who's been through it."

"Believe me. I know. See you next week."

It did make a difference. But would it ever be enough?

She still felt emptier than empty.

CHAPTER 34

F IVE DAYS OF Chelsea giving him the silent treatment every morning was enough. Not that she didn't have good reason. He'd come home later than late for the last week. It was *Dr. Jacobs'* fault. She'd shown up with a big bag of *goodies* the first night. He'd asked her if there was anything left on the shelves in the sex shop. They still hadn't tried all the trinkets and gadgets as yet. That would take a few months. But they each relished discovering which were their favorites to use and have used on them.

Chelsea answered his call after the first ring.

Garrett leaned back in his chair. "Hi, sweetheart. How about a date with your overworked husband tonight? Say the word and I'll cut my day short."

"Really, Garrett?"

"You've got six hours. Pamper yourself however you want to then put on your prettiest dress. I'll make reservations at Chez Pierre's for seven, unless there's someplace else you'd rather go."

"You know it's my favorite."

"I'll pick you up at six thirty. Gotta run."

It took little to arrange for Kimberlie to spend the night at Susan's house. Little to pack an overnight bag and bring it to Susan's mother, Angela, so Kimberlie could go straight there after school.

It took a little more effort and profuse begging and the promise of a huge tip to, at the last minute, get a facial, her hair washed and styled, her makeup and nails—all twenty—done to perfection.

It took dealing with her embarrassment and a tremendous effort not to scream during her first Brazilian wax. She even squeezed in enough time to get a new dress that was more flattering for her figure, as well as one more item.

Chelsea stood in front of the full-length mirror in her closet. "Not perfect, but no one could call me a schlump." Her mother's advice whispered in her mind: *A woman may not be able to be made more beautiful than she is, but she can always be made more glamorous.*

And that's how she felt.

How long had it been?

She also wondered what Garrett would think of the other purchase she'd made. It was impossible to suppress the small smile on her reddened lips.

CHAPTER 35

THE MAGNUM OF Veuve Clicquot had been chilled to icy perfection. Garrett prepped a small toast round with crumbled boiled egg, minced onion, and caviar—just the way Chelsea liked it—and handed it to her.

"Chels, I've never thanked you enough, nor could I ever, for how you've supported me all these years. Even while going through your own demanding curriculum and once you started to practice law. I've never thanked you properly for our beautiful daughter. She's remarkable. And, that's all to your credit."

"Maybe not all. She was a daddy's girl when she was younger, if you recall."

Garrett smiled. "They have to grow up, but I miss those days. Seemed like overnight that she stopped needing me in the same way."

"She still needs you." Chelsea stared at the champagne flute she turned in slow circles. "So do I."

Garrett took her hand. "I'm sorry about all the hours, Chels. It will get better, once I'm over this hump. Once things calm down, we're going to use some of this extra income to take a trip together, just the two of us. Someplace exotic and romantic."

Chelsea's gaze met his. "You mean it?"

"We've earned it. You certainly have. We'll go someplace where staff can pamper you by day and I'll pamper you at night."

Chelsea's eyes welled. "I'd love that, Garrett."

"Nothing but the best for my wife."

CHAPTER 36

GLOWING FROM CHAMPAGNE and attention she'd longed for, Chelsea hurried into her closet. Anxious, and eager, she changed into the sexy gown from Victoria's Secret. Nothing like it had been worn by her since before Kimberlie was born. Her reflection in the mirror didn't match the one desired in her mind, but it would have to do. She straightened her posture. Confidence, Chelsea. You still remember what he likes.

Garrett's pillow was propped behind him, against the ornate headboard, his focus fixed on his iPad.

Chelsea, trembling, forged forward to the bed and cleared her throat.

Garrett glanced up at her and said, "You look beautiful, sweetheart," and resumed reading.

Chelsea pulled the covers back on her side of the bed and positioned herself next to him. She placed a hand between his legs, squeezed, squeezed harder.

"Chels."

"Yes, Garrett?" She tightened her grip, and released. Tightened. Released.

"Another night, babe. I need to relax and get some sleep."

"This is the best relaxant and sleeping pill anywhere." She repeated the action with her hand. Nothing. She threw back the covers and started to move into position, moistening her lips with her tongue as she lowered her head.

Garrett yanked the covers back over him. He put his iPad on the nightstand and turned off the bedside lamp. "Soon. I promise. Now get some sleep." He turned onto his side, with his back to her.

Her eyes filled and her lower lip quivered. "Are you cheating on me?"

Garrett groaned. "*What* does it *take?*"

"Yes, Garrett. What *does* it take? You asked for a date night. You wined and dined me. I arranged for Kimmie to be out of the house. I fixed myself up for you, including this gown that I now feel ridiculous wearing. You could have accommodated me."

"I told you: I'm tired."

"If you find me so revolting, you could have closed your eyes and pretended I was one of your sluts. As long as you didn't call out someone else's name, I wouldn't have known."

"Why do you have spoil the evening?"

"Do you even know how long it's been since you've touched me? I didn't rank so much as a two-minute annual hump on my birthday. I have needs, too."

"I'll get you a vibrator."

"You're a bastard. A lying, cheating—"

"Here we go again." Garrett bounded from the bed. "I'm done. You don't appreciate anything I do for you."

"You know that's not true."

"I bust my ass every day to make sure you're provided for. More than provided for. Yes, I made a mistake."

"A big one."

"Damn it, Chelsea. You can't let go of a simple human error."

"There's nothing simple about what you did to me. To us."

"You'll never let it go, and it's too exhausting to keep trying to make it up to you. I'm sleeping in the guest room tonight. Maybe a night alone in bed will bring home to you what you have."

"I assure you, it won't be much different than any other night."

Garrett slammed the door behind him.

The tears didn't come. No sobbing. No beating the pillow with her fists. She felt nothing. One thing she did know was that feeling sorry for herself was getting her nowhere. After tonight's *failure to launch*, she was certain he 'gave at the office', or anywhere he felt like it, and with whomever he felt like it.

Pen was right. Garrett was the only one having a good time.

She got her laptop from her nightstand, logged on to Goodreads, typed in her cell phone number, hit Send, and turned down the volume of her ringtone. When nothing happened after waiting several minutes, she turned off the light.

CHAPTER 37

TWENTY MINUTES LATER, Chelsea's cell phone rang. She turned on the lamp and grabbed her phone. "Luke. Hi. I wasn't sure if or when I'd hear from you."

"I would have called sooner," Luke said, "but I had to build up the nerve."

Chelsea's cheeks grew hot. A nervous laugh escaped her. "You're doing better than I am. Took me five days to send my reply."

"I thought I'd lost you forever. As a fan, I mean. Sorry. That sounded improper. I suppose I feel … Frankly, I feel foolish. Like a kid who got praise he was starving for. Or a puppy ready to lick the hand of his mistress. Oh crap. Sorry. Again. I'm going to shut up and let you speak."

This time, Chelsea's laugh was genuine, and came with a measure of satisfaction. "Believe me. I understand. You mentioned meeting for coffee so you could get my input. I'm flattered that you even want it. Where and when?"

"Really? That's great. What's good for you?"

"Weekdays are best. As long as I'm back for 3:30, when my daughter gets home from school."

"How old?"

"Fifteen."

"Is she as beautiful as you? What am I saying? Of course she is. There I go, being inappropriate again."

"I'm not offended, Luke. On the contrary."

"If you still want to meet—even though I continue to embarrass myself, I don't start my shift until four tomorrow. Unless that's too soon."

"How about eleven at Books and Brew? If we stay long enough, we can grab a sandwich there for lunch. If you have the time."

"I will. Good night, good night! Parting is such sweet sorrow …"

"That I shall say good night till it be morrow."

"Shakespeare thanks you, and I thank you. See you at eleven."

Chelsea put her laptop and phone away, turned off the light, and settled under the covers. Nervous energy flooded her.

He'd called her beautiful. Again.

Starting above her breasts, she trailed her hands down, feeling the contours of her body and the sensuous silk of the gown. Imagined it was Luke's warm coffee-brown hands stroking her, learning her.

She turned onto her side, bunched the pillow just right under her head and waited for sleep.

CHAPTER 38

G ARRETT WAS GONE when Chelsea woke. A relief, to be sure. It saved her from having to choose to ignore him, be nice to him, or lash out at him. She checked her phone and Goodreads. Luke hadn't reconsidered and canceled their date. She should call it an appointment. Yet, people scheduled lunch dates. They'd scheduled a coffee date. What was the big deal? Luke, the author, could just as easily be Lana, the author.

Tell yourself another one, Chels.

Still in her gown, she went downstairs, fixed one cup of coffee and boiled two eggs, surprised that she wasn't grabbing a package of iced cinnamon rolls from the freezer, ready to eat all eight rolls as usual. If meeting a man for coffee had that effect … She stopped herself from taking the thought further.

Luke had likely flattered her because she liked his writing. Nothing more. Nothing less. She felt the familiar depression start to return. Automatically, her hand yanked open the freezer door. She stared at the frozen sweet comfort. And closed the door, empty-handed.

She grabbed her phone. Scrolled to the desired name and number. "Richard, I know you're at work and busy. I just wanted to say this to someone who really gets it: Your brother's a bastard."

"I have about five minutes before a meeting. Talk to me."

Chelsea checked her reflection in the mirror. Her hair still looked good from the evening before. And, why not? Garrett hadn't messed it up in a fit of passionate intimacy. Even if Luke's wife wasn't a fan of his writing, her hair was probably messed up every night. The jealousy that flared stunned her. She shook it off.

A shower cap was fitted over her hair. She used hot water and scented soap on a loofah to scrub away the previous disappointing night.

If only it were that easy.

What to wear proved more challenging than anticipated. An hour later, she had managed to put together an outfit that appeared somewhat slimming to her eye. At least the colors worked in her favor. And one could never go wrong with silk, especially when it was warm out.

It was ten thirty. Books and Brew was a ten-minute drive away. She didn't want to get there early. Or late.

She paced until it was time to leave, repeatedly tucking her hands into her armpits to save her cuticles from being ravaged.

Ravaged. A word so close to ravished. It's what she needed to be. Maybe that would make her feel alive again, rather than hollow.

CHAPTER 39

CHELSEA EASED THE Bentley into the slanted parking space in front of the coffee shop. She resisted the impulse to look yet again in the visor mirror, as though some metamorphosis—positive or negative—had occurred since she'd left her house. If Luke waited there, watching for her, such behavior would appear anything but casual.

This meeting was a casual one. They were two new acquaintances meeting to discuss his book. Nothing more. If he insisted on flattering her, for whatever reason, what was the harm in that?

She got out of her car and started for the door. The blur of a man rushing to open it caught her attention. Startled blue eyes stared into warm brown ones.

"Luke. Hi, I'm Chelsea." She extended her hand.

Luke pressed his back against the door to hold it open and took her hand in his. "Shall I compare thee to a summer's day? Thou art more lovely and more temperate."

Chelsea felt the heat climb up her neck to her face.

Luke's smile faded. "There I go again. I've made you uncomfortable right from the start."

She gave a gentle squeeze to his hand and released it. "Not at all. I'm just not used to … Do you have a table waiting?"

He pointed. "Just there. The one with my book on it."

"Oh no."

"What is it?" Luke glanced around the room.

"I meant to bring your book so you could autograph it."

Luke relaxed and smiled. "You'd be my first."

"Guess I messed that up for both of us."

"I'd sign this one and give it to you, but it has my notes in the margins."

"My loss." Chelsea sat in the chair opposite his.

Luke remained standing. "What would you like?"

"Cappuccino."

"I'll be right back."

She waited a few seconds then turned to look at Luke. Strong back, strong legs, firm … She caught his reflection in the mirror behind the counter. Caught him watching her study him. He grinned. She smiled, bit her lower lip and faced forward. Cheeks flaming pink, Chelsea picked up his book and pretended to read the first page, and the second.

Luke returned with their coffees. She turned to take her cup and saucer just as he reached to place them in front of her. The back of his hand grazed across her breast, which readily betrayed her by revealing her response to his touch.

He shifted his focus from the front of her sheer blouse to her face. "That was an accident." He put her coffee down, spilling some. "So was that. I'm not usually so bumbling."

"It's all right."

Luke sat. His gaze connected with hers. "Which part?"

Chelsea realized he was waiting for an answer. "Which part what?"

"Which part was all right? Forget I said that. Forget the last thirty seconds. Let's start over."

Chelsea laughed. "Well, here we are."

"Here we are. Cheers." Luke held up his cup.

She tapped his cup with hers, keeping her gaze locked with his, and avoided saying what was foremost in her mind:

The question is, Where are we going from here?

CHAPTER 40

NOT SINCE COLLEGE had Chelsea had such engaging conversation with anyone. Garrett, when he was around, had spoken of little more than his work for as long as she could remember. Kimmie could be a real chatterbox when the mood struck her, but wasn't an adult, even if she attempted to act like one on occasion. Pen tended not to talk about anything deeper than men, herself, men, clothes, men. Her mother talked about her marriage to Garrett, and Kimberlie, more often than anything else substantial.

She'd focused so long on the absence of physical intimacy, the pleasure of intelligent conversation and a person's desire to hear what she had to say, and how much she needed that interaction as well, had gone ignored.

Luke had prodded her for her thoughts, her feelings. Drank them in. Drank her in with his eyes.

They'd discussed passages from his book and how they connected to real life, his gaze intent on her face. His body taut at her every word. Occasionally, he'd touched her hand or arm for a moment. She'd done the same.

It was lovely, a luxury. But that kind of attention doesn't last, she reminded herself. The first blush always fades from the bloom.

"Mom! Are you even listening to me?"

"Sorry, Kimmie. What did you say?"

"Where were you?"

"Thinking about a book I read."

"Must be some book."

"It is."

"As I was saying—"

"Can you say it while we swim?"

"You're going to swim? Like, in a bathing suit? Like, do you even own one?"

"I've got a suit. I've got a pool. Time I use them. Get changed. I'll meet you in five minutes. Then you can talk to your heart's content."

"Who are you, and what have you done with my mom?"

Chelsea laughed and bounded up the stairs.

CHAPTER 41

TIRED, YET content after swimming twenty laps and playing pool games with Kimberlie, Chelsea stood in front of the refrigerator, wondering what to cook. She queued Garrett's number.

As though the previous night had never happened, she asked, "If you'll be home for dinner, what would you like?"

"I'm working late. I'll grab something in the cafeteria."

"Sounds good. See you when I see you."

Chelsea ended the call and looked up the number for a nearby restaurant that delivered. Two dinners of boiled lobsters, steamed asparagus, plus two tomato, basil, and mozzarella salads.

She sent the delighted but bemused young delivery guy away with a twenty-dollar tip. Opened a chilled white Bordeaux for her and a sparkling water for Kimberlie. Set the table, with candles. Dished the food onto her best china. Added music she and Kimberlie could each tolerate and called up the stairs for her daughter.

Kimberlie dashed down. "I'm star-ving. What's for—? What the heck, Mom?"

"These are some of your favorites, right?"

"Yeah, but …"

"Great. Let's eat."

"Sure. But what's eating you?"

Chelsea spun around. She took her time pouring a glass of wine, enough time to let the blush leave her cheeks, prompted by the thought of changing the innocently spoken word "what" to "who."

Dangerous thoughts, Chels. Luke's married.

As are you.

Kimberlie slouched against the chair back. "I'm stuffed. And, I've got tons of homework tonight."

"Better get to it, then. But don't stay up too late. Beauty sleep, missy."

Chelsea loaded the dishwasher then stood at the bottom of the stairs. Kimberlie's door was closed, which meant she was serious about getting her homework done and didn't want to be interrupted short of an emergency or her favorite pop idol showing up to surprise her.

She took her cell phone outside, where she reclined poolside on a lounge chair. The text message to Luke was keyed in and sent.

Any chance you can call me?

She waited an anxious minute. Sighed after five. Then a ping.

Can you give me fifteen minutes?

If I can wait that long. She typed *Yes.*

Twelve minutes later, her phone rang.

"Sorry, Chelsea. I had to make up a reason to leave the house. I could have gone to the basement, I suppose, but I didn't want to chance it."

"I'm sorry. And inconsiderate. The last thing I'd want to do is cause you trouble at home."

"Believe me. I'm happy to leave that noxious atmosphere."

"More than a simple matter of her not liking your writing, then."

"Way more. Let's not talk about that. I'm pleased to hear your voice again, but surprised. I thought you'd be enmeshed in family."

"My daughter's focused on schoolwork. My husband won't be home until late, which is typical."

"He may be smart enough to be a doctor, but the man's a fool. I'd rush home every night to be with you."

Chelsea twirled strands of hair around her finger. "Nothing is more painful than being disappointed by the one person you thought would never hurt you."

"My words. From my book. The question is, do you use them for my situation or your own?"

"From what it sounds like, both."

"Are you disappointed because he doesn't give you enough attention, or are you saying—"

"He cheats. Prolifically, no doubt. Has been for years. However, I didn't catch him at it until two years ago and again last year. He was supposed to mend his ways, but he's at it again. I'm certain of it."

"How?"

"You saw my Bentley. That's the latest guilt payment for my services no longer being required and him servicing others."

"To think I was intimidated when I saw you get out of a car it would take me a lifetime to pay for."

"One of a number of payoffs from a man who believes he's God's gift to women, as long as it's not his out-of-shape wife."

"The man really is an idiot. And the last thing you are is out of shape. I was terrified I'd drool the entire time I was with you today."

Chelsea grinned. "What about your situation?"

"You don't want to hear about that."

"Every word you want to utter."

CHAPTER 42

THEY TALKED FOR twenty minutes, touching briefly on their situations with their spouses. Kept the conversation mostly about their children—a deliberate attempt to stay with safer topics. Luke hated having to end the call with Chelsea. Almost as much as he'd hated parting from her at the coffee shop.

It wasn't fair to compare Brandi to Chelsea, but facts were facts.

Chelsea was a perfect example of "still waters run deep." There were depths to be plumbed, mysteries to be explored and solved. With Brandi, what you saw was all that was there.

Chelsea was animated when she spoke, especially about his writing. So different from Brandi's boredom with him and her ever-increasing bitterness. And there was the fact she'd never read as much as one paragraph of one of his books, reminding him ad nauseam that she didn't care for fiction, whenever he begged her to see what he and his writing were about.

Chelsea was delicate. Brandi thought delicate was a cycle on a washer and dryer.

Chelsea was engaging and conveyed substance. Brandi was brittle and caustic.

And there was the most obvious difference: Chelsea was white. He'd never engaged in an interracial relationship.

The last word of that sentence caused his breath to catch.

It wasn't a relationship. What he had with Brandi was, with all its flaws. He and Brandi had a history. What he had with Chelsea wasn't even a friendship. It was—it was what?

It was only going to make him crazy if he didn't rein in his thoughts.

CHAPTER 43

BRANDI GLANCED UP from the financial magazine she was reading. "I thought you were going to work out?"

Luke dropped his gym bag inside the door of the office. "Too crowded. I'll go tomorrow."

"A better use of your time would be to either work extra shifts or get an extra job. At least until I get one that pays."

"We have enough for now."

"How can you be so damn complacent about the situation we're in? Oh, that's right. I forgot. You're used to having me pay for most of what it takes to maintain our lives. If you can call keeping our heads just above the waterline a life."

"I hope you leave the grimace and bad attitude at the door for interviews."

"You have a damn nerve talking to me like that. After all I've done for you. And for your bratty son."

"For which you never fail to remind me. Don't think I'll forget what you said about me, and about Tim, anytime soon."

"You weren't meant to hear that. I told you, I was frustrated."

"You're frustrated more often than not these days."

"Living with you, I have a right to be."

"If you hadn't needled me into … Never mind."

"Go ahead and say it. Coward. Milksop. That's a word for an author. And it fits you. Maybe I prodded you into marrying me, but you went for it. You could have ended the relationship. Instead, you … I've changed my mind: I'm glad you overheard. I'm just sorry I didn't say it to your face."

"Enough. Before we both go too far. I'm going to work in the basement tonight. Don't wait up for me."

"Don't worry."

Luke stomped down the stairs, placed his laptop on the dented coffee table and dropped onto the ragged sofa. He hated arguing but was equally relieved it had happened. It gave him a perfect excuse to avoid being in the same room with Brandi. And, how could he be expected to sleep next to such a prickly woman after being with Chelsea? Lovely, mellow Chelsea, who filled his mind with thoughts both innocent and not so innocent.

He'd told her that her husband was a fool for not wanting her. For wanting anyone other than her. Men with opinions of themselves too high for their own best interest, tended to be blind to their good fortune. Hall obviously did well for himself, but he had no idea that his true treasure waited at home for him every night.

The moment he'd seen Chelsea get out of her car, he'd known she was more than merely a fan to him. She was a lovely creature. A muse.

Ideas for a new novel came faster than he could type. He shifted from noting ideas to writing character dialogue, writing what he wanted to say to Chelsea. What he desired to hear her say in return. Described how he'd make love to her, and how she'd respond, down to the last ecstatic gasp and moan and cry as he pleasured her to the point of release.

Three hours later, Luke lifted his fingers from the keyboard and read what he'd written.

Just remember, old boy, it's all fiction. Neither you or Chelsea will break your marriage vows. No matter how much you might wish differently.

CHAPTER 44

THE BOWL OF Caesar salad slipped from Luke's hand. He slammed his wait tray down, cursed and got a broom and dustpan from the cupboard.

James entered the kitchen. "Who dropped what?" Saw it was Luke and said, "That's a first. Something on your mind? Woman problems?"

"Yes. But it's not what you think." Luke emptied the contents of the dustpan into the trash. He grabbed several paper towels, a bottle of cleaning liquid, and squatted to wipe up the dressing smeared on the linoleum floor.

"I'm intrigued. Your break's in ten. Wait for me in the courtyard. You can tell me what's going on. Can't have you dropping dishes all night."

Luke nodded. He prepared another salad, added it to his tray then fixed a smile on his face as he entered the dining room.

"Okay," James said, "let's hear it." He handed Luke a cup of coffee.

Luke blew on the steaming liquid, sipped, then said, "I met a woman."

James punched Luke's arm. "Now you're talking. This is my kind of problem. Simple and easy to give advice about."

"It's not so simple. She's enticing, compelling."

"Boring. What's her body like?"

"Head-to-toe gorgeous."

"No problem, so far."

"I come alive when I'm in her presence or hear her voice."

"That's a bonus."

"Her eyes tell me the feeling is mutual. I'm afraid it may get serious."

"Again, no problem. Hit it and quit it."

Luke shook his head. "It's not like that with her. She's not the kind of woman you do that to. She's also not African American."

James shrugged. "Still not a problem. If she's luscious and purple, I say tap that."

"She's married."

"*And*, there it is."

"That's not the problem."

"Seems like a big fucking one to me."

"She's all I think about or want to. I feel like I'm being drawn in and I don't want to resist it. I want to rush in."

James blew out a breath of exasperation. "Okay. She's married. So she isn't going to want this mutual attraction advertised. Bowl in that alley. Rush in, as you said, and knock her pins down a few times. Then turn in those shoes that ain't yours to keep and get the hell out. She'll get the message."

"If she lets me in, I'll never want to leave."

"Then you'd damn sure better get out now. That woman sounds like one of those Chinese finger puzzles. You put yourself in that, you ain't ever coming out."

"It would be a lovely way to live."

"More like die, you mean. Dude, married women have husbands. Some of them have guns. I never took you for stupid. You want a playmate, I'll find you one, any color you want. And single. I know a few who have no ambition to hook a guy. They just want to dabble and be dabbled by someone who knows what he's doing."

"I'm not looking to dabble."

"You're not looking to pay the ultimate price for playing, either."

"Maybe you're right."

"I am." James slapped Luke on the back. "Break's over. Keep your mind where it belongs."

Luke followed James into the restaurant. Of course his friend was right. He needed to do something about this situation. It was best to tell Chelsea he'd started a new novel, so needed his full focus there.

No more texting or calls.
No more meeting for coffee.
She'd forget all about him in no time.
However much he didn't want her to.

CHAPTER 45

SHORTLY AFTER NINE o'clock on Saturday morning, Luke's son, Tim, knocked on the front door. Luke kissed the top of Tim's head as he entered. He watched his ex-wife speed off to wherever, to do whatever. He'd learned long ago that it was best not to ask what Tina was up to.

Tim dropped his overnight bag on the floor. "Where's the step-monster?"

Luke shut the door. "She's at the store. I'll grab a couple of sodas. Wait for me in the basement."

"Why the basement?"

"In case she comes home. You and I need to talk."

"I just walked in and I'm already getting grief."

"That's not what this is about. Go on. I'll be there in a few."

Tim pounded down the stairs. Luke pulled two cans from the refrigerator and joined his son. He handed a soda to Tim, who popped the top, downed half the contents and belched.

"Manners, Tim."

"She's not even around to hear me."

"Manners practiced in private are easier to practice in public."

"Whatever."

"Tim."

"Please excuse the sound I made after ingesting a quantify of this carbonated beverage."

Luke shook his head. "I need you to be polite to Brandi. Things are tense right now."

"What'd you do this time?"

He wanted to say, *I kept breathing.* "Her office downsized. It was unexpected. Things are a little unsettled right now. That's all."

Tim barked a laugh. "The cow got fired."

"I mean it, son. You'll understand such situations when you're an adult working for a living. You lose your income, it can be a stressful time."

"Fine. Whatever."

"Although I'd prefer you got along, you don't have to pretend you like her. Just be courteous."

"You mean don't piss her off."

"Do us both a favor. Please."

"Whatever."

Father and son drank from their cans. Luke rested his soda on his knee. "I never asked how the divorce affected you. Is affecting you. I'm sorry I've waited so long."

"Whatever."

"Tim, please talk to me, and with more than one word, especially that one. Tell me how you feel about what happened, because it happened to all of us."

"It sucks. All right? It's like I'm a wishbone being pulled in two directions. And, it's embarrassing to be the one whose parents split. None of my friends are like that. They don't understand what it's like. Especially holidays. And none of them have to be nice to someone who's not their parent."

"So, you're hurt. Embarrassed. Angry."

"Why couldn't you have stayed together?"

"It wouldn't have worked."

"Because of the affairs?"

Luke stared wide-eyed at Tim. "You knew?"

"I'm not stupid."

"I had no idea. We tried to keep it from you—one thing your mother and I agreed on. Then you understand?"

Tim slouched back and toed a wobbly leg of the coffee table. "You should've just gotten your own thing going. Stayed together doing your own things. You know?"

"That's not how it works."

"It does for some."

"What do you mean?"

Tim shrugged. "Pete's got extended cable."

"I don't want you watching … Look, it wasn't the relationship I signed on for. As hurt as you feel, that's how much what happened hurt me. In a different way, of course. But pain is pain. However, we have to work to heal the pain and do the best we can. Do whatever it takes."

"It took marrying step-monster?"

"Would you *please* stop saying that. And, yes, finding someone to be in a relationship with again helps. But the sting of betrayal can last a while. Sometimes a long while."

"Like that time a hornet stung me?"

Luke ruffled Tim's hair. "More like stepping on a ground nest and getting hit by a number of the swarm."

Tim thought about it and nodded.

"Son, we can't afford it right now, but would you like me to find someone for you to talk to, when we can pay?"

Tim glared at Luke. "I don't need a shrink."

"Of course not. But if you'd like to talk to someone who's objective—"

"Nah. Mom would bug me to tell her what I talked about."

"Guess you're stuck discussing it with me. I'm here for you anytime you need to talk. I love you, son. More than anyone or anything."

"Even more than Brandilocks?"

"You're the bone of my bones, flesh of my flesh."

Tim toed Luke's leg playfully. "That's disgusting." He burped long and loud.

"Tim."

"Please excuse the sound I just made after—"

Luke put his can on the coffee table and launched a tickle attack on Tim, who pretended to fight off his father. The coffee table crashed onto its side. Spilled soda began to spread across the concrete floor.

Tim, laughing, grabbed old newspapers from a stack in a corner and tossed them over the spill while Luke righted the table. "Good thing you-know-who wasn't here, Dad. You'd be in deep—"

Luke strained to suppress a smile. "Son."

"Stuff."

"When am I not?"

CHAPTER 46

T HE VILLAIN IN the movie had been winning, but the hero was about to get his second wind, about to get ice-cold enraged and kick some bad-guy butt. Luke and Tim's attention diverted from the TV screen at the sound of a key in the lock.

Luke looked at Tim. "Remember what I said."

Tim grinned, got up, opened the door, and bit his lower lip to contain the laugh that threatened to escape at Brandi's startled expression. She stood in the doorway, keys in one hand, bag of groceries clutched to her with the other.

Tim took hold of the bag. "I'll get that."

Brandi glanced at Luke, who smiled and shrugged.

Luke had to give it to Tim: The kid could put it on when he wanted to. Although he spent a good portion of the day in the basement with Luke's laptop, when he had to interact with Brandi, he wasn't effusive, but wasn't rude either. It put Brandi on the spot to act better, as well. The tension between the two of them was still palpable, but they made an effort to keep it at an undercurrent level.

Around eleven o'clock, Tim settled on the couch for the night. Brandi went to bed. Luke took his laptop down to the basement to work for a while. No Goodreads e-mail or text from Chelsea. Disappointing, but for the best.

He did find four new five-star reviews and discovered he'd sold ten e-books. It was his best day as an author so far, and he wanted to share the good news.

Luke turned off the lights in the house, turned off the TV Tim had fallen asleep to, and went upstairs. He closed the door to their bedroom and leaned against it.

Brandi looked up from her book. "What are you grinning about?"

He told her.

Brandi put her book down and clutched her hands to her chest. "How wonderful. We can now pay for beans and rice for a few weeks. Maybe I can even buy a stale roll for the boy."

"You're determined not to let me celebrate even a small victory."

"We have very different ideas about what qualifies as a victory."

"I guess this victor can forget about getting any spoils tonight."

Brandi picked up her book. "Tonight and a lot of nights. Until further notice."

"Would you rather I sleep in the basement?"

"I don't care where you sleep."

He wondered if she realized how inciting a comment that was.

CHAPTER 47

A FEW MINUTES before noon the next day, a car pulled up out front, the driver honked the horn. Luke went to the window. Tina. No call to alert Tim she'd pick him up early. Typical.

"Tim, your mom's here."

"I'm not ready."

"Neither am I, but she is. Did you leave anything in the basement or office?"

"Nah. I just need to put my stuff into my bag and put on my shoes."

"I'll help."

"I'll do it. There isn't much."

"Maybe you should run out and tell her you'll be ready in a minute."

The horn honked several more times—two short, one long, one short. Luke opened the door and held up a finger to indicate a minute was needed. Tina held up a finger as well, to indicate her sentiments. Luke shook his head and shut the door.

"You sure you've got everything?"

"Yeah, Dad. Brandiflake going to stay in her room all day?"

"I doubt it."

"Do I have to go up there and tell her I'm leaving?"

"I'm sure she knows by now. Let her stay where she is."

"Permanently."

"Thanks for behaving." Luke wrapped his arms around Tim and kissed him on the cheek.

"Gross, Dad." Tim, smiling, pulled away. Four angry honks sounded from outside. "I gotta go before Mom loses it." He lowered his voice. "If you're lucky, maybe the step-monster will stay up there all day."

Luke opened the door for Tim. Watched his son get into the car, and waved as they drove off. He leaned his back against the door and stared up the stairs. Listened to the silence that filled the space.

He went into his office and opened his laptop. Maybe he could get some writing done before Brandi came downstairs to inflict more wounds or snub him. But he didn't feel like writing more than a text message.

Can you get away for about an hour?

He waited for a reply.

CHAPTER 48

L UKE WAITED IN the last booth at the back of the small diner located just outside of town. The paper napkin in his hand had been twisted more times than it could bear. It shredded into fragments in his hand.

Each time the door opened, his heart raced. The fifth time, a wind gust caught the door and flung it all the way open. Chelsea struggled to pull the door closed. He wanted to get up to help her, but couldn't move. The low-backed sundress she wore revealed a foot of creamy skin, smooth and supple, begging to be kissed and stroked. His mouth went dry.

Chelsea turned and brushed hair from her face, squinted her eyes to find him in the dimly lit interior.

Luke stood and held up a hand. Her expression when she saw him made his breath catch. His eyes devoured her curves as she sauntered toward him.

"Thank you for meeting me, Chelsea."

"You did me a favor."

Luke waited for her to slide into the booth then sat across from her. "I didn't think that on a Sunday—I mean, I hope I didn't cause any problems for you."

"No one else is home today. I won't even be missed."

"I'd miss you."

Chelsea tilted her head and smiled. "That's nice to hear."

The waitress stopped at their booth. "What'll it be, folks?"

They ordered coffee and pie, and carried on mundane chatter until their orders were delivered.

"I wanted to tell you my good news, about my books." Ten minutes passed as he shared what had happened and expounded about some of his dreams.

Chelsea reached for his hand. "I'm thrilled for you, Luke. I told you, it just takes patience. You watch. This is the start of momentum. By the way, I've recommended your book to friends and others. So watch for more sales and reviews to come."

"Your faith means a great deal to me. More than you know."

"I'll keep promoting it, and you, every chance I have. I'm sorry I haven't as yet read the other two, but I promise I will." Her smile faded. "What is it?"

Luke shook his head. "I'm struck by the contrast, is all."

"I think I understand. Not a star in your own home."

"Not even a flicker."

"She doesn't know what she has."

"You understand what that's like." Luke stroked the back of her hand with his thumb. "I don't know how he can think of another woman when he has you. I'm having difficulty thinking of anything but you."

Chelsea let her hand linger in his for a moment then eased it away.

"Seems I continue to do things I need to apologize for. I'm sorry, Chelsea."

"That's the problem, Luke. I'm not."

Over coffee that was sipped and pie that went untouched, they talked about everything but what hung between them.

Luke paid the bill and walked her to her car. "It's going to rain. I hope you get home before it does." He leaned forward slowly.

Chelsea tensed, wondering what it would be like when he kissed her. Would it be brief? On her cheek? Her mouth? She licked her lips as he moved closer. Felt the heat from his body. He stopped, his face inches away. His eyes held her captive, like a skittish bird cupped in the palms of his hands.

Luke opened the car door. "You'd better go."

Chelsea nodded and positioned herself behind the steering wheel. Luke closed the door and stepped back. She reversed the car out of the slot, waved, and drove onto the two-lane highway.

Luke went to his car, rested his head against it and cursed.

CHAPTER 49

S HE WAS A few miles down the two-lane road before Chelsea realized she didn't recall the drive. Didn't recall seeing other cars, pedestrians, or anything other than the replay in her mind of what had almost happened with Luke. An obvious reminder that she was taking risks and needed to get her head on straight. She engaged the Bluetooth.

"Hey, Chels," Penelope said. "What's doing?"

"Did I catch you at a good time?"

"Touching up my toenails, but I can chat and paint at the same time."

"I met Luke for coffee."

"Now you're talking. Tell me."

"Not much to tell about that, other than he's an excellent conversationalist, never dull. And—" How much should she say?

"And?"

"We met up again. In fact, I just left him."

Penelope whooped. "What's he like in bed? Tame and tender, or wild and exotic?"

"We met for coffee."

"How boring. And disappointing. I'd hoped you were going to get properly laid by hot chocolate man, Chels, not caffeinated."

"It may be easy for you to hop into bed for a romp with a man you just met, but it's not that way for me."

"You've always had a tendency to make simple things complicated."

"There's nothing simple about it."

"Doesn't seem to bother Garrett."

"It should."

"It doesn't." Penelope sighed in response to Chelsea's silence. "Do yourself a favor and keep this in mind: It's been a long time since Garrett serviced you. I think there's a statute of limitations about that. You wait any longer, you'll become a virgin and have to be popped all over again."

"Not physically possible or plausible."

"Just saying. If I were you, I'd be having a hot-fudge sundae interlude with an author instead of a hot-and-bothered Sunday."

"There's an essence of sacrilegious about that."

"That's another conflict you self-impose. You can't be naughty *and* nice. And only one of those is fun." When no reply followed, she said, "I need to go. My nails are getting tacky."

"We wouldn't want *that* to happen."

"Was that a dig, Chels? Because if it was—"

"I didn't mean it to sound like that. I'm guess I'm more flustered than I realized. Catch you later."

Flustered wasn't the word for it. She'd been terrified that Luke was going to kiss her, terrified he wouldn't. And when he hadn't, she'd felt like screaming. In frustration. And relief.

It was obvious Luke wanted her, and she wanted him to want her. Surely that alone should be enough to satisfy her.

You're lying to yourself, again, Chels.

Her phone rang, she checked caller ID. "Hi, Richard. What's up?"

"That's my question. Haven't heard from you in a while. You okay?"

"I am. Just decided to start doing some things with myself and my life. Time to stop bothering you every time I feel a twitch."

"You know I'm here for you."

"You're a love. We'll chat another time. I'm almost to my hair appointment."

She hated to lie to him.

Hated that she didn't even have to think about it.

And, that doing so was easier than it should be.

CHAPTER 50

WITH POSTURE STRAIGHT and a wide smile, Chelsea preceded Dr. Moore into the office. She sat in the same place as her last session and slipped off her shoes, tucking her stockinged feet to the side of her on the leather sofa.

Dr. Moore's left eyebrow went up. She got her tablet and pen from her desk and sat on the opposite end of the sofa. "Mrs. Hall, you seem more relaxed than last time. Almost jaunty, if that's the appropriate word for how you appear to be feeling."

"Please. Call me Chelsea. I am more relaxed. Because I do feel better than I have in quite a while."

"I'm happy to hear it. What's that a result of?"

"What you said. You know, about not letting anyone make me feel as though I'm less. How can I expect anyone to think better of me if I don't think better of myself? I knew that once. I'd just forgotten that I did."

"And now you have."

"Yes." Chelsea glanced out the window. A slight smile played on her lips.

"Did something specific happen as a result of this new view of yourself?" Chelsea stayed silent and kept her gaze fixed beyond the glass. "Chelsea?"

Chelsea, blushing, looked down at her hands. "I feel more engaged with myself and my life." She told Dr. Moore about swimming every morning and eating healthier. She prattled on, uninterrupted for a half hour, unaware of Dr. Moore alternating between jotting notes and paying particular attention to her facial expressions and body language.

"... and although I still believe Garrett is seeing other women—mostly because he continues to claim he's working late every night, including weekends, I'm not letting those thoughts control me as I have in the past. After all, I could be wrong, but I doubt that. And if I am right, nagging him won't make him stop. It didn't before."

Dr. Moore put the tablet and pen on the sofa cushion that separated them and looked directly at Chelsea. "Sometimes situations, and people, are not what they seem."

Chelsea sighed. "That's so true."

"We both know what infidelity can do to a relationship. Some relationships survive, but it can take years for healing to happen and for trust to be restored. Most relationships shatter. As do the people affected, especially when children are involved. Sometimes the resultant situation becomes dire, extraordinarily so in some cases, for one or more of the individuals. Do you understand what I'm saying?"

Chelsea's face flushed red. "I understand."

"In my experience it's better to end the relationship rather than destroy it, and others, by traveling the path of infidelity."

Chelsea picked at her cuticles and forced a laugh. "I suppose Garrett's lucky I stayed; though, I don't think he'd appreciate my telling him that."

"Probably not. Chelsea, is there something particular you'd care to share with me?"

Chelsea looked at Dr. Moore then away. "Nothing I can think of."

Dr. Moore kept her eyes directed at Chelsea. "Promise me you'll give serious thought to what I just said."

"Of course."

"Our time's up. We'll pick up on this discussion next week."

"I don't feel that I need to come back. As I said, I'm feeling better."

"And I think you're at a significant turning point in your relationship and life."

Chelsea slid her feet into her shoes. "You may be right about that."

CHAPTER 51

ARRETT'S ATTENTION SHIFTED from the open chart to his pinging phone. He turned the screen toward him and read the text message. *Dr. Jacobs,* asking if he was available to give her a protein injection that night. He chuckled. Replied that his syringe was loaded and ready.

He called the hotel, checked his wallet for hundreds—more than enough for the night manager. Then he called Chelsea.

"I have to work late tonight."

She mumbled, "Okay."

He gripped the phone. "I've told you time and again, it's important that I make a good impression. I wish you'd understand."

After a moment she said, "I do. And I'm sure you will."

"It didn't sound like you understood."

"Sorry. I'd just bit into an apple when you called."

"Oh. I thought—"

"I'm sure you're busy. I'll see you when I see you." She ended the call.

Garrett stared at the phone in his hand. He recalled seeing the bowl of fruit in the kitchen, but thought it was for Kimberlie—some new diet fad, not that she needed to watch her weight. Not like her mother. Other images floated into his awareness: the light tawny tone to Chelsea's usually pale skin, the bathing suit drying in their bathroom.

What was going on?

Maybe his sleeping in the guest room that night had made a dent. Maybe she realized if she wanted to keep him happy, she'd better shape up, in more ways than one.

She might as well. Who else would want her, except some desperate guy looking for whatever was available and easy. Not that Chelsea was easy. She was anything but.

She had it good with him, and knew it. He also knew that whatever small changes she made now wouldn't last. In no time, she'd resume nagging him about his hours, pouting, and stuffing her face.

These thoughts began to dampen his mood. He couldn't have that.

Instead, he pictured some of the toys he and *Dr. Jacobs* had left to try. One in particular lifted his mood and the front of his trousers.

He checked his watch. His departure time couldn't come fast enough.

CHAPTER 52

H I, LUKE. I just learned my daughter is spending the night at Susan's house—school project, and Garrett is, of course, "working" late again, which means he'll get in around one or so. Perhaps even later. Any chance you can meet for a quick drink and a chat this evening? Well, maybe not too quick (grin).

Chelsea chewed on her bottom lip. The most she knew about Luke's schedule was that it wasn't always consistent. It was five thirty now. Luke may be home already, with *her*. She picked at a cuticle and paced. Five minutes. Ten.

Hello, beautiful lady. How about seven thirty at Toby's? It's a quiet, out-of-the-way place, if you don't mind going there.

Sounds cozy. I'll see you then.

Do you need me to tell you where it is?

I'll find it.

She had a little less than two hours. Chelsea looked up the address and directions—too risky to record it in her GPS—then dashed upstairs. The hot shower was supposed to relax her. It didn't.

Then, it was forty-five minutes trying to decide what to wear, trying on and discarding clothing into a pile on the floor. The only thing that soothed her was knowing that Luke liked her fuller curves, obvious by the way he traced them with his gaze. A shopping trip was in order, at least for a few outfits that flattered her figure.

A sleeveless black shift was selected. Feeling emboldened, Chelsea added a belt. She cringed at her reflection in the full-length mirror, hating that her waist wasn't smaller. But this would be a test to prove whether Luke truly admired her body or if it was a matter of wishful thinking on her part.

She went back into the bathroom, fixed her hair into a chignon and took care applying her makeup.

Chelsea closed her eyes and imagined Luke's hands reading her body like Braille. Her body began to tingle. In all the right, too long-ignored places.

She rouged her lips, blotted with a tissue, and warned her reflection:

"People who play with matches, Chels."

CHAPTER 53

TOBY'S LOUNGE WAS easy to find. Chelsea recognized the place, having passed it on the way out of town whenever she traveled that direction, which was seldom. It wasn't exactly a dive, but neither could it be mistaken for elegant. Nor did it make any pretense in that direction. It wasn't Garrett's kind of place. Nothing but the best and most expensive for Garrett. She shook her head to clear away any thoughts of her husband, certain he likely didn't have the same issue in her regard.

The parking lot was nearly full. She pulled in and paused, trying to decide where to park. Driving a silver Bentley no longer seemed ideal. She spied a place that would keep her car from being obvious from the two-lane highway, pulled in, turned the engine off and took a deep breath. The thing to do was start the car and go home, where she belonged.

Too late. Luke was jogging toward her. She waved and got out as he reached her car.

Luke said, "I thought it best if I waited out here so you didn't have to walk in alone and look for me."

"That was thoughtful."

"How do you manage to look even more lovely each time I see you? Or have you cast a spell over me?"

Chelsea laughed. "Maybe we should go in and find a table."

A booth with a semi-circular padded bench, located in a darkened corner, was empty. Luke took her hand and led her through the people crowding the bar. Chelsea glanced around then slid into the booth.

"You okay, Chelsea?"

"A little skittish, if I'm honest. I was trying to make sure no one I know is here."

"One thing is certain: If they see you, they won't say anything if you won't. Sorry to bring you to this kind of place, but I felt it was safer. Maybe I'm being over-cautious."

"More like prudent."

"Since the first time I saw you, I felt compelled to look after you."

Chelsea tilted her head and studied his face. "I believe you mean that."

"I do. As presumptuous as that may sound—"

"Don't, Luke. It's okay. I think I understand."

"I'll get our drinks. White wine?" Chelsea nodded. "I'll be back as soon as I can."

She fought the urge to peek around the edge of the booth. Yipped when she picked at one cuticle too aggressively. Folded her hands on the table and waited and wondered if she was crazy for staying.

Luke returned with their drinks and slid into the booth, keeping a distance of several inches between them.

They sipped in silence, until Luke said, "It's not the same as meeting for coffee, is it?"

"No. But it's okay. The only thing is—"

"It's obvious you're uncomfortable. Maybe this place was a bad idea."

"It's not that. What I meant was that people are glancing at us. Some of them are staring."

Luke nodded. "I noticed. Who can blame them? You're a stunning woman."

Chelsea offered him a small smile. "Thanks, but I don't think that's what has their attention. I thought these days, no one cared if people of different races were together, or at least had the courtesy to pretend not to."

"It was forbidden in so many segments of society for so long, I suppose the idea is still awkward or disquieting for a number of people. Of course, there are some cultural differences, but certainly not so great that they can't be dealt with, if two people know they're right for each other."

Chelsea chewed on her bottom lip then said, "So you're confident mixed relationships do work?"

Luke studied her for a moment. "There's evidence they do, and have throughout history. Not here, perhaps, but attitudes have shifted, just faster in some locations than others. What about you, Chelsea? Do you believe you could ignore those who disapproved? For example, what about the people in here who are watching us?"

Chelsea touched his arm. "They don't know how happy I am when I'm with you, or how unhappy I am when I'm not." She removed her hand and took a sip of wine. "Luke, have you ever been involved with a—I'm not sure how to say it. I don't want to sound ignorant."

Luke smiled. "Have I ever been with a woman who isn't black?" Chelsea nodded. "I haven't. What about you?"

Chelsea shook her head. "It just never happened. I never had a reason to give it much thought."

"And now?"

Chelsea blushed and fiddled with her wine glass. "Maybe."

"Maybe we should change the subject. Do you mind if I talk about my book and the reviews it's getting?"

"Safer topics, you mean?"

"Up to you."

"Better safe, and all that, I suppose."

Chelsea arrived home shortly after nine twenty. At eleven forty-two, Garrett's car rumbled into the driveway. This was followed by the front door being opened and closed. Seconds later, she heard him go out the back door. Soon after, she heard a splash.

She went to the window and peeked through the side of the curtains. Garrett was swimming—nude. She'd heard him do this other nights, and she was fairly certain why. Those other nights, she'd always pretended to be asleep when he sneaked into their room and bed, preferring not to let him know she kept track of the time.

He was earlier than usual tonight, far earlier than she'd expected. Thank goodness Luke had needed to leave when he did. Otherwise, she might have not been home when Garrett returned. Not that he would have suspected anything. Not that there was anything to suspect.

At least, not yet.

CHAPTER 54

GARRETT CLIMBED THE stairs, pausing at Kimberlie's room. The door was open, the bed empty. He turned the corner and saw that at least one lamp was on in the master bedroom, and hoped Chelsea had fallen asleep with the light on.

She hadn't. Her pillow was propped behind her back, her knees bent, holding the book she was reading in position on her lap. He cursed under his breath and readied himself for yet another episode of angry, self-pitying accusations from her.

Chelsea looked up. "You must be exhausted." She put her focus back on the book and turned the page.

"I thought you'd be asleep. You usually are."

She kept her gaze fixed on the page. "You're never home this early, so wouldn't know what I'm usually doing."

"Point taken. Kim's studying at Susan's?"

"She is."

Garrett went into the bathroom and brushed his teeth. He turned out the bathroom light and started toward his side of the bed.

Chelsea said, "I meant to tell you to leave the light on in there." She went into the bathroom and closed the door.

Whatever she was doing to shape up was starting to make a difference. Not enough to his liking yet, but enough to notice. And there was something about her. He couldn't identify it, but there was definitely something different.

She had on the gown she'd bought for their failed date night. That couldn't be mistaken for anything other than a blatant invitation.

Despite his opinion about her overall appearance, despite the sexual gymnastics he'd engaged in earlier that evening, he had an erection. Why not give her a little to make her happy? Put her on her back and maybe it would keep her off his about his hours and all the other things she complained about.

The stiffness between his legs demanded attention. Any port in a storm, as the saying went.

Chelsea returned to bed, slid under the covers and picked up her book. Garrett moved next to her. He took the book from her hands and placed it on the nightstand.

"Garrett?"

He wiggled his eyebrows at her and turned off the lamp. His hands groped her breasts—one squeeze, two. His mouth found a nipple through the sheer fabric—one quick pull and release. He raised her gown to her hips, used his fingers to feel between her legs. "Not wet yet? I'll fix that." He put his fingers into his mouth then rubbed them against the tip of his erection, pushed his way inside her and began to thrust, unaware of the grimace on her face.

I could be anyone, Chelsea thought. She squeezed her eyes shut and played back what happened when Luke had walked her to her car. How he'd held her face in his hands and looked into her eyes with tenderness that made her ache. How he'd kissed her forehead, her cheekbones, her chin. Whispered her name before putting his mouth on hers, gently at first. When she'd responded, his kisses had grown more passionate. As though she was his next breath, and the next. Luke had run his hands from her hips to just on the sides of her breasts, but went no further. Kissing her in a way that made her lightheaded, like the first time a boy French kissed her when she was sixteen. Luke had moaned when she sucked on his tongue and ran her nails lightly up his back as their bodies pressed together.

She imagined Luke's lips moving to her neck, her shoulders, her breasts, trailing down her abdomen, and then between her legs. Chelsea kept the image going. Imagined it was Luke moving inside of her. She wrapped her arms and legs around *him*, and was louder than ever before when her orgasm happened moments later.

Garrett thrust harder and faster. "Oh, yeah, baby, yeah. I'm. Al … most. Oh, yeah!" He collapsed on top of her then rolled off and went into the bathroom.

To wash me off, Chelsea thought. To rid himself of any trace of my essence.

Chelsea said nothing as Garrett strutted toward the bed and climbed in on his side, turning his back to her.

He was snoring in seconds.

It took longer for her tears to stop.

CHAPTER 55

THREE MINUTES AFTER ten the next morning, Chelsea's phone rang. She recognized the number, said hello and listened. A number of emotions flashed across her face. "And you're positive Kimberlie's okay? … I'll be there in ten minutes."

She parked in front of the school, hurried inside, listened to the guidance counselor's explanation, and pleaded in her best, though rusty, professional manner for her daughter not to be suspended.

Kimberlie sat silent and unmoving in the room, arms folded, head down. Twenty minutes later, she trailed her mother to the car.

"Your father isn't going to be happy. I'm not happy. Fighting with a boy. I can't believe you did that. What were you thinking?" They both got into the car. "You look all right. Are you? Did you get hurt?"

"I'm fine. Can we go home now?"

Chelsea put the car in gear and pulled away from the curb. They rode home in silence.

"Get a snack, but stay in the kitchen. I'm calling your father. No telling what time he'll get home."

"Do you have to tell him?"

"You bet I do. He'll likely hear about it from someone, and that someone had better be me."

After two rings, Garrett answered. "Calling to praise me for my stellar performance last night?"

Chelsea rolled her eyes. "I'm calling to tell you that your daughter got into a fight at school. With a boy."

"Is she injured?"

"Thankfully, no. Neither is the boy. I talked the school out of suspending her for more than the rest of the day, but they wouldn't budge about adding the infraction to her record."

"What happened?"

"I'll let her tell you." She handed the phone to Kimberlie.

"Hi, Dad."

"Explain."

"It was his fault. He started calling me names, being really nasty. I told him to stop but he just kept on. He got in my face and kept saying worse and worse things. I had enough so pushed him away. He pushed back, harder. I landed on my a— backside. I was so pissed, I hit him."

"Where?"

"In the schoolyard."

"Where on him, Kimberlie?"

"Arm. Then he hit my shoulder with his fist and I slapped his face. We started to wrestle. Then the yard monitor broke it up."

"I thought you had better self-control than that."

"You didn't hear what he said."

"I don't give a damn what he said. You touched him first. You never strike anyone except in self-defense or in defense of another person who can't defend him- or herself. You hear me?"

"Yeah."

"How many times do I have to tell you that decisions have consequences? This is going on your permanent record. Be damn glad your mother did what she did. Just because your teachers give you all A's, it doesn't mean you're off the hook. You'd better hope the people significant to your future and success overlook that you brawled."

"I *earn* the A's. No one *gives* them to me."

"Sarcasm? Really, Kimberlie?"

"Sorry. Just sayin'."

"What the hell are they teaching kids these days? And what the hell is that boy's family teaching him? Under no circumstances should a man—or boy—ever strike a woman."

"I guess maybe *he* thought it was self-defense."

"He shouldn't have been taunting you in the first place, but he should have turned his sorry ass around and left you alone. And you should have immediately reported him to the monitor instead of letting it escalate. You sure you're not hurt?"

"I'm fine."

"Put your mother on."

Chelsea took the phone. "Go to your room. No phone or computer or any other form of communication the rest of the night." She held out her hand.

"Aw, Mom. That's so not fair."

"Hand your phone over. I'll call you when dinner's ready."

Kimberlie dug her phone from her purse and placed it in Chelsea's outstretched hand. Halfway to the stairs, she turned, her eyes filled with tears. "Am I grounded?"

"I'll think about it." Chelsea blew out a breath and put her phone to her ear. "I don't believe she did that."

"I think I convinced her to never do it again. What punishment did the boy get?"

"I didn't ask."

"You should have."

"The last thing I need is a lecture. Will you be coming home early?"

"I can't."

"Even after this?"

"Chelsea, I'm not going to go through this every time I—"

"Do whatever, Garrett."

She ended the call. And thought about texting Luke.

Not a good idea, Chels.

CHAPTER 56

"I HOPE today is a better one. You know how to behave. Do it." Chelsea kissed Kimberlie's cheek and watched her still downcast daughter nod and close the car door behind her.

She kept focused on Kimberlie's slow steps to the entrance and into the school. Kimberlie really was a good kid. As her mother, it was her responsibility to not let her child off the hook too easily. But she understood how some people can push others to their limit of tolerance. Cause them to do something they might otherwise not have done. Difficult circumstances tended to reveal to people what their limits were. Unfortunately, there was always someone bent on forcing them to that point.

Chelsea's reverie broke when an impatient parent behind her honked. She waved and pulled onto the drive then turned left, onto the road that led home.

The remainder of the day was ordinary, sedate, until later that afternoon. Kimberlie *had* to study for an exam overnight at Susan's house. Garrett *had* to attend a dinner conference that started at eight and would continue quite late because he *had* to entertain some out-of-towners. Penelope had a date.

By six o'clock, Chelsea had drafted several text messages of various lengths and intensity to Luke, each time stumbling over what to say, and each time changing her mind and deleting them. It was better to leave it, and him, alone. Let the dust settle. It was the only way for them to see clearly the precipice they stood on.

Despite caution that prodded her, she wanted to believe he felt something real for her. If she was nothing more than a novelty to him, it was best not to encourage him. Or herself. A half hour later, her phone pinged.

Lady of beauty and grace, how are you today?

Relief, fear, desire to be deemed significant flooded her.

I'm alone and lonely, wishing I was with stimulating company.

If you mean that, I'm available.

Toby's?

What time?

Seven too soon for you?

I'll strive, challenging as it may be, to wait that long.

Chelsea laughed. *See you soon.*

She rushed upstairs to primp. For him. Glanced at the bed and recalled how she'd had to substitute the illusion of Luke over the reality of Garrett. How odd that she'd desired her husband for so long, only to not want him when he'd accommodated her. And that was all it was; though, she had no idea why Garrett had suddenly changed his mind after all this time. As much as she'd wanted to be the one to say no, it seemed too risky to give him cause to be suspicious.

She wondered who Garrett had pretended *she* was.

And wondered if Luke pretended it was she when he made love to his wife.

Neither Chelsea or Luke meant to drink as much as they did. Neither of them had intended to kiss and grope each other in the booth in the dark corner of the dimly lit lounge. Neither did they start the evening with any intention of stumbling to the motel two buildings away from Toby's.

Nor had they intended to consume each other in what could only be described as a raging torrent of need. Twice. Until both were spent and panting with arms and legs entwined.

Luke stroked her back. "We can't fall asleep." He got up and searched. Found his watch under a chair, having cast it off in a flurry of their eagerness to remove anything, no matter how sheer, between them.

He sat next to Chelsea on the bed. Ran a hand from her cheek to the place on her body that had sated them both. "Much as I hate to say it—"

"I know. It would be too easy to stay here all night."

Luke stood. "I'm going to shower."

Chelsea extended her hand. "Not alone, I hope."

CHAPTER 57

C HELSEA DRAGGED ONE of the poolside lounge chairs to the edge of the morning sun. Her phone was next to her, atop the attached small teak table. She sipped her coffee, noting the brew was the same shade as Luke. It took no effort to recall the intimate moments they'd shared the night before. Tender, sweet, sensual, passionate Luke.

She glanced around. The trees lining the perimeter of the yard were high enough, flush enough with leaves. Only a tree cutter, someone in a helicopter, or some annoying, curious neighbor with a drone and too much time on his, or her, hands would see into her backyard. She removed her robe, peeled off her swimsuit, and did the twenty laps naked.

After the last lap, she rested her arms on the side of the pool, relishing the tenderness of her nipples and between her legs. Luke had demonstrated his thoughtfulness in a number of ways, which included shaving before they met up. No stubble burn on her face to contend with or be entrapped by.

What did he feel about what had happened? Was he as confused as she felt?

She swam to the steps and got out, air-drying unclothed on the chair. A glance at her phone indicated a missed call and a text from Luke.

God, Chelsea, I never meant to compromise you as I did last night. Can you ever forgive me?

We compromised each other. Any forgiveness has to go both ways. But, Luke, I've never been "compromised" so well. My body is still humming. Or, perhaps, engaged in a symphony is more accurate.

Woman, what knowing that does to me … However, we're playing with the proverbial fire.

You need me to say it first, don't you? Because of how I feel about you, Luke, I will. It can't happen again.

We both know it. But I feel as though the dungeon door has been slammed shut, enclosing me in icy darkness.

Why don't we stop texting and talk on the phone?

I can't hear your voice right now. It would break me.

She wanted to tell him she was naked and waiting, but he was right. Dr. Moore was right, as well. There was too great a chance of destroying a number of lives.

I value our friendship, Luke. So, if you're still willing to know me, I suppose coffee in broad daylight is the only way.

YES! We'll stick to coffee and innocent conversation. Sorry, Chelsea, my break is over and I have to get back to work. Coffee next week?

I look forward to it.

Chelsea donned her robe and took her phone and cup inside, aware that her moment of bliss, where genuine affection was guaranteed, was gone. Like a prized seashell carried away by a wave. Leaving her to yearn for its return, which would never happen.

CHAPTER 58

EACH NIGHT FOR the next week, Chelsea maintained the pretense of being asleep when Garrett came in during the wee hours of the morning. He'd started coming home even later than usual. Her relief about this was genuine. It allowed more opportunity to replay in her mind, her one and only intimate experience with Luke. And, it prevented Garrett from climbing on top of her again, tainting the memory that would have to last the remainder of her life.

Garrett's—who could call it love-making?—paled in comparison to Luke's. The double-entendre made her smile.

She took care with how she dressed to meet Luke at Books and Brew. And she planned topics to talk about so they didn't sit in awkward silence.

At ten till eleven, Chelsea drove to the coffee shop. Luke waited outside, held the door open as she approached. He went to get their coffees, she found a table against the far wall. Their first meeting here seemed a lifetime ago, when their feelings for each other were still unencumbered.

Luke put their cups on the table and sat. "You look well, Chelsea, except for the circles under your eyes. Aren't you sleeping?"

Chelsea ran a polished nail around the rim of her cup and shrugged. "I have a lot on my mind." She looked up and gave him a half-smile.

"We'd had too much to drink."

"You don't believe that anymore than I do. The alcohol did nothing more than remove our inhibitions."

"You're right. That was a stupid thing to say. Well, we're sober now."

Chelsea chuckled.

Luke smiled. "Want to share what's funny?"

She shook her head. "I shouldn't say it."

"Please. I need to know what you're thinking."

"It's just that I find it difficult to imagine that it would be even better if we weren't somewhat inebriated." Her smile faded. "Your expression tells me I should have kept that thought to myself."

"That's not ..." His gaze held hers. "I was thinking how much I'd like to find out."

"Maybe it won't be as spectacular."

Luke's cup stopped halfway to his mouth. "You said won't, not wouldn't. As in there's a possibility."

"You could get a room at the same place and text the number to me. So we don't show up together."

"There are rooms and parking in back. But we agreed: coffee only."

Chelsea stroked the back of his hand. "Only one kind of coffee I want. And I want it now. If you have the time and inclination, that is."

Luke bumped the table in his rush to stand. "Leave in a few minutes. I'll text you as soon as I get the key."

Chelsea, sheathed in perspiration and breathing hard, started to ease herself up and off of Luke.

He kept his hands on her hips and pressed down. "Don't move," he said. "I want to look at you."

"I must look a mess."

He caressed her breasts. "You're a goddess."

"A sweaty one."

"A radiant goddess."

"Who needs to work out more."

"That's up to you, but I think you're perfect just as you are."

"Thank you, kind sir. But I refer to my out-of-practice thigh muscles."

"You don't hear me complaining."

She trailed her fingers up his chest. "The sounds you made could never be construed as complaints." She reached for his watch and sighed. "Time can be so inconvenient. There's only one thing to do. C'mon. Into the shower. Maybe the hot water and my soaping you will recharge you."

Luke growled and grinned. "You aim to have your way with me again in there, don't you?"

Chelsea crawled on all-fours to the edge of the bed, stopped and looked back. "Are you coming?"

"I don't think I'll be able to help it. But, it may take a few minutes."

CHAPTER 59

PENELOPE PULLED A turquoise silk sundress from the rack and held it up. "What about this? It'll show off your eyes and tan. By the way, is that tan real or spray-on?"

"Real," Chelsea replied.

"Since when do you lay out in the sun?"

"I don't. I discovered I have a large pool in my backyard and decided to use it."

"Looks good on you."

Chelsea took the dress from Penelope. "I like that. I'll try it on. Back in a few."

Penelope followed her to the dressing room and stood outside the closed door. "Okay, give."

"Give what?"

"The glow. Swimming. The inches you've lost—you're looking fabulous, I add. There's also your new interest in attractive clothes, or I should say, clothes that you'll look attractive in."

"You really think I look better?"

"Is all of this for Garrett? Are you trying to rejuvenate his interest in you?"

"Not likely."

"You must have a reason for all of this. What is it? You *are* trying to seduce Garrett. Aren't you?"

"You're dreaming."

"This is me. Your oldest and dearest friend since elementary school." Penelope opened the dressing room door. "What the hell? Since when do you wear a thong? Now I know something's going on."

After a few seconds, Chelsea said. "Not here." She closed the door.

"Ha! I knew it. It's the hunky—"

Chelsea stuck her head out. "I *said* not here."

Chelsea tossed her shopping bag into the back seat and got behind the steering wheel.

Penelope slid onto the front seat and closed the door. "I've waited long enough. It *is* the author, isn't it? I want details. Leave nothing out."

"What kind of details? It's not like you've never had sex before. You know what the parts look like and where they go."

"You know what I mean. Is it true?"

Chelsea started the engine. "Is what true?"

"Are all black men especially well endowed?"

"I wouldn't know about all of them."

"You know what I mean."

Chelsea put the car in gear and pressed on the accelerator. "Any bigger and I'd have trouble walking."

Penelope laughed. "Damn. I really have to try one on. Or, I should say, in."

Chelsea slammed on the brakes and turned to face her friend. "Joking's over. It's not like that. I care about him. I care deeply, in fact."

"Don't get your thong in such a twist."

"Doing this isn't easy for me."

Penelope grinned. "Especially if he's huge."

"Pen!" Chelsea's attempt to maintain a severe expression failed.

"One more question?"

Chelsea blew out a breath. "Go ahead. Otherwise, you won't leave me alone."

"How does his technique compare with Garrett's?"

Chelsea started to drive. "After careful consideration, I believe Garrett's opinion of himself is highly overrated."

"Ouch."

"He used to be better at it. Maybe he is better with his women. All I know is that his most recent effort was a poor demonstration."

Penelope faced Chelsea. "When did this happen?"

"Fairly recent."

"You didn't mention it. Since you refuse to give me specifics about Luke, at least entertain me with ones about Garrett."

"Believe me. I'd rather forget. Where do you want to have lunch?"

CHAPTER 60

D<small>R. M</small>OORE assumed her usual position at the end of the sofa, opposite Chelsea. "You're looking quite pretty. That blue's a good color on you. And, you seem even more relaxed than last time. I'm glad of that. However, I am disappointed that you canceled last week's appointment. I thought we agreed it's important to meet each week, at least for a while."

"I didn't feel it was necessary. Life is improving. In fact, this is my last session. Although, it's not really a session—I'm not staying. I respect you, so wanted to come by in person to tell you that. And to thank you. I'll pay for the hour, of course."

"Are you saying your relationship with your husband has improved significantly? Has he changed in some particular way?"

"I've changed. And because of that, I haven't been angry with him or nagging him about his hours—or about anything—for a few weeks. He's happier. I'm happier."

"I see."

"I knew you would." Chelsea stood. "So, I'll pay for my non-session and be on my way."

Dr. Moore motioned for Chelsea to sit. "I think there's something important we need to discuss. I'd like you to stay. At least for a few more minutes. Please."

Chelsea shrugged and sat. "Such as?"

"The first blush of a new relationship makes us feel remarkable, ecstatic even. Everything is brighter. We're ebullient nearly every moment of the day."

"What are you on about?"

"I don't think it's your husband inspiring this change in you. Or swimming or a diet."

Chelsea's cheeks flamed. "I don't know what you mean."

"I've been there, remember? I bought into the illusion that a new man in my life, one who gave me the attention my husband didn't, was real. It isn't. Or, at least, is so seldom authentic that those infrequent exceptions almost don't count. The majority of adulterous relationships end badly, and painfully for all."

"You're wrong."

"About which aspect?"

"You think I'm cheating on Garrett. I'm not."

"You agreed to be honest with me."

Chelsea walked to the window. Keeping her back to Dr. Moore she said, "I told you why I feel better: I decided to believe in myself. That's all there is to it. We're happier because of it." She pivoted and moved toward the sofa. "I suppose it's the nature of your profession to look for some ulterior motive, rather than the simple truth."

"I meant no offense. Please. Sit down. Tell me more about what you're doing that's making a difference."

Chelsea shook her head. "No need." She grabbed her purse and walked to the door. With her hand on the knob, she said, "I'll pay on the way out. Thank you for your time, Dr. Moore." She yanked the door open.

"Chelsea."

Chelsea sighed. "Yes?"

"I'm here if you need me."

"Thanks. But I'm certain I won't. I'm managing fine on my own."

Before Chelsea closed the door behind her, Dr. Moore said, "We all believe that. And we're always wrong."

CHAPTER 61

SWEAT BLOOMED ON her face as soon as she left the building. It worsened when she got into the sweltering car. Chelsea left the door open and switched the air-conditioner onto High. After a minute or so, she closed the door and directed two of the air vents toward her face. Anything to cool the heat in her cheeks, not solely caused by the unseasonably hot day.

She'd fooled herself into believing it would be easy to lie about what was going on. Dr. Moore had seen right through her. Which felt worse: Lying or getting caught? No ready answer came.

She was, however, aware that anger had flared when Dr. Moore insinuated that what she and Luke felt for each other was infatuation only. There was no point in explaining how moments away from Luke were moments without air. Dr. Moore wouldn't have believed her.

How it was with Luke—how she was with him—added a new dimension to her life, enhanced with sensations and sensuality she'd never explored. Sex had never been that way with Garrett. She had never acted with him the way she did with Luke, had never felt inspired to. This shift in her, this willingness meant something. It was significant. It clearly indicated the path she needed to follow.

Didn't it?

But, what if Dr. Moore was right? After all, look at how she'd fooled herself about Garrett, and for how long.

Maybe it was as simple as not being able to trust what she felt. Some flaw in her that made her imagine things that weren't there, believe things that didn't exist.

Eyes closed, she returned to the moment she'd looked into Luke's eyes as he moved inside her, the love transmitted to her, the affectionate words whispered to her.

What it was like to feel cherished.
She'd believed such things before.
And, they'd proven false.

CHAPTER 62

COFFEE CUP FILLED, newspaper in hand, Garrett took a seat at the small table in the kitchen. Frequently, he peered over the pages to watch Chelsea move around as she prepared Sunday brunch. She'd probably dropped a size or two. Three at the most. Top form would take a while. But if she kept at it … Even her thick thighs were starting to tone and were enhanced by a light tan, especially in the sundress that was shorter than she'd worn since college.

He folded the paper and placed it on the table, walked up behind her, put his arms around her waist, bumped his groin against her backside. Kept bumping, feeling the initial stirrings of an erection.

Chelsea attempted to shift away from him. "I'm busy, Garrett."

"Kim's at Susan's until this evening."

"So?"

He raised her dress. "When did you start wearing a thong?"

"I decided to see what the fuss was about." She pulled her dress down.

"I'll show you what it's about." He pulled her dress up and the thong down. "Move your hips into position, so I can slip it in."

Chelsea yanked her thong and dress into place. "I'm tossing a salad."

"You can do two things at once. Besides, I'll be doing most of the work. All you have to do is enjoy the ride."

"Not now. I want to get brunch prepared. I'm hungry."

He grabbed her breasts and rubbed against her. "So am I."

She shrugged him off. "We're not hungry for the same things. Now, stop!"

Garrett backed away. "Fine. Just thought I'd give you a Sunday Special."

"Maybe another Sunday."

Garrett stomped into the living room. The throbbing between his legs insisted on satisfaction. No way would he go to the master bathroom to take care of it, or use the pool suction outlet. No way would he take care of it himself then spend the rest of the day with a woman who denied him his due.

He pulled his phone from his pocket and sent a text message. Seconds later, the response made him chuckle. He went back into the kitchen.

"You'll have to eat alone, Chels. Just got called in."

Without looking up, Chelsea said, "It is what it is."

Garrett hurried to his car, started the engine and sped out of the driveway.

What was up with Chelsea? After all her whining about him not giving her any often enough, she refused him? More where you came from, sweetheart. More attractive. More willing to do whatever I want, where I want it and when.

At least she'd stopped nagging him about his hours. It always took a little extra to get his mind off his complaining wife. Fortunately, his women knew how to give extra.

The bulge in his pants diminished. Not a problem. *Dr. Jacobs* would have him back up in no time. Nothing like an affair that was especially naughty to get the juices flowing. Plus, her text indicated she had something particular in mind.

He licked his lips in anticipation.

CHAPTER 63

THE WEATHER TURNED cold just before the first week in November. Grateful for a heated pool, Chelsea continued to swim laps every day, as soon as she returned from dropping Kimberlie off at school. On the weekends, she got up before the others, preferring to keep her activity private. Her thoughts, as well. The last thing she wanted was for Garrett to join her, or try to join his body to hers.

Time with Luke was sporadic because of his schedule. And hers, because of Kimmie's increase in school activities before the approaching holidays.

The last time they'd been together was a few agonizing days ago. Luke had told her, "You're looking good, love. But promise me you won't go too far. Your body drives me wild just as it is."

She'd caressed him in the way he liked, and where. "And you're an extraordinary driver."

"Wench!" He lifted her with ease and placed her on top of him. Moaned when she slid him inside of her. "What you do to me, woman."

"Why don't you tell me?" Chelsea began to move.

"Can't talk when you do that. And I'm rendered speechless when you do *that*!"

Afterwards, they lay in each other's arms. Chelsea decided to broach a subject she'd stayed away from but had to know. "Luke, it's an uncomfortable topic, but please be honest with me."

"Of course."

"Do you and your wife still—?"

"Not for a long time. Even before you and I got together. And although she finally got another job, which should have put her in a better mood, we barely talk these days. And when we do, it isn't at all pleasant. Just functional. We're polite when my son visits, for his sake. But I sleep in the basement every night. I write then fall asleep thinking about you. Since we're being honest, what about your situation?"

"I'm lucky. Garrett has one or more women keeping him occupied."

"He doesn't ask?"

Chelsea hesitated. "He's asked a few times, a very few. But it's easy to put him off, because I know he's not really interested. He went a number of years without touching me. So, his occasional interest or, rather, sense of marital obligation, doesn't mean anything. Not anymore. And definitely not since—"

Chelsea's phone rang. She checked the screen. "Damn. I have to take this."

"Who is it?"

"Garrett's brother." Chelsea took the phone to the window. "Hi, Richard. Yes, we plan to be there for Thanksgiving. Yes, all three of us. I'm fine … No, really, I am. But, I'm in the middle of something now. I'll call Anna later, to find out what I can bring so there aren't any duplications. Yes … Later. Bye."

Luke sat up. "It'll be our first major holiday. Together but apart."

Chelsea placed her phone on the nightstand. "It won't be easy for either of us. Kimberlie will be on break, starting Monday, which means when she gets out this afternoon … She may visit friends while school's out, but it depends on who stays around and who travels for the holiday. Susan and her family may go out of town. They haven't decided yet."

"We may not see each other for a week or more. I'm already feeling bereft at the idea."

"I can't stand the thought, either. So," she trailed her fingers up his thigh. "Since we've already had the main course, maybe we should have dessert. Interested?"

"Let me show you how much." Luke pulled her onto the bed and rolled her onto her back. He began at her lips then trailed his mouth lower and lower. He reached his destination and said, "Who doesn't love pie?"

Chelsea cried out and grabbed his head. "Every time you do that to me, I'm certain you'll have to peel me off the ceiling."

He lifted his head. "You're not going anywhere until I'm done."

"You mean until I'm done."

"Just for that, I won't settle for anything less than undone."

"You've already accomplished that."

CHAPTER 64

THE WOMEN CONGREGATED in the kitchen, tending to the tasks of putting up the few leftovers from the Thanksgiving feast, loading dishes into the dishwasher, and scrubbing pots in the sink. Kimberlie, phone in hand, texted someone as she bounced up the stairs to watch TV in her grandparents' bedroom.

Garrett, Richard, and their father plopped onto the sofa and chairs in the den. Garrett switched on the big-screen TV he'd given his parents the prior Christmas.

Thomas Hall unbuckled his belt and opened the top button on his pants. "I ate too much."

Garrett said, "As always."

Richard draped one of his legs over a cushioned chair arm. "Easy to do. Our women can cook."

Theresa Hall came to the door. "Garrett, I need you to help me with something."

"The game's about to start, Mom."

"It won't take long."

"Is it that urgent?"

"You're not too old for me to drag you up by the ear, son."

Thomas kicked a toe toward Garrett. "You're wasting time arguing with her. Better get it over with."

Garrett hoisted himself from the chair. "What's so important?"

Theresa pulled him by the sleeve of his sweater. "It's in the front yard."

"I'll get my jacket."

"We won't be out that long."

He shrugged and followed her through the front door, to a hedge near the sidewalk. "I'm a doctor, not a yardman."

Theresa put her hands on her hips. "You're in trouble, is what you are."

"What are you talking about?"

"I'm talking about your marriage. I'm talking about saving it."

"My marriage is fine." He turned. "This is ridiculous. I'm going back in. It's freezing."

"It's not fine. Not according to your brother. And I'm not blind. You and Chelsea act like a couple that tolerates each other. Barely."

Garrett clinched his hands into fists. "What the hell does Richard know about my business? What did he tell you?"

"Enough."

"He's blowing smoke."

"Not according to Chelsea." She tilted her head up. "That's right. I guess your wife needed to talk to someone who knows you well, and didn't feel it was appropriate for that someone to be your mother."

"She's a whiner. I've spoiled her. I'm telling you, we're fine. Sure, we've had some rough patches. Every couple does. But she gets these bouts of petulance. That's all."

"You can't fool me, son. I know you too well. You're back to your antics, aren't you?"

Garrett shook his head. "You're wrong. You're all wrong. I do my best to provide for my family, and this is the grief I get. Well, Richard's going to get it from me." He started for the door.

Theresa grabbed his arm. "Your brother talked to me in confidence. I told him I wouldn't say a word. You say anything to him, you'll get me in trouble. But I have a precious granddaughter to think about."

Garrett shook her hand off. "My family is my concern."

"Then maybe it's time you start acting like it."

CHAPTER 65

CHELSEA CAST SEVERAL glances toward Garrett on the drive home. He'd worn a scowl since shortly after they'd finished dinner. When the men cheered or jeered during certain plays in the game, Garrett's voice wasn't among them. For the remainder of the time with her in-laws, the only person he'd talked to, with more than brief sentences, was Kimberlie.

Garrett parked the car in the garage. Kimberlie bounded out and used her key to dash inside and up the stairs, leaving the door open to the blustery chill.

Garrett said, "Don't get out yet."

Chelsea removed her hand from the door handle. "What's wrong? You haven't been yourself all afternoon."

He stayed facing forward. "You have no business confiding in Richard."

Chelsea strained to hide her surprise and discomfort. "What are you talking about?"

Garrett pounded the steering wheel. "Don't act like you don't know. I don't want my family's noses in our personal life. What's between us stays there. Richard is the last damn person I want involved in my affairs."

"Not the *best* choice of words."

"Damn it, Chelsea. I'm serious. You have something to say, you say it to me."

"If you're ever around long enough, maybe I will."

"If you want to know why I'm not, listen to yourself. And look in the damn mirror."

"Obviously, I'm not so awful. You wanted me a few nights ago."

Garrett barked a laugh. "I figured the occasional mercy fuck is one of my obligations. Believe me. It's a relief when you refuse me."

Chelsea's eyes filled. "It's a relief for both of us. You're such an asshole. A selfish, arrogant—"

"Get out."

"What?"

"Get out. I'm going for a drive."

"It's Thanksgiving."

"I know what damn day it is. I need to ride around and cool off before I have to spend any more time with you."

Chelsea left the car door open and went toward the house. She heard the door being slammed and Garrett shout, "Bitch," before he backed out.

The tires squealed as he drove away.

"And I'd take a bet—and win—on how you're going to *cool off*."

She went inside and closed the door.

CHAPTER 66

NOISE OF CHRISTMAS shoppers bustling past the landscaped courtyard located at the center of the upscale mall, reverberated in the huge enclosure. Potted palms strategically placed around the perimeter did little to buffer the volume. Chelsea absentmindedly stirred her Bloody Mary with the celery stalk and said, "I have no idea what to get Garrett for Christmas."

Penelope leaned forward to hear her better. "You two getting along now?"

"We're cordial to each other, but that's about it. We make an extra effort when Kimmie's around."

"You've got two weeks to figure out what to get him. What about Luke? What are you getting him? Not that you're obligated to give your paramour anything; though, it's considered a nice gesture."

"That presented a greater challenge. I can't buy something really nice. Garrett might find out about it when he does the accounting. Nor can I give Luke anything that would get him in trouble at home."

"You'll think of something."

Chelsea blushed and grinned. "I did."

Penelope leaned in closer. "You have to tell me."

"I discussed this dilemma with Luke several weeks back. I got creative. In the Ladies room at one of the places we meet."

"Where *do* you go?"

"That's between me and Luke."

"And that was enough? A one-time little bit of risque sex? *He's* easy to please."

Chelsea shook her head. "In the backseat of my car—never the front, because one of you inevitably hits the horn. Against a wall in an alley. A wooded area in the park. A house under construction—when no one was there, of course. In a field. Behind a barn, the second time in the hayloft. There were several more places, and more to come. I've discovered it's fun to think of the possibilities. Even more fun to test them."

"Wow, Chels. I never took you as one who'd be adventurous."

"Luke inspires me in a way Garrett never did. It may sound odd, but anything beyond standard with Garrett would have felt sleazy. It's completely different with Luke."

"Any idea what Luke's going to give you."

Chelsea pinked from her neck up. "He started giving at the same time I did. I express my desires and he fulfills them, and acts on some of his own. Until I can't breathe or think anymore."

"I guess he's stuffing your stocking pretty often."

Chelsea's blush deepened. "Always more than once in the few hours we have. And if I've worn him out on one end, he's still energized at the other."

"I'm getting aroused just hearing about it. I admit it: I'm jealous. But you're getting close to the danger zone, Chels."

Chelsea wrapped her hands around her glass. "I've already crossed into it." She raised her eyes to look directly at Penelope. "I love him. And I want to please him. Sure, it feels a little dangerous, carrying on as we have been, but that adds to the excitement. It deepens our connection." She laughed. "No pun intended."

Penelope shook her head. "You don't really love him. What you're feeling is the thrill of being a naughty girl after being married for so long. Especially because the bloom is off the rose with you and Garrett."

Chelsea shook her head. "That's not it. I mean, it is thrilling, but we really are in love. There's nothing shallow about how we feel."

"I think you're both fooling yourselves."

"You're wrong. We've broached the subject of getting divorced so we can be together."

Penelope choked on the sip of Chablis she'd taken. "Are you out of your mind? Be smart, Chels. Keep the good life with Garrett and boink Luke on the side. No reason to get everyone embroiled in that kind of conflict. And believe me, Garrett wouldn't go easy on you. He might not go easy on Luke, either. Don't ruin a good thing. Enjoy it for what it is and let the rest of it go."

"I don't see why Garrett should care, considering what he gets up to."

"But you aren't absolutely sure Garrett's up to anything." She paused. "Or are you?"

Chelsea shrugged. "I'm not saying he doesn't work a lot of hours, but no one works as much as he supposedly does."

"You can't do this, Chelsea. Don't even think about it."

"It's almost all I think about lately."

CHAPTER 67

L UKE THREW HIS hands up in frustration. "I don't know what you want from me, Brandi. I don't think you know. Other than to bark at me like a drill sergeant or criticize me every time we're in the same space. My patience is wearing thin, frankly."

Brandi flung the large spoon into the pot of beef soup she'd been stirring. She faced him, hands on her hips. "*Your* patience is wearing thin? I don't give a damn about your patience. I work sixty hours a week. You work half of that or less."

"I'm working more hours during the holidays, and you know it."

Brandi harrumphed. "Then I come home and have to take care of things here. I do the shopping. I cook. I clean. I manage the accounting and pay the bills. Mostly with what I earn. You sit in the damn basement writing for pennies. The only one getting anything out of this marriage is you."

"I'd help around here, but nothing I do or the way I do it pleases you, so why bother? You yell at me no matter what. The only time I have anything that resembles peace is when I'm in the basement, not that I don't hear you slamming cabinets or pans, stomping around or cranking up the volume on the TV, or running the damn vacuum to deliberately disturb me."

Brandi clasped her hands and held them to her chest. "I'm so very sorry. The great author must have peace and quiet so he can produce dribble that doesn't sell. How uncharitable of me."

"Since that's the only kind of peace I can get from you, you might at least let me have it. It is, after all, two days till Christmas."

"You can't possibly expect me to be available for sex."

"The only thing I can expect from you is more of this behavior. And since we're laying it out there, even if you wanted me, I doubt I could get it up, considering all that's been going on. No sane man wants to hump a cactus."

"I'm not missing anything. Not much to miss."

"And that's you in a nutshell, Brandi."

"What's that supposed to mean?"

"When a man says 'for better or worse,' he's thinking of circumstances life brings his way that he and his wife work through together. Not the worst in his woman. And not 24/7." Luke grabbed his laptop from his office and stormed to the front door.

"Where do you think you're going?"

Before closing the door behind him, Luke said, "I'm going to find a quiet place where I can work for a while. Enjoy having your kingdom all to yourself."

CHAPTER 68

L UKE DROVE TO the corner, turned right and pulled up to the curb. He drew his phone from his shirt pocket.

I know it's last minute, but can you get away for a while?

A minute later Chelsea replied, *As it happens, I can. Where?*

Start heading to our place. I'll text the room number to you.

See you soon. Every inch of you.

Luke dropped his phone onto the passenger seat and drove a few miles over the speed limit. Toward his destination. His solace. His refuge.

Chelsea tapped on the motel room door and flung herself into Luke's arms as soon as he opened it. They stayed there for several moments, letting their lips speak their longing. She pulled back and studied his face. "What is it?"

"I'd say it was another fight with Brandi, but it's really the same one that never stops."

"I'm sorry, Luke. I guess I'm fortunate. Garrett and I now speak only if we must. He's home so seldom when I'm awake, I barely have to contend with him."

Luke sat on the end of the bed and patted the spot next to him. "I don't want to talk about them. I've got news. Incredible news."

"You're beaming. Tell me."

"It's just as you said. My books are gaining momentum. More sales, more exceptional reviews. All coming fast."

"That's wonderful, Luke. It was just a matter of time."

"It's better than that." He grinned. "My royalties are up to four thousand dollars. For this month. I feel like I'm finally on the journey I always intended to take. Was meant to take."

"You were on that journey when you typed the first word of the first story. I'm thrilled for you, love. And to celebrate," she pushed him back and teased the zipper of his jeans down, "let me take you on a different kind of journey."

Chelsea draped a leg over Luke and stroked his chest. "I love these times with you, but I want more."

"I agree."

"What are we going to do, Luke?"

"I think it's time we do what's necessary to make it permanent."

"Do you mean it? You're not just saying that to—"

"Appease you? I wouldn't do that to you. Why should we live miserable lives with only intervals of joy? I think it's time to switch those quantities around."

Chelsea caressed his face and kissed him. "I'm ready."

Luke pulled her head to his chest. She'd never been through a divorce as he had. At some point he'd have to tell her no one is ever ready for what comes of that action, even if they believe they are. Not during, not after.

Chelsea's phone rang. She checked who was calling. "It's Garrett."

CHAPTER 69

THE CALL CAME at seven forty-five on the evening of the twenty-third of December. Garrett checked caller ID and told *Dr. Jacobs* to stay quiet. He slowed his thrusts and answered. "Chloe, I'm deep into something at the moment." He grinned at the woman beneath him, put his hand over her mouth, sped up his thrusts then slowed again. "I'll have to call you back later."

"Richard's in the E.R. He collapsed or something."

Garrett withdrew from his partner and sat on the edge of the bed. "What happened?"

"Anna was so upset, I couldn't really make sense of what she was saying. But I did understand they're running the usual tests to find out what's going on."

"Which hospital?"

"Mercy."

"I'm on my way. Do you need me to pick you up?"

"I'm in the car with Mom and Dad. Anna's at the hospital. She rode in the ambulance."

"I'll be there as soon as I can." He ended the call and turned to the woman. "My brother's in the emergency room. Get my clothes organized. I've got to speed-shower and get going."

"What's wrong?"

"Too soon to know."

Garrett found his parents, Chloe, and Anna in the emergency waiting room. "Do you know anything yet?"

Thomas Hall answered. "He had a stroke. They found the clot and are prepping him for surgery now, to remove it."

"I'm going in there. I'll be back as soon as I can."

Twenty minutes later, Garrett returned with five cups of coffee and sandwiches for each of them. "They said the stroke happened in the right hemisphere. Not that there's a good side of the brain to have a TIA, but Richard's recovery will likely be easier because of that. I was able to speak to him just before they administered anesthesia and booted me out. I told him he's in good hands. That we're all here and will be when he wakes. He was aware enough to understand. I think. Now we wait."

CHAPTER 70

THE ELECTRONIC GLASS doors slid open. Chelsea rushed to the information desk in the emergency room, heard familiar voices to her left. She joined the family in the waiting area, hugging everyone in turn. Garrett explained the situation. She held up a bag. "I brought sandwiches and sodas."

Theresa Hall looked up with worry heavy in her eyes and face. "We had something not long ago. But thank you, dear."

Chelsea sat next to Chloe. "I'm sure it'll all keep, in case anyone wants any of it later."

They sat in the silence many endure at such times. After an hour had passed, Garrett got up and paced. "Richard and I have had our less-than-perfect moments. I tormented him when we were kids. But if anybody else did anything to him, they didn't do it twice. No one but me was allowed to pick on my little brother. It was my job to look after him, to protect him." He was quiet a moment then said, "Excuse me. I need to make some calls." He went out through the sliding doors.

Ten or so minutes later, he returned. "I've arranged to take the week off. I'm going to make damn sure Richard gets the care he needs, when he needs it. Told everyone they can call if they absolutely need to, but I made it clear that I'm not budging from his side."

Theresa said, "You don't have to do that, son. There's no reason for you to miss that much work. We can manage."

"Mom, the last thing I want you to do is wear yourself out. It's the same for you, Anna. I'll stay with him around the clock. And I'm pretty sure he'll need to go to rehab for a while. Whatever he needs during this first week, I'll make sure he gets it."

Thomas said, "That's good of you, son. It'll ease our minds some-what."

Garrett faced Chelsea. "I'll need some clothes and toiletries."

"I'll bring them in the morning. And, I know it may be too soon to mention this, but we can either postpone celebrating Christmas until Richard's home or we can have it here, with him. If he's well enough."

Garrett glared at her. "I think we can worry about that at a better time."

Theresa leaned forward. "That's thoughtful of you, Chelsea. I say we wait, so Richard can enjoy it more. So we all can. Although, Kimberlie may need to have her Christmas on the day."

Garrett shook his head. "She's old enough to understand. She'll celebrate it when we do." He turned to Chelsea. "By the way, why isn't she here?"

"She's spending the night with Susan. Right now, they and Susan's parents are attending a performance of *The Nutcracker*. There's nothing she can do. I'll call her first thing in the morning and pick her up on the way here."

Anna went to Garrett. She hugged him and kissed his cheek. "Thank you. We'll all feel better if you're looking after him." She glanced at each of them, fixed her gaze on Garrett and said, "I think it's time we all pray."

For once, Garrett didn't argue.

CHAPTER 71

GARRETT STAYED WITH Richard in intensive care, restricting the family to visiting hours only. He ordered them out after twenty minutes on Christmas day. Chloe called him a tyrant then embraced him hard.

He hugged his parents. "Sorry, but it'll wear him out. Too much stimulation too soon."

Theresa patted his cheek. "You know what's best."

Two days later, Richard was moved into a regular room. Garrett bathed his brother, fed him the same way he'd fed Kimberlie when she was a baby, chatted to him about his condition and the improvement he could expect. Told him he'd whup him as he had when they were kids, if he didn't work his butt off to recover.

It took only one flare of his temper to straighten out staff that took too long to show up or did something in a less than proficient manner.

During the times Richard was awake and alert, Garrett read to him in a soothing voice fifteen minutes at a time and had one-sided conversations, until his brother began to make the first sounds that emerged into singular, small words to convey what he needed.

On the fifth day, the rehabilitation therapist showed up. Garrett paid close attention, asked more questions than the therapist was used to answering. He repeated the therapy again later in the day, each day, careful not to overdo it and tire his *patient*.

On the seventh day, Richard, speaking and moving better, was well enough to transfer to a rehab center. Anna and the rest of the family took over. Garrett returned to work, cutting his days short to rush to the center and check on Richard's progress.

He was home by six thirty each night.

Chelsea took her phone into the master bathroom. She locked the door, turned the cold water on in the shower, and keyed in the words of her text message.

My dearest love, life should return to normal soon. Thank you for understanding. Not seeing you or hearing your voice these few weeks is torture. I haven't dared call or text you before now, even late at night. Kimberlie's never had to face anything severe related to family. She's not left my side since the morning of Christmas Eve—the only private time I've had is in the bathroom. She slept with me that first week, when Garrett stayed at the hospital, and woke with every sound or whenever I moved in bed. Now that his brother is in rehab, Garrett's been coming home early every night. Really early! I feel like I'm in prison. Sorry…don't mean to go on and on. It's frustration talking. I know you're in your own hell, as well. But my longing for you passed bittersweet after 42 hours and turned to pure agony. Thank goodness Richard's recovery has been excellent and he goes home in two days. Kimberlie returns to school the same day. I'll scream if I can't be with you soon.

Seven minutes went by before she got a response.

Sorry, my love. Had to wait for my break. Yes, we're both living in a particular kind of hell. We'll make sure that our next Christmas is together and a far happier celebration. Be forewarned: When I'm with you again, there won't be a part of you that doesn't receive my admiration and ministrations. More than once. We both must plan for the time that will take.

I love hearing that, Luke. And it makes this waiting even more frustrating. But you knew that, didn't you? Just for that taunt, I'm going to wear you out when I see you (grin).

We'll wear each other. In. And out. Must get back to work. I'll be waiting to hear from you. Waiting to be with you again. It can't be soon enough.

Chelsea put the phone under her folded towel and got into the shower. She adjusted the water temperature then switched the shower head from spray to jet-pulse and tilted it toward the marble bench. She positioned herself on the bench, knees apart, and imagined the water was Luke, teasing her to her release.

CHAPTER 72

CHELSEA HAD MADE it plain that she missed him as much as he missed her, longed for him in equal measure. Smiling, Luke tucked his phone into his shirt pocket and turned to go back inside the restaurant. He startled when a figure emerged from the shadows.

"James. I didn't realize you were there."

"Thought I'd join you for the break, but you had all your attention on texting. Looking all intense. What's going on, dude?"

"Nothing."

James shook his head. "This is me you're talking to."

"I'm in love. Deep, abiding, all-encompassing, torrential love with the woman I told you about."

"Aw, crap."

"Forget it." Luke started for the door.

"Sorry. I'm listening. I'm curious about a woman who can have that effect on you."

"I told you she's gorgeous. She's also kind, sensual, fun, intelligent. All wrapped in auburn hair, eyes the color of a clear-day sky, skin the color of cream, a body that begs to be appreciated, and the enthusiasm to reciprocate."

"And has a husband. Forbidden fruit, man."

"She loves me as much as I love her. This is the woman I've always dreamed of sharing my life with."

"Dude, you got a big fucking boulder on that path of bliss: You're married. To a hellcat."

"Everything you said about Brandi was right. I made a mistake when I married her. Mistakes can be corrected."

"This pale goddess of yours pushing you to marry her?"

"It's not like that. We know what we want, what we need. When the time is right, we'll both get divorced so we can be together."

"You out of your mind? You better hope her husband doesn't find out, or you may not have to worry about a divorce."

"I'm sure it won't come to that. Besides, he has no right to be offended. He cheats on her. Has for a long time. It's like an addiction with him."

"Doesn't mean he'll give up the little woman without a fight. A lot of men who play around still love their wives."

"Like you?"

James poked Luke's arm hard. "And you. Don't try to smooth over what you're doing by calling it love prefaced by a bunch of high-sounding adjectives. You're a man. Fact is, men cheat."

"Not all."

"The percentage who don't is damn small."

"That's pretty cynical, even for you."

"Truth is truth. I don't make it up. I just recognize it for what it is."

"It isn't my truth."

"Just because you don't want to call it what it is doesn't make it something else."

Luke stayed quiet a moment then said, "I'd do anything for her. I'll do anything to be with her."

"It's not like you to be irrational. And that's what you're being. I know you can't see it, but dude, don't screw up your marriage for a married woman."

"My marriage is already screwed up. Always has been. And you know it."

"This is bad. So bad, I don't know what to say except get out of it while you still can."

Luke shook his head. "You don't search the world for a diamond, find it then cast it away."

"Brandi finds out, she's gonna chop your *diamonds* off, dude. And make earrings out of them."

"You worry too much. I also thought, considering your history, you'd understand."

"Believe me. I understand."

"I don't think you do."

CHAPTER 73

I T HAD BEEN just over three weeks since they'd been together. Once they shed their clothing, there was no gentle segue into lovemaking for Chelsea and Luke. They all but tore at each other, reminded each other repeatedly not to leave marks from the intensity of their passion.

Chelsea flopped onto her back. "That was amazing. I love when you try new things."

"It's my pleasure and destiny to please you." Luke rolled onto his side. "However, now that we've sweat enough to remove your makeup, why don't you tell me how you got that bruised cheek."

"I was looking for something in the kitchen, in one of the bottom cabinets. I forgot I'd left the upper cabinet door open, and *whack*. I saw stars."

"That's your story and you're sticking to it, I suppose."

Chelsea stroked his chest. "Let's forget about that. I can't go this long without you ever again. We need to plan how we're going to resolve this dilemma. I've realized that life is too short not to make the most of it while we can."

"I know. But let's not rush into it."

"I thought you wanted … Last time, you said you were ready now. What's changed?"

He kissed her breasts. "Nothing, and I am ready. But I'm just starting to do well. I want to be in a better financial position than I am right now, before I make a move."

"That doesn't matter to me."

"And I love you for that. But trust me. In the bigger picture, it will matter. I want to feel more stable in my ability to do it right. I want to take care of you the way you deserve."

"As far as a place goes, once we're free and clear, you'll move in with me."

"I don't know how your daughter will feel about that. Or Garrett."

"Once I'm divorced, Garrett will have no say about it. And, no one can tell me my new husband can't live with me. You and I will date for a while so Kimberlie can see how wonderful you are. I know she'll love you. Then, you can move in as soon as we're officially engaged."

"I hope you're right. But I think it's best if you're prepared for it to perhaps not be as simple as you want to believe. There's your family to consider and mine. Even if Kimberlie goes for it, I can't guarantee that Tim will."

"Your son will love the house. And the pool. And I'll love him because he's yours."

"It'll be his second time to go through this; though, it won't be the same as when his mother and I divorced. He still finds it a difficult experience. He's never accepted Brandi—just barely tolerates her; though, I share his feelings about her better now. We also don't know how our children will get along."

"You're over-thinking this, Luke. Kids are more adaptable than we tend to believe."

"I hope you're right."

"Isn't it better to show them an example of what happiness looks like, rather than the opposite?"

"And, there are our exes to contend with. One for you, two for me."

"You and Brandi haven't had children. There's no reason for her to stay in your life."

Luke nodded. "That's true. I'm sure she'll be relieved to be rid of me."

Chelsea rolled onto her side. "You're sounding world-weary, love. That won't do. Time to remind you why we have to get our lives arranged so we can be together."

Luke gasped then closed his eyes to block out any thought but what Chelsea was doing. She was right: this was the woman and life he had to have.

CHAPTER 74

CHELSEA HAD WONDERED how long it would be before Garrett resumed calling her to say he was working late. It took until the night Richard returned home.

She didn't make a big deal about it, because what Garrett did, or *whom* he did, was no longer important to her. What she wanted was to be with Luke.

She understood why he wanted to wait a little longer before announcing their desire to divorce their spouses, but it also frustrated her. Male pride, even in the best of men, always had to be considered. All she had to do was prove to him that they were already set up to start their new life. She'd keep the house and the Bentley. Garrett would pay alimony, child support, and all expenses for the house and car. When she and Luke married, the alimony would cease, but they'd be able to make it. His sales were improving and would continue on that track. She was certain of it. And, she could offer legal advice or provide smaller legal services from home, if they needed extra funds.

Throughout the evening, Chelsea played out various mental scenarios as to how to address this with Garrett. To bolster her courage, she replayed images of her more intimate moments with Luke.

Whatever she decided to do, it had to be soon. Garrett had already taken so much from her. Why give him even more opportunity. He didn't want her. He'd made that clear in many ways for years. How to accomplish this task in a proficient, smooth manner came to her: point out to Garrett that he'd be free to screw any woman he wanted, without guilt or a discontent wife.

This tactic appealed to her. Now it was just a matter of when. There would never be a perfect moment for such a pronouncement, but she'd watch for a more ideal one.

It was a few minutes after two in the morning when Garrett came in. Chelsea went to the window, expecting him to dive into the pool, as was his habit. Instead of hearing the back door, she heard footfalls coming up the stairs. She dashed back to bed.

He didn't go into the bathroom as he usually did. Instead, he stripped at the side of the bed and climbed under the covers. He reeked of sex.

"Garrett, I want a divorce."

"Don't be silly. It's late. Go back to sleep. I'm bushed."

"And I know why. But, the fact is, I'm not happy. I want out. I want a chance at true happiness."

"Not this crap again. You know I was out because of Richard. There's a lot to catch up with at the hospital and my practice."

"I mean it."

"So do I. Look, Chels, I'm sorry about my hours, but it's necessary. I'm sorry you're unhappy, but I do love you, and I have no intention of ending our marriage."

"Right. You love me."

"More than the day I married you, I swear. You can forget about a divorce. It'll never happen. We're a family and we're staying one. End of discussion. Go to sleep."

A new plan formed in her mind.

CHAPTER 75

I T WAS STILL dark out when the racket of a snowblower woke everyone in the house. But at least getting the cars out of the garage, Garrett off to work, and Kimberlie to school was easier because of it.

Chelsea was up to forty laps each morning, and more than a little grateful the yardmen had erected the large tent over the pool. She'd had to wear knee-high snow boots to get to it.

While she swam, and afterwards as she sipped coffee in the kitchen, she worked and reworked the details of her plan.

Her phone rang; her lips stretched into a smile. "Hi, love. Where are you?"

"I'm at the restaurant. On my first break. I couldn't wait to tell you what's going on. *A Dark Walk* is taking off. It made the *USA Today* best-seller list, and is on its way up. Also, I just checked my royalties. Ninety-five hundred on Amazon, seven thousand on Barnes and Noble. I'm still stunned at this dramatic turn."

"As the kids would say, OMG. Luke, I'm so pleased for you."

"For us, Chelsea. For us. If this continues, I'll be able to contribute to the life you're used to. And before you tell me again that it doesn't matter, you know it matters to me. We'll be flush."

"I don't want to put a damper on your excitement, but Brandi may get some of that. Your first wife certainly will, or at least she'll try to."

"I'm not telling either of them."

"They'll find out when you become a best-selling author. Maybe before. And definitely during the divorce settlement."

"Then I'll have to hope they don't find out, until the divorce is over and done with, if ever. You're right about Tina, though. I'd hate giving her more, but will for Tim's sake. Unless we get him to live with us. However, Brandi and I haven't been married long enough for her to claim anything."

"Keeping this secret could become problematic."

"This isn't the time to worry about that. We need to celebrate next time we see each other. Sorry, Chelsea. I have to get back to work. But I want you to keep one thing foremost in your mind and heart: I'm deeply, irreversibly in love with you. I'll do anything for you, anything to protect and care for you. Gotta run."

"I feel the same, love." She ended the call and stared at her phone.

Luke was far too ecstatic at the moment, to see the potential financial fly in that sticky ointment. She'd have to explain things to him another time, when he wasn't soaring. Let him revel in his success for now. There would be plenty of time later for reality to be dealt with.

One thing was certain. This news made her even more resolved to act on her plan. It was the only way to protect her own interests.

CHAPTER 76

A T TWELVE THIRTY, Kimberlie called to say she was doing a study-sleepover at Susan's house and would head there directly after school. Garrett called a few minutes after three that afternoon with the anticipated announcement that he was working late at the hospital.

No reason to wait for a better time to follow through on her plan. This was the time to act.

As soon as that second call ended, Chelsea ordered a rental car. She drove to the place, asked if she could leave her car with them and pick it up within a few to several hours. They assured her that as they were a 24/7 company, it was no problem. She ignored the puzzled and curious looks when she swapped the Bentley for an older model Toyota.

There was only one sure way to guarantee a divorce and good settlement: catch Garrett in the act.

She'd considered hiring a private detective, but decided it was too risky. What if the detective checked on her? The last thing she or Luke needed was to be caught doing the same thing she wanted to use against Garrett. She and Luke would have to be more careful from now on, until they were both divorced. No more motel, unless they found a particularly secluded one in a nearby town.

Chelsea stopped at a convenience store for a few snacks and water. No telling how long she'd have to wait for Garrett to leave work. Unless he'd already left. Her stomach fluttered at the thought of possibly missing this opportunity and having to wait for the next one. She was ready now.

She wended the Toyota through the hospital parking lot. Breathed with relief to see Garrett's car still there. She found a place to park where she could watch for him. Waiting was harder than expected.

At seven forty-two, Garrett exited the front door and sauntered to his car, phone pressed against his ear. He laughed at something the person on the other end said. She started the car and put it into gear. Her foot rested on the brake as she waited for Garrett to drive out of the lot.

She followed him to the edge of town, continuing on for miles, wondering where he was going. Prayed he wasn't going to some last-minute conference meeting instead of to a rendezvous. Followed him all the way to Brookline. Laughed out loud when Garrett turned into the parking lot of an upscale hotel.

Chelsea turned in seconds behind him and parked. As soon as he went inside, she got out of her car, stopping just outside the glass door to watch what he did. It *was* possible she could be wrong. He could be going to a meeting or conference.

His manner was buoyant, casual—he wasn't afraid of being seen, of being caught. Garrett handed his credit card and a number of hundred-dollar bills to the man behind the desk, who handed over a key. It was the confirmation she needed. At least, part of it.

Garrett started toward the elevators. As soon as the doors closed with him inside, she entered the lobby as though she had every reason to be there. Watched the floor numbers, prayed the elevator didn't make more than one stop. It didn't, not until it reached the top floor. Relief flooded her. She pressed the button and waited for an elevator to take her up.

And Garrett down.

CHAPTER 77

THE ELEVATOR DOOR opened. Chelsea stepped into the carpeted hallway. There were only two doors on that floor. One was marked as the Executive Suite, the other was the Presidential Suite. Ordinarily, this would mean she had a fifty-fifty chance of getting one of the rooms right the first time. But this was Garrett.

Chelsea stood in front of the door to the Presidential Suite and took a few deep breaths. Garrett was about to get the shock of his life. She slapped a hand over her mouth when a giggle erupted at the thought. She was ready. And resolute.

This was going to be most satisfying, especially after all the hell he'd put her through. She was prepared for whatever she discovered on the other side of the door. Because this was her ticket to freedom and happiness.

Chelsea rapped on the door. Seconds later, Garrett, leaving the door closed, asked who it was. She lowered her voice and said, "The champagne you ordered, sir." Her cell phone was in her hand, ready to capture the proof.

The security bolt was thrown, the handle turned. As the door opened a mere few inches, Garrett said, "The champagne's already been de—"

Chelsea started recording the video and shoved her way past a startled, naked Garrett, who had a white smudge around his lips and an erection diminishing by the second. She filmed the woman perched on the edge of the sofa, capturing the woman's shocked expression, evident despite the black leather mask covering the upper half of her face. The woman's hand, wrapped around a whip, was still raised.

She noted the smeared whipped cream on the woman's breasts and between her wide-spread legs elevated by knee-high patent leather boots with stiletto heels.

Boots she'd seen before.

CHAPTER 78

NO ONE MOVED or said anything for several seconds. The woman screamed and said, "Oh God. Garrett, do something."

Chelsea started toward the sofa. "You bitch! I'm going to rip every bleached hair out of your fucking head." Chelsea launched forward. Garrett grabbed her arms and held them behind her.

Struggling to restrain Chelsea, Garrett said, "Penelope, get dressed and out of here. Now."

Chelsea strained to break free, cursing at top volume at her husband and her once best friend.

Penelope ran into the bedroom and returned seconds later, maskless. Three stains began to form on the front of her dress. "Chels, I'm—"

"Don't you dare call me that. Don't you dare call me ever again." Chelsea, breathing hard, stopped struggling against Garrett's restraint. "It all makes sense now. And, how very clever you both are. You must have had quite a laugh at my expense, pretending you detested each other. Always referring to her as a slut. The correct label, but a different motivation behind it than I expected." She stomped on Garrett's foot until he released her. Facing him she said, "Don't bother to come home. Not tonight. Not ever."

"Now just a damn minute, Chelsea."

"I mean it, Garrett." She pointed at Penelope and said, "Stay where you are. Both of you stay right where you are. Enjoy your sleazy party. You'll both be paying for it for a long time." She stuck a finger in Garrett's face. "Expect to hear from my lawyer."

CHAPTER 79

CHELSEA MOVED THROUGH the hotel lobby like an automaton, oblivious to the surroundings and her phone ringing, stopping, ringing again. She had to get away.

Panic struck as she searched the parking lot for her Bentley, finally recalling she'd arrived in a Toyota. It took several seconds to remember where she'd parked. More seconds to steady her hand so as to fit the key into the lock, and then into the ignition.

Her phone rang again. She turned it off and threw it to the floorboard. In the enclosed interior, she screamed, "Leave me alone." Go, she told herself.

The drive from Brookline to Waltham took an hour longer than it should have. A result of Chelsea having to pull over several times, until gut-wrenching weeping could cease long enough for her to see the road again.

She parked the Toyota in the garage and walked trance-like into the house. Trance-like, made a call to a locksmith and told him it was an emergency; that she'd pay double, triple even, if he'd get there immediately and change every lock. She told him how many were needed, and how many keys.

Numb, she waited for then watched the locksmith in silence, speaking only when he asked her an infrequent question. The landline rang. And rang. She ignored it. Ignored the raised eyebrows of the locksmith. An hour later, the man hurried from the house with a wad of cash in his pocket as the phone rang again.

Chelsea stood at the back door, gazing at the tented pool. The phone rang four times. Went silent. Rang again, insistently. A light snow began to fall. She shivered, glanced to the right of the pool and nodded. Not bothering to put on a coat, she went to the built-in brick barbecue pit. Within minutes, a fire roared in its recess.

It took a number of trips upstairs and down, and more time than she thought it would take, to burn every article of his clothing, including his briefs. Garrett's presence in her life—up in smoke.

Lyrics from the song by Blackberry Smoke came to mind:

Leave a trail of ashes and a trail of sin.

She wiped her eyes on her sleeve.

CHAPTER 80

I T WAS NEARLY midnight when Chelsea realized her cell phone was still in the rental car. Barefoot, and wearing only an old flannel gown, she retrieved her phone and returned to bed. The last thing she wanted to do was turn the damn thing back on, but there was Kimberlie to consider. If her daughter needed her, she had to be available.

She pressed the button. Missed calls, voice and text messages from Garrett, all of which she deleted. None from Penelope.

Nothing from Luke, either. She needed to tell him what had happened, needed to hear his voice soothing her. Even though he'd said he slept in the basement, she didn't dare call him. After all, there was nothing he could do. One of them should be able to sleep.

An insidious thought surfaced: What if Luke had lied about his arrangement? What if he was next to his wife, and was there every night? Both of them sated after his doing to his wife what he did to her. Everyone important to her had lied to get what they wanted. Why should he be any different?

Don't judge him by Garrett's standards, she scolded herself. Luke isn't Garrett. He had to be different. He had to be. Otherwise, she'd lose what little sanity she had left.

The landline jangled again several minutes after midnight. Then her cell phone—Garrett. She ignored it. Deleted the subsequent message without listening to it. This went on for twenty minutes. Then a text message came in.

For God's sake, Chelsea, and for the sake of our daughter, please forgive me. I swear it will never happen again. I won't even so much as look at another woman for the rest of my life. Let me make it up to you. I'll spend every day, as long as I live, doing that. Whatever you want. Tell me it's okay to come home.

I'm all out of forgiveness, Garrett. You and Penelope don't deserve it. I have to figure out what to tell Kimmie so she doesn't hate you. BTW, you need to go shopping. Tomorrow.

WTF?

When I got home, I felt chilled and thought a bonfire was just the thing, after I had all the locks changed. Some of your clothes took longer to burn than others. If you bother me again tonight or ever show up here without my permission, I'll call the police and file a complaint.

Chelsea didn't wait for a reply. She turned her phone off and lay with her eyes open in the dark. If Kimmie did need her, Susan's mother or father would come to the house if she didn't answer either phone.

There was one thing she shouldn't do, but felt compelled to. She sat up, turned her phone on. And watched the video. She barely made it to the bathroom in time to lose the contents of her stomach. She stayed in there, with a cold wet rag draped on the back of her neck, until the dry heaves ceased.

Her plan had succeeded. She'd been prepared to catch Garrett in the act. But not for what she'd discovered.

What was meant to be simple had become complicated.

CHAPTER 81

CHELSEA DRAGGED HERSELF from bed a few minutes to eleven the next morning. Waited until she drank half a cup of coffee to turn her phone on. There were several text messages from Luke asking if she was okay, and why wasn't she answering him. That if he didn't hear from her soon, he had no choice but to go to her house to make certain she was safe and well. Five more from Garrett, escalating from apologetic to irate and vile. One from Penelope professing her love and begging forgiveness for being weak. For making the worst mistake of her life.

A quick call was made to the rental car place, requesting they bring the Bentley to her house—*Leave the keys on the seat, and take the Toyota*—the keys were inside, on the floorboard. The credit card used the night before took care of the charges. She didn't want to see or speak with anyone.

She ached to tell Penelope off, to verbally rip her to shreds, but there was a hitch: Penelope knew her secrets. Only one thing to do.

I need time, she wrote back.

Time to think. Was it possible to keep Penelope quiet until both she and Luke were divorced? And not have anything to do with her at the same time?

Chelsea wrote and revised a text message to Luke. It took ten minutes to finally arrive at the one she sent.

Sorry, love. Followed Garrett to a hotel last night so I could catch him cheating and force him to give me a divorce. I wasn't prepared for what I saw, or who. He was with Penelope. I don't believe I'll ever be able to erase that image from my mind. The saving grace is that I don't have to see him. I forbade him from ever coming here again, unless I say he can.

God, Chelsea, are you okay?

I will be. Still feeling devastated. I'm going to find a lawyer this morning and get things going. Also have to talk with Kimberlie when she gets in from school. Have to figure out what to tell her. One of us crushed beyond measure is enough.

Not easy. I remember what that's like. I'm here for you. If there's anything I can do, tell me.

If there is, I will. It may be a few days before we can see each other. We're on our way to being together, my love. And I can hardly stand waiting to be with you.

Your move, Luke.

CHAPTER 82

"I DON'T *believe* this! What is *wrong* with everybody?" Kimberlie, sobbing, ran upstairs and slammed her bedroom door.

Chelsea would give her some time, but not too much. The last thing she wanted was for her daughter to feel alone as she went through the pain of this transition.

She'd wait until the last minute to tell her mother, who'd probably tell her to take Garrett back. Again. Would she mention Penelope? At some point, she'd have to. But that could wait, hopefully, for a very long time.

As for Garrett's family, she'd let him be responsible for telling them. Then she remembered Richard. Worried that the news might cause a set-back. He was doing better than expected, but there was no way this wouldn't affect him. She'd have to talk to Garrett's family eventually, especially Richard.

Luke had tried to tell her about the difficulties that might or would present themselves. She hadn't wanted to listen. The only thought she'd wanted to entertain was about the inevitable bliss she and Luke would share. How could she be so naive? There was a long, challenging road ahead before they could legally be together. That left open the opportunity for a lot of pain to travel with them.

At six o'clock, Chelsea knocked on Kimberlie's door. She turned the knob—locked. "How about some soup, Kimmie?"

"I'll never be hungry again."

"I understand how you feel. But you need to eat. C'mon, Kimmie. We need to help each other be strong. I'll start heating the soup."

Chelsea was almost to the bottom of the stairs when she heard Kimberlie's door open.

She looked at her daughter and said, "Chicken noodle?"

Kimberlie shrugged and trod down the stairs as though each step took tremendous effort.

Chelsea waited for Kimberlie and wrapped an arm around her daughter's shoulder as they walked to the kitchen. "We'll get through this. It won't be easy at first. No major change ever is. It may take a while to get everything arranged so life goes more smoothly for everyone. But we'll do our best, won't we?"

"I guess. It's not like I have a choice."

Kimberlie eased onto one of the counter stools while Chelsea dumped the canned contents into a pot. Kimberlie's phone rang. "It's Dad. I don't know what to say to him."

"He's your father and you love him. Just be nice."

"Hi, Dad. Yeah, she told me … She said you guys are splitting up and that you won't be living here anymore … No. I don't want to do that … *No*, Dad … all *right*." She held her phone down. "Dad wants me to ask you if he can come home."

"Let me talk to him." She took Kimberlie's phone. "Garrett, this is a difficult time for all of us, but you will not put Kimmie in the middle again … Yes, I was serious about a lawyer. I met with one this afternoon … You'll find out who in a few days. There's nothing more to say at this time. I'm giving the phone back to Kimmie."

Kimberlie took the phone, slid off the stool, and walked into the formal living room.

Chelsea listened to her daughter talk in soft tones between bouts of sobbing.

She swiped at her eyes and stirred the soup.

CHAPTER 83

THE WARM WATER should have felt good. Chelsea sat on the steps in the shallow end of the pool. It was better to keep moving, to do some activities that were normal, rather than curl into a ball and not move until she felt human again. That could take far too long. Her daughter, and circumstances, required her presence. She completed her laps.

Wrapped in a long cashmere robe, she waited as a tall cup filled with steaming coffee. The cup was just to her lips when the doorbell rang. Through one of the glass panels on the side of the door, she saw an unfamiliar, modest car parked in the circular driveway. Certain someone was either looking for odd jobs or at the wrong house, she opened the door. The slap to her face came fast and hard.

"You *bitch*." Penelope's face blazed crimson.

Chelsea rubbed her cheek. "That's rich, coming from you. Now get the hell off my property. Be damn grateful I won't have you arrested for assault."

"If anyone needs to be grateful about not having charges filed against them, it's you."

"A little early to be hitting the bottle, isn't it? Or has your guilty conscience led you to start drinking your breakfast?"

Penelope balled her hands into fists. "Your innocent act doesn't fool me. I know you too well. You're the one who needs to stay off *my* property."

"You *are* drunk. Go home and sleep it off. And stay the hell away from me." Chelsea pushed the door to close it.

Penelope shoved the door back. "I'm sending you the bill, and you'd better damn well pay it as soon as you get it."

"What bill?"

"Four new tires and a crappy rental car."

"What the hell are you talking about?"

"Just stop it. You ever slash my tires again or do any other damage to any of my property, I will have you arrested."

"I haven't been anywhere near your house or your car. Nor do I intend to be ever again. If someone slashed your tires, it's likely another wife whose husband you're playing whipped-cream fantasy with."

"So, you're going to stick with that poor-little-misunderstood-Chelsea farce. You even have the puzzled expression down to perfection. Probably practice it in the mirror. I've put up with your I'm-so-wounded facade long enough."

Chelsea remained at the threshold as Penelope stomped to the rental car and sped away.

She was sure of two things: she hadn't slashed the tires, and no way was she paying the bill.

CHAPTER 84

CONCERNED STAFF AT the hospital had commented about his appearance, asked if he was ill. Garrett's expression, and the tone used to reply that he was fine, signaled them to drop the topic. He opened the top folder in the stack on his desk then closed it, unable to concentrate. Scrubbed his hands hard over his face.

His cell phone buzzed. Penelope. Again, and still showing up on the screen as *Dr. Jacobs*. How clever he'd thought he'd been when he'd arranged that deception. He'd already deleted fifteen voice and text messages from her in the last hour and a half. He couldn't continue to ignore her, because he knew she wouldn't give up. The last thing he wanted was for her to show up at the hospital. To barge down the hallway, demanding to see him. Time to tell her to stop.

"I'm at work, Pen. I can't just drop everything when you call."

"I need to see you."

"Not a good idea."

"I didn't mean right this minute, Garrett."

"We're not going to see each other again. Ever. Period."

"Just a damn minute."

"I'm out of minutes."

Penelope softened her tone. "You'll want meet with me. Believe me. You'll be glad you did."

"I'm not in the mood."

"When I tell you the truth about Chelsea, you'll thank me."

"What are you on about?"

"Not now. It has to be in person."

If that was the only way to get her out of his life, so be it.

"Where and when?"

CHAPTER 85

I F PENELOPE HAD so much as her shoes off, he was leaving. The woman was poison. Garrett unlocked the door to the Presidential Suite and crossed the threshold.

Penelope, seated on the edge of the familiar sofa, poured wine into the extra glass on the silver tray resting on the coffee table. "It's not a firing squad, Garrett." She held up the glass. "But you'll need this."

He closed the door and walked to her, took the glass and sat in a chair positioned at a ninety-degree angle to the sofa. "Okay. You got me here. What's so damn important?"

"I'll get straight to the point."

"I'd appreciate it."

"Chelsea isn't the aggrieved little spouse you think she is. She's deceived you. And she's quite good at it."

Garrett checked his watch and sighed. "I don't have time for this."

"She's cheating on you."

Garrett took a gulp of wine, swallowed and said, "Bullshit."

Penelope shook her head. "Fact. And it's not the first time."

Garrett motioned with his free hand for her to get on with it. "Okay, let's hear your spiel."

"She's been involved with someone for months."

"If that *were* true, why would you just now be telling me?"

"Because she'll go after you for adultery, even though she's guilty of the same thing."

"Chelsea would never cheat, and we both know it. You're pissed at her because you're guilty and don't like how it feels."

"I only feel guilty that she found out. But I'm not lying. She may have started out having sex with the guy because she was angry with you, but now she believes they're," she made quotation marks in the air with her fingers, "'*in love*'. She had every intention of divorcing you. Guess she figured catching you in the act was the way to go. She just never realized she'd catch you with me, the keeper of her *dark* secrets." Penelope snickered.

Garrett flashed back to Chelsea's statement about wanting a divorce, but he recognized a con when he saw one. Penelope was playing him. Best to go along just to see exactly how far she'd try to take it. "All right. I'll bite."

Penelope formed her lips into a pout. "Don't tease me, Garrett. You know how I love when you bite me. And where."

"That's it. I'm out of here." Garrett stood.

Penelope pulled a book from behind her. She turned it over to the back cover and handed it to him. "That's the guy. Her lover. Your competition. He's her most recent dark secret." She barked a laugh.

Garrett looked at the photo of the author then at Penelope. "How far are you going to go with this charade?"

"It's not a charade. And I'm going to tell you just how far Chelsea *did* go."

CHAPTER 86

GARRETT DOWNED THE wine in one gulp, grabbed the bottle and refilled his glass. "You have proof of any of this?"

"I can give you enough details that demonstrate proof."

"I'll give you five minutes. Tops."

"Let's go back to the first time she cheated on you."

Garrett rolled his eyes. "Here we go."

"Chelsea had an affair with a lawyer in her firm. Eric Eisenberg. You remember him?"

"Vaguely. I only saw him once at the one Christmas party I went to, and just long enough to be introduced."

"Chelsea didn't just have a few thrills with Eric, she got pregnant with him. About a year before Kimberlie was conceived."

"I think I would have known if—"

"Garrett, you're an enthusiastic lover and excellent provider, but totally self-absorbed."

"You're not scoring any points, here."

"You don't pay attention to Chelsea—or anyone, for that matter—unless it suits your purpose to. You're so full of yourself, you can't believe she'd look at another man or that another man would pay attention to her. Go ahead and look as mad at me as you like, but we all know it's true."

"If you're trying to piss me off, it's working."

"Chelsea had an abortion."

"You're really going for broke."

"I drove her to the clinic and to my house afterwards, until she felt ready and able to go home, able to look and act as though nothing had happened."

"Again, bullshit."

"The man's wife, Patricia, found out about the affair. She confronted her. Chelsea hadn't told Eric she was pregnant, but Patricia recognized the signs. Told Chelsea if she didn't get an abortion, she'd report the affair to the firm *and* call you. Chelsea agreed, but also got Patricia to sign a non-disclosure agreement stating she'd never tell, in exchange for seventy thousand dollars. I went with Chelsea to make the withdrawal at the bank. The money came out of her America account."

"We don't have any accounts at that bank."

"You mean *you* don't. If you feel like digging that far back, you'll find proof she has an account you don't know about, in her maiden name, if she still has it, that is. We haven't talked about it since that time. But, I can give you the approximate date of the withdrawal, if you want it. The signed agreement should still be in a safety deposit box at that bank, also under her maiden name. Unless she decided enough time lapsed that it was safe to destroy the evidence."

Garrett went to the window with the book in his hand. He stood silently, seething. A minute passed and he said, "What about this Luke Thompson guy?" He couldn't wait to hear whatever nonsense Penelope was about to spew. It was so obvious: she'd seen the book on the nightstand or was with Chelsea when she bought it.

Penelope filled him in on the details she knew about how Chelsea and Luke had met. "Many of the nights these past few months, when Kimberlie was at a sleep-over and you were satisfying your appetites, Chelsea was satisfying hers. With him. According to Chelsea, he's more than equipped to do that, if you follow my meaning."

Garrett kept his back to Penelope. "Where's this affair supposedly taking place?"

"I asked, but she refused to tell me exactly where. Although, for an untraceable Christmas gift, she came up with myriad places like a public bathroom, the Bentley, out in nature, before it turned cold, of course. I have to give her credit. I never imagined she could or would be so inventive. Maybe you didn't know that about her, either. Vanilla through and through. Your words, verbatim. Or maybe it was you who treated her that way. Maybe she found your technique unimaginative, boring, so why make the effort?"

"Believe me, she wanted it. Still does."

Penelope laughed. "Maybe once. But she told me you can't compete with him. Said you overestimate your proficiency. Or, maybe it has something to do with how well endowed he is."

Garrett walked back to his chair but didn't sit. "How long did it take you to come up with this elaborate lie?"

"Poor Garrett. Your ego is just too inflated to imagine any of this is true. But it is."

Garrett smirked and clapped his hands. "I have to hand it to you. This is quite a performance."

"You want proof? Get it yourself." She waved a hand. "Check her phone for calls and text messages. Maybe she deleted them, but maybe she knew you're too stuck on yourself to ever suspect anything like that from her, or that you'd ever check her phone. Especially because you wouldn't want her to check yours."

"You're not going to give up, are you?"

"I don't know how you can confirm the bank information, since that's private, but the withdrawal was made the first week of April 2004. I gave you the name of the lawyer and his wife. Maybe the wife will spill it to you. Since she can be bought, make her an offer as an incentive."

Garrett studied Luke's photo then tossed the book onto the chair. He headed for the door.

Penelope stood. "What are you going to do?"

He turned. "Not your business. Stay away from us."

Garrett closed the door behind him, but not fast enough to block out Penelope's laughter.

CHAPTER 87

T HE HILTON HOTEL room in Waltham would have to suffice. Until Chelsea calmed down and begged him to come home, that is. And that needed to happen soon.

Garrett tossed the wrapped bundle onto the bed. He detested paying for his few new items of clothing to be laundered. What man drives up to such a place in the most expensive Porsche money can buy and doesn't own a washer and dryer or pay a housekeeper?

It was necessary to put a halt to their temporary split before word got out. He'd made Kimberlie swear not to tell anyone. But that was only one plug for a number of possible leaks. Humiliation wasn't his style.

He kicked off his shoes and ordered a steak and baked potato from room service. Called back and added a bottle of their best merlot to the order.

He turned on the TV. Turned it off. Went to the bathroom and splashed cold water on his face. Did a search on Amazon for Luke Thompson. Three books. He checked the first two. Both had few reviews and two and a half stars. Some author he was. He clicked on the third book.

The reviews for *A Dark Walk* were predominantly excellent or exceptional. Chelsea had once commented about something she'd read in the novel, not that he'd paid any real attention to what she'd said. It was something about the pain of being hurt by someone you thought never would do that. Something about how the author must have felt that way to be able to write about it.

He continued to scroll and read the reviews. Then he saw Chelsea's profusely glowing comments about the book. And about Thompson. He clicked on the book cover to look inside. Saw the author had thanked his wife, Brandi, for being his inspiration. Did Thompson mean his wife inspired him to write, or did he mean she inspired him to feel the pain he wrote about?

Whatever.

But now he knew Penelope was lying. Not only would Chelsea not cheat on him, she'd never do it with a married man, and certainly not twice.

The knock on the door startled him.

The tray was placed on the coffee table, as directed. The tip was put into the hand eager to receive it.

The wine was consumed.

The food left untouched.

CHAPTER 88

ARRETT STEPPED OUT of the shower. He wiped the moisture from the mirror, shaved, and dabbed concealer under his eyes to diminish the dark circles. Donned in new slacks, shirt, and jacket, he brewed a pot of coffee and left a message at his practice that he'd either be in late or not at all. That would inconvenience staff, but they'd have to figure it out for themselves. He took a cup of coffee to the sofa and watched the time.

At five till nine, he looked up America Bank & Trust's main number. He knew who he had to get to help him. Bob Adams was one of the vice presidents and a member of City Club; they'd sat at the same table for lunch many times. It was an informal relationship at best, but it was the only way he'd likely be able to confirm Penelope's story.

At five after nine, he keyed in the number. "This is Dr. Garrett Hall. Bob Adams, please." It took only seconds for the connection to be made.

"Garrett, good to hear from you. You finally decided to give us some of your business?"

"Actually, I want to do some business with you, of a personal nature."

"Okay, you've got me curious."

"I'd rather talk in person. How about lunch today at the club?"

"I can do that. But it has to be between one and two."

"I'll see you at one, then."

"What's this about?"

"We'll talk then. I'll go a little early and get a table. Ask at the desk."

Garrett ordered a light breakfast from room service, made another pot of coffee, and used his iPad to look up Luke Thompson on Facebook.

He found an author page on the site. Found that Thompson lived in Waltham. Personal photos had been posted, along with brief blog-type missives about what it was like to be a novelist. From the photos, it was easy to see Thompson was tall, at least taller than the others in the images where he wasn't alone. People probably considered the guy attractive.

He scrolled down the page, stopping at a photo of Thompson in swim trunks. It showed a man who didn't have an ounce of anything loose on his body and defined muscles in all the right places. He'd be powerful in the sack. If he knew what he was doing. What did Chelsea know about good sex? Not much. Not in his experience. Always wanted him to get it over with.

Garrett didn't hear the first round of knocks on the door. The second round, louder and harder than the first, got his attention. He ate the toast and finished the coffee, leaving the omelet and sausages.

His search for additional information about Thompson continued, with him growing more agitated, based on what he learned. He returned to the photo of Luke in trunks. Images of Chelsea and the author began to play in his mind. No way could he or would he believe they were lovers.

Similar images and others, provoked by imagining Luke and Chelsea engaged in some of his own escapades, tortured him until noon.

At five after, Garrett tucked one of the envelopes provided by the hotel into his jacket pocket and closed the door behind him. There was one errand he had to take care of before heading to the club.

CHAPTER 89

H E'D ALMOST FINISHED his second double Scotch over ice by the time Bob Adams waved then wove his way to the table. Garrett rose and extended his hand. "Thanks for meeting with me."

Adams had his hand on the chair across from him. Garrett pulled out the chair to his right. "Sit here, Bob. If you don't mind." He waved for a waiter, who zipped to the table.

Adams shrugged and sat. Both men gave the waiter their drink orders.

"What can I do for you, Garrett?"

"Let's order first."

"You don't look so good. You okay?"

"Just going through a temporary rough patch."

Adams frowned. "Financial?"

"Personal." He asked and let Adams talk about his family. Not that he listened, just nodded and made proper sounds at the right places in the one-sided conversation.

Garrett sat straight and said, "Finally. Our drinks." They gave their food orders to the waiter.

"Okay," Adams said, "we won't be interrupted for a while."

"My wife has an account at your bank under her maiden name. Johnson. Chelsea Johnson."

"I'm not going to like where this is going, am I?"

Garrett pulled the envelope from his jacket pocket and slid it to Adams. "Maybe twenty-five hundred will help you like it better."

"Garrett—"

"I wouldn't ask you to help me with this unless I was desperate."

Adams glanced around then put the envelope into his inside jacket pocket. "What do you need?"

Garrett told him what to look for.

Adams nodded. "I may need a few hours. I'll have to research between a couple of appointments."

"Whatever it takes. Give me your phone. I'll put my number in."

The food arrived. Adams cleaned his plate. Garrett pushed food around on his. They left together, shaking hands in the parking lot.

Adams said, "I'm not sure what news will be good to hear."

"The truth will do."

Garrett returned to his room, and continued to ignore every call or text except the one he wanted, which came almost two hours later.

"What's the word, Bob?"

"Seventy thousand. Just as you said. Cash. The signed form for the IRS is still on file in archived records."

Garrett ran a hand through his hair. "That account still open?"

"Yes."

"Balance?"

"Three thousand and change. If this is bad news, I'm sorry to be the bearer of it. I need to go. My next appointment just arrived."

Garrett got up. He paced. This couldn't be real. This happened to other men, not to him.

He turned and saw the face of Luke Thompson smiling at him from the iPad. Imagined Thompson's hands and mouth on Chelsea, saw the man humping her, saw her mouth and hands on him. Saw and heard her climaxing—for *him*.

The heavy table lamp was in his hand within seconds. He used it to pummel the electronic *pill* too bitter to swallow, smashed it into fragments, shattered the lamp, battered the coffee table, which Garrett flung across the room, puncturing the Sheetrock. The sounds that erupted from him more animal than human.

CHAPTER 90

"THIS KIND of behavior is intolerable." The hotel manager stood in the middle of Garrett's room and surveyed the damages. "Just look at this mess."

"I had an adverse reaction to a new medication. I'm fine now. I'll pay for the damages. No need to show me an estimate, just take care of it. Add the cost to my card."

"You can count on it. You can also start packing."

"You're not serious?"

The manager punched a number on his cell phone. "Tyler, prepare an Authorization for Payment of Damages form for Dr. Hall and get it to me in 202 A-S-A-P." The manager positioned himself, arms crossed, in front of the door. "I don't see any packing going on."

Garrett pulled a plastic trash bag from one of the waste receptacles and began stuffing his clothes, unfolded, inside.

"No suitcase, Dr. Hall?"

"I'm traveling light."

"As long as you travel away from here."

Tyler arrived, form in hand, as Garrett dropped the last of his toiletries into the bag. He signed the form, grabbed the bag and said, "You're damn lucky I'm not reporting you to Better Business Bureau."

"Likewise."

Garrett drove to the nearest five-star hotel. He stood at the front desk, confused as to why the desk clerk initally stared at him then avoided looking at him as he completed the registration process.

Once in the room, he tossed the bag and the battered iPad onto the bed. Caught his reflection in the dresser mirror. His unwashed hair stuck out on one side and was plastered to the other. When had he shaved last? A cut on his cheek, which he hadn't felt, had left a trail of dried blood on his face and shirt collar.

He needed more clothes, and a suitcase, but no way could he shop in the condition he was in.

The shower was hot but not soothing. He shaved around the cut. Did his best to wash the blood from his shirt. And thought about what his next step needed to be.

He ordered a club sandwich and a pot of coffee from room service. While he waited, he made a list.

CHAPTER 91

I T HAD BEEN easy for Garrett to find a phone listing for Eric Eisenberg's residence, and he was thankful they still used a landline. The last thing he'd wanted to do was show up at their house, but he would have, if that's what it had taken.

It had been harder to make the call the next morning, when he was sure Eric was at work, or should be, and it felt safer to use the hotel phone so caller ID wouldn't give him away and the call ignored. It wasn't until the phone started to ring that he realized he didn't know whether or not Patricia Eisenberg had a job. Whatever it took to find her, he'd do it.

She answered on the fourth ring then made it clear she didn't want to talk to him. A guarantee of five thousand dollars, cash, to meet with him eased her hesitation. She arrived at the diner a half hour later, pinched-faced, eager to get the money and leave, but not until Garrett swore he'd never reveal that she had given him the details she remembered about the affair.

"What else?" he asked.

"Wasn't that enough?"

"If you withhold anything—and, Patricia, I believe that's what you're doing—I'll pull half the cash out of the envelope getting warm in my pocket."

"Fine. It's your funeral. Your *wife* got pregnant. I forced her to get an abortion. No way in hell was I going to let Eric stay involved with her because of his bastard child."

"He knew?"

"I made certain she didn't tell him. I wanted *it* and her to go away. Permanently."

Garrett gripped his coffee mug then swiped it and the dishes and condiments off the table. All heads turned at the clatter and the slew of obscenities erupting from him.

Patricia, pale-faced, escaped from the booth. "I'm leaving. Before you get us both arrested."

The diner manager rushed over. "You need to leave, sir." He handed Garrett the bill. "Put your money on the table and get out."

Garrett pulled a twenty from his money clip and slung it to the floor. He hurried after Patricia, whose hands were already on the door handle. She rushed outside. He caught up to her and grabbed her by the arm.

"Let go of me."

He did. "I'm sorry I lost it in there. You have no idea what I'm feeling." He pulled the envelope from his inside jacket pocket and handed it to her.

She tucked the envelope into her purse. "When you can think straight again, you'll realize how wrong you are."

In one week, he'd been kicked out of his house, a Hilton, and a diner.

Nobody else was going to oust him from where he wanted to be.

CHAPTER 92

H E SPED BACK to the hotel, repeatedly slamming on the brakes when traffic lights turned yellow or red. As Garrett waited for the lights to turn green, he beat on the steering wheel and cursed, ignoring the disapproving and sometimes frightened expressions from onlookers in other cars and on the sidewalks. Ignored those who aimed their phones at him.

Inside the hotel lobby, he grew impatient waiting for the elevator, pounded the button and kicked the doors. "What the fuck is the hold-up?"

The doors opened. An elderly couple with their two young grand-children started to exit. "Take your fucking time," he said. "You're not in a hurry, so why should I be."

He disregarded their shock and admonitions. Hit the button for his floor and the Close button several times, desperate to get to his room and shut everyone out.

His phone rang as he slid his key into the lock. He dug the phone from his pocket, saw who it was and kicked the door. "What now, Penelope?"

"We need to meet again."

"I can't. My schedule's too tight."

"I'm tighter. After all, it's been days."

Garrett scrubbed his hand through his hair. "Pen, please."

"You left before I could tell you more about Luke Thompson."

His shoulders stiffened. "Give me a minute." He let himself into the room and went to the liquor cabinet, removing four small bottles of Scotch. He placed three bottles on the nightstand, opened the fourth then sat with his back against the headboard. "I'm listening. What else do you know?"

"It's not like Chelsea told me much, Garrett, nor did she tell me right away. And I practically had to drag from her the little I got. As for where they did the nasty, I told you what she told me. Why don't you forget her, at least for a while. Let me help you forget."

"I'm not hearing any new information."

"I wanted—needed—to hear your voice."

"I'm hanging up."

"Will I see you soon?"

"Maybe."

"Garrett, don't be like that. Not with me. Not after all these years."

"That's the best I can do right now. I have a lot to take care of."

He dropped the phone next to him on the bed. He had proof of the earlier affair. But he wanted irrefutable proof about what was going on with Thompson. Penelope had been right about Eisenberg. She had to be right about Thompson, as well. No matter how much he didn't want her to be.

Maybe he should see Pen, or at least one of the other women available; though, Pen would be more willing to do what was needed to ease his anger. He hadn't gone this long without sex since he was a teenager. But he knew it was a useless thought as soon as he had it. There hadn't been any action down there since Chelsea had knocked on the door of the Presidential Suite, no matter how much effort he'd expended in the shower. Even the porn movie he'd paid for on TV was shut off after a few frustrating minutes.

He could follow Chelsea, but there was no telling when she'd meet with Thompson. He might follow her for a week and come up dry. He didn't have the luxury of that kind of time. Nor did he have the patience to hire a private detective. Plus, there was the humiliation factor. The fewer people who knew, the better.

The most logical thing to do was what Penelope had recommended: Access Chelsea's phone. He'd find a way. Tomorrow morning. Once he was sure Kimberlie was at school.

CHAPTER 93

T HE LACY FRENCH bra and matching thong were the color of a ripe peach. Chelsea studied her reflection in the full-length mirror. Gone were the days of recoiling at the sight of her fuller figure because of Garrett's preferences. Luke told her repeatedly that he loved every inch of her and demonstrated it in the best ways. And the most erotic.

His text message had said to meet at the motel in thirty minutes. He'd sent another text soon after: *I'm bringing chocolates.* She shivered at the memory of the time he'd done that before, as one of his Christmas gifts. Recalled where he'd chosen to place the chocolates. What he'd done as the candies began to melt on the contours of her body and in the delicate lip-like folds between her thighs. He'd consumed half the box of candy in this way before letting her help him fulfill his own pleasure.

She tried on several outfits, not that they'd stay on long, laughed at that thought then sighed. Winter was not a season that lent itself to dressing sexy the way spring and summer did. No longer was she content to hide under baggy pants and sweaters. Luke had cured her of that, and of so many other things.

Garrett parked in the circular drive. He looked around at *his* property then got out. He inserted his key into the front door lock. It didn't work. Chelsea had told the truth about changing the locks. He punched the doorbell repeatedly and waited. More than a minute went by before Chelsea came to the door with her purse slung over her shoulder.

"As you can see, Garrett, I'm on my way out. And, I'm certain it didn't slip your mind regarding what I said about coming here."

"Did you also use my things from the coat closet for your bonfire?"

"Actually, I forgot about those items."

"Then would you mind letting me get my heavy winter coat and leather jacket?"

"Now's not a good time. I've got to get to an appointment."

"It'll only take a minute."

"I said not now."

He pushed passed her. "And let you come home and burn them too? No way." He started for the stairs.

"Just a damn minute. I don't want you in my house, much less upstairs."

"Your house? Fuck that. What don't you want me to see?"

"You're being ridiculous."

"I need my damn coat and jacket. It's bad enough I have to replace my entire wardrobe."

"Fine. But I'll get them. You stay right where you are."

"Did you torch my shoes?"

Chelsea sighed. "Not yet."

"Then bring me a couple pairs of good ones. Did our daughter see my empty closet? Did you tell her what you did?"

"I don't have time for this, Garrett." Chelsea tossed her purse onto the small table in the foyer and sprinted up the stairs.

As soon as she was out of sight, he grabbed her phone from her purse, read Luke's message to meet him at their *usual* place and when. No wonder she was in a hurry to get rid of him.

He waited until he heard Chelsea open the door to the cedar closet in the hall. It wouldn't take her long to get the items and return. He took screen shots of several of her messages and sent them to his cell phone. But he couldn't resist scrolling through some of the older messages. They went on for months, all the way back to September.

He stopped on what he imagined was supposed to be a poem Thompson had written to her, scowling as he read.

The shoes Chelsea threw at him hit him on the back.

"What the hell are you doing with my phone?"

CHAPTER 94

"CONFIRMING THAT my so-said aggrieved wife is a lying whore." Garrett dodged the second pair of shoes Chelsea flung with force at him.

His coat and jacket fell to the floor in a heap. "Give me my phone." Chelsea flew at him, grabbing for the phone he held out of reach.

Garrett shoved her back, into the foyer table. "After busting my ass to pay for the lifestyle you had to have, this is how you pay me back. You fuck this Thompson guy?"

"I didn't get involved with Luke to pay you back. I'd have to sleep with half the men in this town to do that."

"You actually fall for this crap?" He held the phone high and read from it. "Your magenta lips, honeyed, succulent, call to me. From between your alabaster thighs, they beckon me. I answer the call and from your center, you give forth your nectar. Your sweet nectar feeds my—"

"Stop! Just stop. You're making something offered in love sound vulgar."

"You're not even going to pretend to feel ashamed?"

"Why should I? You don't."

"Are you at least using birth control this time? Or is it your intention to get pregnant with this Thompson prick?"

Chelsea's face paled. She backed up a few feet.

"Or, maybe you want to replace Eisenberg's bastard that you aborted."

"Oh God."

"At least now you're looking as guilty as you are."

"There's only one person who—"

"Leave Penelope out of this. This is between you and me. And Thompson, when I get my hands on him."

"Stay away from him."

"Don't touch your precious Luke?" He threw her phone to the floor. "You got knocked up by another man. A married man. What the hell, Chelsea? You have any idea what knowing that does to me?"

"After what you've done, why should I care? And, how do I know you don't have a few illegitimate children you're supporting?"

"I don't."

"That you know about, you mean. Maybe your women were forced into abortions, as well."

Garrett shook his head. "Never happened."

"You can't be certain."

He fixed his gaze on her. "One hundred and ten percent."

CHAPTER 95

GARRETT SMIRKED THEN threw his head back and laughed. "After Kimmie was conceived, I fixed it so I shot blanks."

Chelsea lowered herself onto the staircase. "You kept that from me? You didn't discuss such an important decision with me? You bastard. You knew I wanted another child. You let me believe it was my fault that I never got pregnant again. That I was being punished because I'd …" She dropped her face into her hands. "All this time."

"Since we're revealing secrets, I have another one for you. You're going to love this one. Remember how you wanted a natural delivery?"

Chelsea looked up. "Where are you going with this?"

"The epidural I insisted you have was for another purpose. So was the screen put up after the birth. I had the delivery doc do a tubal ligation on you. Paid him ten grand, off the books."

Chelsea gripped the railing. "You're lying."

"I wanted to make damn sure I never had to see you blow up into a whale again. I didn't realize you were going to stay one."

"You can't have done such a thing. You're only saying that to punish me."

"And, yet, you never got pregnant again. And you won't. Not now, not ever. Or did you even worry about it with Thompson? If I hadn't done what I did, how were you going to explain a mixed-race kid to me, and to Kimberlie? If your *lover* uses rubbers, he's wasting his money. Money he doesn't have to spare, from what I can tell."

Chelsea pulled herself to her feet. "You're even more despicable than I imagined."

"What the hell were you thinking to do your fucking around in public places?"

"I get it. Your whipped-cream queen really paid me back for breaking up your party. I didn't know you were into such things, not that I would have wanted to. But I was lucky to get it missionary. Lucky if you lasted five minutes. Whereas Luke—"

"Don't even dare—"

"What? You don't want to know that a man can satisfy me? And that you don't?"

"Bullshit. You had one hell of an orgasm the last time we made love."

"If that's what you call making love, you can keep it. I've learned the difference. And the only reason I had an orgasm during your, what can only be described as a rabbit-fuck, was because I imagined you were Luke. Only he doesn't grunt like a pig or paw at me like an amateur."

"You're going too far."

"Let me tell you exactly how far I plan to go."

CHAPTER 96

"ONCE LUKE and I are both divorced," Chelsea said, "we're getting married. We're both finally going to be happy. You, however, will keep on screwing around and die alone."

Garrett glared at her a moment then barked a laugh. "You are a simpleton. You think he's going to leave his wife for you? You're nothing but a piece of ass to him. Both of you have had your fun going exotic. The novelty will wear off soon enough for him, if it hasn't already. Face it, sweetheart, you're not a woman who can hold a man's interest very long. Then you'll realize what you've lost. And believe me, Chelsea. You've lost me."

"I never really had you, though. Did I? I've been unhappy for longer than I care to remember. You could have changed that. I was willing, for such a long time. You did everything you could to crush that dream. So, Garrett, congratulations. You did it. But, I'm going to be happy, cherished, and loved. Finally."

"If you think I'm going to allow that man into my daughter's life, you're fucking crazy."

"Luke is a wonderful man. He's decent and kind. I'm more concerned about the sleazy women, and their S&M preferences, you'll subject Kimmie to. Now, it's time for you to get out of my house and out of my life."

"It's still my house. You're still my wife."

"Only on paper. Now go. I'm already late for my appointment."

"Your appointment to get fucked, you mean. I saw the text, remember?" He grabbed her arm and turned her around. "You're not going anywhere."

"Let go of me." She escaped his grip. "Your touch repulses me."

"I'm going to prove you're lying to yourself about that. I'm going to prove you still want me." He pulled Chelsea to him. He grabbed her breast and squeezed hard, grabbed her between her legs and squeezed harder.

"You're hurting me."

"Pain and pleasure, sweetheart. Maybe that's what you've needed all along." He covered her mouth with his. His scream echoed in the foyer when she bit his lower lip. He shoved her away. Wiped his lip. Saw the blood on his hand.

His fist made hard contact with her face, sending her into the foyer table then onto the floor.

CHAPTER 97

THE EMPIRE GRANDFATHER clock in the foyer chimed. Garrett howled in rage, hit the clock with his shoulder like a linebacker, sending the clock over, destroying the twenty thousand-dollar timepiece. Glass, internal mechanisms, and splintered wood scattered across the marble floor.

He glanced at Chelsea, sprawled on the floor, her hand holding the cheek and bloodied lip already starting to swell. Saw in her eyes something he'd never seen before: terror.

His gaze went to the family photos on the wall, at his daughter smiling at him from each of them. Shame and shock surged through him. Thank God Kimberlie wasn't home, but what would she think of him when she learned what he'd done? He held his head in his hands and ran moaning from the house. His tires screeched his departure.

He ran a red light, unaware of what he'd done until he heard rubber against pavement and horns blaring, and then eased his foot off the accelerator.

It hadn't been that long ago that he'd chastised Kimberlie for fighting with the boy at school. Had lectured her about how unacceptable it was for boys to hit girls. He should have pleaded with Chelsea not to tell Kimberlie what had happened. What would she tell their daughter about that, and about the clock his daughter loved?

Worse, he felt only partial regret for striking Chelsea. She'd deserved it, if anyone did. The things she'd said. And there was the months—make that years—of her deceit.

She hadn't behaved at all as he'd expected. He was sure her shame would be so great that when he insisted she let him move back in, she'd let him. He hadn't gotten that far.

Still, after all he'd done for her, all he'd given her, she should have crawled on hands and knees to him, pleading for forgiveness. He would have insisted she behave the way he expected her to. He would have been able to do whatever he wanted, without further reproach, because she'd never want Kimberlie to learn what her mother had done.

But it hadn't gone that way.

CHAPTER 98

THERE WAS ONE person who might have sway over Chelsea. Garrett dialed the number he didn't want to but had to. "Richard, I'm in trouble."

"You sound terrible. What's happened?"

"Chelsea's been cheating on me."

"I don't believe that. She wouldn't. Someone's lying to you."

"Saw the evidence with my own eyes. In front of her, where she couldn't deny it. Rubbed it in my face, in fact."

"I'm so sorry, brother. And shocked. I know you're in pain, but maybe you can understand what it's been like for her."

"I don't need to hear that now. Especially not from you."

"The truth can hurt, but you need to hear it, not just blow it off as you usually do."

"Knew it was a mistake to call you."

"Wait. What are you going to do?"

"I've already done it."

"Why do I get a bad feeling about that?"

"Because you're right. I struck her. I didn't mean to do it, but she went too far."

"God, Garrett. Is she okay? Did you hurt her?"

"If she puts ice on her lip and face, the swelling will go down."

"I can't believe you did that, no matter what she said. Or did. She's your wife and the mother of your child. What's wrong with you? We weren't raised to hit women. Mom and Dad are going to flip. And what about Kimberlie?"

Garrett pulled into a parking lot and turned off his car. He rested his head against the steering wheel. "I don't need you to tell me that.

But before you're too quick to side with Chelsea, let me tell you what all I learned about the slut I've been married to."

Richard listened in silence for the nearly quarter hour Garrett spoke. "I'm sorry for both of you. But you need to own your part in this. You neglected her. You made her feel unloved and less of a woman. You cheated on her and did it first, and refused to stop. I'm not saying what Chelsea did was right. It wasn't. But I understand how she might have felt pushed into it."

"Leave it to you to see it that way. Right now, I'm more concerned—make that terrified—about what she'll tell Kimmie."

"I'll call Chelsea and see what I can do to smooth things out. In the meantime, stay away from her. You don't want Kimberlie to see her father hauled to jail for assaulting her mother."

"It was unintentional."

"Garrett, it's time you get a grip on reality. You don't live in a world of your own where people do your bidding and let you get away with doing whatever you want to do, no matter who you hurt."

"Is the lecture over, or are you building a head of steam for more?"

"None of us like to be told when we're wrong. You abhor it more than most. Go back to your hotel and calm down. I'll call Chelsea as soon as we hang up."

"Let me know what she says."

"If it's appropriate, I will."

Garrett slammed the steering wheel with his fist. "I'm your brother. Where's your damn loyalty?"

"As usual, I'll see what I can do to straighten up the mess you've made, before you make it worse."

"It's not easy having a saint for a brother."

"I wouldn't know."

"You can go f—" Garrett completed his sentence to dead air.

CHAPTER 99

WHERE WAS SHE? The first flicker of anxiety shot through Luke's body. He returned to the window of the motel room and peered once again through the split in the drapes. Hoping to see Chelsea getting out of her car. Waving at him. Speeding her pace to reach him.

Something wasn't right. She'd never before agreed to meet then not shown up or called.

She'd never so much as called or sent a text message to say she was running late. Always arrived minutes earlier than she said she would.

He called again—no answer.

Texted her again—no reply.

It was almost noon. Chelsea's daughter should be at school, and Garrett no longer lived there. Wasn't even supposed to go there.

Fear welled inside him. He called again, sent another text. No answer.

Luke left the box of chocolates on the bed, closed the door behind him, got into his car, cranked the engine and sat in the chilly interior. He knew what he wanted to do, needed to do, as well as the problems it could cause. He cursed and returned to the room.

He paced. Tried to reach her again. Nothing.

Back to the window. No sign of her. How long was he expected to wait?

He had to act, and it had to be sooner rather than later.

CHAPTER 100

THE ACTION LUKE'S mind prompted him to take was an insane thing to do. But he had to find out what was going on. Confusion and anxiety prodded him. He needed advice.

"James, can you talk?"

"I got a few minutes. What's up?"

"Something's happened to Chelsea."

"The woman who's got your nuts in a knot?"

"Don't talk about her that way. It was a mistake to call you."

"Sorry, dude. What's the problem?"

Luke explained. "She's never done anything like this. I know something's wrong. Something serious. I have to find out if she's okay."

"If she's not answering, I don't know how you can find out. Wait a damn minute. No way. Don't be a stupid fuck."

"It's the only way."

"Man, her husband could be there."

"She kicked him out."

"That's what she told you."

"She wouldn't lie to me."

"All right. She doesn't lie to you. But he could be there getting some of his shit."

"She burned it."

"This is worse than I thought. Get away from her. She's a crazy woman."

"You don't know her like I do."

"That's what you said about Brandi."

"Damn it, James."

"All right. I don't know her. But I know how fucked up this situation sounds. Stay away."

"I can't. She may need me."

"Look, I'm sure it's nothing. Her old man probably went there to get something he needs—papers, checkbook. Who the hell knows. Stay where you are. She'll show up with an apology. Probably broke a nail or something."

"You're right."

"Now you're making sense."

"If he's there, I have to go and make sure she's safe."

"Shit, dude. You're not hearing me. You're not thinking straight. Stay away from—"

Luke ended the call. The motel room door slammed behind him as he raced to his car.

CHAPTER 101

L UKE RANG THE doorbell, waited, put his hands over his eyes and peered through the glass panel on the side of the door. Relief flooded him when he saw Chelsea approach.

He gasped when she opened the door. "Your face! I knew something happened. Were you in an accident? Why didn't you call me?"

Chelsea glanced toward the street and ran a trembling hand over her hair. "You shouldn't have come here, Luke."

"I had to. Now that I see you, I know it was the right thing to do."

"You need to go. Now."

"You *want* me to leave?"

"I want you to be safe."

"Talk to me, Chelsea. I'm not going anywhere until you do."

She glanced toward the street again. "You'd better come inside."

Luke followed her, stepping over the broken bits of clock. "What the hell? You need to tell me exactly what happened here."

"I will. Then there's something else I need to tell you. Something from my past."

"The past is just that, love. We all have one."

She shook her head. "If we're going to be together, you need to know everything."

"You're scaring me."

Chelsea looked into Luke's eyes. "I just hope I don't scare you away."

Luke walked to the French doors and peered out at the tent covering the pool. "The bastard actually hit you." He turned. "Where is he? I'm going to make sure he knows he'd better stay clear of you. I swear to you, Chelsea, as long as I'm alive, no one will ever hurt you again."

"You need to stay away from him. I don't know what he'd do to you. Let me deal with this. Legally. We'll both lose if you confront him."

"Only a coward hits a woman. I want to see how he does with a man who isn't afraid of him."

Chelsea took his hands in hers. "For my sake, don't. I love you for wanting to protect me, but I don't want this situation to escalate into anything worse."

"That's why I want to talk to him, so it doesn't."

"I can promise you it won't happen again. I'm really not worried. Garrett knows if I talk, Kimberlie won't want to have anything to do with him. He knows what's at risk."

"He should have thought about that before attacking you."

"This is the last thing he'd want to go public. What concerns me more is how you feel about what I told you. About what I did."

"As I said, nothing from your past has anything to do with us now. I cheated on my first wife, after she cheated on me. And although I'm still married, it won't be for long."

"And my inability to give you a child?"

"If you want a child, we'll adopt. Otherwise, you'll just have to let me spoil you."

"You already do."

He smiled at her. "You came into my life before I was able to change my situation. Hurt makes us do crazy things. Things we ordinarily wouldn't even think about doing. As for the abortion matter, I'm sorry you had to go through that. I know it wasn't easy for you. As for Garrett, what he did is unforgivable."

"You're a good man." Luke held his arms open. Chelsea folded herself into them. "I don't deserve you."

"You deserve every bit of love I can give you and more. You were dealt a bad hand, love. You believed your husband would honor his vows. He not only didn't honor them, he trounced on them. And on you. He deserves worse than what you're going to do to him."

"I'm terrified he'll come after you."

"Don't concern yourself about that. I'm not. And if it does come to that, I can take care of myself. I'm sure you've noticed that I'm not a small man."

Chelsea looked up at him and blushed. "I noticed."

"Woman, if you weren't injured, I'd make your entire body blush with pleasure."

Chelsea's attempt to smile failed. "I'll hold you to that." She rested her head against Luke's chest and sighed. "Garrett's brother called me. He made every attempt to get me to take Garrett back. To forgive him. Used every angle, including what's supposedly best for Kimberlie."

"What did you tell him?"

"About Kimberlie, I told him I'd lie to her this time, but never again. I'll tell her I tripped and fell into the clock. About Garrett, that it's over. That I put up with Garrett's neglect and infidelity longer than anyone should have expected me to. Even put myself through a good deal of self-abuse. I'm done. God, what he's done to me. I haven't been able to trust him for years. I can't live with a man I can't trust. I can't live with a man who hits me, even if I tell myself he won't do it again."

"We'll do what we need to, to make sure he's out of your life as much as possible. Your safety is paramount."

"Promise me that you won't confront him."

"It's not easy, but I promise. However, if he comes after me—"

"You'll have every right to protect yourself. I just pray it never comes to that. You warned me that this wasn't going to be easy."

Luke hugged her to him. What she didn't realize fully as yet—what he didn't want to tell her while she was this fragile—was that he was fairly certain this was just the beginning.

One thing he was sure of was that this wasn't the first time Garrett Hall had struck her. He hadn't believed the kitchen cabinet story, and he was terrified Garrett would hit her again. Or worse.

It was almost time for Kimberlie to come home. Chelsea started a cup of chamomile tea brewing then went upstairs, splashed cold water on her face, and redid her makeup.

Back in the kitchen, she sipped the tea and waited, grateful Luke had righted the damaged clock. It would either have to be repaired, if that was possible, or gotten rid of, but on another day. There was only so much a person should have to contend with at one time.

At three forty-five, she heard the key in the front door.

"Mom, I'm home."

Chelsea called out from the kitchen, "I hope your day went better than mine."

"*What* happened to the clock?"

"That's sort of a funny story." She listened to Kimberlie's footsteps come up the hall, toward the kitchen. She blew out a breath and pasted a smile on her face.

"Mom! What happened to your face?"

"I'm such a klutz. Get a snack and I'll tell you about it."

CHAPTER 102

THE CLOCK ON the nightstand next to Garrett's bed read 1:13 a.m. Even with the amount of whiskey consumed, he couldn't sleep. Why not take a drive? It was a free country. He could drive through any damn neighborhood he damn well wanted to, at any damn time, day or night. He kicked the twisted bed covers off.

Half-empty bottle of Scotch in hand, he tramped through the inch-deep snow to his car, laughing in his inebriated state at the fog created by each breath.

It took three tries to put the correct address into his GPS. The engine in the Porsche grumbled to life. He put the car in Reverse and pressed down on the accelerator, scraping the car parked next to his, and then drove onto the vacant road. Snowplows had cleared the main streets, leaving the side streets for later or for the sun to melt.

The GPS guided him toward his destination, re-calibrated directions when he made a wrong turn. Once in Luke Thompson's neighborhood, he scoffed at the cookie-cutter houses. No imagination or frills were needed for people who couldn't afford better. Just give them a box with walls and a roof.

Despite the GPS's accuracy, he slowed, checking addresses on mailboxes and house fronts, until he found Luke Thompson's. He stopped the car and strained to focus. Two cars in the driveway, both years old. Chelsea was fooling herself if she thought this Thompson guy could afford her.

Garrett brought the bottle of Scotch to his lips and drank. "My wife's ass don't come cheap, buddy," he shouted inside his car. "And it's not the best ass out there." He laughed. "Trust me. I know. I've tested more ass than you've ever dreamed of."

Garrett took another hit from the bottle, capped it and dropped it onto the passenger seat. He reached under his seat. The metal of the Walther was warm from the car heater. He turned sideways and aimed the pistol at Luke's front door. It wouldn't take much. Just roll down the car window. Honk the horn until the prick came out. Then *pow*. Maybe empty the clip into the bastard. Put an end to it. Right here. Right now.

The window slid down silently. He took aim. It would be so easy. The perfect sitting-duck scenario. Who'd find him guilty? All he was trying to do was save his marriage.

So what if he played around. It was different for men. Everyone knew that. Then he remembered Frederick Starks. Remembered the humiliation of the public trial and media frenzy. Remembered the scars on his friend's body. Scars from knife wounds inflicted by inmates.

His words slurred as he spoke aloud. "You're lucky, Thompson. This time. But you *stay the hell away from my wife!* I've got scalpels. Turn you into a damn eunuch. She won't want you then."

Garrett tossed the gun onto the seat, rolled the window up, and drove back to the hotel, taking out a few mailboxes along the way.

He woke with the sun blazing cruelly in his eyes and his face pressed to the car window, drool dripping from his open mouth. He staggered from his car, through the hotel lobby then to his room, not quite making it all the way into the bathroom when his stomach rejected its contents.

CHAPTER 103

H E WAS TWO hours late for work. It couldn't be helped. After shutting off the alarm clock next to his bed—twice—it had taken that long for Garrett to shower, shave, and force toast and coffee down. And keep it down.

He scowled at hospital staff who stared then looked away. Heard their comments and snickers after he passed them. To hell with them all.

Folders and phone messages crowded his desk. Why didn't everyone just leave him the hell alone.

He opened his brief bag, twisted the cap off the bottle and drank. Fortification was needed to put up with the crap he had to tolerate. He put the bottle away and sifted through the calls, separating them into important and not-as-important piles.

His red-rimmed eyes looked up at the sound of a timid knock on his open door. He motioned for the intern to enter. Tried to remember the guy's name and couldn't. Tried to focus on the name on the badge and gave up.

"Dr. Hall, is this a good time?"

"Why wouldn't it be?"

"I'm sorry, sir, but are you okay?"

"Why wouldn't I be?"

"It's just that you don't look well."

"I'm fine. Unless you have another purpose for interrupting me, I suggest you tend to your business."

"Yes, sir. It's just that—"

"You see this stack on my desk? All these phone messages? Some of us have work to do. If you don't have any, I can find some for you. I'm sure there are any number of bedpans that need attention."

The intern backed out then turned to hurry away. Garrett pulled the bottle from his bag. It was going to be a long day, and another disappointing night. Might as well do whatever it took to get through both.

CHAPTER 104

CHELSEA'S STOMACH TWISTED at the sight of the name on caller ID. Garrett was the last person she wanted to talk to. Might as well get it over with. "What do you want?"

"You're such a clever, lying bitch."

"You sound drunk."

"Not drunk enough."

"I'm hanging up."

"Don't you dare. Who the hell do you think you are to cheat on me? On me! The man who's given you everything."

"I'm lucky you didn't give me a disease."

"Right back at you, babe."

"We have nothing to discuss, especially when you're drinking."

"You said some pretty shitty things to me. For your information, I'm a terrific lover."

"I've already said all I'm going to say about that. But I'm sure you could get many of your women to agree with your assessment."

Garrett laughed. "Like they say, babe, practice makes perfect."

"You're disgusting."

"Don't forget generous. I've decided to take you back."

"That's no longer your decision."

"We're a family, damn it. Think of Kimberlie."

"I am thinking of her. I want her to know she has a right to expect her husband to love her and cherish her. To be faithful to her. And, not to strike her. For any reason. So far, her example is an absentee father who screws anyone who'll let him."

"Not anyone. I do have my standards."

"Which I'm aware of, since I didn't meet them. I don't know why you even married me."

"The practice I applied to preferred it."

"That's clarifying."

"You shouldn't have gotten fat."

"You shouldn't have cheated on me while I was pregnant. Don't try to deny it."

"I won't. Had to do it. Couldn't get it up for you while you looked like a cow. Also couldn't be expected to wait for you to get thin again. I'm still waiting."

Chelsea gripped the phone. "I was carrying our child."

"I'm moving back in. You hear me? You're ruining my life, bitch."

"It's not me doing that, Garrett. It's not even three thirty in the afternoon. Where are you? Are you drunk at work?"

"Don't worry about me. I'm a star, remember? They love me. Everyone loves me. Except you."

"You destroyed my love. It's been dead a long time. Time to bury it."

"We'll see who gets buried. If you think I'm going to let that bastard—"

"That's enough, Garrett. I have had enough of you. Let our lawyers do the talking from now on."

Chelsea cut the phone call off. She fought the tears threatening to spill. And wondered how she was going to make it through the chaos growing worse by the day.

CHAPTER 105

TWO DAYS LATER, Garrett strolled into his office at the hospital and stopped a few feet from his desk. Someone had cleared its surface of all folders. No pile of messages waited for his attention. No stack of charts required his expertise.

He sat in his chair, turned the desk phone toward him, fully intending to find out who'd been in his office, and ream them. Propped against the phone was an envelope, with his name typed on the front. He opened it and began to read the letter printed on hospital stationary and signed by the administrator.

He was under investigation. According to the letter, as a respected interventional radiologist, he wasn't being held personally responsible for the patient's infection following the uterine fibroid embolization, nor for the subsequent complications. But the patient's husband had complained. So they'd been compelled to pursue the matter. Alcohol had been smelled on his breath by those who'd assisted with the procedure. Further reports about the recent change in his appearance and demeanor indicated there was a problem he needed to address.

Suspended. Without pay. Two months. Two months to get treatment or do whatever was required. Two months until a board review. Or face termination without severance.

He slammed the letter down on his desk. Who the hell did they think they were to do this to him?

His hands trembled as he opened his brief bag, fumbled as he attempted to break the seal on the bottle of Scotch. He cursed when he spilled some of the amber liquid on his shirt. Coughed when it didn't go down as smoothly as he needed it to.

To hell with them. To hell with everybody.

CHAPTER 106

GARRETT DROPPED THE bottle of Scotch into his bag and shoved the letter inside his jacket pocket. Staff ducked around corners or kept their heads down as he walked to the elevator, which seemed in no hurry to reach him and facilitate his escape. He watched Nurse Adams hurry into a room to avoid him.

He took the stairs. Tripped. Cursed when the bottle broke and his bag and the stairwell reeked of whiskey.

He raged the entire sixteen minutes it took to drive to the hotel. Once parked, he reached under his seat for the Walther. Started to put it into his bag and realized he couldn't. He tossed the bag onto the rear seat and tucked the gun into his back waistband, fixed his jacket over it and got out.

Once in his suite, he ordered a steak, salad, and a bottle of Scotch. While he waited for his order to be delivered, he stripped and showered. Tipped the waiter, ignored the food, opened the bottle and began to drink.

Everyone around him was losing their minds. If hospital staff knew what he was going through, maybe they'd be more understanding. No way would he tell them, though. They'd already lost respect for him. Otherwise, they wouldn't have snitched about the drinking.

It wasn't as though he'd been drunk during the procedure. One drink to clear the cobwebs was all he'd had. If they wanted to see drunk, he could show them drunk. He brought the bottle to his lips and swigged the liquid, ignoring the burn in his throat.

They'd probably blame him for Chelsea's infidelity. They knew his reputation with the ladies. Hell, a number of them were on his staff. They'd been willing enough to be catered to, to have his money spent on them. He'd have been smarter to find a couple of high-class professionals, since he paid anyway. One way or another, he paid for his entertainment. And theirs.

Damn Chelsea. She'd gotten away with cheating by taking advantage of his absences. If Penelope hadn't told him, how long would it have been before he'd learned the truth? When the damn bastard moved in with his wife and daughter?

He staggered to the window and stared out, without looking at anything in particular. His family would side with Chelsea. At least, Richard and Chloe would. Who was he kidding? His mother would be furious with him. His father, more disappointed than he could stand. What about Kimberlie? Maybe she'd be better off without him. Maybe they all would.

He took a long pull on the bottle. Maybe they deserved to find out what it would be like to have to go it alone, without his money coming in. That's all they considered him good for.

Garrett got the gun from under his pillow and sat on the sofa. It would serve them right. They deserved it, especially Chelsea. Tears streamed down his face. "Be a man, damn it."

He went to the dresser. Studied his face in the mirror—the dark bags under his eyes, the sunken cheeks, the mottled complexion. "Look what you've done to me, bitch!"

Chelsea had said she'd had enough of him. Well, he'd had enough of everyone and everything. Every one of them was stripping him bare of anything that mattered to him.

Garrett raised the gun, placed it against his temple. "Your hand's shaking so much, you might miss, asshole."

He positioned the gun in his mouth and stared into his reflected eyes.

It would be over quick.

He held his breath and pulled the trigger. Heard the *click*. Nothing had happened beyond his bladder letting go.

He'd forgotten to chamber a round.

He lowered the gun. Started to do what was needed and stopped.

Why should I give the bitch the satisfaction? Or her damn boyfriend?

Maybe you don't want a fight, Chelsea Hall, but you're going to get one.

Garrett put the gun on the table and ate the steak, now congealed in its juices.

CHAPTER 107

GARRETT SQUEEZED HIS eyes closed and reached for his buzzing cell phone. "Who the hell's calling me this early?"

The caller cleared his throat. "It's Aaron Logan, Garrett. And it's nearly eleven in the morning. Hardly early."

Garrett covered his eyes with his free arm. "Dr. Logan. Sorry. I thought … Never mind. How's your wife doing?"

"She's doing somewhat better. Thank you for inquiring. I take it you haven't had breakfast. Meet me at Fred's Diner at noon. Sharp. I'm fairly certain you have no other plans."

"I don't know if I can make it."

"You'll make it. If you ever want to resume your position at the hospital, that is. Get up and into a cold shower. I'll see you at twelve. Garrett?"

"Yes?"

"Don't disappoint me."

"I'll be there."

He started the small pot of coffee brewing then stumbled to the bathroom, surprised to find his pants and underwear soaking in the lavatory. He didn't recall doing that. He threw the sopping garments onto the floor and opened the sink drain. Showered, shaved, gulped the coffee, got dressed. Found a place to hide the gun so housekeeping wouldn't find it.

Squinting his eyes against the sunlight, he made it to his car, wondering how damages to various places on the right side had happened. He opened the door, reeled back at the odor, and slammed it shut. There was no way he could drive to his meeting. Twenty minutes to twelve.

He looked up a car service, told them there was a hundred dollar tip in it, if they got him to Fred's Diner by noon or a few minutes before.

He made it there five minutes after. His predecessor, dressed for the office, complete with one of his innumerable, ridiculous bow ties, eyed him from a booth.

"Sorry, Dr. Logan. Car trouble."

"I saw you didn't drive here. I confess I believed the reason was that you were incapable."

"As I said, car trouble. I'll get it taken care of when I get back to the hotel."

Logan arched his eyebrows. "You're staying at a hotel? It's time you tell me what's going on, my boy, because we both know your behavior is uncharacteristic. The bedraggled man sitting across from me is not the man I admire and respect."

Garrett exhaled hard. "My life's in the toilet."

"Crude terminology, but I'm listening."

It wasn't easy at first, to reveal what was going on. It got easier as Garrett talked, uninterrupted. Still, he held back some of the details—there was only so much humiliation he should be forced to suffer.

Aaron Logan sat forward when Garrett stopped speaking. "I'm sorry about your troubles. You should have come to me before letting it—yourself—get to this point."

Garrett ran a hand through his hair. "I realized last night how bad it's gotten, when I thought about ending my life. Then I realized that wasn't a solution. There's too much I want to do."

"We all have misfortune visit us in our lifetime, but I'm glad you came to your senses. Time for you to buck up. Still, I believe you would benefit by getting some form of assistance. If you're relying on alcohol or some drug to cope—"

"I'm not. At least, not relying on it. I just hit bottom."

"My boy, you have too much to offer. You've decades ahead of you yet. Make them count. You've come too far in your career to eradicate all your accomplishments."

"You're right. Time to straighten myself and my life out so I can return to doing what I love and what I'm good at."

"What you're best at."

"Thank you, sir."

"Let's order and get some food into you. You have two months to rest, get your head straight, and your life organized. I'm sure you won't disappoint me. It would be tragic if you were the first person I'd ever recommended for a position who failed to meet expectations." Logan picked up the menu. "Now, let's see what's edible."

Garrett pretended to study his menu. Logan and he had very different opinions about what could be considered tragic. There was, however, one person who understood tragedy better than anyone he knew.

CHAPTER 108

"I KNOW you'll do fine on the test." Chelsea kissed Kimberlie's forehead. "You studied hard enough."

"Thanks, Mom." Kimberlie got out of the car and leaned in. "Watch those feet of yours. My mom, the klutz."

Chelsea faked a laugh as Kimberlie closed the door and sprinted to the school entrance. She pulled the car away from the curb, turned right out of the driveway, and headed toward the superstore. A hearty stew and fresh-baked bread would be perfect for their dinner.

She turned into the store parking lot, glanced left and slowed to watch Penelope drive out and onto the road. Pulse racing, she pulled into the nearest spot, turned off her car, and leaned against the headrest.

Had it always been Pen's plan to destroy her? To reveal secrets she's sworn she'd take to her grave? If Penelope Sanders had visions of Garrett marrying her, buying her a small mansion, an expensive car and lifestyle, she was dreaming. Garrett would never take anyone as gauche as Penelope to a hospital function, especially not as his wife.

She'd allowed both of them, albeit unknowingly, to take advantage of her for years. Whatever Penelope was playing at, she was about to find out that she wasn't the only one who could spill secrets.

CHAPTER 109

THE DOORBELL RANG. It rang again, followed by pounding on Chelsea's front door. Through the glass panel, she saw Penelope's car parked out front, reversed her steps, went up the stairs and turned right, walking until she reached the end of the hallway. She opened the window and shouted, "Leave, or I'll call the police."

Penelope walked to the rear of her car and looked up. "You bitch!"

"Problem?"

"I got fired. Seems my boss's wife received an anonymous call. Anonymous, my ass. Happy now?"

"Guess you should have earned your huge bonuses and flexible work schedule the old-fashioned way. Oh, that's right. You did. The oldest way."

"You went too far this time, Chelsea."

"You know what they say about payback. Guess you should have saved some of the money instead of blowing it on cosmetic surgeries and clothes."

"This isn't over. Whatever I do now, you've asked for it."

"You've already done your worst."

"Don't count on it."

"Don't threaten me. Or I'll tell the police it was you who gave me this face and lip. You *were* responsible, after all. It may have been Garrett who inflicted it, but you set him off."

"Maybe I did. But I'm much better at getting him off."

"If you think Garrett's going to thank you for what you did, you're wrong. Speaking of Garrett, how is he? Have you seen him lately? Has he invited you to spend your lives together in a drunken stupor?"

Penelope stomped to the driver's side of her car. "I'm going to come up with something very special, just for you."

"As long as it doesn't involve whipped cream and whips."

CHAPTER 110

G ARRETT SCROLLED TO Jeffrey Davis' cell phone number. When Frederick Starks was still a free man, the three of them had engaged in weekly rowdy partying. The strip clubs, lap dances, and occasional, more private parties with select women had stopped when Starks had been arrested.

He'd elected to stay away from the mess, and had read in the newspaper that Jeffrey had taken over running Starks's business empire. Because of his self-imposed removal from their sphere, Jeffrey might not want to talk to him. The call was answered after the first ring.

"Garrett Hall. Man, it's been ages. How the heck are you?"

"Thanks for taking my call. I wasn't certain you would."

"Look, I understood. It was easier for me because I'm single. I knew you wanted to keep your wife off your back. But sometimes I miss those days."

"I hear you."

"What are you up to?"

"That's too long a story for the time I have."

"You don't sound good."

"At the moment, I'm not. I need to see Starks. I know you visit him. What's required for me to get in there?"

"Couple of things. Starks has to put your name on his approved visitors list and you have to be vetted. Takes a couple weeks. Maybe even months. Red tape and all that."

"I can't wait. I need to see him as soon as possible."

"Sorry, but that's how it goes. Wait a minute. Starks said you treated him when he had the transfusion."

"I did."

"That should work. Call the prison and tell them you're Starks's doctor and you want to check on your patient. I doubt they'll refuse you. Don't know if they'll have to vet you or not, but it's your best shot. Since they have a doctor on staff there, want to tell me what's up?"

"Another time. Maybe I'll buy you dinner one night soon."

"I'm in. Just let me know when. And, let me know how it goes."

"Will do. One more thing. Do you have the number of the prison handy?"

"Sure. I'll text it to you soon as we hang up."

Seconds after the call ended, the number for Sands Correctional Facility was added to Garrett's phone list and called.

CHAPTER 111

G AINING APPROVAL TO check on Starks had been easier and quicker than Garrett had anticipated. Traffic was light that Saturday morning as he made the two-hour trek in three hours to the maximum security prison. The snow wasn't yet as heavy as it was predicted to become, but only those determined to get somewhere they had to be were on the roads.

He turned onto the long drive that led to the parking lot provided in front for visitors. Counted the guard towers, felt squeamish at the sight of the multiple coils of razor wire atop the tall wall enclosing the property's perimeter.

It took twenty minutes to be checked in, scanned for potential or actual weapons, and his medical bag searched. A guard whose belt was loaded down with a holstered pistol, blackjack, and Taser gun escorted him through the gray interior and heavy electronic barred doors, to a private room. Garrett sat at the small table. And waited. Nearly fifteen minutes later, he stood and extended his hand.

"Starks. You let your hair grow back. I like it better than the shaved head."

"Made Steve, the barber, pretty happy. He cried when I had him shave it off and cried when I had him give me a trim."

"How are you feeling? Anymore health problems since I saw you last?"

Starks shook his head. "So far, so good. I didn't know doctors made prison calls for patients they treated at a hospital."

"They don't. This was the easiest way to bypass the long vetting process for approval. I'll check you, of course, but I'm here for a different reason. One only you can understand better than anyone else."

"You look like crap. What's going on?"

"That's primarily why I came. To discuss my situation with you. Get your input. It'll take a while to tell you everything."

Starks slouched back in his chair. "I've got fourteen years to listen, unless my attorney can work some magic to get me out sooner."

CHAPTER 112

S TARKS STARED HARD at Garrett. "Booze and guns don't mix. In your case, get rid of both. As for going after this Thompson guy—don't. Take it from me: Sands isn't a place where you want to take up permanent residence."

"I get that. It's why I didn't go through with it and decided to talk to you. But I also understand why you went after Ozy Hessinger." Garrett slammed his fist into his palm. "I want to take the guy out."

"That wasn't my intention when I went to Ozy's house that night. I only meant to inform his wife, in front of him, about what he'd been doing. I'm glad the bastard lived. Saved me from getting life in here. Now, he gets to lose everything he cost me. Except his freedom, that is."

"Hardly seems enough of a penalty for him to pay."

Starks shrugged. "It's all I'm going to get."

"Finding out what Chelsea's done has damn near destroyed me. My faith in her and our marriage was based on lies. Since your experience is similar, I need to know how you coped with your feelings about Kayla, once you learned the truth."

"Obviously, not well. The Bible warns us about such women, but we don't listen."

"Not a book I've ever felt tempted to read."

"I was the same way. Until I got here and had lots of time on my hands, plus working in the library. I memorized a specific passage I came across. It starts at Proverbs, chapter five, verse three. 'For the lips of an adulteress drip honey, and her speech is smoother than oil; but in the end she is bitter as gall, sharp as a double-edged sword.'"

"Maybe Chelsea's lips dripped honey with her lovers, but I got the gall."

"I'm not done yet. 'Her feet go down to death, her steps lead straight to the grave. She gives no thought to the way of life; her paths are crooked, but she knows it not.'"

Garrett stood and paced. "That's the thing, though, isn't it? Chelsea knew it was wrong, as did Kayla. And I certainly feel like I'm dying. Every day, some part of me withers."

"I know what you mean. And you want to punish her severely for doing this to you."

"Damn right."

"I wanted to rip Kayla from one end to the other. There weren't enough vile things I could say to her or about her. I wanted everything bad that could happen to her to happen. I'm thinking you feel the same way about Chelsea."

"She deserves it."

"It's as though her actions erased a large portion of who you are, in your eyes and the eyes of others. The humiliation is unbearable."

"I'm diminishing under the weight of it."

"You feel shredded because she deceived you, particularly in the ways she did it. What you believed about her and your life was all a lie. Because of that you feel you can never trust her again."

"Exactly."

"Even if you want to."

CHAPTER 113

"WHY THE hell would I want to ever trust Chelsea again?" Garrett faced Starks, his expression made plain his disgust.

Starks crossed his arms at his chest and leaned back in his chair. "Even with all the emotions I had—the anger, rage, bitterness—I still considered Kayla my wife. The mother of my children. My exclusive property. Twenty years of my life had been invested in my relationship with her."

"Yeah. No return on that investment for me, either."

"It's not that easy to let go of what you believed you had."

Garrett slammed a hand down on the table. "I trusted her."

Starks fixed his gaze on Garrett. "And she trusted you."

"Whose damn side are you on?"

"I know, right? Every time I pointed my finger at Kayla's perfidy, there was always someone around who was ready to twist that finger toward me. I was indignant as hell."

"Those people are fucking idiots. Probably never had anything like this happen to them. They don't get it."

"Maybe. Too bad they were right."

"I don't believe I'm hearing this. You've been brainwashed or something." Garrett placed both hands on the table and leaned forward, until his face was a foot away from Starks's. "Maybe you're ready to cave, but I'm not. I don't deserve what she did to me. I worked my ass off. Gave her everything she wanted. Instead of staying lower middle-class, her life is luxurious because of me."

"You're preaching to the choir."

"Let me show you something that may change your tune." Garrett pulled *A Dark Walk* from his medical bag. He flipped the book over and pushed it toward Starks. "That's the guy she's been screwing. That's the guy she's so sure she loves and plans to marry. Plans to move into *my* house with *my* daughter."

Starks whistled. "That's an added element I didn't have to deal with. At least, not that I'm aware of. Kayla went with so many men, who knows?"

"Sorry to say it, but I'm relieved I'm not dealing with that same level of treachery. Still, it would make more sense to me if Chelsea had fallen for someone wealthier than me, whatever the color of his skin. What the hell was she thinking? That I'd pay for their life? She's fucking crazy. This guy," he jabbed his finger on Luke's photo, "must have seduced her. That's the only way this crap could have happened."

"You sure about that?"

"I can't believe Chelsea would have gotten involved with him otherwise. He can't afford more than an old car with rust spots and a box for a house in a neighborhood of tacky boxes."

Starks nodded. "How many times have you driven by his house?"

"Just the one time."

"You did better than I did. Every night I couldn't sleep, I took a drive by Ozy's place, which turned out to be nearly every night for months."

"I had my gun with me. I aimed it at his front door, wishing hard he'd open it."

"You want to beat him to a pulp or end him."

"Yes."

"Because your life fractured into pieces you'll never be able to put back together, and you believe he's responsible."

"I just fucking said so."

"Sorry, buddy. He didn't break your life. You did."

CHAPTER 114

GARRETT GRABBED THE book and shoved it into his medical bag. "It was a mistake to come here. I thought you, if anyone, would get it."

"I know some of what I'm saying isn't what you want to hear. I sure as hell didn't, when it was said to me. But you came here for the voice of experience. That's what I'm trying to give you. You need to get off that gilded throne you've put yourself on and let me talk."

"Why don't you say something worth hearing?"

"Why don't you sit the fuck down and keep your mouth shut for a minute."

Garrett scraped the chair across the floor and plopped into it. He folded his arms and stared at the table. After a moment he said, "All right, I'm listening."

"We're both successful men. At least, I was before I screwed up royally. You've screwed up, too, but you still have a chance. What you need to do is get yourself off the booze. You have to have a clear head going forward. You want to get reinstated at the hospital, don't you?"

"I'm worried that may not happen."

"Any reason it shouldn't?"

Garrett shrugged. "How the hell should I know? Nothing makes sense anymore."

"Let's deal with one issue at a time. If you lose your position there, you still have a practice. You can still make money from that. Build the business and open another practice on the other side of town. Then open another in another town."

"Great. Now, what about Chelsea?"

"What about her?"

"How do I deal with her, after learning who she really is?"

"Each of us eventually shows people who we are. Or who we choose to be. Or who we blame others as having forced us to be. There are two sides to every situation."

Garrett dropped his head into his hands. "I loved her."

"Men like us don't know how to love. At least, not at first. Maybe not ever, for some. Possessiveness isn't love. Taking a person for granted isn't, either. Men like you and me have to learn what love isn't before we learn what it is."

"I don't understand where you're going with this. Sounds like a bunch of damn dribble. I expected more from you."

"Maybe it's time you do something I didn't—see a counselor. There's a good one here. Name's Matthew Demory. Maybe he'd consent to see you as a private patient. Off-site, of course."

"I don't think that's the way for me to go."

"And I think you'd get something out of it, if it's with the right person. One thing about Demory: He's big on forgiveness. A pill I personally found more than difficult to swallow."

Garrett laughed, but not with amusement.

Starks raised an eyebrow. "What?"

"I've badgered Chelsea for years to forgive me. She couldn't. Or wouldn't. Now, others will expect me to do that? Everything is fucking twisted."

"Bites, doesn't it? I had the same problem." Starks shifted forward. "I'm serious about you moving on with your life. Because here's what I know: Every time you look at her, you'll see Thompson. See them together. At least until time allows the images to fade."

Garrett ran a hand back and forth across his forehead. "That's happening now. I can't shut the damn films off."

"If you can't live with that, you need to let go. Those thoughts are poison, buddy. They'll taint every moment you're around her."

"How am I supposed to stop them?"

"Maybe now you can understand what it's been like for Chelsea."

"If I hear that one more time—"

"You ought to repeat it to yourself several times a day. Until you finally comprehend the truth. As for the thoughts, try as best you can to let them go when they pop up."

"How the hell am I supposed to do that?"

"Keep busy. That's why I said time has to take care of making them fade. But only if you don't fuel them by playing them over and over, or inventing new versions."

"Not easy."

"Neither is forgiving her. Or yourself, when you're finally able to get that far."

"I don't see how that can ever happen."

"You never know. The main thing is to not do anything stupid. That's why it's crucial you let go of any such thoughts. When you see the brutality in here and deaths that result, as I have … when you're on the receiving end of that brutality or hold your broken, dying son in your arms as I did—that's a story for another time—those types of experiences wake you up to reality. Especially the reality about yourself."

Garrett shook his head. "Look, Starks—"

"You and I are cut from the same cloth. I get what you're thinking and feeling. You know I do."

"I know you're trying to help. It's just there are times I wish that Thompson bastard was dead. Chelsea, too."

"You only feel that way because it isn't a fact. I promise you'd feel different if it were. At least about Chelsea." Starks looked away. He exhaled hard and cleared his throat before facing Garrett.

Garrett studied Starks's face. "What aren't you telling me?"

CHAPTER 115

"KAYLA HAS cancer. She's dying," Starks said. "As much as I've hated her, as smug as I felt when she miscarried her boyfriend's baby and he left her—which, I always said he would, I never thought I'd get news that she had months to live."

"But won't that fix things? I mean, isn't it better if she's out of the picture for good? Out of sight, out of mind kind of thing?"

"As much as you might want to harm Chelsea, and him, imagine what it would be like to realize your daughter was about to lose both parents—you to prison and her mother in death. You think you feel tortured now? This hell you're in would get a lot worse. You'd also get the perspective shift you've resisted and still want to."

"Look, Starks, I appreciate what you're going through. It sucks, and I really am sorry. But it's not the same."

"It's similar enough for you to pay attention. There is one significant difference. Kayla said she married me for what she could get, not for love—I'd promised to give her the world, and she meant to hold me to it. Maybe she meant that, and maybe she was lying to herself because she was afraid to trust any man, after being abandoned by her father. But I loved her, in my own way. Always did. I just didn't realize how much until it was too late, and now it's really too late. I abused anything she felt for me by basically abandoning her to long hours working so we could buy expensive stuff, and with all the women I slept with, and crap even she doesn't know about, and I hope she never does. The only woman I ever really loved … I'll never have a chance to make it up to her. It's too late for me, but it isn't too late for you. Chelsea loved you from the start."

"I wish I could believe that."

"I said you and I are cut from the same cloth. That material is an egregious level of pride fueled by overfed egos. We did exceptionally well in business and convinced ourselves our wealth and status entitled us to do whatever the hell we wanted. We were wrong. One thing we didn't consider is that there's always an expiration date that smacks you hard."

Garrett shook his head. "Prison's really changed you. This isn't the fun, freewheeling Starks I partied with."

"Those behaviors have been purged out of me. But, God, what it took for that to happen. What I had to lose. And the price others had to pay, especially my children. Trust me, Garrett, you don't want to follow in my footsteps."

"How am I supposed to get on with my life? Act like it never happened?"

"See the truth about what you've done, who you've become or always allowed yourself to be. It's the only way to avoid making the same mistakes or worse ones. Whether that's with Chelsea or someone else."

"You're saying I should take responsibility. Mend my ways."

"The sooner the better."

"I don't know if I can do that. I've tried to stop being with other women. I can't let go of how good it feels. Monogamy is monotony has been my motto. Yours, too."

"Then prepare for the price you're paying now to increase. Until there's nothing left of you to pay with and no one left in your life who wants anything to do with you. Because they can't trust you."

"You're saying that unless *I* change, I'm fucked."

"I'm saying you have a choice. Which one are you going to make?"

CHAPTER 116

GARRETT DID A perfunctory check-up on Starks, thanked him, and left, once again escorted by a correctional officer to the reception lobby. It was a relief to get out of that oppressive atmosphere. How did Starks do it, day after day after day? The answer came to him: he doesn't have a choice, and that's what he was trying to drum into you.

Snow came down in large, wet flakes that stuck, but snowplows did a good job of keeping up with it on the highways. Still, the roads were slick. He kept his speed under thirty-five.

It hadn't been easy hearing what Starks said. The man's words, for the most part, ran counter to everything he'd ever believed.

Where had those beliefs come from? Not from his father. His father had always been a family man. Sure, he'd been fairly successful, but only enough to provide a moderate, comfortable life for his wife and three children. Garrett had wanted more. Always had. It was all about the money and what and who you could buy with it.

He'd started doing odd jobs for neighbors when he was ten. If a program was on about the rich and famous at a time when he could watch, he parked himself in front of the TV, promising himself he'd be like those men one day.

For years, he'd checked out biographies from the library about the most successful men in history and contemporary times, absorbing the information, as though if by osmosis, he'd become like them. How many of them had wives *and* mistresses? Nearly all of them. A seed got planted: Wealthy, successful, prominent men were seldom fulfilled by one woman. Nor could they or should they be. They worked hard. That gave them the right to play. They had more energy and lust for life than most. It had to be expended somewhere.

His practice of this belief started when he turned sixteen. He had money saved from six years of yard work and bagging groceries at a local store. Enough to attract girls willing to put out if they were treated to a nice dinner and a few relatively expensive trinkets, relative, that is, for someone their age. As soon as a girl got clingy, he moved on to another one. Or he'd string a few of them along at a time. Once he began to succeed as an adult, he ignored his father's example and latched onto other examples, like Starks's. Every cosmopolitan city was rife with guys like him.

Then it struck him: Very few of those men he'd admired had remained married to their first wives. Many had multiple wives, and children with each one. Despite the people they'd accumulated over the years, a number of these men died alone.

What had Chelsea wanted from him? What he'd promised in their wedding vows. Instead, he betrayed those vows. Betrayed her. Sending her into the arms of two men. He was way ahead of her, count-wise, if anyone was keeping score.

She'd also had to face getting pregnant with one of them, and an abortion. Not easy for someone who'd wanted more than one child. Chelsea could have tried to pass the kid off as his, but didn't. He could be raising Eisenberg's kid, instead of his own, and never known it unless something happened to him as had happened to Starks. That would have been some kind of fucking karmic backlash, for sure—cut off her ability to have more kids, only to realize he'd done the same thing to himself. Except, she'd have a kid that was hers, and he wouldn't.

Chelsea might have made her decision about the abortion from fear, but more likely from integrity. He'd pushed her into that situation. And had kept pushing her, including away, despite her efforts to save their marriage.

Starks was right. He'd been a damn fool. A selfish prick who didn't deserve a second chance. More like a third, fourth, or fortieth, if he really wanted to be honest with himself.

Maybe it wasn't too late. If he could just talk to her, explain that he'd come to this realization. Maybe she'd hear him out.

She had to.

CHAPTER 117

"PICK UP. Pick up. Pick up." Garrett tread back and forth as he waited for Chelsea to answer his call, certain he'd soon hear the voice mail recording. Instead, she answered on the fourth ring. He gripped the phone as relief flooded him. "I'm sorry to call so late. I wasn't certain you'd answer. Thank you for doing so."

"The only reason I did was to make it clear there's nothing left for us to say to each other."

"Please don't hang up, sweetheart."

"Don't call me that. You gave up that right ages ago. I let this farce go on long enough. It's over. Finally."

"No. You were right. Our marriage was worth saving. *Is* worth saving. Chels, I can't tell you how sorry I am. But I'd like to try. I want to make it up to you."

"After what you did to me?"

"I've been a selfish bastard. Everything is my fault. I realize that now. I didn't want to admit that to myself, but reality smacked me in the face. Let's start over, from where we are. Let's agree to forget the past and begin fresh, as though none of it happened."

"Broken record, Garrett."

"I swear it's different this time. Let me prove it to you. I'll do whatever it takes to fix this. We'll find a marriage counselor—a good one this time. One who won't let me off the hook. I'll keep every appointment. I'll do whatever's recommended. And I'll resign from the hospital. My income will decrease somewhat, at least for a while, but we can make it. I'll hire more doctors for my practice so I have more time to spend with you and Kimberlie. Like a family is supposed to do. This time I'll treat you the way you always deserved."

"How many times did you practice this speech before calling me?"

"I'm speaking from my heart."

"Keep your heart. It's been running on fumes. But, you've bruised mine for the last time. There's someone in my life now who loves me the way a man is supposed to love his woman."

"That relationship isn't real. What we have is."

"You're wrong."

"It's an affair, Chels. An illusion."

"You'd know all about that. But I repeat: You're wrong. What we had was the illusion. Or, rather, my delusion. Reality smacked me, too, Garrett. And the sooner I remove you from my reality, the better."

"You feel that way now because I've hurt you."

"Hurt me? You altered me."

"I want to make it right. I'm begging you to let me. Will you at least think about it? For the sake of our daughter and what we could have as a family? You didn't give up on us before. I'm pleading with you not to give up on us now. For all our sakes, Chels. Please. At least think about it. Neither of us have the right to throw our relationship away without at least giving it serious consideration. We need to give it—us—a real chance."

Chelsea sighed. "I'll think about it. But don't expect much to come of it."

"That's all I deserve."

"You don't deserve even that much."

"Thank you, Chels."

"I'm hanging up now. It's after midnight. I'm exhausted."

Garrett placed his phone on the nightstand and stretched out on the bed. The way their conversation ended, he could see the proverbial light at the end of the tunnel. Maybe it was a tiny pinprick of light now, but it could grow. It had to.

The old him would have rushed to buy her something wildly expensive, something that would show off how successful he was, in order to win her back. Not this time. This time he'd have to give of himself. As long as he wasn't allowed to live at the house, how was he supposed to do that?

Answers to that question eluded him.

CHAPTER 118

WAS THIS A case of too little, too late? Chelsea propped her arms under her head and stared up at the dancing tree shadows on the bedroom ceiling. Cold wind whistled across the window glass.

The truth was that she still caught herself, at times, waiting to hear Garrett's key in the front door lock, followed by the back door opening and closing, the sound of his body piercing the water in the pool, then minutes later, his footsteps coming up the stairs and down the hall to their bedroom. Could still easily recall the feel of the mattress shifting when he got into their bed, believing she was asleep. There were times, when half asleep, that she felt his body depress the mattress, only to turn over and see his side of the bed still made. Empty. As it had been when she'd climbed in.

Her body grew tense, as it had all those nights. She inhaled deeply and released the breath. He'd promised there would never be nights like that again. If he was fooling himself, and her, could she go back to living like that?

Garrett had called her relationship with Luke an illusion. Could an illusion feel so real?

Of course it could. She'd lived it with Garrett for years.

He'd sounded so sincere about their reconciling, about his guilt, and wanting to make amends. He'd sounded sincere before. But this time, there was something different in his voice, and in his words.

Luke was the better man. Wasn't he? He was kind, empathetic, compassionate, creative. With words and with lovemaking. He made her feel the way she'd always wanted to. Learning about her past hadn't deterred him in his love for her, hadn't angered him. Not like it had Garrett.

But didn't Garrett have more right to be incensed? He was her husband, the one who'd been wronged. She knew how much the truth had to have hurt him, having been on the receiving end of his consistent infidelity and deception. And, now, spouting his latest revelations about what he'd done to her, sounding genuinely, confusingly, contrite.

She rolled onto her side, facing where Garrett had always slept, and placed her hand on his pillow. Garrett was the father of her daughter. Her daughter needed stability in her life. And they both needed to be better examples for Kimberlie.

Garrett's desire to repair their relationship meant he was willing to forgive her past indiscretions, and this recent one. He'd said so. Maybe he *had* changed, or was at least willing to do his best.

Perhaps he'd realized what he was about to lose. Maybe it mattered now. More than the ego that let him believe he could screw around and get away with it. Screw with people's lives without consequence.

Garrett had abused her love and her faith. He'd stolen her ability to have more children. And hadn't told her. Let her blame herself and feel the shame of it all this time.

But he was her husband.

But she loved Luke and didn't want to hurt him. He didn't deserve it.

But Garrett was her husband.

CHAPTER 119

GARRETT'S PHONE PINGED. He moaned, pulled the comforter up to his chin and opened his eyes into slits. Soft sunlight glowed from the top edge of the heavy drapes in the otherwise darkened room. The digital clock on the TV showed it was six fifty-three. By the third ping, he recalled his conversation with Chelsea. It had to be her. She'd taken the night to contemplate his offer and was willing to take him back. Was willing to make it work. But why send a text message rather than call? Unless it was bad news.

His pulse raced as he grabbed the phone and checked the screen. It was bad news, but a different kind. *Dr. Jacobs.* What the hell did Penelope want? The woman had to be dealt with once and for all. He read her text message: *I e-mailed a few photos to you. You'll want to see them.*

The last thing he wanted to see was *more* naked pictures of Penelope. He opened his e-mail and started to delete them, unopened, then decided to see how far she was willing to debase herself. He'd look, laugh, and then he'd tell her to get lost. He opened the first photo, and the next, and the next.

What the hell was going on?

CHAPTER 120

THE HOTEL PHONE rested between Garrett's ear and shoulder as he studied the images on his cell phone of Chelsea and Richard—Richard hugging her to him, Richard kissing her cheek, Richard holding the door that opened into a hotel lobby. "All right, Penelope. You have my attention. What's this supposed to be about?"

"A picture's worth a thousand words. Isn't it obvious?"

"You woke me up. I'm still groggy. Why don't you explain it to me."

"A few years ago, you and Chelsea had a huge argument. She had Kimberlie go to Susan's house then stayed away for a couple of days and nights."

"I remember. So what? It happens to the best couples."

"What isn't supposed to happen is for a man's wife to screw his brother."

"I'm hanging up."

"Photos don't lie."

"I don't believe it. Not for a moment."

"Who could blame you? But the evidence is right there."

"I don't know what that was about, but you're wrong."

"I never considered you a fool, Garrett. Until now. When are you going to get it into your head what kind of woman you're married to?"

Garrett sighed. "I don't understand why you even have these photos?"

"Chelsea ran to me after the argument, complaining about you yet again. Big yawn. I went into the kitchen, and heard her call Richard, heard her ask him to meet her at their usual place. She'd never revealed anything about her involvement with him before, or ever—she's so secretive. Anyway, I followed her. When I saw where their usual place was, I took those photos. Figured I might need proof one day. Today's the day."

The words "usual place" stuck in Garrett's mind. The same words Thompson had used. Still, he couldn't believe it. He didn't want to. "What kind of a friend are you?"

"I stopped being her friend a long time ago, especially after you and I started enjoying each other. I tolerated her. So I could make sure she didn't find out about us, and so I could be near you. I put up with her whining about you, whining amid her expensive house, cars, furs, jewelry, and trips. She never appreciated you. Not like I do. I knew she had you hoodwinked. And that it was only a matter of time before she couldn't hide who she really is. It's time to get her out of your life, Garrett. It's time you have a woman who loves you, who understands you and what you need."

"And you're ready to jump into that role?"

"I've been ready for years."

"The thing you need to understand, Penelope, is that to me, you're nothing more than a sex toy."

"You're only saying that because you're upset. We're alike. We belong together, particularly in bed. Or anywhere you want to—"

"I said it because it's a fact. And I'm nothing like you. I'm not a whore."

"Takes one to know one. Face facts, darling. Your wife and your brother have been at it for years. These past few months she's been doing him, Luke, and you. I never realized how industrious the little woman could be. I suppose you're sloppy thirds these days."

Garrett slammed the receiver down. He studied the images. Zoomed in on the expressions on the faces. Penelope had been right about Luke. Right about Eric and the abortion. But this?

He'd been worse than a fool.

He found the number he wanted. "Anna, where's my brother?"

"Hi, Garrett. It's good to hear from you. I'm sorry about your troubles with Chelsea. Why don't you come over for dinner one night soon? We'll eat, we'll talk, and we'll pray."

"Where's Richard?"

"He went to your parents' house to help them with—"

Garrett pressed Off. He grabbed his keys and rushed to the elevator. In minutes he was in his car, foot pressed hard on the accelerator.

CHAPTER 121

GARRETT'S CHEST HEAVED with breaths that came in rapid, ragged intervals. He turned into a convenience store lot, put his car in Park, and attempted to get himself under control. He pulled up the photos on his phone.

He'd hated learning that Chelsea had been confiding in Richard. Hated learning they'd both kept that from him. Hated that his mother had known. But it explained why Richard knew as much as he did about his and Chelsea's relationship. Why hadn't he figured it out before?

But this?

It was inexcusable. Nearly incestuous.

Did they talk about him before or after they had sex?

Did Chelsea compare the techniques of all her lovers, or did she just enjoy their differences?

Richard—acting holier than thou, all the while betraying him. This was the ultimate disloyalty, and he wasn't going to put up with it. What had been cleverly kept secret was about to be revealed.

More questions flooded his mind. There was only one way to get answers. He put his car in gear, leaving tire marks on the pavement.

CHAPTER 122

RICHARD'S CAR WAS in the driveway. Garrett parked behind it, blocking any opportunity for his bastard of a brother to run. He rushed to the front door, turned the knob. Locked. Forget using his key. He pounded on the door with one hand and repeatedly pressed the doorbell with the other.

Richard flung open the door. "What's happened? Are you okay? Anna said you called looking for me and hung up without saying goodbye."

"You sonofabitch." Garrett aimed his fist for Richard's jaw. Richard dodged. The hit connected with Richard's shoulder.

Theresa hurried toward them from the kitchen. She grabbed Garrett by the arm. "What do you think you're doing?"

Garrett lunged at his brother.

Thomas rushed down the stairs. "Stop this right now. Have you lost your mind, son? Whatever the problem is, we're going to sit down and discuss it." He pointed to the living room. "Now, Garrett."

Garrett stomped into the room and dropped heavily into a chair a few feet from the fireplace. Thomas sat on the sofa. Richard eased warily into the chair across from Garrett.

Theresa said to Richard, "I'm going to get something to ice your shoulder with. I'll be right back." She returned moments later with a frozen bag of peas. "Now, Garrett, you'd better have a good explanation for what you did."

"Better than good." Garrett glared at Richard and started to speak. He told them about Eric Eisenberg—all of it. He told them about Luke Thompson. He held up his phone, displaying the photo of Chelsea and Richard entering the hotel. "You met my wife at a hotel."

"You had her followed?"

"Did you meet her there more than once?"

"Yes, but let me—"

"Over a few years?"

Richard stood up. "Calm down, Garrett. Let me explain."

Garrett tossed his phone to the floor and launched at Richard.

Richard tried to block the punches to his torso that came hard and fast. "Garrett, for God's sake, let me explain what—"

Garrett's fist landed in the center of Richard's chest. Richard buckled over and collapsed. The sickening crack of his head hitting the raised marble hearth brought everything to a halt.

CHAPTER 123

GARRETT STOOD WITH his fists raised and ready. There was only a little blood on the marble. "Get up, Richard. I'm not done with you."

Theresa grabbed Thomas' arm. "Why isn't he moving?"

Thomas ran to Richard. "Son? Richard?" He looked up at Garrett. "You're a doctor. Do something." When Garrett didn't move, he said, "I'm calling nine-one-one." He hurried to the phone.

Theresa said, "Thomas. Wait."

"There's no time."

"Wait just a few seconds." She spun Garrett around. "You need to get out of here."

"What?" He glanced over his shoulder at Richard. The small amount of blood expanded into a puddle, spread across the marble, spilled onto the carpeted floor. He turned back to Theresa. "I didn't mean to—"

"I know. But you have to leave before the ambulance gets here. We'll tell them he slipped. A freak accident. We don't want the police to get involved." She looked back at Thomas, who after a brief pause, nodded.

Garrett shook his head. "I can't leave him like that."

Thomas picked up the receiver. "Son, you listen to your mother. Go back to the hotel and wait for our call. Let us handle this."

"Let me just—" Garrett pressed two fingers against Richard's neck. "Thank God. Give me a towel."

Theresa tugged his sweater. "Go, Garrett. Now." She pushed his phone into his hand and shoved him forward.

Garrett staggered to the door and to his car. He backed out of the driveway without looking, hitting the brakes with a jolt when a driver behind him held his hand on the horn.

He didn't remember driving back to the hotel. Didn't remember how he got to his room. What he could remember was the sound of Richard's skull hitting the hearth, how pale his brother's skin had been as he lay unmoving on the living room floor, the sound of his father shouting into the phone for an ambulance, and his mother begging Richard to wake up.

CHAPTER 124

GARRETT SLUNG OPEN the door to the mini-bar. He couldn't afford to get drunk, but needed something to take the edge off. To make his hands stop shaking. To make the icy chill inside him go away. Just one airplane-size bottle of Scotch would do it. He broke the seal, twisted the cap off and drank.

He drank. Paced. Began the tedious process of deleting photos of Chelsea from his phone, until he couldn't stand to look at her face any longer. He put the phone down and stood at the window.

Why didn't his parents call and tell him that Richard had come to minutes after he left? That the EMTs checked him and all was fine. That aside from a few stitches and a fierce headache, Richard was okay. And willing to forgive him. So they could forgive each other. It was a call that, if received as desired, could stop the anguish tormenting him.

Garrett went to the lavatory, splashed cold water on his face, avoided looking at his reflection in the mirror. His cell phone rang. He dashed back, scooped up the phone and cursed. "I don't want to talk to you now, Chelsea. I'm waiting for a call."

"So much for putting me first, now and forevermore."

"Forget everything I said."

"You didn't sound drunk last night, but apparently you were."

"I'm hanging up."

"I should know better by now than to trust you."

He clutched the phone. "You're the last damn person to talk to me about trust."

"You always were nasty when you had a hangover."

"What I do no longer concerns you. I don't want to hear your voice or your lies ever again. And, don't fool yourself into believing that

I don't mean it. You were right about one thing: our attorneys are to do the talking from now on."

"Why are you acting like this?"

"Because you're a poisonous, lying bitch. I'm going to instruct my attorneys to get you out of *my* house as part of the divorce settlement."

"You'd make Kimberlie leave the only home she can remember?"

"I don't care where you go or what you do. Or who you do. You can go to hell, as far as I'm concerned. But Kimberlie stays. With me. I'm going to ask for full custody. I'll fight however I have to, to get it. And, I intend to win."

"For your information, Garrett, as far as the courts are concerned, Kimberlie's old enough to choose who she lives with."

"She'll choose to live with me. In *my* house. Especially once she knows her mother's nothing more than a whore."

"You wouldn't—"

"Do us all a favor: Run away with your latest penis-puppet and never contact any of us again. Better yet, die and leave us in peace."

Garrett ended the call and stood at the window. Noted the crisp blue sky and the clear cold day. His phone rang again. If it was Chelsea or Penelope calling with more of their crap, he'd rip them from one end to the other.

He stormed to his phone on the coffee table. It was neither woman. Nor was it whom he'd expected. "Chloe?"

Garrett lowered himself onto the sofa as he listened to his sister's voice, tears streaming down his face.

CHAPTER 125

G ARRETT CRADLED HIS forehead with his free hand. Chloe shouted his name over the phone several times. He took a few ragged breaths and said, "I need to hear you say it again."

"Richard is doing okay. The prognosis is good, but they feel it's best to keep him under observation for a few days."

"Thank God. On both accounts. I've been going crazy waiting to hear from someone."

"From what Mom and Dad told me, you went crazy before that."

"Anna must hate me. You all must." Garrett began to pace.

"We don't hate you, and Anna doesn't know anything other than Richard tripped. She doesn't even know you were at the house. She did ask where you were and we told her you were doing a procedure; that we'd tell you later what happened."

"I was terrified I'd killed him."

"You didn't. And before you ask, Mom and Dad got Richard to agree to that story, once he was conscious and talking in the E.R. They told *me* what happened before Anna got there. They don't want her to know. Any of it. Especially your part in the accident."

"Accident. Don't be so gracious. I don't deserve it. This is all my fault. I was furious about what he and Chelsea … what they've done."

"They haven't done anything."

"If Mom and Dad told you everything, then you know that's not true."

"You're the one who has the facts inside out. Nothing like what you believe happened between them ever did."

"I understand why you're defending Richard, but—"

"I'm defending him because I was there."

Garrett pivoted and stopped. He gripped the phone. "What are you saying?"

"First, tell me who took those photos and then sent them to you after all this time."

"What does that matter?"

"Just tell me, G."

"Penelope."

"That *bitch*. But, now it all makes perfect sense to me."

CHAPTER 126

"I DON'T understand, Chloe. What makes sense?" Garrett returned to the sofa. "Please get to the point a little faster than you usually do."

"I knew my suspicions were right about her. I never liked or trusted her. Penelope's so … artificial. In every way, if you get my meaning."

"Chloe."

"It was after that big fight you and Chelsea had."

"I know."

"As you also know, she decided to stay at the hotel a few days to think things over. But she needed someone to talk to who knows you well, so reached out to Richard. I called Richard while he and Chelsea were talking over coffee in the hotel restaurant. I could hear it was a restaurant and figured I could meet him and he could buy me lunch."

"You're approaching the too-much-information zone."

"Anyway, I bugged him until he told me where he was and why. I told him it was all in the family and that I was coming over there. To wait for me."

"How can you be sure it was that time and not another time they met there?"

"I remember what they were wearing—Mom told me what she remembered from the photos."

"I'm going to grow old waiting for you to tell me why Penelope's involvement in this makes sense."

"Chill, G. I'll get there. Richard and I walked Chelsea back to her room, you know, to see if there was anything else she needed."

"She didn't deserve it."

"We didn't know that then. Anyway, that's where they always met to talk. I sat in on a couple of those conversations."

"Why? Why would Richard even let you do that?"

"I told him you were my brother, too, and I had a right to know, or didn't I count? Guilt sometimes works. Anyway, I did want to know what was going on, but I also considered it a life-lesson."

"Not what I'd want my baby sister to learn."

"Then you should consider setting a better example from now on. And you need to realize Richard isn't like you. He honors the vows he made before God. He never pays lip-service to his faith. He lives it."

"Penelope set me up."

"Believe it."

"Why would she do something that egregious? Why lie about my brother and my wife?"

"It's obvious."

"Not to me."

"Then let baby sister tell big brother the other facts of life."

CHAPTER 127

"I'M WAITING." Garrett kept the phone pressed to his ear as he got two miniature bottles of whiskey from the mini-bar.

"Penelope's always wanted you. Well, I don't know if she actually wants you, but she wants what Chelsea has, and that starts with you, and your wallet. Every time I was in the same room with her, especially at your house, I'd watch her ogle the house and what's in it, the pool, the cars, Chelsea's jewelry and stuff. Despite the makeup she wears, it couldn't hide that she all but turned green."

"I never noticed."

"She followed every move you made. Kept her eyes on you longer, and more longingly, than she should have. Sure, she acted like she couldn't stand you, but I'm not female for nothing. I know the signs. She was straining her brain to figure out a way to seduce you. I'm just grateful you never returned her interest. The image churns my stomach."

Garrett twisted the cap off one of the bottles and downed the liquid in one gulp. If Chloe didn't know about him and Penelope, maybe no one in his family did. Maybe Chelsea hadn't told anyone. Yet. "Penelope lied about Richard. My own brother."

"Told you. She's a bitch. Chelsea needs to be rid of her."

"I'm pretty sure that's a done deal." Garrett blew out a breath. "I need to apologize to Richard. I'll clean up and head over to the hospital."

"Wait until tomorrow. They want him to rest, and without any excitement. They even kicked us out."

"I won't do anything to disturb him, but I need to tell him how sorry I am. The sooner the better."

"G, I love you, but you tend to put your interests first."

Garrett sighed. "That stings, Chloe, but I'll wait."

CHAPTER 128

THE BREAKFAST GARRETT ordered could have fed two people. Not a bite was left on his plate. He showered, shaved, got dressed, checked the time. Ten forty-five.

He called Chloe. "I'm getting ready to go to the hospital. How about riding with me? Maybe having you there will help Richard relax about my being in the same room with him."

"Sorry, G. I just left there. But it's okay. I told Richard about our conversation. He understands how the confusion happened and who caused it."

"What did he say?"

"You know Richard. He had me take his hands and bow my head while he prayed for you and Chelsea. And Penelope. He believes every lost soul can be saved."

"Even mine?"

Chloe laughed. "Especially yours."

"What's his room number?"

"Four twenty-five."

"Sure you wouldn't like to go again? I'll buy you lunch. Anyplace you want to go."

"You're a big boy. Go there and take your lumps. And if Richard asks you to pray, do it without any complaint."

Garrett chuckled. "I'd deserve that, as well."

He slipped on one of his new jackets, dropped the phone into a side pocket, and left the room feeling both trepidation and relief. Richard could always be counted on to forgive everyone. How could they be from the same family, he wondered.

A quarter hour later, he dropped his car off at valet parking and made a stop at the hospital gift shop. Armed with balloons and the largest box of chocolates the shop carried, he waited at the elevator with several others. Once inside, he asked the person nearest the buttons to push Four.

The elevator stopped at each floor, finally opening on the one he wanted. Three nurses pushing a crash cart sped past him. Someone had coded, and the staff's mad dash was an attempt to save a life. If he were Richard, he'd say a prayer for the person whose life hung suspended between this one and the next, if there was anything that came after. Richard was adamant there was. He wasn't so sure.

Nurses and cart turned right. Garrett checked the signs for room numbers and turned right as well. He watched the nurses rush into a room on the left side of the corridor, where the odd-numbered rooms were. He picked up his pace, checking room numbers for each door he passed. "No-no-no-no."

Room four twenty-five was abuzz with activity and orders being conveyed rapid-fire. From the other side of the door left ajar, one of the nurses shouted, "Clear." He heard the familiar sound of electricity zapping the heart to get it to beat again. Pushed open the door.

A nurse turned him around and shoved him toward the corridor. "You can't be in here."

"That's my brother."

"Please wait outside."

"I'm a doctor."

"Then you know the rules." She softened her tone. "I'm sorry, sir. Please wait here. I have to get back inside."

Garrett leaned against the opposite wall, balloons in one hand, candy in the other, his expression one of fear and anguish. What was taking so long?

Damn you, Richard, do what you know you need to. Get your heart pumping. Take a breath and the next and the next. I'm standing out here waiting to say I'm sorry. Waiting for you to forgive me.

I need to hear you say you forgive me.

The door opened. The nurse who'd evicted him walked to him and put her hand on his arm.

"Is he okay now?" he asked.

"I'm so sorry."

Garrett looked at her then at the door as the other two nurses moved the cart over the threshold.

The nurse said, "We have things to do for him, but would you like to go in and be with him awhile?"

Garrett nodded. He stepped toward the room and stopped. "Please give these to one of your patients." He handed her the balloons and box of candy, entered the room, and closed the door.

CHAPTER 129

S IX-YEAR-old Richard Hall tightened his grip around the bedpost. "C'mon, Garrett, lemme stay. If you don't, I'll tell Mom you won't let me in your room. She said you had to be nicer to me."

Garrett struggled to pry Richard's hands loose then gave up. "Go ahead, crybaby. Tell her. But it's my room. Why do you have to pester me, anyway? That's all you are. A whiny, bratty pest."

"Mom said you shouldn't oughta talk to me like that. She said I'm your little brother and you should be nice to me, 'cause we're *family*."

"You're a bug. You know what you do with bugs, don't you? You squash 'em. You don't get outta here and leave me alone, I'm gonna squash you."

"Aw, Garrett, lemme stay. I won't bother you."

"You're bothering me now."

"Chloe keeps breaking my toys and screaming when I take 'em back."

"Go outside and play."

"It's raining."

"So maybe you'll drown and put me out of my misery."

"Why can't I stay?"

"Because I'm busy."

"Yeah. And I know what you're busy doing. I'm gonna tell Mom."

"You do and I'll clobber you every day for the rest of your life."

"Where'd you get it, anyway?"

Garrett's face flooded with color. "What?"

"The icky magazine you shoved under the bed when I came in."

"You've been diggin' in my stuff. I told you I'd break your head if you ever did it again. Keep your grubby hands off my private stuff."

"*You're* the one who needs to keep your *hands* off." Richard yelped when Garrett punched him in the arm. "It's nothin' but a bunch of naked girls. That's so gross. So was what you were doing. I'm gonna tell Mom. Then you'll really get it."

"You're too young and stupid to understand."

"I'm telling Mom you called me stupid again. You know what she said."

"Seems like that's all you can say—'I'm gonna tell Mom.' Well, little baby, just remember what she said about being a tattletale. She may punish me, but she'll punish you, too." He dragged Richard to the door and shoved him out. "But it won't be in my room. Now stay out!"

He slammed the door in his tearful younger brother's face. And thought about the shame he'd feel if Richard really did tell on him. He opened the door. "All right. You can come in. But only if you never tell Mom, or *anyone*, about the magazine and—you know."

Richard grinned and bounced into the room. "I won't tell. What do you wanna do?"

"I dunno. Wanna start on that big puzzle I got for my birthday?"

Richard extended his arms and imitated a jet, with sound effects, making a four-point *landing* on the floor.

Garrett poured the hundreds of puzzle pieces onto the middle of the carpet covering the varnished oak boards. He watched Richard study the image on the box, his tongue running back and forth across his lower lip, evidence he was determined to do a good job, good enough to impress his older brother. Richard caught him watching. Garrett shook his head as Richard's goofy smile dented his chubby cheeks, as it always did when his big brother agreed to play with him.

They'd worked on the puzzle until they were called downstairs for dinner. The puzzle remained in place for months, unfinished, until his mother told him she was tired of getting pieces stuck in her vacuum cleaner. He'd put the remaining pieces of the puzzle that would never be complete back in the box and the box on the shelf, where it remained until he'd thrown it away.

God, he'd thrown so much of his life away.

Garrett was exhausted from the day's events—arriving too late to see Richard alive and hear his voice one more time, calling his parents and Anna to tell them Richard was dead, feeling like a leper in a room of saints as the family wept over Richard's shell, the shell he'd caused to empty and never have life again. He closed his eyes and rested his head against the back of the sofa in his hotel room.

He stayed in that position, letting tears stream unresisted down his face. Until his cell phone buzzed. He left the memories behind, wiped his eyes, and read the text message from Chelsea. Read that Chloe had told her about Richard. And about his part in the accident. About why it had happened. Had sworn her to secrecy. Read how sorry she was that Penelope had used them to this end, and her plea for him to call her.

Why had Chloe told Chelsea the truth?

What the hell did it matter?

He turned his phone off and brought the bottle to his lips.

CHAPTER 130

C HELSEA'S TEXT MESSAGE to Luke, asking if he could talk, received a response seconds later. He'd take his break early and call her in about fifteen minutes. The quarter hour dragged by.

"Hi, love. Missing me as much as I'm missing you?"

"Luke, I have something to tell you." She told him everything, with little emotion, still numb from the shock, as well as too afraid to fall into what she believed might be an emotional abyss. Made him promise to tell no one.

"I'm so sorry, love. It sounds as though you were close with your brother-in-law."

"I was. God, I hate talking about him in past tense."

"Are you okay, Chelsea?"

"Nowhere near it."

"Is there anything I can do?"

"There is something."

"Name it."

"We need to slow everything down. I've got a lot to take care of, things you can't be involved with, starting with telling Kimberlie about her uncle when she gets in from school. I'm not going to tell her about her father's part in what happened, but she's never had to face this kind of loss before. I need to be there for her, and for Garrett's family. No telling how long all of this will take. It may be a while before you hear from me."

"I understand why you feel that way, but I'm not comfortable about it. I'm worried about Garrett and that volatile temper of his. I don't want him to have the opportunity to batter you again, especially if he partially blames you for what he did."

"Whatever else Garrett is, he's not a violent man."

"Chelsea, he killed his brother in a fit of temper."

"It was an accident."

"He tried to rape you and struck you when you resisted. That was no accident."

"And was ashamed. You'd know that if you'd seen how distressed he was when he left. He'd never done that before and never will again."

"You're saying that because you don't want to believe or admit what he's capable of. You still want me to believe your bruised cheek wasn't from him."

"Because it's true."

"Damn it! Why do so many battered women think they have to protect the bastard who hits them? I won't be able to stand knowing you're living in fear, even for a short while."

"You've got it wrong, Luke."

"Are you trying to protect me or him?"

"There's nothing to worry about. I'll be fine. Garrett definitely wouldn't do anything like that again, not after this tragedy."

"I don't want anything to happen to you, not as long as I'm able to protect you. You have to let me do that."

Chelsea rubbed her forehead. Exhaustion was setting in, and she had a long road to travel over the next several days, or longer. "I appreciate how you feel. Please don't worry. There's nothing to worry about. I need to go now. But I had to explain why I may not be available for even text messages for a while."

"I hate the thought of you going through this alone."

"You know how it is. You're seldom alone until the funeral is over and everyone has gone back to their lives. Besides, Kimberlie will be with me."

"Text or call me when you can. I need to know you're okay."

"I will."

Chelsea ended the call but kept her phone in her hand. She knew Luke had been waiting to hear that she loved him, but the words wouldn't come. At least, not at the moment. She should at least text that message to him. But it would be too much like swearing in church.

He was wrong about Garrett, and had no cause to concern himself with her safety. Luke had no way of comprehending how Richard's death would devastate Garrett. Had no way of understanding that although the brothers' relationship sometimes went off the rails because of the differences in their beliefs, Garrett was protective of his family, especially in the role of older brother. He'd demonstrated the depth of his sense of duty and devotion when Richard had been in the hospital in December.

Whatever her feelings were for Luke, in family matters such as this one, for now at least, he was an outsider and had to remain one.

She checked the time. Kimberlie would be home in a few hours, the start of a long night.

Chloe had said she'd call later with details about the arrangements. That it was better if she, Chelsea, waited until the right time to see the family. That all things considered, it might not be until the wake. She hated being excluded to this extent, but understood Chloe's reasoning. If she needed another reason, her last conversation with Garrett was enough. She hadn't told Luke about it, because it would have amplified his concern. There were only so many burdens she could bear at one time.

However, there was one thing she could do.

CHAPTER 131

C HELSEA LISTENED AS the call went to voice mail. Again. Penelope, it seemed, was wisely choosing to ignore her calls. Or perhaps she was afraid to take them. Not that it mattered. But once Penelope saw Richard's obituary in the paper or word reached her from someone who knew them both, she might delude herself into thinking she needed to be available to console Garrett. And buddy-up to the family.

The last thing she'd allow was for Penelope to show up at the wake, the service, or graveside.

Twenty unanswered calls later, made one after the other, Chelsea started a string of text messages.

You lied to Garrett about Richard and me.

You knew what that lie would do to Garrett.

Richard is dead—a horrible accident.

Because of this and because of you, Garrett is destroyed.

But he knows the truth now—the real truth, which has nothing to do with your lie.

Richard's death and how Garrett feels after misjudging his brother is on YOU.

How many lives will you need to ruin before your perverse appetite for destruction is sated?

Forget making any kind of apology.

Not one of us can or will ever believe anything you say—it's too deadly to do so, so leave us alone.

Can you really live with yourself, after all you've caused?

If you can, then you're even more evil than I or anyone imagined.

Stay away from me and every member of my family.

Be clear about that—they're MY family.

They'll NEVER be yours, especially not after what you've done to us. Stay away, or pay the price.

She didn't expect or want a response from Penelope. Would the woman even be that stupid? Perhaps her text messages would prevent Penelope from contacting Garrett; though, she knew him well enough to guess what he'd tell her, if she dared to call or show up where he was.

Dr. Moore would have told her not to contact Penelope. She wouldn't have been able to have a fraction of peace had she not informed Penelope about the consequences of her actions.

Tears turned to uncontrollable weeping.

They were all paying for the consequences of their actions.

Including the innocent.

CHAPTER 132

I T TOOK MOST of the next morning for Garrett to help his parents and Anna make arrangements at the funeral home, setting the services for Friday—two days of waiting that he dreaded. He stopped at the superstore and loaded up his back seat and trunk with prepared foods from the deli, beverages, and paper supplies—anything he could imagine they might need. Anything to free his family's time to mourn and be comforted by others.

He pulled into their driveway. Richard's car was still there. The urge to back out and run gnawed at him. Sweat beaded across his forehead. He had to go in. Facing this time with his family was part of his penance.

He turned his engine and cell phone off. The only people he wanted to speak with were inside his childhood home.

That was a lie.

The one person he wanted to speak with had been silenced.

By him.

He'd made it to the house an hour or so before streams of relatives and friends started to arrive or trickle in to pay respects. He was grateful for that time because it gave him and his parents and Chloe an opportunity to say what they each needed to say. And to agree about what wasn't to be said to anyone outside their immediate family, including Anna, about how *it* had happened.

Being there with his parents and sister was the hardest thing he'd ever done. Until they asked him to kneel with them at the hearth and pray. He lasted a few minutes then ran from the room, apologizing between sobs.

His mother, father, and sister finished their prayers then wrapped their arms around him. Told him all was forgiven. That they loved him. That Richard would want him to forgive himself rather than punish himself for an accident.

Their compassion was unbearable.

Garrett kept busy tending to their many guests who came with more food, running out with his father's giant umbrella to cover those who arrived in the steady rain that showed no sign of stopping. Did the same when anyone left. Made sure everyone had something to eat and drink. Stayed out of the living room. Fell apart when Anna arrived with her parents. And again when she, now his brother's widow, because of him, knelt in prayer at the place where the beginning of the end had happened.

At eight minutes to midnight, exhausted and seated in his car, Garrett turned his cell phone on. Ignored the numerous missed calls and text messages. He got the bottle of Scotch he'd hidden under his seat and opened it. Took several hard pulls before he tucked the bottle between his legs and turned the engine and windshield wipers on high. He drove. Sipped. Wept. Cursed himself.

He got onto the highway and drove past the exit that would take him to the hotel, drove past the next town, and the next.

Rain pounded the windshield. Loud, but not loud enough to drown out his thoughts. Came down so hard he couldn't see more than a few feet past his hood. At the last minute, he saw the sign for a rest stop a few miles ahead. He drove until he pulled off the highway and into a slot.

The wipers beat a message on the glass—you *killed* him, you *killed* him, *you killed him.*

Where's your arrogance now, you pathetic sonofabitch?

There weren't enough statements of condemnation he could tell himself. His actions had impacted so many lives, for so many years. He'd polluted the *pond* then caused ripples that would last decades.

A text message would reveal his plan too soon. A voice mail might be deleted without ever being listened to. He grabbed the small notebook and pen in the glove box, turned on the overhead light and wrote *Dear Chelsea, I—*

What the hell could he say to her? To anyone?

He put the notebook and pen back into the glove box. Took a hard swig of Scotch then put his car in gear.

Garrett pulled onto the mostly empty highway and pressed on the accelerator—70, 75, 80, 90, 110 miles per hour. He said the words *I'm sorry* aloud, kept repeating them, until he was shouting them.

He ignored the tears that blurred his vision, put the bottle to his lips and pressed his foot down as far as it would go. It was imperative he reach his destination as soon as possible.

CHAPTER 133

CHELSEA WOKE WITH a start and her heart drumming in her chest. She sat up in bed, checked the time—just after three in the morning. The doorbell rang, followed by several hard knocks.

She slipped on her robe. It had to be Garrett. Drunk, and in more pain than he could bear. How could she blame him for wanting to be with his wife and daughter at this time? She'd talk with him a while then put him to bed so he could sleep it off. She'd spend the night in the upstairs guest room. Or should she lie in the same bed and hold him while he cried? While they cried together.

Kimberlie would be relieved and comforted to see her father there in the morning. She'd attach herself to Garrett and not leave his side. It had confused and angered her not to be with her father and the family. She'd explained to Kimberlie that the family had to take care of arrangements and such; that the two of them would go to the house immediately after breakfast.

Chelsea reached Kimberlie's room and closed the door, not wanting her exposed to an inebriated, wrecked Garrett. She continued to the stairs then down, flicked on the light in the foyer and opened the door. She blinked, confused. "Can I help you, Officer?"

"Are you Mrs. Garrett Hall?"

"Yes." What had Garrett done now? "Please come in. It's so cold and wet out. Would you like a cup of coffee? It'll only take a few seconds to make."

"No, ma'am, but thank you. I'm sorry to bring bad news, Mrs. Hall. Your husband was in an accident."

Her hand went to her chest. "Oh, God. Is he okay? Which hospital was he taken to? I need to wake my daughter. We'll get dressed and down there as soon as we can. Where is he?"

"Maybe there's a place we can sit."

CHAPTER 134

CHELSEA REMAINED WHERE she was in the foyer. She bunched the lapels of her robe together, gripping the fabric closed at her throat, as though to shield herself. "How bad is it? Is he conscious?"

"I'm sorry, Mrs. Hall, your husband didn't make it. He was already gone when we found him."

"Oh God. Oh God." Chelsea reached for something—anything—to support her.

The officer took her by the arm and led her into the living room, easing her into the nearest chair. He took a seat on the sofa, a foot away from her. "Mrs. Hall, although we're certain of his identify from his license, we still—"

"Need someone to identify his … confirm it's him."

"Yes, ma'am. Are you able to do that now? Would you prefer to wait until seven or so?"

Chelsea shook her head. "No. I have to make sure. I have to see him." She looked up at the policeman. "How did it happen?"

"Car crash. Mrs. Hall, had anything happened recently that might have made Dr. Hall depressed?"

"Why would you ask that?"

"Anything at all you can tell us?"

"His brother died yesterday. He felt responsible." She added quickly, "Because he always felt responsible for his younger brother. But why are you asking?"

"We found a note in his car."

"A note to whom?"

"To you, ma'am."

"What did it say? Let me see it." She thrust out her hand.

"I don't have it with me, ma'am. He didn't actually finish the note. Just started with dear and your name, followed by *I*. That's all. There was also a bottle of Scotch in the car. We're pretty sure he'd been drinking, ma'am. Heavily. Did he usually drink a lot, or maybe was an alcoholic?"

"No. Don't say such things."

"I apologize, Mrs. Hall. But you see why I had to ask about his mental state."

"You're saying he killed himself. I can't believe that."

"I'm sorry, but that's what it looks like."

"I can't breathe. I can't—"

Tears streamed from Chelsea's eyes. She folded her body over, gulping for air to ease her lungs and tightening throat.

The officer leaped up. "Stay like that. Where's your kitchen?"

Chelsea pointed in the general direction. The officer returned a minute later with a glass of water and a roll of paper towels. He handed both items to her and waited for her to regain composure.

"Would you like me to drive you to the—to where he is, Mrs. Hall? Or is there someone you can call to drive you? This weather's nasty. I'd rather you not drive yourself."

"I need to get someone to come here and stay with my daughter— I don't want to wake her. I don't want her to go with me. I don't want her to see her father like ... not until I know ... I'll call her friend's mother. It shouldn't take long for Angela to get here. Then, if you don't mind, please take me to my husband."

Chelsea pushed herself up from the chair. She glanced around, as though unsure about how to walk, to move, to breathe.

There was only one thing about this that was a relief, if it could be called that: Garrett had died in a car crash. It would be hard enough to tell Kimberlie. It would be too brutal to tell her, or Garrett's family, that he had committed suicide. If she could manage to keep that from them. The two Hall brothers gone, in two days.

The house of cards they'd constructed out of their chaotic lives was collapsing.

CHAPTER 135

RAIN TURNED TO sleet. Tiny frozen pellets beat against the glass of the French doors. Chelsea checked the time again. Six thirty. She brewed her fifth cup of coffee since the policeman had brought her home at four fifteen. It was a lonely vigil, but she wanted Kimberlie to get as much sleep as she could. Before she learned her life had changed dramatically. That no chance remained for it to ever be the same again.

Angela had left at almost five that morning, promising to wait until noon to tell anyone other than her husband—and swearing him to secrecy—about Garrett's death. The last thing Chelsea wanted was for Susan to call or text Kimberlie, before she'd had a chance to talk to her. To break the news to her. To break her heart.

While there was time, while everyone remained uninformed—because she was determined to tell Kimberlie before any of their family or friends, there was one thing she had to do. She sent a text to Luke, telling him she needed him to call her immediately.

She answered her phone and squeezed her eyes closed. Before he could ask how she was, she said, "Garrett's dead. He killed himself last night. He got drunk and crashed his car. The police notified me just after three this morning. I went to the morgue to confirm it was him."

"I'm so sorry, love. What a horrible ordeal for you to go through. Who's with you? Who's looking after you?"

"I'm alone. For now. I'm keeping it quiet until I tell Kimberlie, which I'll do when she gets up."

"Let me come to your house—as a friend. There must be something I can do."

"I know you want to help, but your being here would do the opposite. After I tell Kimmie, I'll tell my and Garrett's family. Then I'll start to notify others. I'll have people here soon enough to help out. There's so much to take care of."

"When will I see you again?"

She cupped her forehead in her hand, swallowed hard. "You won't."

"Chelsea—"

"It has to be this way. What happened to Garrett is my fault. I caused all this grief."

"You're wrong about that, and you know it."

"I should have never … I should have tried harder to save our marriage instead of—"

"Getting involved with me."

"I'm sorry, Luke, but it's true. Garrett may still have been cheating on me, but he'd be alive. My daughter would still have her father."

"Chelsea, please don't do this. You know what we have. Don't let Garrett rob you of anymore happiness than he already has."

"I'm sorry. And I need to go. I hear Kimberlie moving around upstairs."

"Chelsea, I'm begging you."

"I can't. I wish you the very best, Luke, but this has to be over."

She ended the call as Kimberlie called for her. "I'm in the kitchen, Kimmie." She listened to her daughter's heavy footfalls on the stairs. Dread of the burden that was hers alone welled in her chest.

"Mom, why'd you let me sleep so long? You knew I wanted to get to Gram and Gramp's house early."

"Sit here by me, Kimmie."

Kimberlie yawned and shuffled to the chair Chelsea pulled out.

She took Kimberlie's hands in hers. "There's something I need to tell you."

CHAPTER 136

B RANDI SUSPENDED HER hand a foot above her plate then dropped her fork onto the ceramic disk. A clump of scrambled egg bounced from the plate to the table. Luke didn't react as she'd anticipated. "What's wrong with you?"

Luke kept his eyes down and continued to push the eggs around on his plate. "Nothing's wrong with me."

"I realize we haven't been getting along—we barely speak to each other these days. But you're acting like someone died."

Luke shook his head and tossed his fork to the table. "You're suddenly concerned about me?"

"More annoyed than anything."

"So, same old, same old."

"I don't have time for your moodiness. I need to get to the office." Brandi rinsed her dishes in the sink then arranged them in the dishwasher. She grabbed her keys and purse, and said, "You could make an effort, you know. That's always been your problem. You make only the effort you want to, not the one you need to."

"You don't want to be late."

"If you're not careful, Luke, you're going to find you're living alone."

"I'm already there."

Brandi stormed from the house, slamming the door behind her.

Luke stayed at the table, unable to muster motivation to move or do anything. His cell phone rang. He bounded to the desk in his office, praying it was Chelsea calling, praying she'd come to her senses. His shoulders sagged when he saw who it was. "Hello, James."

"Hey, dude. I need you to come in a few hours early today."

"I was going to call. I'm not coming in."

"Don't do this to me, Luke. I'm shorthanded."

"Something's happened."

"Tim okay? Brandi?"

"He's fine, she's fine. It's Chelsea."

"Aw crap. I told you she was bad news. You gotta end it now."

"She did that. This morning."

"Okay. It hurts. It sucks. But problem solved, and bigger problem avoided."

"Her husband offed himself last night."

James whistled. "That's some bad shit, man. Better you're out of it."

"I understand she's got to deal with all of that, but she's free now. Why can't she see that? It's a clear path for us to be together. It's what we said we wanted. What she said she …"

"You definitely need to avoid that situation."

"You don't understand. I've lost the love of my life."

"Luke, listen to my words: Love is what we make it. Brandi's pissed, but she hasn't left or kicked you out. That means there's still a chance with her. You never had a real chance with this Chelsea chick. Put this affair out of your mind and make it right with your wife."

"It wasn't right to begin with, as you pointed out a number of times."

"I've been known to be wrong. Not often, but it happens." James cut his laugh short when Luke didn't join him.

"I can't lose Chelsea."

"Toxic territory, my man. Leave it alone. Now why don't you come in. Nothing like hard work to take your mind off troubles."

"I can't."

"Keep it together, Luke. You may have lost her, but there's a lot more you could lose if you don't get your shit together."

"I'll see you tomorrow."

Every few minutes, Luke checked to see if he'd missed any calls or texts from Chelsea, knowing he hadn't.

This wasn't how it was supposed to be.

CHAPTER 137

THE FUNERAL HOME had worked fast to accommodate a family grieving the loss of two of its members a day apart. Chloe had been the go-between, begging Chelsea, when Chelsea had pleaded her case, to let Thomas and Theresa make the arrangements for their sons, adding that they all felt it was a good idea to keep Kimberlie out of it, at least until the private viewing for family. She'd resented the repeated request, but agreed. They were hurting. These were, after all, Theresa and Thomas' sons, their children, no matter their ages.

Chelsea wrapped an arm around Kimberlie's shoulders as they entered the brick and glass building. She suppressed her humiliation and guilt about not having been involved until now and told the receptionist who she was. "Has the family already gone in?"

"Yes, Mrs. Hall. We opened a partition to make one large viewing room so both of your loved ones could be in repose near each other."

"Thank you." Chelsea hugged her daughter to her. "Ready, Kimmie?"

Kimberly nodded and began to weep. "I'm scared, Mom."

"I know."

They stopped outside the entrance to the room, each in turn signing their name in the guest book before crossing the threshold. Floral arrangements already lined two long walls. Chelsea's stomach recoiled in response to the cloying scents permeating the space.

Thomas Hall stood stoop-shouldered at Richard's open casket, with an arm around Anna, who leaned into him, one hand stroking Richard's hands now positioned one over the other for eternity. Chloe clung to Theresa Hall at Garrett's closed casket. Chelsea and Kimberlie joined them.

Kimberlie touched Theresa's shoulder. "Gram?"

Theresa turned and clutched Kimberlie to her. "My precious girl. Your daddy's gone. My boys are gone." They hung onto each other as their tears flowed.

Chelsea stroked the framed photo of a smiling Garrett that rested atop the casket. "Be at peace now."

Theresa screeched, "Don't touch him. Don't you dare touch my boy."

Thomas rushed to his wife's side. "Not now, honey."

"Yes, now. Okay, you've seen him, Chelsea. You've seen what you caused. I've lost both of my sons because of you."

Chelsea's face drained of color. "Theresa, please don't do this."

"Garrett told us what you did. All the way back to—"

Paul and Janice Johnson walked up to them. Janice said, "What's going on here?"

Theresa turned to her, her expression livid. "Your tramp daughter did this. She's seen the results of her actions, now she needs to get the hell out of my sight."

Kimberlie glanced from Theresa to her mother and back. "Mom? Gram?"

Theresa pulled Kimberlie to her. "You're going to stay here with us, and with your father and uncle, but your mother is leaving."

Kimberlie's face grew even more pallid. "Mom, what's going on?"

Janice said, "Just a damn minute."

"No, Mom." Chelsea touched Janice's arm. "Theresa's within her rights. I may not have directly caused their deaths, but it's because of me that they're gone."

Janice slung her purse onto a chair. "Chelsea, I don't understand any of this."

"I know. I'll explain it to you and Dad later." She turned to Kimberlie. "Stay with the family today. One of them will bring you home tonight, or you can call and I'll pick you up."

Paul said, "We'll take Kimmie home. We planned to spend the night at your house, as it is."

All eyes focused on Chelsea. "I'm so very sorry. For all of us." She glanced toward Kimberlie then faced her mother-in-law. "Theresa, I beg you not to—"

"Get out. Now. I can't mourn my sons with you anywhere near me. Maybe the day will come when I'll pray for you. But right now, I don't know when my heart will be open enough to do that."

Chelsea kissed Kimberlie and her parents. She left the room, walked sobbing through the lobby. Ignored the receptionist's queries offered in kind tones, tones that sent her running from the building to her car.

She rested her head on the steering wheel, unable to move. Unable to catch her breath. Unable to stop the ache in her chest that threatened to overtake her.

CHAPTER 138

SUNLIGHT FADED THEN disappeared. Chelsea turned on the gas fireplace, now the only illumination in the living room, or house, for that matter. She returned to the same corner of the sofa, where she'd stayed motionless for hours.

The telephone had remained remarkably silent. Or perhaps it wasn't so remarkable. It was a given that people who went to the funeral home would ask where she was. What wasn't certain was what they were told about her absence, or who told them. If Theresa had her way in the state she was in, they'd know everything. Unless Thomas and Chloe were able to keep her contained. As for Anna and Kimberlie, it all depended on how much Theresa wanted them to know at such a painful time.

Time. It was only a matter of it before everyone knew what she'd done. It was only a matter of time before Kimberlie came home. And when that would be might depend on what she'd learned.

It was nearly ten o'clock when she heard the key in the front door lock. Chelsea turned on the lamp next to the sofa and went to the foyer. She switched on the light and opened the door.

A swollen-eyed Kimberlie dashed past her and up the stairs. Janice and Paul Johnson followed, each kissing Chelsea on the cheek. Paul put a small suitcase on the floor next to him and draped a suit bag over it.

Chelsea flinched when Kimberlie slammed her bedroom door. "How is she?"

"As you might guess," Janice said, "Theresa Hall couldn't keep her mouth shut."

"What you must both think of me."

"Whatever your father and I might think, I know you well enough to know it's minimized by what you think of yourself."

Chelsea nodded. "I'll go up and talk to her."

"Maybe you ought to wait until morning. She's upset and exhausted."

"Who isn't? I prepared the upstairs guest room for you, when you're ready for it."

Paul took Janice's hand. "I'm more than ready. What do you say, honey?"

"You go on. Chelsea may need help with Kimberlie."

Paul shook his head. "That's between mother and daughter. I'm sure Chelsea will call if she needs you." He hugged Chelsea to him. "Try to get some sleep, my girl."

He draped the suit bag over his right arm, grasped the suitcase handle, and then took Janice by the hand. The two trudged up the stairs.

Chelsea waited until the guest bedroom door closed behind her parents then started up, each step heavier than the one before it.

CHAPTER 139

CHELSEA RAPPED LIGHTLY on Kimberlie's door. No answer. She turned the knob, surprised the door was unlocked. "Kimmie?"

"Go away. And stay away."

"I can't do that." She closed the door behind her and sat on the bed next to Kimberlie, who moved to the other side. "How much did Gram tell you?"

"Enough to know I can't ever go out in public again."

"God. Did she tell everyone?"

"Just me and Anna. Well, and Grandma and Grandpa Johnson. But Penelope knows, since she's the one who told Dad. She'll tell everyone." Kimberlie pulled a pillow onto her raised knees and buried her face in it to muffle her sobs.

"You have nothing to be ashamed of, unlike me. All of this is my fault."

"Damn right."

"Language, Kimmie."

Kimberlie looked at Chelsea. "Seriously? After you acted like a— a—whore, you're going to call me on *that*?"

"I'm still your mother. I'm obligated to get you to behave properly."

"You mean, 'Do as I say, not as I do?'"

"I deserve that."

"Again—damn right."

"Will you ever be able to forgive me?"

"Don't count on it."

"I don't know how I'll live with what I've done, and without your father's forgiveness, much less without yours."

Chelsea faced the opposite direction. She slid from the bed to the floor and buried her face in her hands. There was no way to stop the sobs that came so hard they left her breathless. She stayed there, unable to move, until she felt a hand on her shoulder.

Kimberlie dropped down beside her. Chelsea looked into her daughter's eyes then tentatively opened her arms. They clung to each other in their shared misery.

CHAPTER 140

A T SEVEN THE next morning, Chelsea, still in her robe, started a pot of coffee, made toast, scrambled eggs, fried bacon, juiced oranges—anything to stay busy. Anything to do something that might make a difference. Or remind her that her purpose in life hadn't ceased altogether.

At 8:32, her parents finally opened their bedroom door. One of them knocked on Kimberlie's door, which opened soon after. The three of them came down the stairs together, dressed appropriately for the day's solemn events, one of them with eyes more swollen and red than the other two.

Her parents consumed coffee, Kimberlie toyed with a small glass of juice. Conversation was all but non-existent. Because three of them were going to greet visitors who wished to pay their respects. Three of them would share memories that made them laugh or weep, and say final goodbyes to loved ones, while the one who wasn't invited stayed away.

Chelsea kissed her parents and Kimberlie as they left at nine that morning to attend the services. They'd be gone all day, first to the church service and burial, and then to the Hall house afterwards, likely for hours into the night.

She stood in the doorway. Watched her father's car turn onto the street and disappear from sight. Went back to the kitchen, where she tossed the uneaten food into the garbage. Meandered from the front of the house to the back, up the stairs, into each room and out again, back down the stairs.

She couldn't stay home.

Alone.

Not again.

CHAPTER 141

"I DON'T have an appointment, but I have to see Dr. Moore. It's urgent."

"I'm sorry, Mrs. Hall. She's booked solid today."

"Please. I'll beg if I have to."

"Have a seat. As soon as I can interrupt her, I'll see if anything can be done."

Fifteen minutes to ten, a silver-haired man entered the lobby, checked in with the receptionist and took a seat. He gave Chelsea a brief glance then put his attention on a magazine taken from the stack on the small round table in the middle of the room.

At five minutes to ten, Dr. Moore's patient came through the door and left. The receptionist used the phone to speak in low tones to Dr. Moore, hung up the phone, told the man he could go in then turned to Chelsea. "Dr. Moore will see you during her lunch break. Come back a few minutes before noon."

"I'd rather stay here."

"That's three hours."

"Please."

The receptionist stared at her a moment then said, "Would you like something to drink?"

Chelsea declined. She rested her head against the wall and closed her eyes.

Several minutes later, the receptionist came through the door with a mug in her hand. "Chamomile tea. Drink it, Mrs. Hall. You look like you need it."

Chelsea took the mug and thanked her. The tea was cold and untouched when Dr. Moore called her in.

CHAPTER 142

"NOW YOU know everything. Every sordid, grotesque detail," Chelsea said. "I'm sorry I lied to you before. I can't afford to do that again. Not to you. Not to myself."

Dr. Moore studied Chelsea for a moment. "It took a great deal of courage to tell me all you did."

"That wasn't courage. It was desperation. I may have felt insecure before, but now …" She laughed without amusement. "Funny. I feel so removed from those earlier feelings. I thought they were so serious. So life-shattering."

"You're saying your perspective has shifted?"

"Shifted? It's been annihilated. Like my life. My husband is dead. His brother is dead. My daughter is trying, but what's been done will stick with her for who knows how long. Or how it will affect her and our relationship for the rest of her life. My parents are ashamed, though they try to hide it. My in-laws want nothing to do with me. My best friend, or so I thought, betrayed me and triggered these events. When details trickle or flood out—and they will, the list of people who detest me will expand exponentially. My life is over. I abandoned my right to it."

"What are you saying, Chelsea?"

"Nothing. I'm rambling. Forget it."

Dr. Moore shook her head. "When a patient makes such a statement, the last thing I'm supposed to do or will do is forget it. If you're thinking of doing anything to harm yourself, I—"

"I'm just talking off the top of my head."

"I have to be certain."

Chelsea walked to the window. "I've become certain of a number of things over the last couple of days. Certain Garrett and Richard would still be alive, except for me. Certain that I was so angry with Garrett I forgot how much I loved him. Certain that he meant it when he said I should die so he could be free of me. Certain that life sometimes has a particularly cruel sense of humor or justice. Rather, injustice."

"So often, people don't realize what being unfaithful can lead to. They don't grasp how weighted the burden of deception and lies can become."

"You tried to tell me, but—"

"But everything else you were feeling got in the way. Prevented my words from reaching you."

"You were like a gnat I needed to swat away, and did."

"There are some consequences of our actions we could never anticipate. As for others," Dr. Moore shrugged, "we're aware of what they may potentially be. But we can be stubborn when we feel we're in the right, or at least, when we feel wronged. We ignore the inevitable. That's one reason I wrote *The Anatomy of Cheating*. Did you ever finish reading it?"

"I was too busy ruining everyone's life, including mine."

"I hope you will. After my own trials and years of professional experience, where I've seen the damages infidelity can cause, my hope was to reach people and inspire them to think before acting. There are some terrible stories in there, including about how children are affected. The worst case was when one of my clients refused to hear anything I said. She murdered her husband's lover. Granted, some of us may toy briefly with the idea of killing our spouse or his or her lover in reaction to our pain, but as a rule, we keep it solely in the realm of imagination."

Chelsea turned and leaned against the wall. "I didn't kill Penelope, but I'm responsible for—"

"You're not responsible for these deaths. You were at fault in some of the circumstances that triggered them, but not *for* them."

"I don't know that I'll ever be able to believe that."

"It will be easier with time, as long as you don't tell yourself the wrong things day after day."

"How do I forget the last conversation I had with Garrett? How do I forget how much he detested me?"

"He was hurt. You understand how that feels as much as I do. Sometimes we say things when we're in pain that we'd never otherwise say. What also is hurting you now is that you never had a chance to make it right."

"Or to say goodbye. Isn't that what the wake and services are about—a chance to face the fact of a loss? I didn't have that chance. Not that I deserved it."

"Those rituals are for that purpose, but they're also a way to start the grieving process. You've already stepped onto that path. Now you just have to keep putting one foot in front of the other."

"Easy to say, but I'm terrified of where it might lead."

"Where it leads is up to you." Dr. Moore put her pen and tablet down. "I'm sorry, but we're out of time."

"Thanks for fitting me in."

"I'd like to see you three times a week for the next few months. Longer, if needed."

"I don't know."

"Chelsea, you came to see me today for a reason. What was it?"

"I felt like I was going to disintegrate. I felt alone—quarantined, is more like it—and that you might be the only person left who wouldn't judge me."

"Then, work with me. Let me help you."

Chelsea scooped her purse from the floor. "I'll set the appointments on my way out." She turned at the door. "I'm sorry I didn't listen to you before it was too late."

"That's a boat most of us have shared at one time or another. Try to get some rest this weekend. Promise me you'll make a genuine effort not to tell yourself the worst things you can think of. I'll see you on Monday."

Chelsea nodded and closed the door behind her. It wasn't that she felt better for having talked with Dr. Moore—she wasn't entitled to feel better. It was more about making a full, unfiltered admission of her sins to someone.

That effort went only so far. Everything felt far, and moving farther away with every heartbeat.

CHAPTER 143

LUKE POSITIONED THE bulky Sunday newspaper under his arm and took it, a mug of coffee, and his phone to the basement. Garrett Hall had been in the ground for nine days. Surely Chelsea would soon realize being alone wasn't in her best interest.

Who was he kidding? When she'd said it was over, she'd meant it. He understood she felt guilt-ridden, but he wasn't prepared to give up. He couldn't. Not after everything that had transpired.

He'd just started to scan the best-selling books list when someone knocked hard on the front door. He listened to Brandi's footsteps cross the room above him, heard the door open, heard muted voices, heard the front door close. Heard Brandi yell for him to get upstairs. Now.

He put the newspaper down, slipped his phone into his shirt pocket, and started up the stairs. Nearly to the top he said, "What is it? Who was at the door?" Brandi didn't answer. His annoyance grew. What was she going to chew him out about now?

Luke entered the room and stopped. "What's going on? Is it Tim? Has something happened to my son?"

Two policemen walked toward him. "Luke Thompson?"

"Is it my son?"

One of the officers pulled rubber gloves from his pocket and started to put them on. "Face the wall. Place your hands on the wall, above your head."

"What's this about? Get your hands off of me."

The officer doing the pat-down removed Luke's phone, wallet, and keys, dropping each into an evidence bag.

"Brandi? What's going on? Did you—" He turned his head to look at her. Brandi's terrified expression made it clear this wasn't her doing.

"Luke Thompson, you're under arrest for the murder of Garrett Hall."

"You're crazy."

"You have the right to remain silent."

"Get these cuffs off of me."

"Anything you say may be used against you in a court of law."

"I haven't done anything."

"You have the right to an attorney before and during questioning."

"There's nothing to question me about."

"If you cannot afford an attorney—"

"I'm warning you."

"… one will be appointed for you at public expense, before any questioning, if you wish."

"Brandi, do something, for God's sake."

"Mr. Thompson, knowing and understanding your rights as I have explained them to you, are you willing to answer questions without an attorney present?"

"I have nothing to say, other than I'm being set up. Someone's going to pay for this."

"All right, Mr. Thompson, let's go."

Each officer gripped one of his arms and started for the door. He avoided looking at Brandi as they passed her.

"Luke, what have you done?"

What could he tell her?

CHAPTER 144

H ANDCUFFED TO THE metal table in the interrogation room, Luke waited for whatever would come next. Police had taken his front and profile photo shots first, and then his fingerprints electronically, before securing him to the table.

He glanced up, again, at the video camera mounted to the ceiling in one corner of the small space, wondering if he was being watched. How long he'd been in there was unknown. It could have been a few hours or many. It felt like forever, an eternal nightmare he'd fallen into.

He faced the door when it opened and glared at the blond-haired man with the jacket missing from his suit, his shirtsleeves rolled up. The man didn't look at him, but instead, read something in the folder he carried.

The man plunked the folder onto the table and sat across from Luke. "Mr. Thompson, I'm Detective Maddox." He gave a too-often practiced few lines about the interview being video recorded.

"This is a farce," Luke said. "Someone's set me up."

"You understood your rights as they were read to you?"

"This is ridiculous."

"Do you understand your rights?"

"Yes."

Maddox leaned back in his chair. "No priors. Not even a parking or speeding ticket." Luke shrugged. "Says here you're an author."

"Right."

"How's that going?"

"I'm off to a slow start, but I'm determined to do well."

Maddox flipped to a printed page in the folder and ran a finger down a column of numbers. "Better than well, I'd say."

Luke leaned forward, straining to see what Maddox was looking at. "What's that?"

"Records of your sales for the last six months. You're right about a slow start, but then they took off like an F-16. Funny thing about that. Your wife had no idea you were doing so well."

"You talked to her?"

"Why didn't she know, Mr. Thompson?"

Luke looked away. "I wanted to surprise her."

"You did that. Yessir, she was truly surprised. Shocked, I'd say." He fixed his gaze on Luke. "How well do you know Garrett Hall?"

"I don't. Didn't."

"You're saying you never met him?"

"That's correct. Now, give me back my things and let me go."

"You said 'didn't.' So, you are aware he died recently."

Luke shrugged. "I read the paper."

"Based on the circumstances of Dr. Hall's death, we determined it was suicide."

"What does that have to do with me?"

"Fortunately—for us, that is—one of our officers who was at the scene has some automotive knowledge." Maddox leaned back and linked his hands behind his head. "Now, me? I wouldn't know brake fluid from antifreeze." He stared hard at Luke. "But he does. Forensics found a clean thin slice in the brake line. Said it would have taken hours to cause the brakes to not function. Just a steady *drip*, *drip*, *drip*. Until they failed."

"As you said, I'm an author. I don't know anything about cars except where to put the gas in."

"I always understood that authors do research for their books?"

"I don't write those kinds of books."

Maddox smiled and rested his elbows on the table. "That's true. I checked your work. You write about matters of the heart, including betrayal. Guess that's a popular topic, as well as a practice. You're packing in the good reviews. Building quite a fan base, from what I could tell. Especially for *A Dark Walk*. Intriguing title."

Luke shifted in his chair. "I've been fortunate."

"Maybe your fans will keep the faith.

"Now, Mr. Thompson, why don't you tell me when you and Mrs. Hall decided to take your own dark walk together?"

CHAPTER 145

L UKE LINKED HIS fingers and stared unseeing at them. His world had, in only a few seconds, narrowed to a pinpoint of light. Dizziness overtook him, he strained to get air into his lungs. "I need some water."

Maddox went to the door and called out the order. Moments later, a uniformed officer twisted the cap off of a plastic bottle and put it in front of Luke, who gulped half of the contents. He wiped his moist forehead on his shirtsleeve.

"Mr. Thompson, I know the affair between you and Mrs. Hall didn't start out that way."

"It was that damn Penelope Sanders who talked, wasn't it? Of course it was. She's had a hand in all of this."

Maddox added the name to his notes. "We'll be sure to talk to her."

"You mean—?"

"Never heard of her, but thanks for the tip. You see, Mr. Thompson, we're pretty thorough when we investigate a crime. For instance, I've seen Mrs. Hall's review of your book and the exchanges you had on Goodreads, which is where your relationship kicked into gear."

"You're lying. Trying to trick me. You need my password."

"Your wife provided it. I've spent the last hour or so with your phone, reading the text messages you and Mrs. Hall exchanged. Seems you became quite intimate."

"It was just texting. It was stupid, but that's all there was to it."

"This is a relatively small town, Thompson. It took a little legwork, but you and Mrs. Hall were identified as being together at," he read from a page, "a coffee shop, a seedy lounge, an even seedier motel, and a few other places. Turns out there's only one silver Bentley like hers in the area. Plus, a redhead always stands out."

"You did all that since I've been here?"

Maddox shook his head. "We've had a busy week tracking down all we did. Would've been easier if we'd had your phone from the start."

"All right. We had an affair. What does that have to do with anything?"

"Looks like Mrs. Hall considered it to be more than just an affair. So that leaves me wondering if she asked you to get rid of her husband so you two could build your own love nest."

Luke tried to stand but couldn't. "You leave her out of this. Neither of us had anything to do with his death."

"Maybe she didn't. Maybe." He pointed a finger at Luke. "But you did. You'd think anyone, especially in this day and age, would know not to leave fingerprints, like on the brake line and a few of those other engine bits he had to touch to get to it. Guess you thought if the crash was bad enough, no one would notice.

"But I'm curious about something. Did you know Dr. Hall had been drinking heavily or speeding? Did Mrs. Hall, perhaps, contact you about her husband's condition, tell you that circumstances were ideal to carry out your plan?" When Luke didn't answer, he said, "Maybe Mrs. Hall will fill in the gaps. Time to get her in here." He started to stand.

"Wait. Chelsea's innocent. She's been through enough. Leave her out of it. It was me. She knows nothing about what I did. Before I explain, does my wife know about Chelsea?"

Maddox returned to his chair. "Not yet. But it's just a matter of time." He picked up his pen and twirled it between his fingers. "Okay, I'm listening."

CHAPTER 146

"I DIDN'T do it," Luke said, "to get Hall out of the way for the reason you think. Chelsea and I had decided we were going to get our divorces and get married, after an appropriate amount of time, especially because we both have children. She'd already told Garrett she wanted a divorce. It was my turn." Luke focused his gaze on Maddox. "We're perfect for each other. We knew it from the start."

"Very touching."

Luke balled his hands into fists and said, "Hall cheated on her all the time, for years. He was an addict or something. He never treated her right. Berated how she looked until she believed him. Seems he had a type and she didn't fit it. Such a beautiful woman, inside and out. He dragged her down and wouldn't let her up."

"That's not a reason to kill him."

"No, it isn't. But fear for her safety was. He battered her. The first time I saw her injured, she tried to convince me it was an accident in the kitchen. A cabinet door. The second time, she told me the truth. He tried to rape her. She fought back. He didn't like it. When I saw her an hour after it happened, her lip was split and swollen. So was her face on that side, where he'd slugged her. She moved slow, so I know there were bruises on her body she didn't tell me about.

"During that fit of temper, he also destroyed a clock that cost around twenty grand. I moved it and all the broken pieces out of the foyer. She wasn't strong enough to do that."

"You went to their house?"

"We were supposed to meet. Chelsea didn't show. Didn't call or answer my calls or texts. I had to make sure she was okay. It was so unlike her, you see. So, I knew something had to be very wrong. As I just explained, I was right."

"How many times have you been to the Hall house?"

"Just the once."

"Mrs. Hall should have reported her husband's abuse. But that didn't give you the right to kill him."

"You say that because you don't know what I know. It's why I was terrified for her safety."

"Enlighten me."

CHAPTER 147

"GARRETT HALL killed his brother." Luke filled Maddox in on the details. "After Chelsea told me what happened, I tracked him the rest of the day. I figured he'd go to his parents' house. There were so many cars parked up and down the street, no one paid attention to mine. I waited and watched all day and into the night. Once it was dark enough and the visitors had cleared out, I took care of his brakes. You're right about the research. I did it on my phone while I waited.

"My original plan was to use my fists when he went to his car to leave—give him a taste of his own, you know? But that would have created more problems. He would have gone after Chelsea. The solution had to be permanent. I couldn't risk his losing his temper again and killing her, as well."

"So, he drove off to his death and you went home to get a good night's sleep after a job well done."

Luke shook his head. "I followed him, which was easy, because of the weather and how late it was. Until he decided to hit the gas. No way could my car keep up with his. That's when I realized messing with his brake line wouldn't have been necessary. Way he was driving, he was determined to kill himself."

Maddox put his pen down and stood. "We'll look into his brother's death."

"Why bother? They're both dead and buried."

"There's a matter of the family's complicity in covering it up. Too bad you were determined to get involved."

"For God's sake. Haven't they suffered enough?"

"Find yourself a good lawyer, Mr. Thompson. You'll need one. But I think you'd better get used to the idea that you're going away for a very long time. Murder gets life in Massachusetts. Don't worry, though. Lots of authors write their books in prison."

"The most I'm guilty of is assisted suicide."

"I doubt a jury will see it that way." Maddox opened the door and motioned to the officer who'd brought the water. He looked back at Luke. "Seems ironic, in a way, to say this about an author." He handed the folder to the officer. "Book him."

CHAPTER 148

C HELSEA DESCENDED THE stairs, started toward the front door and stopped. From recent experience, an unfamiliar car parked in the circular drive meant bad news. She considered ignoring whoever it was, but the person rang the doorbell again then knocked and kept knocking. She turned on the outside and foyer lights, smoothed her unkempt hair, pulled her robe closed at the neckline, and opened the door. "Can I help you?"

A badge and ID were held open at eye-level by a blond man in a gray suit. "Mrs. Hall, I'm Detective Maddox. From homicide. Sorry to call on you on a Sunday night. I'd like to come in and get a few questions answered."

Homicide. She glanced back at the landing to make certain Kimberlie hadn't gotten up in response to the racket. The bedroom door was closed, as it had been for the last four hours, since she'd brought a sandwich to her daughter. This *visit* had to be about Richard. The last thing she wanted was for Kimberlie to hear that her father had killed her uncle, even if unintentionally. There was nothing they could do to Garrett now.

"Come in, Detective. Would you like coffee, water, juice?"

"No thanks."

She gestured toward the living room. "Let's talk in here." Chelsea turned on a floor lamp, sat on the sofa and tucked her robe around her legs and feet. Maddox took the chair opposite her.

"How can I help you, Detective?"

Maddox pulled a small notebook and pen from his jacket pocket. He flipped the notebook open and said, "Your husband died recently." Chelsea bit her lower lip. Tears welled and spilled down her cheeks. "Sorry, Mrs. Hall. I imagine this must be hard for you."

"We were together nearly two decades. I'm finding it difficult to adjust to the reality. It's particularly challenging because of our daughter."

"How old?"

"Fifteen." Her smile was small and sad. "Kimberlie's intelligent, like her father. She's a straight-A student. Beautiful, but not full of herself. Precocious. Although, at the moment, all of that is dulled by her grief."

"Not easy. Where's your daughter now?"

"Upstairs. Likely going through the family photos again." She sighed. "I'm sorry, Detective, but as you might understand, I'm exhausted."

"You'd like me to get to the point."

"Please."

"Tell me about your affair with Luke Thompson."

CHAPTER 149

C HELSEA'S FACE DRAINED of the little color it had. She buried her face in trembling hands. After a few moments, she said, "How did you find out?"

"I'd like to hear what you have to say."

"I don't understand the relevance."

Maddox shrugged. "Maybe there is none. But when we find a loose thread, we follow it. Your husband's death has a loose thread."

"Again, I don't understand."

"I can tell you're shocked."

"I am. I thought this was about—"

Maddox cocked his head. "About what?"

"Never mind. I suppose there's no way to avoid this." She glanced at Maddox, who shook his head. "I'll start at the beginning." She told the truth, careful to omit certain details.

Maddox took notes as Chelsea spoke. He nodded a few times and prodded her to continue whenever her pauses lasted too long. Waited patiently for her to get control when she broke down more than once. "Anything else you'd like to add? Now's the time."

"There's nothing else."

"You're certain?"

"Quite."

Maddox chewed on the end of his pen as he studied her. "Your husband's death made it convenient for you and Mr. Thompson to be together, didn't it?"

"You must have missed when I said I ended it with Luke."

"I heard. You did that after your husband died."

"I was heading in that direction before the tragedy happened. Too much was being lost because of our involvement."

"Still, there's an element of convenience regarding the outcome."

"From your perspective, perhaps."

"How much life insurance did your husband have?"

"What?"

"Would you like me to repeat the question?"

"I can't believe you asked it."

"Still waiting for the answer."

Chelsea went to the fireplace, flipped the switch, and watched the flames flicker to life.

"Mrs. Hall?"

She turned around. "I don't actually know."

"You haven't made a claim yet?" He glanced around the room. "Granted, you've obviously got it good, but that's one of the first things most widows usually do as soon as the funeral's over. Some of them don't wait that long."

"I hadn't even thought about it."

"That's hard to believe. Nearly impossible, actually. Why don't you try the truth this time."

CHAPTER 150

C HELSEA GLARED AT Maddox. "Are you always this cynical? It must be a challenge for any normal person to carry on a conversation with you."

"An effect of the job and what and who I have to deal with. Especially when I'm trying to drag the truth out of someone."

"That is the truth. You don't know what we've been through. Garrett's brother had an accident and died the day before Garrett did. We were all very close to him. Then, this happened."

Maddox kept his eyes focused on her. "Another auto accident?"

Chelsea rubbed her arms as she spoke. "Richard fell and hit his head. He died not long after that. The next day, in fact, even though the doctor thought he'd be fine. He'd had a serious stroke in December. Maybe it weakened something. I don't know." She looked at Maddox, whose expression was quizzical as he watched her. "It was a double funeral. One was going to be painful enough."

"Still."

"Detective, I was the one who confirmed it was my husband. I had to see him in that condition. Do you have any idea what that's done to me?"

"I have a pretty good idea."

"I see him like that every time I close my eyes. Even when they're open. Maybe you can understand that everything about our lives has been turned inside out. We've had nothing but grief, with no reprieve, for nearly two weeks. And it isn't going to go away anytime soon."

"That's a tough situation to be in."

"I don't see a ring on your left hand. Are you married, Detective Maddox?"

"I was."

Chelsea nodded. "Divorced."

Maddox compressed his lips into a thin line. "Widowed."

"I'm sorry. Maybe you understand what it's like for us."

"I'd like to get back on topic."

"I have a question, Detective."

"If I can answer it."

"Why is homicide interested in my husband's accident? I'm sure you read the report and know what happened that night. In his grief over his brother, he mixed alcohol with speed and rain."

"Just crossing the T's and dotting the I's."

"I'm sorry, but your questions seem irregular. And insensitive."

"That's how it goes sometimes."

"Is there anything else?"

"That'll do it. For now." Maddox tucked his notebook and pen into his pocket and stood. "Just one thing, though. Stay in town. I may need to speak with you again."

"I don't understand any of this."

Maddox, keeping his face expressionless studied hers. "Maybe. Maybe not. I'm certain everything will be clear soon enough."

Chelsea walked ahead of him to the door. Maddox stepped across the threshold, reached into his jacket pocket and turned. "Almost forgot." He held out a plastic bag. "Your husband's keys, watch, wedding ring, phone, wallet, and money clip with six hundreds in it."

"I don't understand why we couldn't have these items sooner." Chelsea held her hand palm up.

Maddox placed the bag into her hand, all the while keeping his gazed fixed on her face. He opened his mouth to speak then changed his mind.

Once the door was closed, Chelsea pressed her forehead to it. She didn't believe his explanation for coming to her house, especially at this hour. Nor did his questions make sense. Garrett had been drinking and driving like a madman in heavy rain. He'd done it deliberately, had crashed his car on purpose as a way to escape everything and everyone. Including himself.

There was only one way the detective had known about Luke. Penelope had to have told him. Yet another trap set for her. But why?

She doubted Penelope informed him about her affair with Garrett. Or maybe she had. The woman was shameless. And bent on wreaking as much havoc in her life as she could, with no thought of how it would hurt Kimberlie. And why would she think of that? Penelope wasn't a mother. She was a feral cat, perpetually in heat, claws out.

Chamomile tea might calm her before climbing into bed for another mostly sleepless night. Or a glass of wine. Chelsea started toward the kitchen. She glanced toward Kimberlie's door. It was open.

Kimberlie, tears flowing, sat halfway down the stairs. "It was one thing to hear Gram say it. But to hear you talk about it …"

"Kimmie. I—"

"Daddy killed himself. Didn't he? Because of you. I didn't even get to tell him goodbye. I hate you!" Kimberlie ran to the landing, slamming the door once inside her room.

Chelsea started to follow then stopped. She lowered herself onto the third step, unable to move as despair overwhelmed her.

CHAPTER 151

"I'M LEAVING to go to Susan's house. Miss Angela's taking us to school." Kimberlie, dressed for school, stood in the doorway of Chelsea's bedroom.

"You didn't tell me you were going back today."

Kimberlie shrugged. "I don't want to stay here."

Chelsea sat up in bed. "I know. You have a lot of catching up to do. I'll drive you."

"I don't want anyone to see me with you." Kimberlie cupped her hand over Garrett's wristwatch.

"You found your dad's watch, I see. He'd like that you're wearing it."

"I took his wedding ring, too. You broke your vows, so no reason for you to keep it."

"Kimmie, please."

"I want to stay with Susan tonight."

After a pause, Chelsea said, "I'll pack some things for you and get them to her house."

"I already did that. My bag's by the front door." Kimberlie's cheeks flushed. "I may stay longer than one night. Miss Angela said it's okay."

Chelsea got up and started toward Kimberlie. "I can't stand for us to be like this. Not at such a time, when we're both hurting."

"Should've thought of that before you … I just came to tell you what I was doing so you didn't act stupid. You've already done enough of that." Kimberlie, head down, pivoted and walked away.

Chelsea stayed where she was, listened to the front door open and close. She ran to the hall window and watched Kimberlie walk away, until the hedge blocked her daughter from view.

She trudged down the stairs to the kitchen and started a cup of coffee brewing. Arms folded, she stared out the French doors as she waited. There was no urge to swim laps. There hadn't been for weeks. How odd it was to be in familiar surroundings, yet feel like a stranger in her own life.

Not a stranger—an outcast.

Her choices had contributed to this moment. But she hadn't gotten there by herself. She'd had help.

She went into Garrett's office, found the gun safe and opened it, surprised at how steady her hand was on the combination lock. Surprised again when she saw the Walther was missing. Only the Beretta Storm was there. Garrett had to have taken the other gun. They were the only two who knew the combination. When had he removed it, and why? Where was it now? She made a mental note to report to the police that the gun was missing. Then laughed at how ridiculous she was being, considering what she had planned.

The Beretta felt awkward in her hand. It had been ages since she'd practiced with Garrett at the gun range, and even then, she'd hated touching the pistols. She removed the clip—it was full. Gun in hand, she went upstairs to dress.

Penelope had wanted her life. And in the process, had done what she could to deconstruct it one person at a time; though, she obviously wasn't done yet.

Not if I have anything to do about it, *dear friend*.

CHAPTER 152

CHELSEA PLACED HER purse with the Beretta inside it on the seat next to her, started the engine, drove to the end of the driveway then turned left. It was a few minutes after eight. Penelope, unemployed and a late sleeper, would still be in bed.

If she didn't stop her, the woman would keep chiseling away at their lives until there was nothing left but dust. Kimberlie's rejection was the last straw. It was one thing for Penelope to go after her, another to adversely and repeatedly impact her daughter. If she had to go to prison or die in order to save Kimberlie from anymore pain caused by Penelope, so be it.

Kimberlie had made it plain—had stated it as a fact—that she hated her. Garrett's family hated her. It wouldn't be long until nearly everyone she knew felt the same way. She had news for all of them: she hated herself even more.

Penelope had danced. Now it was time to pay.

The car wasn't in the driveway. Still, Chelsea rang the doorbell and beat on the door. She turned and scanned the cars parked along the street. Penelope's wasn't there.

She got back in the Bentley and drove slowly around the blocks nearest the small rented house. The familiar car was nowhere to be seen. It was probably parked in some hotel or motel parking lot, while its owner slept off a raunchy night.

It was eight thirty-eight. Her appointment with Dr. Moore was at nine. If she wasn't going to be arrested for murder, she might as well keep her appointment.

CHAPTER 153

C HELSEA PLODDED INTO Dr. Moore's private office. Her purse *thunked* when it landed on the floor as she dropped into her usual place on the sofa.

"How are you, Chelsea?"

"Not good." She recounted the interview with Detective Maddox. "And there was Kimmie, having heard it all, or at least enough. I tried to protect her from the truth about Garrett's suicide. Of course she blames me. She's right to do so."

"We discussed how you're not at fault. Just a few days ago."

"It didn't take. How can it when my daughter wants nothing to do with me?"

"I think you should bring Kimberlie with you to your next appointment."

"She's in school. Decided to return today and didn't tell me."

"We can schedule it for late afternoon. It's important for Kimberlie to get the help she needs, and imperative we heal your relationship. You're the only parent she has now. I know it isn't easy, but you need to be strong for her. She needs to talk to me or to another therapist."

"I'll see what I can do." Chelsea turned her tear-filled eyes toward Dr. Moore. "She doesn't want anything to do with me. She's staying at a friend's house, starting this afternoon."

"All the more reason to get her in here."

"She may not talk with me in the room."

"Let's see how it goes. Then we'll schedule appointments for you both, individually." Dr. Moore extended her hand. "Now, why don't you let me have what's in your purse."

Chelsea's eyes widened, she leaned back. "What do you mean?"

"Hand it over very carefully, Chelsea. Guns make me nervous."

"How do you—"

"You're not the first patient to have one. Now, please."

Chelsea retrieved the gun from her bag and handed it to Dr. Moore, who deposited it in her middle desk drawer, which she locked. She returned to the sofa. "Why did you have it with you?"

"To put Penelope out of our misery."

"Was it your intention to scare her or to—?"

"Kill her. It seemed like the only way to get her to stop."

"What stopped you?"

"She wasn't home and I didn't know where to find her."

"After all Kimberlie's lost, you were going to cause her to lose you as well?"

"Maybe she'd be better off. She has my parents or Garrett's she could live with."

"It may not seem like it now, while the wounds are fresh, but she'll come around. She just needs help to deal with all she's feeling. But she'll need you again, and she'll want you there when she's ready."

"Do you really believe that? Because I don't."

"We three have a lot of work ahead of us. I'm not going to tell you it'll be easy, just worth it."

"What am I supposed to do about Penelope?"

"Nothing, and especially nothing violent. You and Kimberlie have been exposed to too much of that already. Avoid Penelope at all costs. If you think about it, there isn't much more she can do."

"I hope you're right. But I don't feel as confident about that as you seem to."

CHAPTER 154

CHELSEA FINISHED HER session with Dr. Moore and decided to follow the therapist's advice regarding closure; though, she doubted the effectiveness of what had been prescribed.

A quick stop was made at a florist shop before heading to the cemetery. She parked in front of the office and went inside. With great humiliation, she asked where Garrett Hall's grave was located. Map in hand, she got back into the car and drove to the proper section.

Wind whipped her hair across her face. Despite the blistering cold, she left her coat unbuttoned. What right did she have to concern herself with her own comfort?

She found the grave and stood at the foot of it. Read the headstone's engraved words—*Beloved son, brother, and father.* Not husband. Her presence in his life had been removed. His family's rejection of her forever etched in stone.

The full reality that Garrett was gone crashed down on her. The full reality that Garrett was buried in the family plot, where there was no room for her, registered. Chelsea crumpled to the ground, crushing some of the flowers in the lavish bouquet.

She had believed there were no tears left in her, but it seemed to take forever for the weeping to cease. She picked up the flowers and placed them at the headstone, and sat so that she could rest her face against it.

"Any apology I give you now is wasted breath. I feel beyond forgiveness, Garrett. Let's face it: You were a bastard for cheating on me the way you did, and with whom you did. And, the other matters, which I prefer not to mention, since I'm supposed to be making peace with our past. But my mistake—*mistakes*—were worse. Because of what they led to.

"Before, it was just the bed that was empty. Now it's everything. You might think it's silly, but I sleep with your pillow wrapped in my arms. I sprinkled some of your aftershave on it so it smells like you. Remember how we slept that way when we were first married? What happened to us, Garrett?

"Why is it that it's only after we lose someone that we grasp how much they meant to us? How can we be so unthinking and unfeeling toward one another, instead of choosing love? Why do we cause those we're closest to so much pain? Why do we choose pain over what we could have, if we just chose to do better? To be better?

"Kimmie wants nothing to do with me. She can hardly stand to look at me. I can't blame her. And if you didn't like my appearance before, you'd be appalled now. I don't remember the last time I showered or brushed my hair or put on makeup. What's the point?

"I never told you how many nights I got out of bed to watch you swim nude. Pride and fury got the best of me. If I could turn time back, I'd join you, naked, in the pool. That would have surprised the heck out of you, wouldn't it? I should have done that every night, no matter what you'd been doing before you came home. Until you started coming home after work to be with me. Instead, I gave you every reason to stay away.

"Now you're here, where I can only pretend that you can hear me, hear how sorry I am. How much I loved you and still do. How much I appreciate and thank you for all you did for us. To thank you for Kimmie. She's all I have left of you that matters. She's all I have left, period. But I'm afraid I'm losing her, as well.

"I'm going to go now, Garrett, but I'll be back." She stroked his name engraved in the marble.

Her gloveless hands were too numb from cold to hold the steering wheel. The temperature was dropping. Snowflakes drifted onto the windshield, staying where they fell. She turned the heater on high and warmed her hands in front of the vents. She'd go home, run a bath in the Jacuzzi, and soak until she warmed up. She'd wash and style her hair, put makeup on, be presentable when she went to Susan's house later in the afternoon to tell Kimmie about the counseling sessions. No reason to cause her daughter anymore shame by looking as bad as she had been.

It was eleven twenty-seven when she arrived home. She picked up the newspaper from the driveway, went inside and ordered twenty dollars' worth of Chinese soup.

It took less than fifteen minutes for the food to arrive. Chelsea ladled soup into a bowl, grabbed a spoon and went to the table. She unfolded the newspaper. The headline on the front page blared in large bold letters:

LOCAL AUTHOR, LUKE THOMPSON, ARRESTED. CONFESSED TO MURDER OF PROMINENT DOCTOR, GARRETT HALL.

By the time her screams ceased, Chelsea lay unmoving on the floor where she'd collapsed, as a new keening of grief uncoiled within her.

CHAPTER 155

D ETECTIVE MADDOX HAD said everything would become clear. But she'd never expected this. Chelsea read the brief article several times, still not wanting to believe the facts in print. Yet, there they were, for her and everyone who knew her to see.

According to the article, during the interrogation, Maddox had revealed irrefutable proof of Luke's guilt. Luke had then confessed.

Nothing about Garrett's death had been deliberate on his part or an accident. Yes, he was being reckless that night, but he might very well have come to his senses, slowed down, perhaps pulled over and slept it off.

She called Angela. "Did you see today's paper?"

"God, Chelsea. It's horrible."

"It's worse than that. This is going to destroy Kimberlie."

"Is there anything I can do?"

"Let her stay with you a while. Maybe a week, maybe two. I'll gather everything I think she'll need and get it to you before she gets in from school."

"Should I keep the news from Kimberlie?"

"Everyone else will know. It's possible that some classmate or teacher mentioned it already. My poor baby."

"There's one redeeming thing about this."

"Please tell me, because I can't see it."

"Kimberlie will know Garrett didn't kill himself."

"It wasn't for lack of trying. Not that knowing her father was murdered will be any easier, but I want her to believe he didn't even try to kill himself. It'll save her. But I don't think it will save us."

"Chelsea, I'm sure—"

"I need to make a call. Then I'll get Kimmie's things to you."

Dr. Moore was with a patient, the receptionist told her. Chelsea left a message that she'd resume her sessions the following week, at the earliest, and would figure something out later about Kimberlie's appointments.

"Mrs. Hall, what reason should I give Dr. Moore for this change of schedule?"

"Tell her to look at today's paper. She'll understand."

She, however, never would.

CHAPTER 156

LOCAL NEWS THE prior night had been excruciating to watch, and contributed to another sleepless night. Still, Chelsea had to know if anything else had been reported about Luke's arrest and Garrett's death, no matter how painful or humiliating.

Her biggest concern was Kimberlie. It was imperative to know anything reported about the case that her daughter might be made aware of. Not that there was much she could refute about anything factual that might be revealed. Besides, Kimmie had already overheard most of the truth from her own lips.

She started her morning coffee brewing then stepped outside to get the newspaper. Cameras clicked and flashed. Several reporters, some with assistants aiming video cameras at her, shouted questions from both ends of the circular driveway and along the front hedge that bordered the sidewalk.

Chelsea rushed back inside and pressed her back against the bolted door. Her landline phone rang, and kept ringing. Anyone important in her life would call on her cell phone. She put the newspaper on the kitchen table then went around the house unplugging phones from their jacks.

There had to be a way to get rid of the reporters. She took her coffee and phone to the table, looked up the phone number for the local precinct and keyed it in.

"Detective Maddox, please. This is Mrs. Garrett Hall." It took only seconds to be connected.

"Mrs. Hall. My apologies. The story leaked before I had a chance to tell you."

"There are a number of vultures with cameras at the end of my property. Is there anything you can do to get rid of them? I have my daughter to think about. At least do something to protect her."

"No guarantees, but maybe I can make a statement that'll get them off your back."

"What kind of statement?"

"For one, that you're innocent. That you had no knowledge of Thompson's plan and, therefore, no collusion."

"That's why you questioned me. Isn't it?"

"He said you didn't know anything about it. I had to be sure."

"And talking with me did that?"

"That and talking with others."

"What others?"

"Family. Friends. Your therapist."

"How did you know—?"

"I followed you. Just long enough to confirm what I needed to."

"I want to feel affronted by this intrusion into my privacy, but I gave up that right months ago."

"People slip, Mrs. Hall. The good ones learn from their mistakes, get back up, and keep going. I'm a pretty good judge of character, so feel confident you fit into that group."

Chelsea began to cry.

"Mrs. Hall? What's going on?"

"That was a considerate thing to say, Detective Maddox. That's all. I know you're busy. Anything you can do to get the reporters to leave me and my daughter alone will be appreciated."

"I can't make any promises, but I'll do what I can."

"That's all I ask."

Throughout the day, Chelsea peeked through the curtains, watched the number of reporters diminish until the last one left at almost three o'clock. Nothing about her was on the news at six or at ten. Kimberlie wouldn't have to be humiliated yet again by seeing the image of her disheveled mother in her robe looking stunned then terrified outside their home.

No reporters were outside the house the next morning. And there was only one small paragraph in the newspaper about Luke waiting in the county jail, without bail, for his arraignment.

The matter of Luke moved at speed, completed within a few weeks. Because of overwhelming evidence of his guilt that satisfied the grand jury. Because he'd confessed. Because Luke entered a plea of guilty at his arraignment. Because of this, no trial was needed, according to the reporters. Because of Luke, she wouldn't have to degrade herself further by giving her testimony on the witness stand.

At his arraignment, Luke was sentenced to life imprisonment at Sands Correctional Facility. In local news videos, he turned his face away from the cameras. His wife did the same, as did his son. His ex-wife posed and blathered at every opportunity about how he'd cheated on her, as well. There was one fleeting glimpse of Penelope, hiding her face with an over-large purse while rushing from her car to her house, to avoid reporters who shouted questions at her. One or more reporters had to have dug deep to learn about Penelope's involvement, or was the result of another leak, as her name had not previously been mentioned on TV or in the newspaper.

How long would Luke last in prison, Chelsea wondered, especially once Frederick Starks learned he was there. She shoved the thought to a deep recess in her mind, where facts too overwhelming to deal with get hidden in the shadows. Denial sometimes had to be used as a safety valve. She had issues closer to home to concern herself with.

CHAPTER 157

THE TEMPERATURE AT 8:46 a.m. was thirty-four degrees—Luke had asked. Sleet made the roads slick during the couple-hour ride that slowed to nearly four hours because of conditions. Despite protestations from other prisoners in the van taking them to Sands Correctional Facility, no heat came on in their secured section of the vehicle. Adding to the unpleasantness was the fact someone had left the roof vent open. He was certain it was a deliberate oversight.

The long underwear under the orange jumpsuit, both provided by the county jail, did nothing to block the cold. It was the same with the socks they'd given him, hardly thick enough to prevent the chill of the metal shackles around his ankles from seeping past the fabric. Or the steel cuffs chafing his wrists.

Once inside Sands, still shivering from the near-freezing ride amplified by fear, Luke stripped, took a supervised cold shower with harsh soap and a harsher brush, and then faced the humiliation of a body cavity search. Thankfully, at least one of the items the correctional officer loaded into his arms was a coat, too thin against frigid temperatures and wind, if he decided to go outside, whenever that was permitted, but better than nothing.

Dressed in one of three yellow scrub sets the guard handed to him, his arms loaded, he followed the CO through multiple floor-to-ceiling gray halls, closed off with electronic doors—so many doors. Other guards they passed memorized his face. Inmates studied him. He could feel their assessments, see their estimations of him forming in their eyes.

"Best not to stare at any of these guys," the guard said. "Some of them take that as a confrontation. Or an invitation."

"You could have mentioned that sooner."

The CO shrugged and kept walking, pointing out where the chow hall was located, the library, giving minimal information about prison routines like mealtimes and protocol in the chow hall. "That way takes you to the infirmary," the guard said.

"Thankfully, I'm healthy."

"That's not why some of the guys in here usually end up in there."

Luke needed no clarification. His body shivered harder.

The CO stopped at an open cell in Block D. "Here we are. Your new residence. Unless we move you."

"Move me to where?"

"Another cell."

"You mean, in case I have problems with my cellmate."

"Or just because."

"Because of what?"

The CO shrugged. "I do what I'm told. Don't need to know why for something like that. Top bunk's taken. Bottom one's yours. Get settled in. And don't cause any shit."

"I don't intend to."

"That's what they all say."

The guard left him standing in the otherwise unoccupied cell. Luke dropped his items onto the bed and sat next to them. The thin plastic-covered mattress flattened under his weight, allowing him to feel the hard surface that did a poor job of mimicking a bed.

The space comprised of concrete blocks painted dull gray was larger than the master bathroom in the house he'd shared with Brandi, but not by much. One window a few feet high and a few inches wide, centered in the back wall, provided minimal natural light.

There was a shelf on the wall at the foot of his bunk, and two small plastic desks and chairs squeezed into the space. One of them was being used by whomever occupied the upper bunk. He wanted to know who that person was—to get the introduction over with, but also dreaded it.

Luke groaned at the sight of the stainless steel toilet located at the entrance end of the cell. Noted the missing lid and seat as part of the design, as though lack of privacy wasn't punishment enough.

Atop the toilet, as an all-in-one fixture, rested a stainless sink that might hold a quart of water. The contraption had been bolted to the floor, as well as to the small wall portion where most of the electronic gate was housed when open. Above the sink, a tiny mirror, held in place by heavy screws in the concrete wall, hung at a slightly crooked angle. He backed up to the distance he'd have to go if he ever wanted to see his entire face at once again.

Luke shuddered and began to put his items away, clothing on the shelf, toiletries on the desk.

"They told me I'd get a new cellmate today."

Luke swiveled and took in the short, scrawny man with a blond crew cut and light brown eyes. Unsure about handshake protocol, he kept his hands at his side. "Luke Thompson."

"Chris Cage. People call me Chunky."

"No offense, but you're anything but that."

Cage chuckled. "I know, right? People here got a twisted sense of humor, if they got a sense of humor. Some of them got none. Best to learn who they are, fast, and avoid them, if they let you. What'd you do before you landed in this oasis?"

"Author. Novelist, to be specific. What about you?"

"Jockey." Cage sauntered to his chair and plopped into it. He propped his feet on Luke's bunk. "Who'd you kill?"

"What makes you think I killed anyone?"

"You're here, aren't you? Okay, I'll go first. I took out another jockey."

"Why?"

"He was screwing my wife. Your turn."

CHAPTER 158

LUKE STALLED GIVING an answer. He continued placing items on the desk, as though their exact position was paramount. If he lied and was found out, it could mean trouble. If he told the truth, he might get the same result. Cage was half his size. Unless the guy was some kind of Ninja or knifed him in his sleep, he could handle him. But Cage might have large friends. Better to get it over with. No harm in fudging the truth a bit, for safety's sake.

"I contributed to the death of the estranged husband of the woman who was the love of my life. He'd already hurt her and had killed his brother in a fit of rage. I wasn't going to wait for him to do that to her."

"You're a writer, all right. You used a lot of words slanted to your advantage. So, you're *that* guy."

Luke stopped what he was doing and faced Cage. "You know about me?"

"Some of us watch the news and read the papers. We like to be informed about who might be joining our exclusive club here."

"Should I expect trouble because of what I did?"

Cage grinned. "Not from me. I try to stay out of trouble, but I'm usually around when there's a show."

Luke leaned against the desk. "Should I expect a 'show'?"

"Guess we'll see."

"Who here would have a reason to confront me? I don't know anyone here."

"Ever heard of Frederick Starks?"

"The name is vaguely familiar."

"It may become more than familiar."

"Why? What reason could he have to be concerned with me?"

"Hall was his friend."

CHAPTER 159

LUKE STOOD AT the entrance to the cell and peered into the corridor. Several inmates watched him—one smirked at him. Others ignored him. "Is Starks in this Block?"

"Next one over. Block C."

"That's something, at least."

"Don't mean shit. And don't stand there looking around. Damn. You got a lot to learn. Guess it's up to me to teach you so you don't invite trouble into my cell."

"You said Starks and Hall were friends. Good friends or casual acquaintances?"

"Pretty good, from what I understand."

The loudspeaker crackled and an authoritative voice barked, "On the count."

Luke looked at Cage. "What does that mean?"

"As I said, you got a lot to learn, fish."

"Fish?"

"New inmate."

"Why fish?"

"'cause new guys are like fish in a barrel. Easy to get to. Follow me."

Luke bumped into Cage when he stopped just outside the cell.

Cage pointed. "Stand there. The count is when they count heads. Unless you got official permission to be somewhere else, you gotta be right here at eight, eleven, three, and six every day. They do a count at ten, once we're locked in for the night."

Luke glanced around, attempting not to return the stares aimed at him. Two correctional officers came around the corner. One held a clipboard, the other carried a small box. As the CO with the clipboard checked off names, the other CO handed out mail. Or didn't.

Cage received a letter. Grinning, he waved it at Luke. "From my wife."

"She stays in contact with you?"

"You bet. Says I proved my love for her."

"Do you get conjugal visits?"

"Nah. Only a few states allow them. This ain't one of them."

"Sorry."

"Yeah. I should have thought of that. What about the Hall widow? She going to visit and write to you?"

"I hope so."

"Long as her name's on the calls and visitors' lists, she can see you and you can call her. If she visits, and Starks is in the room, I'd pay money to see that.

"Good. Count's over. We got about a half hour before we amble our way toward the chow hall. You're in for a treat, there."

Luke started to follow Cage into the cell but stopped. "There's an inmate at the end of the corridor watching me."

"Does he look pissed?"

"No. Just intent."

"What's he look like?"

"Between my height and yours. More slender than not. Dark wavy hair worn short. Dragon tattoo that runs from his hand up under his shirtsleeve."

"*That* would be Starks."

CHAPTER 160

I F THREE WEEKS already seemed like three years, life was going to be unbearable. Luke had asked about the possibility of parole. Maybe in ten years, maybe in twenty, he'd been told, if his record at Sands was blemish-free.

It had taken only a day to discover money, even inside a maximum security prison, was a necessity. One trip to the chow hall had changed his mind about ever going there again, or at least, for as long as possible. Not only was the food inedible, the energy of the dining hall crackled with pent-up negativity.

Sandwiches sold through the commissary, with their thin slices of white bread and one paper-thin slice of ham or turkey, was what he chose to make do with. He'd never eaten so poorly in his life. Even in harder times, he could get a bag of beans to simmer and fresh fruit, even if bruised and dented, at a local open market.

Extra money or exchanges for packaged foods, toiletries, or other goods had kicked into gear soon after some of the inmates learned he was a writer. His skills were respected, as well as needed. The demand for assistance with letters to loved ones, enemies, lawyers, and more created a near-constant stream of inmates to his cell.

His goal of working on a novel crashed and burned when he found out Starks worked in the library, the only place where computers were available for inmates' usage. Until he learned which days Starks didn't have a shift. Even that was tricky, because the schedule could be inconsistent. So far, he'd managed to delay what he believed to be inevitable interaction.

Luke kept to himself as much as possible. He went to the commissary when it was necessary to restock food items, checking first to make sure Starks wasn't in there. The shower room was avoided altogether. It took only one time of getting as far as several feet past the entrance to hastily turn around. The two inmates engaged in a sexual act hadn't so much as flinched when he'd walked in. Not to mention the strong bleach odor, which Cage informed him was the only way to clean the blood off the tiles that resulted from fights and executions that sometimes occurred.

It was the same for the laundry room, which was no safer than any other enclosed space in the building. There was a prominence of brown splotches on two walls in a corner of the room that had yet to be painted over. He recognized dried blood when he saw it, but tamped down any curiosity about how it got there.

Body and clothes were washed at the tiny lavatory in his cell. Cage told him he'd have to get over himself eventually, or risk being marked as a wimp, and wimps didn't do well inside.

Luke lay on his bunk, thinking about what he would have been, should have been, doing instead on a typical Saturday morning. He'd usually be getting ready to go to his restaurant shift that would last into the evening, when diners were plenty and tips were generous.

Cage yawned and jumped down from the upper bunk. "I'm going to see what's happening in the yard. Maybe someone's got a basketball game going. What about you?"

"I'll stay here."

"You'll have to mix with the guys eventually."

"I mix with those who need my services. And so far, my self-imposed near-isolation is working for me."

"Only a matter of time before someone approaches you to see what you're made of. Or for sex."

"I'm not interested in either."

"Never said interest was a requirement." Cage stretched his arms over his head. "Later."

Luke sat up and positioned himself at the narrow window. His view included a guard tower and a twenty-foot concrete wall painted white, topped with numerous interwoven strands of three-foot-high steel razor wire.

He reached under his pillow for the letter he'd received from Tim that week. His first and only correspondence with anyone from the world he used to inhabit. The paper already showed wear from being read first thing every morning, multiple times while in his cell, and last thing at night.

The knot in his throat returned as he read his son's words—*How could you do this to me, Why'd you leave me alone with Mom.* And, *Miss you, Dad.* He'd tried calling Tim a few times, but Tina prevented him from talking to his son. She refused the collect calls, whether they came to her cell phone or the landline in her apartment. The woman's cruelty was stunning, but thankfully, could last only until Tim was old enough to move out.

He went to his desk, took a sheet of paper from his small stack and began to write. The brief letter went into an envelope, which he sealed. He'd just added Tim's name to the front when a nightstick struck the cell door.

"Thompson."

Luke looked toward the entrance. "Yes, Officer?"

"Visitor. Get your shoes on and get going."

"Who is it?"

"Do you care?"

"I might."

"That makes one of us." The guard turned to leave.

"Wait." Luke slid his feet into the lace-less tennis shoes and grabbed the envelope from his desk. "Where do I go?"

"You go with me."

Luke wanted to scream at the CO's unhurried pace. He was desperate to know who'd made the trip to see him.

After what seemed an hour of twists and turns and off-handed comments to inmates and other COs, the guard stopped at the entrance to the visitors' room. "No physical contact. Behave yourself."

"Of course." Luke stepped into the room and scanned the faces of those seated in beige vinyl chairs positioned around beige vinyl tables. He found his guest, next to the wall at the right, waving and trying to look unaffected by the surroundings and the people.

He wound his way through the tables, his smile broad. "James."

CHAPTER 161

LUKE EXTENDED HIS hand then drew it back. "I guess handshaking is considered physical contact."

James nodded. "I got the drill as I was being patted down after emptying my pockets and being scanned."

"Sorry you had to go through that. But I'm glad to see you. More than you know."

"I'd have been here sooner, but the vetting process took awhile. Good thing I've kept my record clean. Shit. Sorry, dude."

"It's okay. How are things at the restaurant?"

James shook his head. "I'm embarrassed to tell you."

"That bad?"

"The opposite. People wait hours for a table. We had to start making reservations all the time. We're booked solid for a couple months. Almost no one cancels. It's the sensationalism. You know?"

"Because of me."

"Your regulars aren't happy you're gone, but they show up to brag about how they knew you when."

"If you're bringing in more money, I can live with that."

"I warned the wait staff not to get used to it. The novelty will wear off, and it'll be back to business as usual." James glanced around. "You doing okay in here?"

"I'm coping." They sat in silence for a few moments. Luke pulled the envelope from his shirt pocket. "Do me a favor. Somehow get this to Tim. Tina's preventing me from speaking with him, so I'm not certain she'd give him any letters from me."

Luke tapped the envelope. "I told him I'll mail my letters to him in care of you, at your home address. I hope that's okay."

"I'll see that he gets them, whatever it takes. I'll keep an eye on the little dude."

Tears welled in Luke's eyes. He looked away, cleared his throat and said, "Knowing he can rely on you will make my time here easier."

"I'll make sure he knows he can contact me anytime, if there's anything I can do for him. Or if he wants to talk or get away from Tina for a while."

Luke pressed his fingers against his eyelids. "Talk about irony. I was hard on Tim because I was afraid he'd end up in prison." He dropped his hands to his lap. "I made the biggest mistake of my life when I decided to end Garrett Hall."

"That was the second biggest mistake. The first was when you got involved with his wife."

Luke shook his head. "I'll never agree with that. You'll never understand what we had, what we were meant to have together."

"You got involved in a cluster-fuck, dude. I know you don't like hearing that, but it's a fact."

"When I'm not thinking about Tim, I'm thinking about Chelsea. Missing them is an ache so deep, I can't reach it. The void inside me expands every day. I'm afraid that one day I'm going to disappear into that emptiness."

"Man, I tried to tell you that was a pit waiting to swallow you. And it did."

"It isn't her fault. It's all on me."

"I know you want to believe that. Maybe I'll let you, if it does something for you. But you have got to get over her. You don't have a choice."

A skirmish erupted on the other side of the room. Guards rushed to pull the inmates apart.

James, motionless, watched with wide eyes. "That shit happens often?"

"I don't know. You're my first visitor, and I stay as much to myself as possible."

"I hear that."

"My cellmate says my isolation has a shelf life." Luke faced James. "The only time I'm not terrified is when I'm asleep."

"Understandable. But, you're a big dude. Bigger than or big as some of these guys or the ones I saw on my way into this room."

"Size counts for only so much here. I'm not going to repeat the stories I've heard."

"Don't. It'll shrivel my *boys*. Still, you won't bother anyone. No reason for any of them to bother you."

"It doesn't work that way inside, from what I'm told." Luke leaned forward and lowered his voice. "I said I'm terrified. It's more than that. I discovered on my first day that Frederick Starks is here."

"That supposed to mean something to me?"

"He and Hall were friends. As in close friends."

"Shit."

"I don't know that I'll be given the chance to serve my life sentence. Every morning I get out of bed, I don't know that I'll be given the chance to live through the day."

James rubbed the back of his neck. "I don't know what to say."

"Give Tim my letter. I need him to know how sorry I am, how sorry I am to have brought shame to our family. He'll read it, but tell it to him from me. It may make a difference if you say you saw me."

James shook his head. "I'll tell him. But, Luke, you gotta get some protection in here."

"How exactly do I do that?"

"Hell if I know. But you gotta hang in there, man. If the fear keeps you sharp, that's one thing. If it keeps you from being able to act, if you need to, that's no good."

"Talk about something else. Anything that has nothing to do with this place or my life before I came here."

CHAPTER 162

THE ANNOUNCEMENT OF lights-out blared over the intercom. Luke climbed into his bunk. He'd hated for the visit to end, but James had to get to the restaurant before three o'clock, and needed time to make the two-hour drive, allowing for traffic. How long would James make the effort to see him? Maybe his visits had a shelf life, as well. He wasn't obligated to alter his life to accommodate a friend.

At least he knew Tim would have James looking out for him. Tim would have someone to talk with about his father, someone who knew his father well. At some point, maybe James would bring Tim to see him. If Tim wanted to do that. If Starks or some other inmate allowed him to continue to breathe that long. And if Tina allowed it. Or didn't know about it.

Cage snorted and snored from the overhead bunk. Luke scooted up to the window to peer out. The stars were in the sky, but he couldn't see them. Outdoor lights obliterated them from view. He might never see stars again, or the moon, unless it was out during the day and in a position in the sky where he could see it, if he ever went into the yard. One day he'd have to be courageous enough to go outside, even if it resulted in him taking his last breath. He craved the warmth of the sun on his skin. And air that smelled of something other than real and false bravado, desperation, and sorrow.

Cage moaned in his sleep. Although the sound was certainly different, it triggered his memory. Chelsea—moaning as his tongue traced various parts of her body. Moaning every time he slid into her, and with every measured or deep thrust. Moaning as he lathered her body in their shared showers, making sure every tender part of her received his tantalizing touch. Teasing her with his fingers and mouth.

The expression on her face and how she cried out when she climaxed. He'd made certain they never went their separate ways without her having that experience more than once.

His erection throbbed with an unrelenting ache. He didn't dare do what would relieve it. There was no relief for his longing for her. He'd have to quell such thoughts if he was going to survive. But those thoughts kept him going, even though they tortured him.

He slammed his fist into the wall. Love had cost him repeatedly in his life. He'd been right: Love came with too high a price to pay.

Unless Chelsea chose to prove him wrong.

CHAPTER 163

THANK GOODNESS, Chelsea thought, for Angela—a sympathetic and loyal friend, as well as a mother who understood the protective instinct. Kimberlie was welcome to stay at their house as long as necessary. There had been no argument from Angela's husband. A compassionate father, no persuasion was required for him to agree to the arrangement, calling Kimberlie his other daughter, as both of them had, since the two girls had become nearly inseparable friends at the age of four. Neither would they accept any money to go toward the extra expense of an addition, albeit temporary, to their family.

At least, she hoped and prayed it was temporary.

It had been almost a month now. As wrenching as the separation was, she respected her daughter's preference to stay away, to not spend time with her. Eventually, that would have to change. It had to.

Considering the fact that her affair with Luke had been included in the paper and on the news, though, the coverage was finally dwindling, it was better if her daughter stayed with them. At least for now. Kimmie needed someone to vent to about this hideous mess, needed to be as removed as possible from it. Needed motherly attention, even if it was someone else's mother providing it.

She, however, had heard nothing from anyone other than her parents and Angela. Not so much as a scathing remark from Garrett's family. Nothing from people Garrett had worked with at the hospital or his practice. At least she knew the families were in touch with Kimberlie. Her mother had confirmed this.

Just after two in the afternoon, the mail slot opened. A number of envelopes hit the floor. Chelsea got up from the living room sofa—the cushion now permanently dented from the hours she spent there—and picked up the mail. She took the envelopes into the kitchen, dropped them onto the table, and fixed a cup of tea.

Seated at the table, she blew on the steaming liquid, took a sip, and opened the first envelope.

It was from the mortgage company. The request for payment was stamped *Past Due* in bright red ink. So was the utility bill. The phone bill. The cable bill. The monthly payment request for the Bentley. The credit card statement with new charges of over ten thousand dollars.

What was going on?

CHAPTER 164

I T TOOK SEVERAL minutes of digging for Chelsea to find Garrett's checkbook and register. He'd been old-fashioned about two things: Handling all the financial matters in their marriage and paying by check, debit, or credit card, the latter which he paid in full each month. He'd also been meticulous about keeping paid invoices in the oak filing cabinet tucked into a corner of the room used as an office.

She compared what was in the files to the check register and unpaid bills—nothing had been paid since two weeks before she'd kicked him out. She gathered receipts for her recent purchases and cash withdrawals, and the last three bank statements, two of which were unopened on the desk. She vaguely remembered putting them there with the other mail she'd not felt up to dealing with. Listed among the many amounts subtracted on the statements, were weekly cash withdrawals by Garrett, of fifteen hundred dollars. It took too much out of her to reconcile what was in their joint account.

A call to the bank, and proving who she was, resulted in learning there was only a little over two thousand dollars in the account. No deposits had been made for almost two months. There should have been three or four substantial deposits from his hospital salary and a salary draw from his practice. The only person she knew well enough from the hospital was Aaron Logan. She found his cell phone number in the Rolodex on Garrett's desk.

"Dr. Logan, this is Chelsea Hall."

"My dear, I've been meaning to find out how you're doing and express my sympathies, but it seemed rather awkward. I'm sure you understand. So sorry about Garrett. Such a tragic loss."

"Thank you. I'm sorry to bother you, and I know you're retired, but—"

"I came out of retirement temporarily when Garrett was suspended. I'd hoped he'd be reinstated at the end of the two-month probationary period. It's tedious finding a qualified replacement."

"He was suspended?"

"Oh dear. I thought you knew."

"When?"

"Several weeks before his untimely demise. I did speak with him about pulling himself together, getting off the alcohol. Such a waste of talent."

"Dr. Logan, the last thing I want to do is sound trite, but it seems the last several pay deposits he should have received didn't get into the bank. It's set up for automatic deposit, so—"

"They wouldn't have gone in."

"What do you mean?"

"Garrett was suspended without pay. This really is a kerfuffle."

"I see. I apologize for bothering you."

Chelsea ended the call. She dropped her head into her hands. Everything about her life was spinning out of control.

CHAPTER 165

D ETECTIVE MADDOX HAD asked about Garrett's life insurance. She'd forgotten about it, again. That money would save her. She'd call each company owed and explain the situation. As long as the insurance company paid quickly, she and Kimberlie would be okay.

She found the policy, exhaled in relief at the amount, and dialed the number on the cover letter. The agent listed on the letter, whose office was in Manhattan, picked up his phone after two rings. She told him about Garrett's death, lying when she claimed it was by auto accident. Thanked him for his profuse condolences. Gave him the policy number. Waited while he looked it up.

"I'm sorry, Mrs. Hall, but Dr. Hall sold his policy several months ago."

"Sold it? What does that mean?"

"It means there's nothing to pay out."

"Why would he do such a thing?"

"According to my notes, he needed the money and that as soon as he got things settled, he'd purchase a new policy."

"How much did he receive?"

"Seventy-five thousand dollars."

"It was for two million. Why so little?"

"The policy was a relatively new one. The buyer paid Dr. Hall what he'd paid into it."

"What am I going to do?"

"I'm very sorry, Mrs. Hall. If we can assist you with any other matter, please call."

Chelsea carefully began the tedious process of going back chronologically through the check register, line by line. Why hadn't she asked the agent for the specific date?

She came across a transfer of eight thousand dollars to Chloe, made in autumn of the prior year. She continued to trail her finger through the register, back to the prior January, long past the several months the agent had mentioned. The insurance deposit wasn't listed, only prior salary and draws were. What had he done with the money?

She called the office manager at Garrett's practice.

"Yes," he said. "Seventy-five thousand went into our account fall of last year, to pay toward the salary and benefits for a new doctor, a down payment on a new piece of equipment, and marketing. Business wasn't coming in the way we needed it to, to keep up with everything, so we had to stimulate interest from potential and existing clients."

"I didn't realize you were having difficulties."

"I'm sorry to say it, but as bad as it was, it got worse fast as a result of Garrett's absence. He basically stopped coming in. We would have managed better had there been preparation, but his disappearance was abrupt."

"But as owner, he still received his draw, right?"

"He stopped taking it, since, as he told me, his hospital pay was enough. Then he stopped all contact with us. Told us to handle it and leave him alone. We didn't understand what his reason was, but we had to carry on. It's our livelihood, you know."

"Is there any chance you're doing well enough now that I can get what he usually drew? Or, perhaps, an advance?"

"The most we could spare is a couple thousand dollars, if you really need it more than we do. I could ask the doctors to hold off on depositing their checks for a few weeks, until the funds are replaced."

"No. Don't worry about it. I hope business picks up soon."

"Improvement's been slight, but we're optimistic." The manager paused then said, "Mrs. Hall, now that you've called, what are you going to do about the practice?"

"I suppose that is my decision. Please keep it going, for your sakes, and mine. I'll give more thought to this when my mind is clearer."

Chelsea stayed motionless at the desk long after the light outside diminished and disappeared.

CHAPTER 166

T HE FIRST THINGS Chelsea sold or pawned were the fur coats, followed by the most expensive pieces of jewelry Garrett had given her, with the exception of her wedding rings. Those would be saved for Kimberlie.

It was easier than expected to let the items go—they'd been given to her out of Garrett's guilt rather than love. It was harder to learn that the price paid for such items was so much more than what you could get for them when you were desperate for cash.

What she received helped to pay for the more minor household expenses, as well as for her and Kimberlie's separate sessions with Dr. Moore three times a week. She would have begged on the street for the money to pay for them. Not a lot was needed for groceries, as her appetite was all but gone. Coffee, tea, juice, and soup didn't add up to much at the store.

Her car was next. But that was a trade-in for a compact car from the dealership's used collection and forgiveness of the balance owed on the Bentley.

She'd also had to face reality about keeping the house. The mortgage payments were too steep. Despite her tearful pleading, the bank refused to wait for the house to sell; foreclosure was their only offer. They gave her a month to move.

After an excruciating, tear-filled conversation with Kimberlie, Chelsea began the arduous process of setting aside what she'd keep and what she'd sell or donate.

Her parents ignored her refusal of their help to sort through furniture, furnishings, and personal items.

"I should sell it all. I need the money," Chelsea told them.

"Nonsense," Janice said. "You'll get back on your feet one day, and you'll need some of these things to get started. Better that than having to start from scratch. You have to think of the future."

"What future?"

Paul put an arm around Chelsea's shoulders. "None of that. You listen to your mother. Figure out what you'll need at our house and decide what you're going to keep. We'll put the rest in storage."

Chelsea shook her head. "I can't take on another bill."

"We'll handle that, for as long as necessary." He turned Chelsea to face him. "One day you'll want to have some things from your life with Garrett. At some point in time, the memories won't be as wrenching. You also want to keep some of it for Kimberlie's sake."

"Of course. I wasn't thinking."

Janice said, "How are your therapy sessions going?"

Chelsea shrugged. "I suppose they're helping. Dr. Moore can't tell me how Kimmie's are going, and Kimmie won't." She looked at her mother. "Does she tell you?"

"Not yet. I hope she will. But you do feel like yours are working?"

"Yes, but I think it helps more when I talk to Garrett."

Janice's gaze met Paul's. "What do you mean?"

"After every session, rain or shine, I visit his grave." She shook her head. "It's a shame that's it's easier now to talk to him than when he was alive."

"I don't think that's healthy."

"Dr. Moore suggested it initially, for closure, and approves of my continuing to go there. Even if she didn't, I'd still go."

Janice patted Chelsea's arm. "Whatever it takes, I suppose. Well, if we want to make headway, we'd better get back to work." She and Paul resumed wrapping and packing anything marked with a yellow sticker.

She knew her parents meant well. But they didn't understand. How could they? Even if they'd had their issues over the years, they had each other.

The only thing she had to look forward to were weekends, once she moved in with her parents, that is, when Kimberlie would come to stay with them. They'd agreed to that arrangement, at least until school was out for the summer. Kimberlie still preferred to have nothing to do with her, and limited her responses to yeses and noes, as much as possible, during the infrequent times they spoke. That first weekend would be uncomfortable for all of them, and she knew her parents would feign a level of optimism that would make her want to scream.

However Kimmie treated her, she was only getting what she deserved.

CHAPTER 167

C HELSEA MOVED FROM room to room in the emptied house, checking closets and built-in drawers and cabinets to make sure nothing would be left behind, made sure windows and doors were locked. She was alone yet not alone: years of memories accompanied her.

In Kimberlie's en suite bathroom, she heard giggles of delight echo from her daughter's first bubble bath when she was two, saw an album of images flash in her mind of the different décor changes as Kimmie grew from a toddler, when they'd moved in, to now.

Angela and Susan had helped her daughter decide what to keep and what to discard. Kimmie had insisted Chelsea be anywhere but there while this task was accomplished. She'd relented, understanding what it took, as well as took from a person, to disassemble one's life.

Her final check of the master bedroom was a different matter. More tears had been shed in that one room than any other in the house. Now, all physical traces of her and Garrett's presence were gone. It reminded her of grammar school days when she'd erase what she'd written on a page, only to still see the ghost lines reminding her of what she'd decided to change. Pale reminders of what she hadn't considered good enough.

Chelsea ran her hand along the oak railing as she walked slowly, step by step, down the stairs; memories flooded her mind. Each cabinet and drawer in the kitchen was opened and closed yet again. She checked the lock on the French doors then stood looking out. The bank would have to arrange for someone to take down the tent over the pool as soon as weather allowed. It was a relief of sorts that the pool remained covered, as though it obscured her vision of another lifetime that was best forgotten.

How easy it was to want the impossible.

Her cell phone rang. These days, only her parents and Angela dialed her number. Without checking who the caller was, she answered. The operator had to ask twice if she would accept a collect call from Luke Thompson. He hadn't believed her before that it was over. This time she'd make it plain.

"What do you want, Luke?"

"It's so good to hear your voice. I've wanted to call but was afraid to. How are you?"

"What do you want?"

"A chance to explain."

"I don't want to hear it. There's nothing you can say that can make up for what you did."

"I'm begging you—please forgive me." When she didn't respond, he asked, "Are you taking care of yourself?"

Chelsea's laugh was false. "Seems local authors were meant to play a role in my life. You. Dr. Moore."

"Doctor? Are you ill?"

"She's a therapist. Mine and Kimberlie's. Dr. Moore thinks she can help us. My daughter wants nothing to do with me, because of what happened to her father. Because of us. Because of me she's lost her father and now her home."

"What about your house?"

"No life insurance. No money in the account and none coming in. I've lost everything."

"God. I had no idea he wouldn't … I never meant for this to happen. For you to be in this situation. This is my fault. But please understand, Chelsea. I did what I did because I love you and was afraid for you. I was wrong, but that's why—"

"Never contact me again."

Chelsea turned her phone off. And wished she could do the same with her thoughts. She finished the walk-through, closed and locked the front door, and dropped her key through the mail slot as the bank had instructed. Only they knew why that last insult was required. She was certain the locks would be changed by the end of the day.

En route to her parents' house, she made a U-turn. Dr. Moore's warning about avoiding Penelope had to be ignored. It would be the last time she ever drove on that street, but she needed to do it. What she didn't know was why. It wasn't that she wanted to say anything to Penelope. Words were wasted on a woman like her.

Chelsea turned onto the street and slowed her car. There was a For Rent sign in the front yard and an overflowing trash receptacle at the curb. Penelope's next door neighbor was outside. She double parked and got out.

"Mr. Green, you may not remember me."

"I may be old, but I'm not addled."

"Of course not." She nodded toward Penelope's house. "She's moving?"

"Moved. A week ago. Packed a U-haul and took off. Said she got a job offer in New York City. Must have had to start right away. She packed all night. Kept me awake. If I hadn't gotten up to see what the racket was about, she probably wouldn't have even told me she was going. Left most of her furniture. More like getting the heck outta Dodge, if you ask me. Didn't leave a forwarding address, if you're looking for one."

"That's not a problem." Chelsea shook his hand. "I need to get going. Thanks for the information."

She got into her car and started toward the home where she'd grown up. As to why Penelope chose New York City, if that was the truth, her guess was that there were lots of wealthy married or divorced men for Penelope to suck dry—literally and financially. The last thing she could imagine her former friend doing was getting an actual job again. And unless Penelope intended to continue her torment from a distance, perhaps the campaign against her was finally over.

Not that there was anything left that could be taken from her.

CHAPTER 168

HER PARENTS MEANT well. Chelsea understood that. They knew how difficult it would be for her to have to live with them, as well as how tension-filled it would be for Kimberlie's first weekend visit at their house, since losing her own. Rather than deal with the anticipated silence between mother and daughter, and as a way to show her that not everyone was ready to reject her, they decided a rooftop party at their ranch house was just the thing.

She'd tried to dissuade them then gave in when they said it would take the pressure off Kimberlie. Besides, they'd said, the weather would be pleasant enough, especially with the number of chimeneas they'd have going.

Guests comprised of the Johnsons' closest friends greeted her then fell into awkward silence. Chelsea directed them to the bar and buffet, each of them relieved not to have to search for something to say beyond *Hello, nice to see you again.* But they fawned over Kimberlie, for which she was grateful; watched her daughter move from being uncomfortable with the attention to warming to it. Absent, of course, was Garrett's family.

Chelsea took a bottle of beer with her to a far corner, away from the throng around the bar and food. She observed the guests, and tried to decide which was worse—being alone with no one around or alone when surrounded by others.

Garrett had always enjoyed the rooftop parties. Often, he'd tend bar for a while because, as he'd said, it was a great way to talk to everyone. It was an opportunity to brag about his success and promote his practice. In the early days of their marriage, she'd enjoyed it as well. She'd been so proud of him—her handsome, suave husband who promised to be a shining star in his field. It was the one promise he'd kept.

Then Garrett had begun to ignore her. Evidence he was cheating surfaced, but she chose not to say anything then. Instead, she had that disastrous affair with Eric. And later, the affair with Paulo, which she'd never told anyone about, including Penelope. Then Luke. How had she dared to judge Garrett?

She focused her gaze on Kimberlie, who laughed at something someone said, laughed for the first time in more than two months. As though evidence that the bond between mother and daughter can exist even when damaged, Kimberlie looked at her then away. The laughter and any hint of a smile disappeared.

The first paragraph of Dr. Moore's chapter on the perils of infidelity came to mind:

It may be only two people in bed, but everyone they know gets trapped in that web. All are ensnared in some measure. The closer the others are to the web's center, the more certain they are to be consumed by the outcome.

She'd never finished that chapter, or the book. She didn't need to. She was living it.

However, that was only one option.

CHAPTER 169

THROUGHOUT THE WEEKEND, conversations between Chelsea and Kimberlie were all but non-existent. With the exception of the party, Kimberlie ate her meals either in the den, where she watched television, or in the bedroom she used.

Their rooms were next to each other, the walls thin enough for Chelsea to hear her daughter sobbing through most of the two nights spent at her grandparents' house.

Three somber adults sat around the table for breakfast Sunday morning. Janice soon abandoned her attempts to start or keep casual dialogue going.

"I'll take care of the dishes," Chelsea said. "You and Dad get ready. I know Kimmie's eager to get back to Susan's."

Janice nodded. "We'll take her back then go to church and the grocery store. We'll be about three hours or so. You'll be all right?"

"I'll be fine, Mom. Take longer, if you like. You and Dad need some time away from here."

"I wish you'd change your mind and come with us."

"Kimmie wouldn't appreciate sharing such a small space with me, even for the time it takes to get to Susan's house."

"You could follow in your car."

Chelsea shook her head. "I intend to rest."

"No denying you need it."

"More than you know."

Twenty minutes later, Chelsea hugged and kissed her parents. Yearned to do the same to Kimmie, who waited in the car with her face averted. She stood in the doorway until her father's car was no longer visible.

Dr. Moore had said she needed to be strong for Kimmie. Sometimes strength had to be demonstrated differently. Her presence—her very existence—only served to torture her daughter, who had a right to feel better, unencumbered by a mother she was too ashamed to know.

She'd betrayed Kimmie as much as she had Garrett. Had she divorced Garrett and then gotten involved with Luke, it would have been different. Still painful, but everyone would be alive. Hindsight wasn't worth a damn.

Chelsea wandered from room to room, ran her hand over, around, and across favorite items. Lingered in front of family photos accumulated over the years.

In Kimmie's room, she picked up the pillow from the unmade bed and pressed it to her face, inhaling the scent of her child. She cradled the pillow in her arms, rocking from side to side, as she'd done so many years ago when Kimmie needed to be soothed. The pillow was replaced, the bed made.

She went into her bedroom and felt around at the bottom of her purse. Garrett's keys were still there. His car key, the original key to their house, and a third key, which had to be to his practice. She dropped the keys back into her purse and slung her purse strap over her shoulder.

The engine turned over easily in her Toyota. She put the car in Drive and headed for Garrett's practice.

As expected, the parking lot was empty. No lights were on inside. She drove around to the back, where staff parked, and let herself inside the building. It had been years since she'd been there, but recalled the layout, which hadn't changed.

Someone else's framed family photos rested on Garrett's desk, but his certificates remained in their frames on the wall. She opened the middle desk drawer and searched for the key she needed. It was there, shoved all the way to the back.

The door to the small room down the hall was locked. The building key, when tried, worked. Equipment and supplies were stored on slotted shelves positioned on the left side of the room. A metal cabinet that contained medications stood against the wall to the right. She unlocked the metal cabinet and searched the shelves until she found a large bottle marked *Narco*. How many of the class-four narcotic pills would it take to suppress her respiratory system, to turn out the light inside her that had diminished to less than a glimmer?

She opened the bottle and emptied six pills into her hand. Returned the bottle to its place on the shelf, locked the cabinet and room, replaced the key in the middle drawer of Garrett's former desk. The pills went into an envelope found on the receptionist's desk, the envelope went into her purse. Chelsea locked the back door and started for her parents' house.

It seemed only right to end her life where it had begun.

CHAPTER 170

CHELSEA CHECKED THE time on the dashboard clock. Her objective had been accomplished with time to spare. The drive back to her parents' house occurred by rote, her mind on other matters.

She let herself into the house. Put her purse in her room, taking the envelope with her. Went into Kimmie's room, took the pillow from the bed. Took a favorite photo from the hallway wall of Garrett, three-year-old Kimmie, and her—all of them laughing, with their arms around each other. Took a bottle of water from the refrigerator and went up to the roof.

One of the lounge chairs positioned under the arms of an oak tree would be the perfect place. She put the items on the end of the cushion and sat, much as she would have had her sole objective been to relax in the shade and fresh air.

Chelsea leaned back with the photo in her hand and studied the faces captured in one moment in time. Kimberlie's was awash in the joy every child the age of three should feel, secure in the arms of parents who adored her. Garrett's expression revealed his arrogance, pride, love of life, and love for his daughter, even if his feelings toward his wife had lessened. Her own eyes couldn't hide the disillusionment she'd felt then and would for years to come, despite the smile flashed for the camera.

She'd stolen her daughter's joy. Had robbed her of her father. And her home. She'd stripped Kimmie of security that should have been guaranteed. Had ended a measure of her innocence.

So many endings. All caused by her.

Chelsea downed the first pill, and the next, continuing until the envelope was empty. No need for a note. The photo would convey her final message well enough.

Gaze fixed on her daughter's image, Chelsea brought the pillow to her face, bending it so the photo remained in sight. How long it would take for the pills to work was unknown. But the last thing she'd see was Kimmie's laughing eyes.

Her daughter's essence would fill her last breath.

CHAPTER 171

H ER THROAT FELT scorched. Chelsea opened her eyes and squinted against the harsh florescent lights overhead. Something stung in her left arm. She lifted her arm, saw the IV dripping saline into her system. This wasn't right.

The effort to sit up exhausted her. Faced with extraordinary weakness, she abandoned the attempt.

Someone said in soothing tones, "Let me help you."

Dr. Moore got up from the foam-cushioned sofa and pressed the button on the upper bed railing to raise the head. She plumped the pillow behind Chelsea. "Better?"

Chelsea's voice rasped when she said, "My throat's sore."

Dr. Moore poured water into a plastic cup, unwrapped and inserted a straw, which she held to Chelsea's lips. "That's from the tube used to pump your stomach. More?"

Chelsea winced, shook her head, and rested back on the pillow.

Dr. Moore placed the glass on the tray table, moved the table and sat on the bed. "Why didn't you call me? If you'd reached the point of taking your life, why didn't you contact me so I could help you?"

"How did I get here?"

"Lucky for you, your mother forgot her grocery list at home and insisted she had to have it. Your father found you and called an ambulance. You nearly died."

A spasm of despair flickered on Chelsea's face. She looked away. "A failure even at death."

"For which many are relieved."

"I doubt that, but I know you're obligated to say it." Chelsea raised the head of the bed higher, reached for the glass of water, which Dr. Moore handed to her. She took a sip, grimacing as she swallowed.

"Kimberlie went back to Susan's house this morning, so she doesn't need to find out about this. Make sure my parents don't say anything. Promise me you won't tell her when you see her at her next session."

"Aren't you wondering how I knew to be here?"

"Now that you mention it."

"First, you need to know this isn't Sunday. That was three days ago. I found out what you'd done when your mother called me this morning. Kimberlie was—is—distraught, as you might imagine. She refused to leave here. Refused to eat or sleep. Your mother begged me to come here and talk with her. I finally got Kimberlie to go home with your parents an hour ago by promising to sit with you until they return, in case you woke up."

Chelsea squeezed her eyes closed and ignored the tears. "I keep hurting my daughter."

"Then you need to stop it."

"That's what I was trying to do."

"The mistake people make, unless they're terminal, is to believe they want to end their life, when what they actually want to end is emotional pain. You owe it to Kimberlie to do better than this. You owe it to Garrett to live for the sake of your daughter. Not to mention your parents, who are also beside themselves. You can't continue to be this selfish."

Chelsea pulled a tissue from the box on the tray table and pressed it to her eyes. "What's that supposed to mean?"

"Causing everyone who loves you to be shattered by your choice of action is nothing *but* selfish. Your pain may have been over had you'd succeeded in ending your life, but theirs would never have left them. Your daughter is overwhelmed with guilt, as are your parents."

"I need to see her."

"She's coming back in about an hour or so. Said she'd only go to your parents' house to shower and eat, but not to stay there overnight."

"I want to see her, but I'm afraid."

"So is she. Afraid you won't forgive her. But, before she does return, there's something I need to give to you." Dr. Moore retrieved an envelope from her purse.

"If that's your bill, I don't have any money on me."

"Humor. I'll take that as a good sign. However, it's a letter from Luke Thompson. He learned about me from you, apparently, and was sure you'd tear his letter up without reading it. So, he sent it to me."

"He's right. I'm not interested. I told him never to contact me. I didn't think I needed to be more specific."

"He begs your forgiveness. I believe he's sincere. I think you'd benefit by reading it."

"I don't care, and I don't want to hear anymore about it."

"Maybe not now. But at some point, you'll need to forgive him so you don't carry this burden forever, even if you never tell him. You also need to forgive yourself, so you can put what's happened behind you and move on."

"Easy to say."

"Anything negative from our past will always be too heavy to carry with us into our future. Our hurts accumulate, and the burden becomes intolerable. We trap ourselves into believing we're obligated to carry them. We're not. What we must do is—"

The door flung open. Kimberlie hurried in and stopped, her gaze fixed on Chelsea. Dr. Moore slipped the envelope into her purse.

Chelsea swallowed hard. "Kimmie. I'm so sorry."

Kimberlie, sobbing, ran to the bed and flung her arms around Chelsea's neck. "Mommy."

CHAPTER 172

A FTER A FEW more tearful episodes and apologies and catching up as Kimberlie snuggled next to Chelsea in the bed, her daughter had finally agreed to go to her grandparents' house and get some sleep. Janice and Paul's relief regarding their daughter and grand daughter was evident, as was their exhaustion. Chelsea slept, but not well.

She took the last bite of oatmeal she could tolerate—the only thing on her breakfast tray that didn't irritate her throat. Someone knocked on her door. She called out "Come in" as loudly as she was able. Unsure that whoever was there had heard her, she started to say it again when Theresa Hall entered the room, followed by Thomas.

"May we come in?"

"Of course. Please." Chelsea pulled the bed covers a few inches higher.

Thomas cleared his throat. "How are you feeling?"

"Better. There's talk of releasing me tomorrow."

"Excellent." Thomas took a seat on the sofa, folded his arms and nodded at his wife.

Theresa stayed near the end of the bed, wringing the straps of her purse. "Funny how asking a person for forgiveness can sound so trite at times, but I hope you'll consider it. Please forgive me, Chelsea."

Chelsea moved the tray table to the side. "I know something about that. Won't you sit? You look uncomfortable."

Theresa placed her purse on the foot of the bed. "I am uncomfortable. Because of how I treated you. After reflecting on my behavior at the funeral home, and the many weeks that followed, I'm appalled. I never imagined I'd ever treat anyone in that manner, especially not … Can you even still think of me as family after what I've done?"

Chelsea patted the mattress. Theresa walked around the bed and sat next to her. Chelsea took Theresa's hand and said, "I'm the one who's grateful you want to forgive me, or want to include me in your life. Mom."

They wrapped their arms around each other, tears streamed down their cheeks. Thomas fished his handkerchief from his back pocket and blew his nose so loudly they couldn't help but laugh.

Theresa said, "When you feel well enough, I'd like to take you to where Garrett is, so you know where to find him. In case you want to visit his grave."

"I've been there. I go several times a week, in fact."

Theresa cringed. "Oh God. The headstone. I'm so sorry. I was furious, out of my mind, really, and wanted to … Thomas tried to talk me out of it, but I was bent on being stubborn. That's not the whole truth. I was determined to hurt you."

"Let's not think about that. I find comfort in bringing fresh flowers and having long talks with him."

"Those *are* your flowers. We weren't sure. We thought maybe it was …" Her face flushed crimson.

Thomas winked at Chelsea and said, "I knew it was you." He looked at Theresa. "Told you."

"It was a good guess, Thomas, and you know it."

"I never guess. I may not say what I know, but I know it."

"Keep it up and you'll be guessing what you cook for your dinner."

"I'm taking you, Kimmie, and the Johnsons out. Kimmie wants a jumbo grilled burger and fries from Burger Bliss." He looked back at Chelsea. "Now that you're on the mend, I hear her appetite's returned."

"Speaking of Kimmie," Chelsea said, "I wonder where she is."

Thomas answered. "She'll be here. I called your mother before we came over. Wanted to make sure it was okay to visit. Kimmie was still sleeping when I talked to Janice. They'll bring her by once she wakes and eats. Said her appetite kicked on around nine thirty last night. That daughter of yours put away seven large pancakes and six thick slices of bacon. Your mother said Kimberlie was snoring fifteen minutes after the last bite."

"My daughter doesn't snore."

Thomas chuckled. "Have it your way. She was purring like an electric saw in her sleep."

Theresa stood and draped her purse over her arm. "We're going to go so we don't tire you. You'll need your energy for when Kimberlie and your parents get here."

"Thank you, Theresa. Thomas. I feel like I'm being given redemption I didn't earn and don't deserve. I'm truly grateful."

Theresa kissed her cheek. "That goes both ways, dear."

Thomas kissed Chelsea's other cheek and followed Theresa out of the room, blowing his nose in his trumpet-like manner before the door was all the way closed.

Dr. Moore had once told her that the true measure of a life is evident in the love—the sustaining kind—shared with those we're closest to.

Her loved ones were willing to give her a second chance.

If only she knew how to merit it.

CHAPTER 173

NEAR THE END of February, Chelsea sold Garrett's practice to the doctors, agreeing to accept two thousand dollars a month, until they rebuilt the practice and could pay more, as well as obtained their promise to make Garrett's legacy a good one.

Yellow daffodils erupted at the end of April. Lawn mowers buzzed or roared into summer, sending the scent of freshly mowed grass into the air each Saturday morning up and down her parents' street.

Chelsea and Kimberlie spent hours on the rooftop of the Johnson home, engaged in long talks interspersed with intervals of laughter, once Kimberlie moved there. Their sessions with Dr. Moore were taken together, punctuated at times with belly-laughs at how ridiculous humans can be. Especially Kimberlie's pantomimed stories of how her occasional first dates went with various teenage boys.

It was mid-August when Chelsea finally decided to tackle the unopened forwarded mail that had accumulated in a cardboard box in her bedroom closet. There had been no rush to deal with it. No bills to worry about other than the sessions and her and Kimberlie's cell phones, both which her parents insisted on paying. She'd tried to get her parents to at least accept some money for household expenses but they refused.

She was with the people she cared about most, so there was no one writing to her or sending postcards from exotic locations, especially not with the standard message, *Wish you were here.*

Chelsea separated each envelope into piles of what was important and what could be disposed of, who she needed to notify of a change of address and who could be ignored.

After an hour, all that remained was the thin stack of bank statements for her personal account in her maiden name. It seemed like both an eternity ago and only yesterday that Garrett revealed what he'd learned. She shook off the thought and organized the statements into chronological order, with the most recent statement at the top. She'd save the older months, but the most recent statement would tell her what she needed to know.

She opened the envelope, believing the statement would merely confirm what she had loosely calculated in her mind to be in there, which should have been around nine thousand or so. The ending balance was over ninety-six thousand dollars. The bank had obviously made a mistake.

She checked the deposits on the first sheet—two bank transfers were listed. The monthly one for two thousand from the practice and another for ten thousand from Special Fund. She ripped open the other envelopes. Ten thousand had been deposited each month on or around the twentieth. There was no way the bank would make such a consistent error. She found the local number for her branch.

"Mrs. Hall, these deposits are legitimate. So, I'm not sure what your question is."

"Who is the larger one from?"

"The Chelsea Johnson Hall Special Fund. Are you saying you didn't set this up?"

A sense of who it was that had, surfaced, but she had to be certain. "Sorry. I got confused. Everything seems to be in order. Thanks for your help."

Chelsea sat on the floor with the statements spread out in front of her. Only several people currently knew about that account besides her: Her parents, Kimberlie, Penelope. And Luke. It had to be him. He'd told her once that his sales were improving, but she never imagined it to be by such a large amount.

Using her phone, she checked his Amazon page. There were thousands of reviews. All raves. Being incarcerated had boosted his success rather than demolished it.

She checked his author page, fought the urge to become over-whelmed when she saw him smiling back at her in his photo. He'd updated his bio. The last paragraph explained that a portion of his royalties went to a special fund, anonymously, to help a family in need.

How he'd gotten her account information to set things up would have to remain a mystery. She wasn't going to ask him or the bank. He was surrounded by criminals now. It was likely a few of them knew a few tricks.

Luke was paying his debt in a two-fold fashion. He sought her forgiveness without her knowing about it. And a way to forgive himself.

She had to do something about that.

CHAPTER 174

CHELSEA'S TASK HAD to remain hidden from her family. A place was needed where she would be uninterrupted, with no questions asked. The thing to do was reserve a half hour of computer time at the library.

Two days later, seated at the desk, she was now obligated to either do what she intended or abandon the idea and leave. But how to begin what she wanted to say? And, how to say it? Her fingers hovered suspended over the keyboard for a few minutes, not that she hadn't contemplated her words the prior night and on the drive over. She nodded once and began to type.

Luke,

I forgive you. I've forgiven Garrett, as well as asked for his forgiveness—and Richard's. I'm still working on forgiving myself.

As for forgiving Penelope? I know it's important to do that for my sake, and I will, but I'm not feeling rushed about that as yet, not that I have any intention of telling her, if and when that may happen. Not that she thinks there's anything she needs forgiveness for. Maybe that's changed, but I have no need to know it. However, I don't allow thoughts about her, when they infrequently pop into mind, to ruin even one moment of my day. The Bible says we are to ask God to bless our enemies. I'm still working on that one, in her regard.

I also need to ask you to forgive me for involving you in my misery and marriage. Both were mine to attend to, and I placed them into your life to fix for me, rather than facing and fixing them myself. When you're able to forgive me for that, please also forgive me for *not wanting us to communicate in any way, ever again, after you read this letter. I ask this for the sake and well-being of my daughter. She's doing well, but still healing. Like the rest of us.*

Receive ... that word is what forgiveness is about, isn't it? We can ask for forgiveness from ourselves, others, and God, if that's our belief system. Asking for it can feel and be difficult. Receiving it, when it's been given, and allowing ourselves to feel forgiven, can be much harder. I'm struggling with that one myself, but that's what I ask you to do. Go beyond my words and receive my forgiveness. Then do this for yourself.

It's an odd thing to tell someone in your circumstance that you wish them well, but that is my wish for you. Don't allow what's behind you to dictate what's ahead of you—who you can be from this moment forward. Advice I find challenging to follow, but it's still good.

Sincerely,
Chelsea

She thought about thanking him for the deposits then quashed the idea. He wanted the fact that he was the provider of the funds to remain anonymous. She'd honor his wish, especially for Kimmie's sake and future. She'd already taken so much from him, as it was. Leave him with a measure of dignity. What person who managed to survive the human condition didn't deserve at least that?

CHAPTER 175

T HE NEXT SEVERAL years passed in some ways quickly and in other ways not, in Chelsea's assessment. Sessions with Dr. Moore ended for Kimberlie, but not for her; though, became Wednesday-only time spent together. Because Dr. Moore was the one person who understood her, didn't judge her, knew how to encourage her.

Chelsea uncurled her legs from under her on the sofa in Dr. Moore's private office. "Today's session marks the end of our seventh year of working together. Seven's supposed to be a lucky number."

Dr. Moore smiled. "Are you feeling lucky, or superstitious?"

A slight smile formed on Chelsea's lips. "A little of both, I suppose."

Dr. Moore cocked her head. "Something's happened."

"You remember my telling you, years back, about Detective Maddox's interview at my house?" When Dr. Moore nodded, Chelsea said, "I bumped into him this weekend."

"Awkward or okay?"

"Awkward, for me at least. He asked how I was doing. He was polite, chatty, in a friendly way, which was so different from how he was that night. It made me feel off-balance. Then he did something that … I'm not certain how I feel about it." She looked directly at Dr. Moore. "He asked if he could take me to dinner this Friday night."

"And?"

"I hesitated so long before answering, it made him uncomfortable."

"And?"

"I said yes."

"How do you feel about going out with him, particularly because of the role he played at such a difficult time in your life?"

"He did what he had to then, in order to reveal the truth. I don't begrudge him that. I also don't think it'll be included as dinner conversation. Still, I'm not sure about going. I think I should cancel. What right do I have to do anything like that? So … normal?"

"Because Garrett died?"

Chelsea nodded. "I don't deserve more happiness than I have now—and I am happy, or at least content most days. If this were Medieval times, with Kimberlie as old as she is now, I'd join a nunnery."

"So you could escape what? Temptation? Life? Yourself?"

"Something like that. It would be a way to avoid making more mistakes. I think I proved without doubt that I'm no good at relationships."

"Life doesn't work that way, and you know it. We can't avoid making mistakes, no matter what our best intentions are, especially in any type of relationship. Everyone deserves however many chances they can get, to do life and love better than they did before."

"Garrett deserves more from me. It's only right I live out my life single. For his sake."

"He isn't here. You are." Dr. Moore leaned forward. "Listen carefully to me, Chelsea. When a loved one dies, some of us forgive them for any hurts they may have caused us. We wipe the slate clean. There's nothing wrong with that. In fact, it's healthy, if that's how we really feel.

"What we shouldn't do is convince ourselves the person was better than he or she was. Garrett was flawed, just like every other human. That fact doesn't have to diminish how you choose to relate to his memory, but neither should you see yourself as so imperfect that you deny yourself the right to have and create the most fulfilling life you can. No one has the right to deny that for anyone."

"I know what you're saying, but I'm not there yet."

"It may be disquieting for you to open yourself to the possibility of another relationship, but not to do so is just a matter of punishing yourself."

"It's my penance. I'm getting off easy."

"How much punishment will be enough? It won't change anything that's happened. Something else you need to keep in mind: any relationship with another person is always, foremost, about the relationship you have with yourself."

"That's not a comforting thought."

"It can be, when you allow yourself to understand how important it is. You have to eventually decide to accept this gift called life. You were saved that day for a reason. You've done well since then, but what else are you going to do as you move forward?"

"That's a good question. One I don't have an answer for, in some respects. Other aspects are easier to address."

"It's just dinner, Chelsea, not a commitment. You have to learn to trust yourself again, as well as others outside your immediate circle. Your life is in danger of becoming too circumscribed."

"You're right. But my courage about that is pretty much nil."

"So do what you know you need to, and do it afraid. That's all courage is. And for your information, it's what you've been doing, without realizing it, every morning you wake up and get out of bed."

Chelsea walked to the window and rested her forehead against the glass. "You sound like Kimmie."

"Did you talk with her about your date?"

Chelsea turned and smiled. "Had to, didn't I? She told me it was about time. Said to go with her blessing and have fun. My child is healthier mentally and emotionally than I am. Thank God." Her smile faded. "I asked if who it was bothered her. She said no. Because he proved Garrett didn't take his life."

"But she knows the whole truth."

"Kimmie said that sometimes the best thing to do is rewrite history, or at least our perspective about it, just enough to help us keep going."

"Smart girl."

"She also told me not to act like a dork on the date, because dorks don't get asked out twice."

Dr. Moore laughed and placed her tablet and pen on the cushion next to her. "She has your best interest at heart.

"Our time's up. Are you going to the grave site when you leave?"

"I have one stop to make before going." Chelsea picked up her purse from the floor. "It's just dinner, right?"

"A baby step. With food and wine and, hopefully, pleasant conversation with someone interesting."

Chelsea smiled and opened the door.

"Chelsea." Dr. Moore grinned. "Do you even know his first name?"

"Mike. He told me after I called him Detective Maddox the fifth time."

"Wear something you feel comfortable in, but don't dress like a nun. It's okay and safe to feel like a woman again, one a man might find intriguing *and* appealing."

"Kimmie already picked out my dress and accessories. She's more excited about this date than I am."

Chelsea shut the door behind her. That's what she was being asked to do by Dr. Moore, Kimberlie, and Detective Maddox—Mike: Close one door and open another. Why did it feel so difficult to let go?

The answer was immediately obvious: guilt.

CHAPTER 176

C HELSEA GATHERED THE fragrant gardenia sprigs from the back seat. She carefully arranged the branches filled with buds in the small urn she'd bought and placed it next to Garrett's new headstone. As she did each visit, she ran her fingers over the words: *Beloved husband, father, son, and brother.*

She hadn't asked Theresa and Thomas to replace the headstone. A few months after Theresa had asked for forgiveness, she and Thomas had invited her, Kimberlie, and her parents to go with them, Chloe, and Anna to pray at the grave sites, barely containing their anticipation of how she'd respond to their surprise.

Chelsea got comfortable on the grass and rested her hand on the grave. "So much to tell you, Garrett. Chloe opened her third massage therapy salon this past weekend. She called it Hall's Heaven. She asked if I thought the name was too shmaltzy. I told her it was perfect. And as she did with the other two salons, dedicated it to you and Richard. I cried when she got to the part in her speech where she said, "Through my brothers' lives, and their deaths, I learned how important it is to help others heal and be whole." Chelsea pulled a tissue from her pants pocket. "There I go again."

After several moments, she cleared her throat. "Chloe said she told you she'd make you proud. She's done that and more.

"Kimberlie keeps demonstrating that she inherited your drive. She's moving through med school the same way she used to move through the water in the pool. Remember how we called her our little angel fish? Four years old, zooming around underwater as though she'd always lived there.

"She's going to make an exceptional radiologist. Staying up nights with you when she was little, while you dictated reports, made an impression on her. Although, I think it was the MRI films. To think I fussed at you for bringing work home. I should have kept quiet about that, and so many other things, so you'd have come home more often.

"Kimmie told me there were two reasons she stayed up with you. One was that she was interested in whatever interested you so intently. The other was that she loved falling asleep in the chair so you'd carry her to bed and tuck her in. There was a third reason that showed up when she was a few years older. She wanted to be like you so you'd want to spend more time with her. You were absent so often, you see. The moments we waste, Garrett."

Chelsea gazed into the distance for several moments before speaking again. "My small law practice is going well. But I intend to keep it as part-time as possible. For good reason. You see, I didn't tell you about something I did, because I wanted to wait until I was sure I could give you a positive report.

"About a year ago, I took in a foster child. A boy. Five years old, with brown hair that sticks out no matter how often I comb it. His was a case I was handling. There was something about him that reached right into my heart and wouldn't let go.

"He was removed—saved, really—from his mother, who was addicted to heroin. You know what else tends to go along with that scenario. She overdosed a few months ago. No other living relatives.

"He's such a bright boy, and creative. You should see his artwork. Every kitchen appliance in my house is covered with his pictures. It's the same at our parents' houses. A budding artist. It's about time we introduce someone with that talent into our family.

"And that's exactly what I did, Garrett. I had a talk with him and he agreed to let me adopt him. It'll be official next week. He wants to meet you, but wanted to wait until the adoption was final. He said he wants to stand here with me and say—wait until you hear this, 'Dr. Hall, my name is Gary Hall and I'm your new son. I hope you'll watch over me from heaven. If my mom's feeling better, ask her to watch me, too.' I catch him practicing it in the mirror. And his name—it's as though he was meant to be a member of our family.

"Don't worry about how Kimberlie feels about it. Those two fell into mutual admiration from the start. When Kimberlie's around, Gary follows her like a baby duck. She loves it. And, he's got two sets of grandparents spoiling him. I keep thinking I should to talk to them about that, but they deserve the joy it gives them.

"Anna and Jason are doing well. Of course they were at Chloe's salon opening. Anna told me Jason isn't Richard, but he's so kind and loving, she's sure Richard sent him to her so she wouldn't be alone. She hasn't said anything yet, but I'm pretty sure I noticed a baby bump. Another gift from Richard?

"There's one more thing. I'm uneasy about telling you, but I can't not tell you. Someone nice, respectable, asked to take me to dinner this week. I don't want to say who, but maybe you already know and understand why I hesitate about that.

"Frankly, I'm anxious about it. My first date in ages. Your parents assured me that you'd want me to live my life. Yes, I asked them how they'd feel. Theresa reminded me about Anna, how she had a right, if not an obligation, to have the best life she can, and why was I supposed to be any different? I know you can imagine how your mother sounded.

"Kimmie and Dr. Moore think it's a good idea, as well. I can't believe I asked so many people what they thought. Now I'm asking you. Your opinion matters. That probably shocks you, but it's how I feel.

"That's all I have to say for now, Garrett."

A breeze wafted across the gardenias. Chelsea breathed in the scent. She turned her face to the sunlight, closed her eyes and let birdsong soothe her. She stayed that way, taking in the quiet and peace of the place.

A half hour later, she inhaled deeply and opened her eyes. Two buds at the top of the sprigs had bloomed.

ABOUT THE AUTHOR

Nesly Clerge received his bachelor's degree in physiology and neurobiology at the University of Maryland, and later pursued a doctoral degree in the field of chiropractic medicine. Although his background is primarily science-based, he finally embraced his lifelong passion for writing. Clerge's debut novel, *When the Serpent Bites*, has received exceptional reviews, as has the second book in The Starks Trilogy, *When the Dragon Roars*. The trilogy books explore choices, consequences, and the complexities of human emotions, especially when we are placed in a less-than-desirable setting. *End of the World: The Beginning*, is the first book in a new serial and became an Amazon #1 Bestseller two weeks after publication. When Clerge is not writing, he manages several multidisciplinary clinics. He enjoys reading, chess, traveling, exploring the outdoors, and spending time with his significant other and his sons. For more information regarding his books, please visit Clergebooks.com.

Made in the USA
Columbia, SC
22 April 2017